Barry Waters was born in 1947 in Norfolk and educated at Wellington School and Cambridge. A former journalist and foreign correspondent (in Brussels, Madrid and Belgrade), he has been an EC official since 1979. He lives near Brussels with his wife, two children, and against their better judgement, several pairs of skis.

COMPLETELY PISTE

PISTE

A Bumper Omnibus
Containing
Piste Again
Back on the Piste
and Totally Piste

BARRY WATERS

HEADLINE

Illustrations by Graham Thompson

Piste Again first published in 1982
by Queen Anne Press
Back on the Piste first published in 1985
by Queen Anne Press
Totally Piste first published in 1988
by Pelham Books/Stephen Greene Press
This edition first published in paperback in 1993
by HEADLINE BOOK PUBLISHING PLC

10 9 8 7 6 5 4 3 2 1

ISBN 0 7472 7882 2

Printed and bound in Great Britain by
HarperCollins Manufacturing, Glasgow

HEADLINE BOOK PUBLISHING PLC
Headline House
79 Great Titchfield Street
London W1P 7FN

PISTE AGAIN

Contents

Introduction

'May I take this opportunity of thanking all of those who
went skiing last year while drawing dole money and social
security. This not only proved my long stated opinion that
it's cheaper to go skiing than to stop at home, but also
helps me to persuade the hoteliers to share my optimistic
view of Britain's sound economic future . . .'

Letter from a West Midlands travel agent to his clients in 1981

There was a time when the Alps were the preserve of mountain folk, convalescents, British milords and a few eccentric members of the upper classes who went in for something called ski-running.

Times have changed. Ski-running has turned into skiing and the sport has long since lived down its exclusive origins. The Alps in winter have become the Central Park of Europe and the Abominable Townsman is there in force, making his strange tracks across the snow, pimpling the slopes with his moguls and finding all the satisfactions of the rat race on the overcrowded *pistes* and lifts.

For most of us there is now no escape. Far from being something few can afford, there are few today who can afford *not* to put in an annual appearance on the slopes. A winter holiday is as obligatory as a summer one, the snow tan as socially necessary as the beach tan, and parallel skiing as vital a skill as driving a car.

Normally sensible people have now come to regard it as perfectly natural to spend at least two weeks a year on the high ground, wearing a fortune in gaudy, uncomfortable clothing, risking broken limbs and cracked ribs, exposing themselves to frostbite, frozen lung and snow-blindness, and being advised by the sons of local crofters how best to slide down hills with boards strapped to their feet.

Even devout cowards can be seen hurtling downhill at close to terminal velocity, icicles up their nostrils, snowflakes attacking their eyeballs, and then voluntarily repeating the experience.

Skiing is now permanently established in the middle classes' conversational Top Ten and it may not be long before most of us have a plug-in miniature mogul slope in the back bedroom so that we can practise rolling our knees in the off-season. They have even fitted up glaciers for year-round sliding for people who miss their two winter weeks or can't bear to hang up their boots for the summer.

Surprisingly, perhaps, there has not so far been much organised resistance to all this. Few people complain openly about their annual ordeal on the slopes and some even profess to derive a bizarre pleasure from it. Suggestions that there are more enjoyable ways of stretching your legs in the mountains seem to have gone unheard.

So it looks as if we may have to learn to live with this new burden in our lives, condemned to spending two weeks a year on the snow and the other fifty talking about it — a penance we pay for comparative prosperity.

But things are not as bad as they sound. Techniques for getting by on the slopes have evolved rapidly in recent years and the reluctant *piste* basher need despair no longer. He or she may never be able to ski, but that is no reason not to succeed on the slopes. The art of Survival Skiing, as it's known, has transformed the sport for the millions who have discovered that there are plenty of ways of getting to the top of a mountain and down again with a minimum of effort and a maximum of kudos. Winter holidays are no longer a pleasure reserved for *piste* beasts and people who don't like having things easy. The Survival Skier can keep his end up with the best of them and, indeed, probably finds more challenges and enjoyment in his version of the sport than the Real Skiers do in theirs.

This book is intended as a guide to some of the basic Survival Skiing techniques, unorthodox in some cases, but effective none the less, and decidedly less strenuous than more conventional ways of skiing. It is written in the belief that most skiers, deep down, or perhaps not so deep down, are not that young any more, don't like heights or snow, would be upset if they broke a leg and just want to get through the day with a flush on their cheeks, a few tales to tell and their skiing ego intact.

1. Skiing and Being Seen

> 'Parallel skiing . . . I indulge in now only as I stop in front
> of a restaurant.'
>
> *Irwin Shaw*

Anyone who has been to a ski resort will know that there is a lot more to skiing than merely sliding about on snow. It is not just a nifty way of travelling from A to B in winter. For one thing, when done with an all too common panache, it's an extremely flamboyant method of getting around.

It does not take long to dawn on most beginners that the chap who has just swished down the slope to a snow-spraying deadstop in front of the restaurant terrace, pushing his glasses on top of his head, need not have done so in quite such a distastefully showy fashion.

Nevertheless, it must be admitted that to some people this is what skiing is all about. The so-called 'Look, Ma' mogulfields in front of the restaurant or under the chairlifts at some American resorts were not idly named. Many people ski simply to be seen. And we may as well concede that most of us aspire to ski in a way that would be worth being seen. To judge by the average skiing conversation, of course, most of us already do.

Survival Skiers soon learn, however, that discretion is the better part of exposure on the ski slopes and that it is not wise to try to beat the exhibitionists at their own game. This does not necessarily mean, though, that you have to defer to the showmen just because they can ski better than you. The point is that you don't really need to ski like that in order to feel that you can ski like that.

The secret of it all is that 'skiing is believing'. And to make belief in yourself as a skiing ace possible there is a universally accepted code among Survival Skiers

---

Rules of Skiing

SELF-KNOWLEDGE

No-one skis like he thinks he skis.

Most 'parallel skiers' can't.

The best skiers talk the least.

Anyone who says he knows how to ski probably can't.

Anyone who says he gets by is probably very good.

Every skier has some advice for every other skier.

If you try to show someone a thing or two, you will be shown up.

which, put simply, amounts to: 'You believe in me and I'll believe in you'. So, provided you feel the part, and most do (the gear is a great help in this make-believe), and provided you get the ego-boosting support of your comrades in adversity, there is no reason to let lack of ability cramp your style.

The Survival Skier is much helped in all this by that fundamental principle which applies to most sports — if not most human activities — that more enjoyment is derived from talking about it than from actually doing it. It is easy to be misled into thinking that skiing is an action-packed participatory sport. And, for obvious reasons, enthusiasts try to put this around. But don't be deceived.

The confusion arises because skiing provides a thousand opportunities for talking about it while seeming to be doing it. This may indeed be the secret of the success of skiing. Most of the time is spent standing in queues or admiring the view or listening to the instructor or taking refreshment. Yet everyone involved in these activities claims to be 'out skiing'.

However, although this apparent active participation is, in fact, essentially passive, there will be certain Moments of Truth. The Survival Skier's aim must be to keep these to an absolute minimum. Your first step should be to plan your holiday very carefully, bearing in mind that the Survival Skier's success or failure is often determined well before he reaches the ski-station.

Don't make the mistake of trying to limber up for the slopes by going to the local dry ski-school. This will only undermine your confidence, and to the Survival Skier, confidence is all. Besides, that plastic matting is jolly hard and it hurts when you fall. Instead, devote your time to selecting the right kind of resort.

The best bet is still the traditional type of ski village — not the purpose-built ski-straight-from-your-balcony resort. The reason for this is that you need to spend as much time as possible actually getting out to the slopes. The old style of village is more likely to ensure this and to provide plenty of plausible reasons for delays *en route*. The modern resort with its ubiquitous conveyor belts and buggy carts and snow-mobiles and mini-trains and lifts of all types to transport you around (why walk anywhere when you can waste a little more of the world's energy resources?) provides far fewer excuses.

You should also check the snow reports over a period of several months. Look for resorts with consistently bad weather. The worst possible conditions for the Survival Skier are bright sunshine, perfect visibility, no wind and excellent snow.

If you pick a sufficiently low-lying station, you may even be lucky enough to find there is no snow at all, or at least, not enough to ski. If you go much below 1,000 metres, though, people may begin to wonder if you ever wanted to ski in the first place. Be careful, however, that this doesn't backfire on you. A shortage of snow can mean all the skiers being concentrated in one area in full view of one another. This is fatal for the Survival Skier who generally wants as much space,

as much tree cover, and as many mountain hideaways as possible.

So study the *piste* maps in the brochures carefully. The Survival Skier will want good access to other neighbouring skiing areas, with plenty of scope for darting from bar to bar and lots of interconnecting routes, ideally via sheltered woodland trails. Above all, try to find somewhere with as many ways down as possible. Finally, always try to pick a resort where the standard of skiing is likely to be low.

2. Gear

'Do you sell ski-wear?'
'Yes. But not really the kind you can ski in'
Overheard in mountain ski boutique

The main thing to think about before you go is gear — no minor matter and, for many, one of overriding importance. Indeed, to some skiers, equipment is all. Even when you've got to the resort gear is likely to occupy rather more of your time than skiing. For if one tenth of your holiday is spent skiing, you can be sure that at least three tenths of your time will be spent dressing and undressing, fiddling with your equipment, discussing it and, of course, shopping for more gear.

The latter is one of the principal *après-ski* rituals, usually taking place between 4.30 and 8.00 pm, thus getting the evening off to an expensive start and giving you something to talk about during dinner. Basically, the aim is to duplicate items you already have on the pretext that the new acquisition has some indispensable additional refinement. Thus you end up with a hat featuring an even louder motif, goggles fitted with windscreen wipers or boots with temperature controls.

Many of these articles, in turn, will be quietly discarded at the end of the year so that the whole cycle can begin again next season. In the ski game disposability is all, and few industries can boast a better trained set of throwaway consumers.

You will gather from this that ski-wear is closely related to fashion — and often

to be found leading the way rather than following. Whereas once town togs were adapted for the mountains, ski-wear now sets the trend in the towns. Do you know anyone who does not wear an anorak for Saturday morning shopping? A ski manual published not so long ago advised skiers to 'travel out wearing a lounge suit, overcoat, gloves and scarf which may all be used for evening wear'. Do you know anyone now who would dare to dress like that in a ski resort?

We are not just talking here about High Street fashion. Ski-gear is *haute couture* as well. There is almost certainly more interest in which is 'the ski' this winter, whether ski lengths are up or down, and whether the new boots are rear entry or side entry than in what Dior or Cardin are doing with hemlines.

In fact, it's very hard work keeping up with the fashion, flitting as it does from striped boiler suits to puffy jackets, from sleeveless overvests to sweaters or from baggy pants back to the traditional *Keilhosen*.

One of the sport's many agonies is deciding which items in your ski wardrobe to pack. Will the jockey look still be in? Will you look out of place this year in your balloon silk windshirt and your pants with the gathered ankles? Should you take your gaiters with you this time – and if so, the plain or the striped, and which way striped? Those damned 'go faster' stripes will keep changing direction, depending on whether it's broad chests or long legs that are in.

Colours complicate things even more. At one time blue on the slopes was as standard as the black of Henry Ford's Model Ts. Now everyone's in technicolour, doing their best to keep up with the shade of the month.

The purpose of all this pantomime, of course, is to take the average skier out

---

Rules of Skiing

CLOTHING

Every skier wears at least five different colours.

One of your zippers will jam often.

You are constantly in search of some new item of clothing or equipment.

Anyone with top-of-the-range gear is probably not a top-of-the-range skier.

Any gear you buy in the resort can always be found cheaper at the pre-season or after-season sale in your local ski shop at home.

All glasses and goggles are guaranteed to mist up in bad weather.

You will rip, stain or lose an item of clothing every few days. It is most likely to be your most recent purchase.

of himself, to encourage him in his delusion that on skis he really is a different person, and a bit of a hotshot at that. Most Survival Skiers go along with this approach and take advantage of the props available. It is, after all, easier to swap technical talk if you are the possessor of items like a skin-tight suit, a pointed helmet, mono-ski wings under your arms and skis which let the air through the aerodynamic holes in the tips.

The Old-Timer

But there are exceptions. One is the Survival Skier who achieves excellent results by dressing 'down' rather than 'up' for skiing. He clings resolutely to his old lace-up leather boots, Telemark era skis and cable bindings. His outfits also are suitably dated – knickerbockers and knee-socks are a great favourite. The colours he chooses are neutral and well faded; pale blues or khakis are the most popular as they are easy to get lost in and have a vaguely military flavour – perfect for muttering about high mountain training in Norway after the war.

Anyone who decides on this sort of outfit must be prepared to see the part through. The aim is to come over as the self-reliant loner who has seen a lot of snow. These types of Survival Skier are usually irrepressibly cheerful and distinctly unimpressed by the latest ski technology. ('I'm a bit of an old ski-tourer, myself . . . How do you get on with those new plastic boots? Not much to chew on if you get buried somewhere. Do you think they're here to stay?')

Another favourite prop is a sealskin strip, tucked in the belt, for ski-walking uphill. ('Never know when you may need it . . . don't trust these lifts much.') Their only colourful indulgences are a multi-coloured set of waxes and a bloodstained kerchief, once used as a tourniquet and kept as a souvenir.

Old-Timers also specialise in interesting homemade refinements to their equipment – every bit as good a talking point as the latest in fuel-injected skis. Some, for instance, do without ski-stoppers or *lanières*. ('Anyone silly enough to lose a ski deserves to walk.') Others remove the straps from their sticks. ('Never again – not since I failed to slip them in an avalanche in the old days and broke both my wrists.')

Skilful use of the bum-bag is another stock-in-trade. Theirs usually contain a fascinating jumble of bits and pieces which they lose no opportunity to tip out and display. Standard items include maps, compass, avalanche cord, crêpe bandages, spare ski-tip, splint, whistle, various kinds of twine, klister, assorted clips, Factor 15 suncream and the occasional real curiosity like a ball of grimy fat. ('Yes, it's yeti-fat. My sherpa gave it to me in the Himalayas one year – works wonders if your eyelids are beginning to go in a whiteout.')

Some skiers amass such a collection of bum-bag material that they graduate to the full skiing back-pack, as worn by guides and instructors. These are invaluable for denoting authority and are a worthwhile investment for all types of Survival Skier.

Whatever approach to gear you adopt, however, the basic rule is to have a lot of it — burdensome as this may be on the journey out. Even in this respect the extra effort involved will be more than compensated for by the lasting impression made on your fellow skiers if you travel out *en groupe*.

It is well worthwhile to invest in several pairs of skis of varying lengths. These can be picked up quite cheaply as most Continental or American skiers change their skis, on average, every twelve days. By contrast, British skiers, because of economic circumstances, are often forced to hang on to the same pair of skis for months at a time. It should be noted here that despite the money-no-object cachet attached to skiing, some Continental/American spending can be excessive; and if someone does persist in going on about their new micro-chip bindings and battery-operated centrally heated boots with built-in telephone and cocktail cabinet, there is surely no harm in remarking that in the end there is no substitute for good technique.

The Ski-Room

On arrival, when setting yourself up in the ski-room, your main aim should be to use your equipment to dominate as much of the room as possible. In addition to taking up plenty of storage space, you should try to establish a permanent working area for your waxes, portable burners, iron, clamps, files, scrapers and other assorted instruments.

An excellent space-taker which can almost serve as a landmark in 'your' sector is a pair of old ski-jumping skis. The only people who ever see these close to are championship ski-jumpers, and, in an ordinary hotel locker room towering above a forest of 175 cm compacts, they can have quite an unsettling effect on the competition. A pair of Scandinavian Fjell skis can be used to much the same effect. And you might as well have a pair of Scorpian mini-skis along with you 'just for fun'.

Don't just use the ski-room at the beginning and end of a day's skiing. If you can spare the time, three-quarters of an hour spent in the ski-room in the evening playing with your waxes and your implements can only enhance your reputation. You are sure to gather round you a small but respectful audience to whom you can explain the importance of a razor sharp 18 inches of inside edge under the boot.

Above all, take gear seriously. The Survival Skier should on no account admit that he doesn't ease the springs on his bindings from one year to the next. When

someone tells you that they ski so much better with the S26A5 binding than they did with the S26A4, or that they must be at least two per cent faster since they started wearing the latest wonder ski-socks, it is as well to believe them. You will win no friends by suggesting that the magic numbers and words written all over our skis, like 'elite', 'slalom' and 'competition' are simply there to make us feel good. Don't take these totems lightly. A man who has just spent a month's salary replacing his old 848 GTS Slalom Elite Specials with the improved 848 GTS Slalom Elite Extra-Specials is not likely to take kindly to having them mocked.

The only people who can sometimes get away with the deprecating approach to gear are the down-dressing Old-Timers. ('I remember how when I was a child we used to just strap a pair of barrel staves to our feet.') Only he can afford to be slightly irreverent in asking whether your bioelastic aerodynamic ski-suit really makes you ski faster, whether your shatter-sure hyper-reflectant sunglasses were specially designed for wearing on top of your head or whether your maximum angulation knee-high racing boots can possibly be more comfortable.

3. Bed and Board

'Sleep faster, we need the pillows'

Yiddish saying

Once you've picked your resort and got your gear, the next big decision is where to stay. In the Grand Hotel Vachement Cher or the Flophouse Familiale? In a Mod Cons Mountain Hut or Pack 'Em In Pension? Or perhaps in one of those modest establishments which seem to have sprung up behind most decent hotels these days, commonly known as The Annex. Wherever you end up, you can be sure that your home from home will have been designed to put Skiing Man to the test every bit as much as slopes.

Your *après-ski* hours will be full of little challenges, like trying to persuade the pension *patronne* to part with the bathroom key; discovering the half-hour in the day when the hot water is actually hot; sneaking upstairs past the receptionist wearing your ski-boots, in spite of all the notices saying you mustn't; working out how to adjust the heating in your room so that the temperature is somewhere between freezing and ferocious; or persuading the manager to move you out of the room next to the lift shaft or disco.

Not, of course, that all these little pleasures are exclusive to hotels in ski resorts. You probably have about as much chance of finding no coat-hangers or bath-plug or a fast-fading 15-watt bulb in your bedside reading lamp in a hotel at the bottom of the mountain as you would in one at the top. Nor do skiing hotels have a monopoly on switchboards which are *incommunicado* with the outside world, laundries that are guaranteed to savage your clothing, or chambermaids who are duty-bound to ignore your 'Do Not Disturb' sign.

However, it is true that skiing hotels are judged by different criteria from hotels down below. The three acid tests are:

a) size of breakfast
b) proximity to ski-lifts
c) the plumbing

In other words, do they give you an egg for your breakfast and enough to stoke up on for the rest of the day? Can you hear the clank and squeal of a nearby ski-tow when you wake up in the morning? Are the pipes noisy and do they offer a reasonable flow of hot water (neither trickle nor torrent) at the time of the day when you most need it?

It should be said, though, that these are tests applied more by Real Skiers than Survival Skiers, who are not usually as raring to go as they tend to make out.

There is often a certain masochistic streak in Real Skiers which can lead them to put up at some rotten hotel with no cons, let alone mod, on the grounds that it is a hotel 'for Serious Skiers'. In fact it's all a clever ploy by a hotelier who doesn't like being disturbed by his guests and has devised this way of attracting the 'early to bed, early to rise' crowd.

One quality common to all kinds of skier is that they are frequently skint. As we've seen, skiing can have serious side-effects on one's bank balance. This has meant that in today's hard times skiing accommodation is much affected by what is known as the Sardine Syndrome.

What this amounts to is more and more people staying in self-catering apartments and chalets and 'apartotels'. These are full of bunks and convertible couches and pull-down or fold-up beds which transform the place at night into one great dormitory where people can slumber amid the intoxicating odours of one another's socks drying out on the radiators.

If you're lucky there'll be a Chalet Girl to do the cooking. If not, there'll be a 'kitchenette' where you can heat up your own baked beans, which you then eat

sitting cross-legged on cushions in the area cleared during the daytime for communal activities.

There is something to be said for this lifestyle. Your booze (bought on the 'plane or from the supermarket) is cheaper than in the hotel bar. There are all the school dorm fun and games (pillow fights and tying people's pyjama legs together, and putting snow in their beds). And there's the constant challenge of trying to get into the bathroom.

But, on balance, the Survival Skier is advised to go for a more classical form of accommodation. This could be the quaint and cosy family-run Hotel Post (there's one in every village — all *Luftmalerei* and shutters outside, cuckoo clocks and doilies inside). Or it could be the ultra-modern over-equipped Hotel Sporting (often, for some mysterious reason, called the Hotel Golf, despite being perched on top of a mountain with no golf course for miles around).

What it will have, though, within its pine-clad walls, will be any number of saunas and solariums and pools (with whirlpools and underwater massage) and gymnasiums and games rooms and ski-wear shops and illuminated boards on the walls of the lobby showing all the *pistes*. All this and a sterilised polythene-wrapped tooth-glass in your bathroom, too.

This sort of place is often a good bet for the Survival Skier, who does need a certain amount of room for manoeuvre — a decent-sized ski-room to perform in, somewhere big enough to get lost in, and a selection of bars where he can sound off.

And even if the other skiers won't listen to you, there'll always be Mine Host or Hostess behind the bar busy with the cocktail shaker or brewing up the *Glühwein* while patiently lending an ear with well-feigned interest as you describe the local skiing terrain and your exploits upon it. (He or she will have been skiing this area since birth but don't let that hold you back.)

4. Ski-Talk

'The greater the lie, the more chance of it being believed'

Joseph Goebbels

This brings us to what is perhaps the Survival Skier's most vital requirement — the chat. For, as we've already remarked, skiing is a sport more for discussing than doing. It is not simply a question of making up for incompetence on the *piste* by grandiloquence off it. Ski-talk is definitely an acquired skill and there is probably more difference between novice and expert exchanging stories at the bar than there is between them on the slopes. One important point is that, initially anyway, you should try to confine your *braggadocio* to skiers of your own level.

Remember the unwritten code of mutual support among skiers which runs: 'You believe my stories and I'll believe yours. I won't go out the next day and look too hard for all the precipices, walls of death and giant man-eating moguls we spent last evening talking about.' However, this applies mainly among skiers of a similar ability. If you move up a couple of levels and try spinning the same yarns, you are likely to find undisguised contempt rather than the encouraging nods, the sucking in of breath, and the whistles of wonderment you can expect from your peers.

Styles of story-telling vary from level to level. The beginners' tales, for instance, are all breathless outpourings of hazards encountered, without much technical data: 'You know that ledge just by the baby T-bar, where everyone always falls on that big bump; well, I was doing a *schuss*, and really going, when, you know that woman with the red suit . . .'

The experts are more sparing and technical in their language, only pulling out the stops on a subject that clearly sets them apart from other groups (powder, for instance).

One general rule is that the tone of most ski conversations should be upbeat and enthusiastic. Your friends will not thank you for putting a dampener on their spirited accounts. Remember the basic convention of mutual acceptance of exaggeration and the need to be supportive.

An important part of this convention concerns accepted ratios of self-delusion. These should on no account be challenged. Most skiers, for instance, believe themselves to be travelling some 40 per cent faster than they actually are (for the novice this can be as high as 60 per cent). Do not attempt to put anyone right on this — you may find them doing the same for you.

Similar ratios apply to skiers' views of themselves in most other aspects of the sport. This may be a reason for the unpopularity of ski-schools which offer video as a teaching aid — filming pupils in action and then playing back the tape at evening self-criticism sessions. These are not usually well attended — most skiers clearly want to preserve their flattering misconceptions of themselves.

It is, of course, as true for skiing as for anything else that it's not what you say but the way you say it. Whatever the subject, whether it's gear, mountains, snow or technique, it's vital to dress it up in the right technical terms, ideally with key words being said in a foreign language. *'Wedeln'*, *'angulation'* and *'passo spinto'* all sound much better than 'wiggling', 'bending forward' and 'skating step'.

That is not to say that English has nothing to offer. The Americans have brought in a lot of good hot-dogging jargon in recent years – words like triple daffy, flamingo, spreadeagle, royal christies and backscratchers; not to mention doughnut, twister, wongbanger and helicopter.

Advice

The use of technical language both confirms your status as an experienced skier and has the advantage of being very flattering – even when you are discussing a comrade's weaker points. 'You're getting a lot of air through the moguls, John' is likely to be far more acceptable to John than 'You seem to be bouncing around out of control' or 'You don't seem to know how to handle bumps'.

Think twice before advising someone to 'Turn left and try to keep your balance'. He or she would much prefer 'Get an even weighting on your edges, then slide into maximum *angulation* to bring you round and flick your heels as you turn'.

When a novice skier lurches past you, struggling against the forces of gravity, say 'Hop, hop' or 'Go, go'. He will appreciate this more than 'Look out, you'll fall'.

The point is that the specialised vocabulary for what you are doing ('heel push using frictional gravity as you counter-rotate') sounds a lot better than what you are doing looks. Developing a facility for this kind of technical language and applying it liberally to your fellow skiers can be well worthwhile. You may feel you are spending an awful lot of time building up other people's egos, but in the end it pays. If people like what they hear about themselves they will tend to defer to you as the *maestro*.

Complex formulae and diagrams of forces are ideal for these conversations – either sketched out in the snow with your ski-stick or drawn in beer on the bar. Someone who can hold forth credibly on the appropriate mathematical formula for adjusting bindings for champagne powder as opposed to fluffy powder need probably do nothing more to establish a reputation.

The use of suitably obscure technicalities, however, can be a double-edged sword. While immensely flattering, if that's the intention, they can also serve as a put-down which can shatter another skier's morale.

The secret here is timing as much as tone. Obscure advice given *before* rather than after someone tries to execute a particular manoeuvre is almost certain to guarantee its failure. If that is, in fact, the aim, it's important for the advice to sound specific but really to be very vague. Above all, don't attempt to demonstrate. Just gaze on, shaking your head sadly as the victim tries to put the advice into practice and fails. This technique is commonly used to exclude a skier who is seeking to move into a higher league but is not showing the proper deference.

It is also important never to let your ski-talk lapse. Never say bump when you can say mogul or *bosse* instead. Never simply lose your balance and fall over – you catch an edge; you tried one slip turn too many; or you should have known better than to try a left-hand mogul before going into reverse camber.

It all helps to keep skiers cocooned in their own exclusive world and to enhance the general air of mystique. For skiers like to be in awe of their activity. They even apply their sense of wonderment to the inanimate objects which help them in their labours. They have reverent technical conversations about lifts, pylons and cable cars – idolising, in short, the whole range of teles (*télésiège*, *téléski*, *télébenne*, *télécabine*, etc.) that get them up the mountain.

People who would not spare a second thought for the engineering triumphs of the car or the aeroplane that got them to the resort in the first place, or to the construction of the skyscraper hotel in which they are lodging, will watch with undisguised awe as the cable car docks or pulls away. 'Just look at that', they will say excitedly to one another. 'It still hasn't taken up the strain on the third pulley. And that cabin must weigh at least three and a half tons!'

Amongst these inanimate objects you must certainly include mountains. Peak-worship is an important time-filler on the slopes and you can usually reckon that a good 25 per cent of the people on upper ski-slopes at any one time will be engaged in admiring, pointing out, identifying and making general obeisances to the surrounding mountain-tops.

You should not get too carried away, however. While it's important to use your terminology convincingly, the Survival Skier should be careful not to follow those people who actually begin to believe their own ski-talk and who feel there is a real relationship between what they say and what they do on the snow.

The ski neurotic has become a very familiar phenomenon on the slopes, worrying about whether his *angulation* might be a couple of degrees off or his skis five centimetres too long. (He's the one who studies his ski manual during the coffee break and anxiously consults the instructor after every lesson with questions like: 'Should I downweight on the uphill ski before or after I've reached maximum *angulation*?')

The ski neurotic has perhaps learned rather too well one of the basic lessons that all Survival Skiers have to master — that nothing is ever quite right. While it's true that the general tone of ski conversations is one of enthusiasm and excitement, they are invariably qualified by dissatisfaction with something or other. Either the equipment has not been set up right, or phases of certain manoeuvres are not coming off properly, or the snow conditions are wrong.

The Weather

Weather is one of the commonest gripes. The snow is never exactly as it should be. It has been perfect on nostalgically remembered occasions in the past, but it is never right *today*.

Make the most of this. Other skiers are always looking for something to blame and they'll be grateful if you can supply it. If someone is having a rough time on a perfectly prepared *piste*, he will be very happy if you suggest that although it

---

Rules of Skiing

WEATHER

The snow conditions are never right.

The snow reports are always wrong.

The weather always gets worse.

The weather in the village is never the same as the weather on the mountain.

The weather was better the week before you arrived.

You are never dressed to suit the day. You either sweat or you shiver.

The one day when snow conditions are ideal will be the day you decide to stay in bed.

The bumps are never in the right place.

If it's expected to snow, it won't.

If there isn't enough snow, there won't be any more.

looks easy, that sort of snow is very difficult to ski on. He will also welcome suggestions of other slopes where the snow may be better. Skiers are a bit like surfers, always willing to set off on that search for the perfect wave/slope, always fantasising about some mythical unskied dreamland of crisp, white powder.

Don't just talk about the weather. Get stuck in to it. Peer knowingly down crevasses. Point out potential avalanches. Put up a finger to test the wind. Taste the snow to examine its composition. And always shake your head and look dissatisfied.

It's also as well to be suitably reverential about the weather. For mountain weather is not to be thought of as ordinary weather — it's there to put you to the test. It can even put you to the test before you leave home; snow reports bear little relation to the truth and can take some deciphering.

Weather tends to be a big favourite with our friend the Old-Timer. He is always harking back to the great whiteouts of yesteryear, and other great battles against the elements.

The Way It Was

At this point it might be worth looking in more detail at how our Old-Timers apply themselves to ski-talk generally. They are often among the more effective exponents of the art and most of the principles they apply also hold good for other types of Survival Skier.

As already explained, the Old-Timers do a lot of their talking through their gear, which always looks suitably ancient. They fill out the picture with appropriate references to the old pre-cable days — leather thong bindings, home-made waxes and so on. Their dated equipment also has the advantage of providing a handy excuse should their performance on slope not seem immediately impressive. This doesn't happen all that often, though, as they are past masters at being seen outside as little as possible. They prefer to do most of their reputation-building work in the ski-room.

Their most common theme is that skiing has got too easy. So much of the challenge has been taken out of it. In the old days you used to have to endure to survive. Remember what it was like having to put on skins to get up a slope? Remember those ribbed hickory skis? And what about the early leather boots – you used to have to take them off every couple of hours and rub your feet in the snow to restore the circulation.

Working as he does mainly in the ski-room, the Old-Timer can easily make use of the full range of his props. He will drop in on a suitable ski-room conversation, choosing an appropriate moment to rummage around in his bum-bag allowing a number of intriguing items to spill out. It is not usually long before he is forced to explain about the seal gut used for binding fingers together in extreme cold and the whale-bone chips for propping eyes open in a blizzard.

Other Approaches

If the Old-Timer's line in chat doesn't appeal to you, you could base your own brand of ski-talk on the novice, who excuses himself by claiming to be more of a cross-country skier; the name-dropping member of the exclusive Club 8847 at Piz Lagalb; the adventure merchant ('Any Big Skiing around here?'); the latest technology buff, specialising in arcane talk about wedging; the hardened loner ('I spent most of the afternoon birdsnesting up over the top ridge); the skied-everywhere dilettante ('I like to do the Hahnenkamm-Streif once a year and usually try to make it for the Inferno at Mürren'); the low-profile Nature Lover ('I like getting in among the trees – did you know that slalom was originally a substitute for racing through woods?'); or the deckchair expert who never goes out at all ('I used to be a bit of a wall-skier until I lost my nerve').

Whatever role you adopt, the underlying precepts of ski-talk – a healthy disrespect for reality, mutual congratulation and flattery – remain the same at all levels. The only time when a somewhat different set of rules apply is in 'Anything you can do . . .' conversations. These are normally started by comparative novices who have rashly abandoned the conventions of mutual support. The Survival Skier should avoid such conversations at all costs as they often lead to an embarrassing escalation of claims.

If you do get involved, your aim should be to kill the conversation as early as possible. Our Old-Timer would probably trump his opponent with something like: 'Ever skied in Tibet? They have a curious sort of turn there – very similar to one I saw the natives in Patagonia using years ago.'

Finally, a little advice about pacing yourself. Whatever kind of ski-talker you are, it's important not to use up too much of your energy skiing during the day. You have to reach the bar in the evening with enough gusto left to tell your tale. You also, of course, need to keep something in reserve for your après-ski turns like the disco gyro and the bar-stool twirl.

Get your priorities right with regard to skiing and ski-talk. Never let your skiing impair your *après-ski* performance. A depressing day when you've skied yourself into the ground can so easily destroy your confidence and credibility. You need all the aplomb you can muster if you are to carry your ski-talk off.

5. Instruction and Group Skiing

'I trust I make myself obscure'

A Man For All Seasons

Up to now we have concentrated on those activities which will take up most of your time – basic *pre-* and *après-ski* work such as talking, shopping, posing and dressing up. But you will also have to spend a certain amount of time actually on the snow. Most of us, in fact, find ourselves strapping on the boards nearly every day.

When you do get out there you've two basic choices – skiing solo or *en groupe*. On the whole, Survival Skiers are advised to steer clear of classes. When you think about it, it really is a bit much to have to pay just to learn to slide downhill. Skiing is hard enough without some rubber-legged farm boy shouting at you all the time and without eight or ten other people being invited to sneer at your efforts. Can there really be any point in this chap, with no bones in his legs, teaching normal people with proper legs how to bend their knees? The answer is No. But it is one way of getting through the day and some people, even Survival Skiers, do seem to enjoy classes.

So let's look first at a typical ski-class in action. The group are lined up on a hillside, most of them facing the same way, listening, apparently attentively, as the instructor gives his lecture. There is no point, incidentally, in trying to understand the fellow. He's probably a goatherd by trade and he almost certainly won't speak much English – though he may have some Skinglish in the style of the American catch-phrase: 'Plant your pole, bend your knees, that'll be 50 dollars please.'

His patter is usually something along the lines of *'flexion . . . extension . . . planter les batons'*. Most pupils catch about every fifteenth word. The rest is lost because of the instructor's obscure pronunciation; or is drowned by the wind; or by the loudspeaker blaring out *Una paloma blanca*; or by the whispering of the two individuals in the group who think they know what the instructor is saying and have volunteered to translate. Don't listen to these people, by the way. They usually get the wrong end of the *baton*. In fact they are quite capable of missing the *baton* entirely and imagine, for instance, that an instructor talking about *'cannes'* is talking about his holidays in the South of France. Whatever the instructor says, actually, doesn't much matter. He talks mainly to give the class a breather and to make him feel he's doing his job properly. For him, this is the hard part.

Next comes the demonstration. The instructor executes a series of turns or exercises while the group all ooh and aah to each other and say 'Doesn't he make it look easy'. The class then proceed to make their own way down, one by

Rules of Skiing
PROGRESS

You won't be able to understand the instructor.

The older or less comprehensible the instructor, the more talking he will do.

Whatever it is you are doing wrong, the instructor will probably tell you to bend your knees more.

Most people don't think they are in quite the right class for their class of skiing. Very few think they should move down a class.

All skiers are aiming to reach a particular level of skiing ability where they imagine their problems will be over. No-one ever does.

The turn you learned last year will be out of fashion this year.

Whenever you think you are getting the hang of it, you are doing it wrong.

Several times during your holiday you will ask yourself: 'Why am I doing this?'

Each year you learn about as much as you've forgotten since the year before.

one, starting off at the instructor's signal. If you are somewhere like Austria the group will do as it's been told and peel off from the top of the line. If you are somewhere like Italy the starting order is likely to be the subject of some discussion, but will in the end be totally random. You can also be sure that at some point two members of the class will attempt to set off at the same moment.

The main point to note, though, is that whatever manoeuvre the instructor has performed, the class is unlikely to make any concession to it. They will all ski down in exactly the same way as they always do, each with his or her own distinctive style – rolling the shoulders, sticking out the bottom in the classic potty position or failing to plant the pole.

While the members of the class perform their specialities, the instructor usually amuses himself by chatting up a passing female. He breaks off briefly as each pupil arrives to explain how he or she should be doing more *flexion*, more *extension* or more planting of the *batons*. He then gives the signal for the next pupil to come down and resumes his conversation with the girl. To be fair, as everyone always comes down the same way it doesn't really matter whether he watches them or not.

The whole exercise will then be repeated. The class regroups, the instructor gives his lecture, demonstrates a different movement and skis down until he disappears out of sight beyond the brow of a hill. He then waves his stick in the air, a member of the class spots the tip of it poking up in the distance and the class proceeds to come down one by one, exactly as before. Occasionally, the whole class will go down together – usually after discussing, at some length, whether this was or was not what the instructor intended. The only real change, though, might be that this time the instructor is talking to a different girl.

There will be times when your group will contain a girl who is sufficiently desirable to interest the instructor. In this case she will normally perform first, carefully watched by him. She will then be given a 20-minute commentary on the progress she is making, plus any help she may need at adjusting her gear, and possibly an offer of a private lesson in Duvet Skiing. The others will then follow on down in quick succession while he continues to entertain her, breaking off as each of her classmates arrives for a quick word on more *flexion*, *extension* or planting of the *batons*.

When the instructor decides it's time for a change of pace he will lead you all on a long knee-slamming run, probably over an area of corrugated hardpack. The critical formula for the Survival Skier here is '*après vous*': try to go last and make sure the group does not go off in an orderly fashion. As people fall you can then stop and ask them if they are all right. This gives you a chance to take a breather and earns you a reputation as a solid type. If, by some mischance, nobody falls, you can easily bring down the person in front of you by skiing on his or her heels.

Usually, however, the instructor will ensure that mishaps take place. In order to maintain his superiority he will have chosen a piece of ground that only he can properly negotiate. Ski instructors have a vested interest in making you ski badly, if only to prove that you are in need of instruction. It's a favourite trick of theirs to ski a bit too fast or a bit too slow to enable you to perform properly on a given piece of ground. Even though instructors vary a good deal there are no exceptions to the rule that power corrupts. And the most likely victim of their tyrannical streak is undoubtedly the Survival Skier with his probable recalcitrance and incompetence.

If it becomes apparent that the instructor wants to take it out on you ('Why you always fall?') there is no reason to be intimidated. You are perfectly free to ask him when he's got to go off and milk the cows. Don't feel obliged to show the sort of fawning deference that most pupils go in for. The worst he can do is deprive the group of essential items of equipment, like sticks, and make them ski down in silly ways. You can also get your own back by reminding him that those who can, do and those who can't, teach. Most of these lads once saw themselves as the Killy, Stenmark or Thoeni of their neck of the woods but never made it into the big league.

It is perhaps worth mentioning that the real Killys, Stenmarks and Thoenis of this world do cause considerable problems for your humble tutor. This is because the instructors, like us, are the victims of the pet theories of the people who can really ski. If, for example, next year you find yourself being solemnly taught to lift the rear of your trailing ski on the turn, it will be because one of the top racers has sparked off a fashion by winning races that way. The superstars are the ones who really move ski technique on, forcing the establishment to keep on rewriting all the manuals and issuing new sets of instructions. These are supposed to apply to you and me but, as we just tend to ski on as we have always done, it tends to be the poor instructors who get most confused by it all.

All this explains why one year you get told to keep your skis together all the way through your parallel and the next that you'd do better to keep them eight inches apart; or why one year you are supposed to hop both skis around simultaneously and another to do most of your work on the outside leg, lifting and sliding the inside one round to join it. Not that any of this has much effect; if you watch a busy ski-slope for a while you will see that there are almost as many styles as there are people. Not even the instructors ski in the same way.

In fact, if you could ski a little faster, your particular variation would probably stand as much chance of becoming the new orthodoxy as did Killy's little quirks. The jet turn became acceptable because Jean-Claude started winning with it. The scissors turn, now as redundant as its high jump equivalent, could become *de rigueur* tomorrow if you started beating the world with it. We would surely all find ourselves going back to the Arlberg crouch if someone came along who could do it a little better than they could in the 1920s. If you won the Olympic Downhill chewing gum, they'd all soon be chewing away on the slopes. So, next time the instructor goes on about your excessive shoulder-rolling, point out that what you are doing is really a primitive version of shoulder swings or mambo, now found in all the best textbooks.

Instructors, however, are not usually very tolerant of individualism. The only time they are slightly indulgent towards eccentricity is when confronted with someone who's obviously from an earlier skiing era — like our old-time ski-tourer. If you are playing this role, you can usually enlist the instructor's sympathy for your unorthodoxy by saying you just can't get out of what is basically a Telemark action. You're reasonably safe here because none of the instructors have much idea what a Telemark actually looked like. The instructor may indeed even develop a sort of respect for you and be reluctant to break this link with the past. If he tries, just shrug your shoulders and say: 'Once a Telemarker, always a Telemarker — I just can't get the hang of this modern technique.' If you try this approach always remember to refer to the instructor as a guide.

The principal advantage of these tactics is that you don't have to start from scratch again every year. For even though it now takes seven days instead of

seven years to become a skier, you have to go back to the beginning every holiday because a new method has evolved in the intervening year. It often seems as if there's a conspiracy among ski-schools always to keep technique one jump ahead of the pupils.

Whatever theory your instructor goes for, he will almost certainly have a repertoire of catch-phrases which vary little from year to year. Many relate to a particular part of your anatomy that is supposed to be the key to it all. Thus we get:

'Ski-lauf ist Knie-lauf.'
'You ski with your head.'
'You ski with your big toe.'
'You ski with your nose.'
'Grip the snow with your toes.'

Italian and French instructors are also rather fond of sexual references, usually, of course, directed at the instructor's favourite girl in the class:

'Skiing is like making love — easy when you get the hang of it.'

Instructors are also inclined to keep evoking that mythical beast, the Fall Lion, which, strangely enough, you are always advised to turn into and attack even though it will always bring you low.

Your tutor may also have a penchant for drawing immensely complex diagrams in the snow, usually for the benefit of a particular member of the group. 'Kennst du ein Bisschen Mechanik?' he will say and proceed to detail the plethora of forces acting on you at any one time.

To vary the pace a bit, the instructor will sometimes stop to admire the view or pass round some *saucisson* and white wine for refreshment. How long this takes tends to depend on the interest shown by the aforementioned girl in the names of mountains or the varieties of local *vino*. Needless to say, it's as well to encourage her to show an interest. Any time the group goes up by T-bar, by the way, it will always be the instructor who goes up with the girl.

Another variation is to break things up with slalom practice. This can be quite fun and is not necessarily all that strenuous. It is usually a good time-waster as it involves preparing the course. This means fetching the sticks, planting them at appropriate intervals and then spending time side-slipping or snow-ploughing down to smooth out the course. It is not too hard to bow out of the slalom itself by claiming some religious objection to competition. Anyway, people are always needed to tidy up the course and put back the sticks that get knocked down, so you can remain involved with the proceedings by doing that. To get the maximum benefit from all this you must insist on the class taking the time and trouble to set up its own course — some instructors have an unfortunate tendency to 'borrow' courses set up by another group.

Selecting Your Class

This is one of the reasons why it's worth choosing your instructor very carefully at the start of the week. Don't let the ski-school make this important decision for you. If the school organises one of the usual mass selection sessions, getting everyone to go through their tricks so they can sort you into classes, make a point of being absent. If challenged you can say you were delayed because you had to make some vital adjustment to your gear. Then, when it's all over, you just latch on to the class that suits you best.

You may as well abandon any notions you may have of a sort of logical progression in skiing. There is simply no point in progressing just for the sake of it. It's best to find a level you like and stick to it. If you are happiest traversing, pick a class that does nothing but. If you enjoy stemming, always seek out the stem class.

People are often misled by the apparently hierarchical nature of the sport, divided, as it is, into groups ranked on a scale from one to six. You will find, however, that in practice there is very little difference between the grades. It's just that each class is nominally engaged in a different series of manoeuvres as they carry on assiduously practising their faults.

One class to avoid, though, is the beginners' class. The disadvantage here is that they are not allowed to use the lifts much, so you have to do an awful lot of rather exhausting walking uphill. All that snow-ploughing can also be rather tiring.

Some people, it is true, do engage in *après-ski* one-upmanship based on the number of your class. But if you do get picked on in this way, it's usually fairly easy to cloud the issue, given that countries vary in their ranking systems. In France, for instance, class one is the top class and class six for beginners, whereas in Italy it is the other way round.

Classmates

Finally, a word about your classmates. You can be sure that most of them will not take such a rational view of things as the Survival Skier who just slots himself into the most accommodating class. Instead they will worry a great deal about where their class is ranked in the general scheme of things, and where they rank in the class scheme of things. Most will believe that their talents are undervalued and that they have been put into the wrong class. 'But I've done all this', they will say, regardless of whether they are still able to do it, or indeed whether they were ever able to do it. 'I mean, we were on to pedal-jump turns last year.' When giving vent to such expressions of dissatisfaction they will always hark back to some Golden Age when their parallels (sic) were out of this world. It all comes down to that capacity for self-delusion which most skiers have and which often makes it all so amusing. Try watching someone who thinks he's doing a *wedel* but isn't.

The Survival Skier is best advised to support his fellow pupils in their beliefs, although there are always one or two who are beyond the pale as far as expressions of sympathy or solidarity are concerned. There is, for example, the chap who always insists on being the first to perform and who, when you are skiing as a group, monopolises the Number Two spot behind the instructor. He invariably feels he should be at least a couple of classes higher up and that bagging the Number Two spot reflects his status in the class. There is, incidentally, no advantage to be had from being the best in the class — it just means the instructor will find even more to criticise.

The chap who is convinced he's a real bomber is even more of a menace. He never follows the rest of the class in their attempts to weave a curved path behind the instructor. He hurtles straight down, usually parallel to the group but sometimes across its path, huddled up in his version of the egg position, clearly imagining he's doing the Kilometro Lanciato. He usually arrives breathless, about half a second before the rest of the group, expecting to be congratulated. When skiing down to join the group, he will never ski past and tack on to the group from below. Instead, he tries one of his racing stops, aiming to fall in at the top of the line but invariably crashing and collapsing the whole group like a row of dominoes.

Whatever differences they may have during class, most groups manage to put up a common front to the outside world during *après-ski* time. They will all rally round and back each other up on stories about the arduous and extensive skiing they have been doing.

Most instructors realise how important a conversation piece the group's travels are, so they usually endeavour to move the class around as much as possible in the course of a day. Thus, when asked that standard dinner-time question, 'Where did you go this afternoon?' you have no difficulty in replying:
'Well, we went up the Black Buzzard and down the White Crow at least 15 times. Then we skied over to the Spitzenspitze, did the Wall of Death a few times, then took that long double drag which connects with the Devil's Cauldron. Up there we found a superblack with no-one on it at all, skied it half a dozen times and then bombed down to Hochgurgl; from there we went over to Obergurgl, down to Untergurgl and finally took the cable car to Übergurgl just in time to catch the last lift back.'

6. Solo Piste Bashing

'If you don't have it in your head, you have it in your legs'

Serbian Proverb

'The Survival Skier should reverse this'

Author

Most Survival Skiing techniques are, in fact, better suited to individual *piste* bashing than to group skiing. It has already been made clear that the Survival Skier usually relies on not making himself too conspicuous. He knows he's only as good as his last turn in public and, to ensure that these are few and far between, he will have picked terrain with plenty of cover, a variety of interlinked ski areas and lots of escape routes.

A properly prepared Survival Skier should never find himself in a situation where he is forced to perform under the critical gaze of others. If necessary, he can outwait anyone on the mountain and he has plenty of time-wasting props at his disposal — camera, suntan cream, screwdriver, waxes, map and so on.

Above all, the Survival Skier will rely on what's called 'just off *piste*' technique — basically the art of standing around beside the *piste* in any one of a number of suitable poses. Probably the most common position is to lean back, perhaps supported by the ski-sticks, arms folded, glasses on head and eyes closed, facing the sun. In the absence of sun the poser might be looking out across country, scanning the neighbouring peaks, marvelling at Mother Nature.

Alternatively, he can go in for a somewhat more active routine, like shuffling off to inspect some nearby unskied powder. That doesn't commit him to skiing in it — he can always come back and say he hasn't got the right kind of wax handy.

The average Survival Skier can do a lot to develop his standing about technique by just watching and imitating the Real Skier. For although attempts to emulate the motions of good skiers in action are almost certainly doomed to failure, their motions when more or less stationary can be copied very successfully.

The most common expert postures tend to depend on ways of leaning backwards or forwards or sideways on the sticks. There is also a good deal of simulation of skiing positions — bending the knees, leaning into imaginary turns and so on. Other characteristic routines are standing still, stork-like, holding the back of one ski off the ground or, by contrast, making impatient little bunny hops. For relaxation, there's sitting down or lying back on the skis, sometimes flexing oneself into a semi-prone limbo position. Skis are kept together throughout, of course. But whereas keeping them together leads to disaster while skiing, you will be surprised how easy it is when you are not moving.

Rules of Skiing

GETTING AROUND

If you start out in the morning 15 minutes later than usual, you will arrive on the slopes an hour later than usual.

The most exhausting part of skiing is getting from the hotel to the slopes.

Skis and ski-boots weigh more at the end of the day than at the beginning.

Most skiers give themselves away by how they carry their skis to and from the slopes.

When you set out from one point on the mountain to another which appears to be on the same level, it will turn out to require much tramping uphill.

A more energetic way of hanging around is to go in for on-the-spot exercises. There are a variety of these, but perhaps the best are the ones which involve using the sticks in an imaginative manner. You can pick up some interesting examples by watching a German or Scandinavian group at one of their early morning knees-bend sessions or, even better, an Inner Skiing ('*Ski Psychologique*') class in action.

It goes without saying that all of this activity is best undertaken on a flat piece of ground. You will be surprised at how many movements which are impossible while steaming down a slope can be elegantly executed when you are on the level. Ability to make good use of the flat is one of the main characteristics of the successful Survival Skier.

But however accomplished your 'just off *piste*' technique you can't, of course, stand still for ever. So when the time comes to move off, pick your moment carefully. Don't hesitate to condescendingly '*après vous*' anyone who tries to nudge you into action before you are ready.

Starts can be difficult and very revealing, so a growing number of Survival Skiers are putting a lot of effort into perfecting imitations of the starting style of Real Skiers. This usually involves choosing the steepest slope available to gain immediate momentum and then casually falling into the first turn, adjusting the straps of the ski-sticks around the wrists at the same time.

Some Survival Skiers can even do a catapult racing start, jumping skis off the snow and pushing off with the sticks as if leaping out of a starting gate. A lot of practice is needed to get this off properly, but it can be worth it. It's another example of how, by working hard on a limited repertoire of special manoeuvres, one can enhance one's reputation as a skier without actually skiing.

To get about on the *piste* our Survival Skier will rely principally on traversing. So, having performed his super-start, he may possibly execute just one turn before sliding into his habitual traverse/sideslip position, tracking across country looking suitably detached until he finds another appropriate vantage point or convenient hostelry. Many Survival Skiers, in fact, spend the day traversing from refreshment stop to refreshment stop. This can make them a bit of a liability to other skiers when they roll down the main concourse to catch the last lift down at the end of the day.

If you feel that almost constant use of the traverse doesn't seem quite the thing after your professional 'just off *piste*' performance and flying start, the best face-saver is to look worried and keep stopping. It's a good general rule anyway to be constantly fiddling with your gear, adjusting it and complaining. So simply traverse off as if you are about to launch into a spectacular run and suddenly pull up short, looking puzzled, as if something is wrong. Then traverse on till you find a suitable spot and start making some vital adjustment to your equipment.

On no account allow yourself to get carried away by your own 'just off *piste*' performance. Don't be tempted to try to imitate some *Pistenjaeger* who has followed his flying start with a quick *wedel* through the powder at the edge of the *piste*. The accomplished Survival Skier must be aware of his limitations. Stick to the traverse. It's easy to execute, looks elegant enough and, with a bit of practice, the Survival Skier can perform it almost as well as the expert. And don't overdo the banana or comma position: some instructors get their pupils to hold the sticks out like a *banderillero* and this really does look as if you are trying too hard.

The great thing about the traverse, apart from being easy to execute, is that it does carry you across and away, rather than down. This means you can usually stay well clear of the main action and, since you are generally up on the valley sides, you also appear appropriately aloof from the proceedings.

However well you plot your evasive course you are almost bound, on occasion, to run across a group of people you know. Your approach here will vary according to their skiing ability, but in general it's a good idea to get in first and suggest that they are the ones who have been making themselves scarce all day: 'Ah, there you are – and where have you been hiding?' Try to stop beside them as sedately as you can. If you've been traversing this can usually be done by simply turning uphill to run out. Then get to work putting some of your standing around technique into practice. Unless they really know what they are doing, you can afford to remain somewhat detached, standing aside from the group and nodding encouragingly if they start practising their turns.

It's usually wise to let them go off first, but if they show no signs of moving pick a suitable moment and just traverse on, adopting your best 'seen it all, done it all' expression. Unless you happen to be hopelessly lost, never be tempted to join one of these groups. If you should have to for some reason, make sure you go last and then peel off at the earliest possible opportunity.

7. Queues

'E pur si muove'

Galileo Galilei

So far we have looked at how to get down the slope and how best to make use of stops *en route*. But the true secret of Survival Skiing is to ensure that you spend most of your day going not downhill, but uphill – or rather, attempting to go uphill. You will, in fact, spend most of your time queuing – so much so that a skiing holiday often seems like a misnomer for a queuing holiday.

Some people even spend as much time before they go on holiday studying the queuing facilities (checking there are bars nearby, that queues are south-facing) as they do studying the slopes. This sort of detail is, of course, very important to Survival Skiers who depend a lot on queues.

It's as well, therefore, to be wary of some of the newer purpose-built resorts which seem to be doing their best to eliminate queuing. This is a pity as skiing would not be skiing without the queuing. Think of all those magic moments spent shuffling forward, getting new designs scratched on to your skis by other skis, and exercising your elbows.

There are many Survival Skiers whose queue technique is well in advance of their slope technique. Indeed, there are some who find meeting the challenges offered in the ski queue far more rewarding than performing on the slopes. It would be a pity if all the years spent perfecting their technique were to go to waste should queuing ever disappear.

Queuing, of course, is an activity particularly well-suited to the English, who get a lot of practice at home, and who don't mind getting their skis scraped since they usually rent their equipment. Living up to their reputation for fair play, they are among the best at spotting and denouncing the Queue Sneak. These loathsome individuals are normally to be found trying to slide past on the outside, which is where the queue moves fastest anyway, or pushing through the middle pretending they are with someone further on.

Some like to sit innocently on the railings at the side of the queue and slide along a metre or so when no-one's looking. There are also a good many who have no hesitation in making straight for the front of the queue. They either say they are with a special group up ahead or that they lost control when stopping and found themselves at the head of the queue. Some just bribe the lift man to turn a blind eye to their activities.

The important thing is to challenge them early enough. It's not much good coming out with: 'I say, I was before you' once it's all a *fait accompli*. Nothing is a surer confession of impotence. Your best bet is to get the crowd on your side before challenging the Queue Sneak. Whip up a general feeling of indignation

Rules of Skiing

LIFTS AND LINES

The other queue moves faster.

Someone will try to jump the queue.

Someone will stand on the back of your skis.

You will stand on the back of someone else's skis.

Whenever you assume the attendant won't want to see your lift pass, he will.

The attendant will only ask to see your lift pass just as you're about to step on to the lift.

Someone will fall off the tow.

The other tow moves faster.

If there are two tows running parallel, one will break down.

You will always be on the one that breaks down.

If the tow stops and you abandon it, it will start to run again almost immediately.

and if possible prompt someone else to take the lead in denouncing the offender. Then come in as the back-up man: 'That's right, mate, you tell him.'

Once war has been declared, the confrontation usually turns into an interesting tussle of wills. Some sneaks quite shamelessly stand their ground, but others can be made to retreat, though not necessarily right to the back. They often manage to save face by reinserting themselves into the queue half way down.

If you can spot the sneak early enough, it is much more likely to be a straightforward physical contest. Don't hesitate to use force. This is one of the reasons for having ski-sticks. The proverbial poke in the eye with a sharp stick can be an excellent deterrent, although unfortunately very pointed poles are now being outlawed at some resorts. You can also use your sticks for blocking someone's way or to pin down their skis until you can plant your own skis on top of theirs. Sharp elbows and rugby-style hand-offs are also very useful. A certain amount of goose-stepping in the lift queue can also pay dividends.

Don't be afraid to use any of these weapons on children. They are the worst sneaks of the lot, usually attacking in groups and often wearing crash helmets to protect them from blows to the head. Despite the smiling indulgence these brats will be shown by some members of the queue – presumably those with similar offspring – make sure you stand your ground. These wowsers will be the *piste* beasts of the next generation. Now is your chance to settle scores with them. Don't be intimidated just because they can ski better than you.

8. Going Up

'Ski slopes are great places for running into people'

Snoopy

Every good queue eventually comes to an end and when you reach it you'll probably find a tele-something-or-other to transport you uphill.

There's an astonishing variety of teles, but the most common is probably some sort of drag-lift. So the Survival Skier needs to devote a good deal of time to developing his *tire-fesse* technique. The way you slide on and off the drag and just how you allow yourself to be hauled up can be very revealing.

This is particularly true of T-bars, where you usually go up with somebody else, thus providing you with an unrivalled opportunity to vent your skimanship on a captive audience.

Unless you know otherwise, it is best immediately to assume you are the senior partner. If your companion really is a novice it makes things very easy. You can offer encouraging looks, tell them to relax and be generally patronising. Always let the other person make the important choices – like who should get off first at the top. Try to seem indifferent towards the whole thing – except for the odd worried look if your partner seems unsteady at any point.

If your companion does not seem to accept your captainship, try to talk or frighten him or her into submission. A good start is to give advice about snow conditions. The weather is one of the standard topics in T-bar conversations. Point out remote mountains and perhaps more obscure geographical features. Turn around a lot to look back. Jiggle about on the bar. Swap hands with your sticks. Steer wide to avoid bumps or dips. Rummage through all your pockets in search of lip salve or cigarettes and then get your companion to hold your gloves while you cream or light up. Do anything, in fact, to unsettle your partner. Don't allow yourself to be side-tracked by the so-called 'romance of the T-bar'.

Another good idea is to make patronising remarks about good skiers who pass you on their way down. There are usually a few talented performers who enjoy bombing down immediately alongside the tow. Shake your head sadly when some supreme *wedel* artist flashes past and say something like: 'I'm sure that boy had potential . . . once. He'll never get rid of those bad habits now!'

If at the top there is any sort of pile-up or confusion – whether caused by you or otherwise – stick to the same drill as for motoring accidents. Assume it's someone else's fault and curse about the number of incompetent novices about. You'll probably get away with it, as the rules about who does what at the top of T-bars are far less clear than the Highway Code.

It's also a good idea to extricate yourself as quickly as possible from any *mêlée*. That way you can use the other bodies to lever yourself up. If you end up as the

Rules of Skiing

FALLING

Falling isn't fun.

The more you fall, the more you are likely to fall.

The closer you ski to the fall line, the more likely you are to fall. That's why it's called the fall line.

You are most likely to fall when someone you know is watching.

Most falls will be blamed on equipment, the snow or someone else.

If you put two novice skiers well apart on an empty slope, at some point on their way down they will collide.

The skier you most want to see fall never does.

last one on the ground you can have a hard time getting on your feet.

When you go up a drag-lift solo, rather than *à deux*, a different approach is called for. Here your performance is for the benefit of the world at large, not another individual. Use the opportunity to mask your skiing incompetence by showing off one or two eye-catching manoeuvres you have perfected.

Simple examples include all kinds of snappy ways of carrying or trailing the ski-poles. Some people like to flick the snow with them. Somewhat more advanced is the rhythmic swaying motion, so that you go up in a series of S-bends, interspersed with shuffling or leaning forward on your sticks which are planted somewhere in your bindings. For the very advanced, there's a technique of catching an edge so that you sway sideways and trail one ski behind you across the track for a while before hauling yourself back on course.

If you slip up on a drag-lift, the best thing is to pretend you were doing the *pisteurs'* job for them and smoothing over a bumpy bit. As you stagger to your feet, mutter to the people coming past you: 'Well, at least that hole won't be bothering anyone else for a while.'

When it comes to cable cars and cabins you depend less on actions and more on that Survival Skier's speciality – words. The talk tends to revolve around gear since you have to take your skis off and are usually huddled together as you wait. Thus everyone has the chance to inspect what everyone else is wearing or carrying at rather close quarters.

These are often the times when you realise how battle-scarred your skis have become and decide that you need a new pair. It is also when someone with short skis will be made to feel markedly inferior. Stare contemptuously at anyone with compacts or mini-skis. These are the big giveaway and no Survival Skier can afford to take them seriously. If you happen to have a pair you'll have to try to pretend you borrowed them.

Although opportunities for action are limited in cable cars, they are not completely excluded. One highly successful Survival Skier has even managed to build his whole reputation around a well-rehearsed trick at the middle station of a bubble-lift. It involves leaving his skis at the middle station the night before so that he can then stage his little drama when he collects them the next morning. As his cabin approaches the middle station, he opens the doors from the inside by forcing a ski-stick between them and turning the locking lever outside. Then, as the cabin passes slowly through the middle station transferring from one cable to another, he jumps out, grabs his skis, stuffs them into the empty ski-holder and rejoins his three bemused companions in the bubble. To maximise the value of this ploy he arranges to travel up with a different group of people every day.

All this depends, of course, on the connivance of the lift men at the middle station, and it costs him a bottle of Glenfiddich a week. Never underestimate the importance of keeping in with officials and the value of a good bribe. Always make a point of shaking hands with these chaps. Even if they don't know you, they will pretend to recognise you — they know an accomplished Survival Skier when they see one.

The advantage of developing one of these more elaborate gambits is that once you have it taped there is very little else you need do. In fact, it is positively unwise to do much else. There is, for instance, one very successful Survival Skier whose whole reputation rests on the fact that as he skis down to stop outside an hotel or restaurant he gives a little jump and manages to flick himself out of his bindings, boots together, to land neatly a couple of feet away from his skis. His bindings, of course, have to be on a very loose setting, but this doesn't matter as he doesn't ever ski. He just comes up to the slopes twice a day to perform his trick. The point, though, is that he has got his act off to perfection. He spent a whole year practising it in his back garden before trying it out on the slopes.

By contrast, there are other Survival Skiing techniques which can also make a lasting impression but which require hardly any practice at all. Try skiing down carrying ski-pickets or flags or some other piece of equipment over your shoulder. It's surprisingly easy to do but it looks deceptively difficult to the majority of people who never have occasion to try it.

Even something as simple as wearing a pack on your back (preferably one of those red ones used by Austrian instructors) can help to establish seniority — particularly if you offer to carry things for other people in it. If they take you up on the offer use the opportunity to show off the compass and map and other bits and pieces you keep inside.

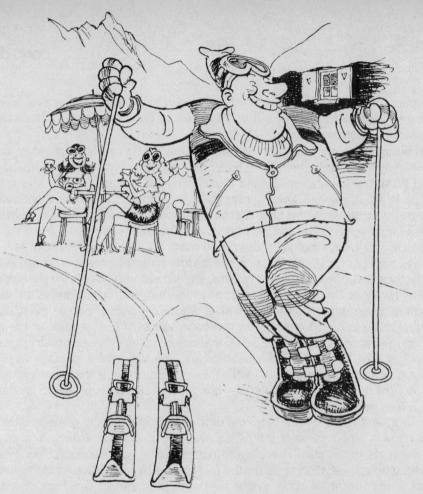

You don't always need to actually possess the props. Often all you need do is refer to some of the items at hand on the slopes. For example, some Survival Skiers like to remark whenever they see a blood wagon: 'Ever tried pulling one of those?' If anyone comes back with 'No' and then an impertinent 'Have you?', our Survival Skier is ready to bluff it out with something like: 'It's okay if you've got the weight right and have someone behind who knows what he's doing.'

However well practised your routines are, though, you are bound on occasion to come a cropper and end up with your nose, or some other part of your anatomy, in the snow. There are all manner of possible face-saving remarks, but perhaps the most satisfactory are those that suggest you were attempting something very difficult which did not in this instance quite come off. You were, for example, practising your 'recovery skiing' but didn't manage to get back on the rails this time. Or you were working on your snow-shoe walking technique ('It's difficult to do on skis, of course, but very good exercise'). Or you were doing your bit for nostalgia by trying the old one-stick Zdarsky swing.

Don't hesitate to blame your equipment: 'I made a mistake with the wax and they just stick at all the wrong moments.' Claim that *Schnee* magazine asked you to test out some new bindings to see how suitable they would be for Mr Average. Or pretend you are on very unsuitable ultra-modern equipment ('That's the trouble with this high technology gear — may be okay for wind tunnels, but not on the slopes').

A final word on falling: when you do go try to make it as spectacular as possible. As in judo, tumbles are well worth practising. If you go down in a mushroom cloud of snow, people may assume, particularly if you help them to, that you were doing something rather ambitious. On the other hand, if you just wobble along and quietly sit down sideways after staring at your ski-tips and making them cross, you are not very likely to be given the benefit of the doubt. And don't be deluded by all those brochure pictures of a smiling lass collapsing into the powder that suggest falling is fun. It isn't.

9. Avoidance Skiing

'Include me out'

Sam Goldwyn

Although most Survival Skiers find themselves spending their time *piste* bashing, there is, for the really advanced, another possibility – Avoidance Skiing. The purest form – TAS (Total Avoidance Skiing) – means not going out at all. This, however, is only for those very exceptional types who can say 'Don't know if I could ski or walk first' and leave no doubt in people's minds that they are telling the truth.

It's no good the average performer thinking he can bow out by pleading a 'dicky cartilage' or even by trying something more ambitious like 'Never been much good since I split my shin on the Eiger'. He just won't be allowed to get away with it.

But it is possible to spend a day 'out skiing' without putting in much of an appearance *en piste*. This usually means slipping away via some little known route, usually off *piste*. You then go to ground in some mountain hideaway beyond the main skiing areas and spend your day sampling the landlord's *Glühwein*, usually in the company of other Avoidance Skiers.

Much depends, though, on first-rate preparation. Since no-one is going to catch sight of you on the slopes you must work very hard to establish and explain yourself before setting out. This means that at the hotel ski-room or the main departure point on the mountain you'll have to talk loud and long about the joys of skiing in the wilderness. Your gear, of course, will reflect this taste for getting off the beaten track. You wouldn't go far wrong with the sort of garb worn by our Old-Timer.

Incidentally, this communal preparation for the day's endeavours is one of the principal skiing rituals, as is the story-swapping off-with-the-boots session on returning to base in the evening.

The sort of line the Avoidance Skier will take is fairly obvious:

- 'Don't go in much for this *piste* bashing. Always was more of an endurance skier. Like to get stuck into the heavy stuff!'
- 'Never ski down the same hill twice if I can help it!'
- 'Always was more of a cross-country skier – like to get away from things, you know!'
- 'I prefer to get lost somewhere – never could stand much waiting around in lift queues.'

The drawback of Avoidance Skiing is that to escape you nearly always have to go off *piste*. As a result there is a danger of running into trouble and finding

---

Rules of Skiing

LOSSES

Every day, you will
a) forget something; b) break something; c) lose something

This is most likely to be
a) your lift pass; b) sunglasses; c) ski pole basket

If you lose a ski or a stick in deep snow, you will never find it where you thought you lost it.

The chances of losing any given item are in direct proportion to its importance and replaceability.

You never manage to lose the item you most want to lose so that you can justify buying a swanky new one.

You won't remember after lunch where it was outside that you left your skis.

---

yourself limping back to civilisation looking like the abominable *Homo Nivium* emerging from a snow war. But if you have the gall you can sometimes turn the situation to advantage with remarks like:

- 'Been practising my avalanche technique — it's fun trying to stay ahead when they break!'
- 'I was cruising around looking for a good avalanche and one found me!'
- 'Ever done any stunt skiing?'
- 'I think next time I'll play it safe, take out my ballet skis and quietly practise my royal christies.'
- 'I always was stronger at the shooting side of biathlon.'

Should anyone be intrigued enough to try to follow the Avoidance Skier, they can usually be put off with: 'If you try it, old boy, stay clear of the crevasses. You can usually feel the texture of the snow change, but not always . . .'

This spine-chilling approach is worth developing. It only needs the odd remark to create a picture of a wilderness beyond the *piste* full of bodies buried in drifts or impaled on trees. Try:

- 'What's your crevasse rescue drill like?'
- 'I was really looking for a spot of *couloir* skiing — I need a bit of a challenge these days!'
- 'I went over the top this morning. There's some real over-the-head Rocky Mountain-type powder in the dips.'

The odd reference to helicopters does no harm: 'Pity there's no heli-skiing around here!' (Be sure to check first that there is none.) Some people need do no more than say 'I ski alone' to conjure up a vision of a hardened loner with a phial of morphia in his bum-bag.

But there are less hazardous ways of Avoidance Skiing. One approach, if you can get up early enough, is to catch the first lift up (being careful to stay clear of any early morning German skiers or even the occasional group of hearty 'first run' Brits) and then appear back in the ski-room to wind up your day just as the others are getting ready. You then proceed to tell them, sounding as exhilarated as you can, that for you there's only one time of day when the mountain is at its best. That's the early morning. And for someone who wants to work on their ice or powder technique there's no better time. Snow conditions can be so interesting early in the morning and it's such a pleasure to be off *piste* when all the animals wake up. Once you've established all this you are free to go back to your hotel room for the rest of the day.

For those who don't feel safe off *piste* and who can't get up early, there's always the lunch hour. Aim to get up the mountain just as the others come in to eat and then head straight out saying you like the uncrowded slopes. Be careful, however, about where you go. Many mountain restaurants are situated to provide a view of the more spectacular *pistes*. Avoid these areas at all costs.

It is clear that Avoidance Skiing, at least in its purer forms, does presuppose a certain level of ability, particularly to get about in off *piste* areas. And however attractive the idea, especially if you can find some convivial hostelries to do your avoiding in (one reason, by the way, that Brits often confuse off *piste* with off pissed), it may be wise to be a bit less ambitious.

10. Skiing à l'Anglaise

**'In spite of their hats being terribly ugly, God damn! I love
the English'**

Pierre Jean De Béranger

Considering that Britain invented modern downhill skiing (that's our story) and produced many of the great Alpinists (the names of Whymper and Roberts of Kandahar are not forgotten in the Alps) it might be said that the British have let things slide a bit since. Not a bit of it. It's true that since those early days when only the British were racing downhill other nations have come to dominate championship skiing. But this has now developed into a rather crude form of the art, flashily commercial, with all the subtlety of old sacrificed to speed, and where the only important thing seems to be winning. The Englishman instead has chosen to stay aloof, remaining true to his amateur tradition and making his contribution on the holiday slopes. It is here that he has continued to excel, foregoing the glamour of the World Cup perhaps, but contributing mightily to that range of Survival Skiing know-how that the package deal *piste* basher depends on.

Much has been said of the advances made by Killy, Thoeni and Stenmark, but not enough, surely, of the achievements of Watkins, Thomas, Smith and others. Yet these are the men who, with their inventiveness and determination, have made the more important breakthroughs, forging the techniques which enable the fortnight-a-year man to keep his end up.

Perhaps one day, when someone adds up all the trophies, badges and diplomas won in ski-school end-of-week races, the immense contribution of these unsung heroes will be recognised.

In some respects, in fact, it is the Stenmarks of this world who have been shown the way by the Smiths. It is only fairly recently, for instance, that the speed merchants have learnt the lesson that the big races are won not on the steep bits but by how well the flatter parts are negotiated. However, an appreciation of the importance of the flat has long been conventional wisdom among the Smiths. Indeed, it is on the flat that you will most often find the Smiths working and practising their technique.

Much of what is said about the Smiths, of course, applies to Survival Skiers in general. Nevertheless, there's no question that the British do stand out from the rest and that one can legitimately talk about a clearly recognisable *style Anglais*. Let's try therefore to analyse this style in more detail. These are the main postural characteristics:

a)   *Absence of forward lean.* The British skier tends to stay fairly erect.

b) *Bottom sticking out*. Believed to add stability.
c) *Fiercely rotating shoulders*. Gets a bit of movement into the action.
d) *Stiff lower leg*. Particularly on steep bits or moguls. Shows character, too.
e) *Loose lower lip*. Ideal for recounting experiences at the bar.
f) *Tendency to wave sticks about*. Helps to add interest to the action.
g) *Intermittent rhythmical swaying*. Invariably after refreshment stops and at the end of the day.

The British skier will usually be found on shortish skis, wearing a distinctive hat and with his sunglasses worn correctly over the eyes rather than on top of the head. His boots will be Italian and his anorak or knee-length cagoule (well waterproofed as he goes out in all weathers) will have extra large pockets for carrying *The Sunday Times Ski Book* around. He will certainly have a bum-bag, often on the large side, in which, being safety-conscious, he will keep things like crêpe bandages, a whistle and salt tablets. Somewhere about his person, St Bernard style, he will also have a brandy flask for those all too frequent emergencies.

Even in the old days the British set the sartorial tone on the slopes. You need only look at those Victorian photographs of gallant Englishwomen climbing in their long skirts and red flannel petticoats. For the very cold weather there were undergarments called 'toasties' and headpieces called 'snuglets'. An additional whiff of refinement came from the bamboo perfume sprayed on the mittens.

So it seems fair to say that the British have always stood out in the mountains. The mere title of Sir Arnold Lunn's anthology *The Englishman on Ski* (you went out on ski in the old days, not skis) makes clear that an Englishman in the Alps was in no way to be confused with a Frenchman in the Alps, or anyone else for that matter.

But the English skier has undoubtedly evolved considerably over the years. It began with the almost regal English 'milord'. He was followed by the gentleman tourist who sent letters to Lunn for his yearbook. Today the more distinctive types are chalet-dwelling Hooray Henrys with their Sloane Ranger molls and *piste* clogging package dealers with Union Jack hats and compact skis.

One thing has changed little, however. The British have always seen it as their role to try to *amuser les autres*. Perhaps it can be traced right back to when Colonel Napier set the whole of Davos laughing by arriving at the Grand Hotel with a Norwegian butler and two pairs of skis (quite a novelty at that time). The butler's party piece was to ski down the slopes near the hotel holding aloft a tray with a cup and saucer on it.

Another characteristic of the skiing Briton, from ski-running days to the present, has been his determination to go out in all weathers, and not to take the soft

options. Lunn, for instance, was highly contemptuous of the sort of 'Cresta skier who never climbs a yard if he can help it'. Today, too, the British continue to live up to their 'mad dogs and Englishmen' reputation, venturing out in the most atrocious conditions to do battle with the elements. Cynics might say that this is not just a matter of mere fortitude since, as most Brits only manage two weeks skiing a year and each day represents about a week's salary, they can't afford to miss out. A week's lift pass alone probably costs as much as an annual season ticket from London to Brighton. Anyway, Britons continue to be contemptuous of those continental 'fair weather' skiers who believe in taking the third day off to rest.

This attitude may also have something to do with the rugged traditions of Scottish skiing, an unsung heritage where Skiing Man is truly put to the test. This, you will hear Brits hold forth, is 'real' skiing, bearing little relation to that namby-pamby *piste* bashing on well-manicured slopes under bright blue Alpine skies. Just take your average *Pistenjaeger* and park him on Glenshee and you'd soon find out what he was really made of. Alternatively, perhaps, put him on one of the other skiing surfaces like mud, grass or water; that would be a test of his mettle. It takes a good man to outski a Brit on one of these surfaces.

Certainly, there are no apologies to be made for Scottish skiing. After all, the Scots had mountains when Switzerland was as flat as a bedboard. Don't forget to keep mentioning that the Alps are very 'young' mountains.

This does not mean to say that privately British skiers may not hope things turn out a little better for them during the next Ice Age. Either that or bring back the Empire so that skiing in the Saltoro Range of the Karakoram in the Himalayas would again be like skiing in one's own backyard.

Not that the height of mountains need necessarily have all that much to do with skiing pedigree. It can be pointed out that the day the first British skier strapped sticks to his feet and slid was as far back as Saxon times and that these modest beginnings are still celebrated every year at the feast of St Swooshius in the Somerset village of Steep where the locals dance about with burning brands tied to their feet. One theory has it that the practice was brought over by the Vikings. But there is also what looks like a Roman ski-jump at Bath, so it is possible that one can trace things back even further. There's no guarantee that anyone will believe this, of course, but there's no harm in trying.

In fact, the British skier is rather good at pointing things out and putting Continentals right on some of the more common misconceptions. When not cutting a dash on the slopes he will often be found performing with even greater distinction at the bar, offering his advice, his wind unchallenged. There's many a Champagne Charlie who can dominate a big hotel by his voice alone. Similarly no-one can take over a whole resort as effectively as a group of hard-drinking young Scots looking for some opposition in a 'boat race'.

And why not blow the trumpet a bit? There may have been a few Swiss resorts, like Gstaad, that the British didn't start, but not many. And just because a man can't stem christie, that's no reason to restrain him from talking about how his grandmother went up the Matterhorn with Whymper.

Ski-talk, like queuing, seems to suit the British. One reason may be that much of what's said is about the weather. Brits are also good at kindly enquiries about other people's welfare: 'Did you have a good day? Have any falls?'

The British are equally at home in more erudite conversations. They may have fewer active skiers than other countries, but they almost certainly have a higher percentage of experts and theorists. British skiers have made a contribution to ski lore and verbiage well out of proportion to their numbers.

Amongst themselves, British skiers have been known to indulge at times in somewhat crude xenophobia — like making rude remarks about the quality of the machinery in Italy and Spain and its probable ancestry. There is also a frequently expressed conviction that somehow the British skier is getting a bad deal and it mightn't be a bad idea if the Continentals moved aside and let the British organise things for a change.

One feature of most British ski-talk is a determination to take the whole business very seriously. This may be because, despite the illustrious skiing heritage we have outlined, British mass skiing is still in its infancy and is therefore still undertaken with the earnestness of the novice.

This may also account for the unflagging enthusiasm of most Brits; coming to skiing later in years they find they have an exciting lifetime challenge ahead of them. By contrast, people born within range of the Alps who have skied from the

Pleasures of Skiing

EQUIPMENT

Wearing ski-boots. Ideally they will pinch in at least three places, be tight enough to guarantee that your toenails drop off at the end of a week, and ensure that a layer of skin is removed every two days.

Wearing *après-ski* boots. A less acute sensation, but memorable nevertheless. As with ski-boots, there is the pleasure of clumping along like an astronaut. And there's the added delight of giving your feet a sweat bath. Most *après-ski* boots are synthetic and it's not long before they get all nice and squelchy, especially in overheated hotels.

Carrying skis. This is particularly enjoyable while walking uphill. Instructors generally have a groove dug into their shoulder to make it easier.

Getting a poke in the groin with a sharp stick. The attacker will be one of those people who carry their ski poles parallel to the ground and pointing backwards.

Getting a bash on the head. Usually happens when someone in front of you carrying skis over his shoulder suddenly swings round to ask for a light.

Worrying. Generally about whether someone is going to walk off with your skis in the lunch-break or remove your newly-purchased Dream Boots from the ski-room overnight.

---

cradle can usually do everything perfectly by their teens and find it all rather a bore. They then have to go in for ballet or hot-dogging or something equally undignified to generate any interest.

Like the Americans, the British are equipment-minded and take a lot of pleasure in the mechanical side. They always have a lot of sensible points to make about things like edges and if there's repair work to be done on the slopes it's normally the Brit in the group who will produce the screwdriver. Unlike most Continentals, who don't touch their equipment from one year to the next, the British skier is likely to spend the other 50 weeks of the year cleaning and oiling his bindings and performing the necessary surgery on the rest of his gear.

Part of this safety-consciousness may be because the British feel that much more vulnerable on skis. If your chances of being injured are rather high, you are more likely to produce the sort of chap who goes to the ski injury seminar and who knows the avalanche drill backwards and who is always worrying about where the nearest first-aid booth is. Or it may be just another hangover from those early days when the original Alpine Brits were invalids and convalescents. There is also, of course, no forgetting Whymper's grave at Chamonix.

The Whymper tradition has lived on in other ways, too. Like him, his countrymen are not frightened to take a tumble now and then — if only to help *les autres* feel more at ease. Some of the Continentals, on the other hand, tend to stand on their dignity somewhat and make rather a fetish of not falling down.

Everything considered, the British skier is a good all-rounder and certainly has no need to apologise for his performance. On the contrary, he should not be afraid to sound off a bit about the British School. Remember that everything that was worth saying about skiing was said as far back as 1910 by Vivian Caulfeild in *How to Ski* — even though he may have been a bit contemptuous of British efforts on the slopes.

So next time someone asks you about the length of your skis, why not reply in feet and inches?

11. The Rest

'The instructor was grimacing and gesticulating at me. "Ski parall-el, ski parall-el, m'sieu." That was only the beginning of his tirade. When his oration, which was almost political in its vehemence, was over he ran over to me, picked me up, shook me and put me down again. He was certainly agile. I wish I knew what it was he wanted me to do. I felt very gauche. My knees quaked and from the position in which he had left me, I fell.'

S. P. B. Mais, British Ski Year Book 1949

Although familiarity and appreciation of the British approach may help boost your ego, it's a knowledge of the various Continental styles that are more likely to help the Survival Skier get through his day successfully.

This is particularly true for group skiers who must choose a style of tuition that suits them. *Skilehrers, moniteurs* and *maestri* differ considerably, and the pros and cons need to be weighed up carefully. An instructor who enjoys talking, for instance, may bore and confuse but does have the advantage that he doesn't make you do so much skiing. A *poseur* of an instructor may be very irritating but he is going to spend less time looking at you and finding fault.

Let's look therefore at the main national approaches. Very broadly there are two main groups – the Latins (Italians, Spaniards and French) and the Mittel-Europeans (Germans, Austrians and Swiss).

The Latins

The Latins, in general, seem prepared to accept that you should enjoy your skiing and are less inclined to throw the rule book at you. Italians and Spaniards in particular are inclined to favour the 'follow me' approach. They know that, in the end, it's mileage that counts and that the real reason they can ski better than you is because they've put in a couple of million miles on skis since the age of three. They accept that you are unlikely to understand, let alone absorb, anything much of what they say, so they don't waste too much time on explanations. That doesn't mean they don't spend time talking; they do, but it tends to be about the sunshine and the mountains and how they got on when they went over to London as a demonstrator at the *Daily Mail* Ski Show. They also manage to touch base at a fair number of refreshment stops in the course of a day and they don't mind too much if you decide to take rather more extended breaks or even slide off for the odd half day. After all, if they weren't getting paid for it, they'd do the same.

Pleasures of Skiing

MEMORABLE MOMENTS

When you realise you're heading for an Almighty Fall but haven't yet hit the ground.

When you get to an *omigod* precipice and realise that the only way to go is down. This moment is at its most poignant when you are holding up a lot of impatient people behind you.

When you try to put your skis back on in deep snow and keep trapping a thick wedge of snow between boot and binding. This is nearly as enjoyable as that pleasure from the past of lacing your binding cable under the lugs with freezing fingers after a fall.

When you get a boot or collar full of snow. Especially satisfying when the snow takes some while to melt.

When you lose your ski or ski-stick in deep snow. This can provide hours of fun and keep a whole class amused digging away.

When the instructor makes you spend the afternoon walking uphill on skis — especially when he makes you do it herringbone-style.

When you get shown up by an infant who's only been skiing for a matter of days — a constant pleasure since the slopes today are full of small people.

When it dawns on you that you'll probably never become quite as good as Jean-Claude Killy.

A disadvantage is their enthusiasm for departing from the straight and narrow. They often fail to perceive the class's reluctance to get involved with the *neve fresca*, or to get lost in the woods or to jump from patch of melting snow to patch of melting snow in order to ski right down to the village. (They are the ones who jump from patch to patch, of course — you just gouge out the bottom of your skis on the gravel in between.) Needless to say, all this considerably increases the possibility of casualties and people do from time to time get lost in crevasses and buried in drifts.

The French differ somewhat from the mainstream Latin approach. They also accept that skiing can be fun, but they are a lot more intellectual about it. Big talkers, they spend time explaining their personal philosophy of the art, and very often try to inflict upon you *avant-garde* techniques dreamed up by some Grenoble professor. Provided, however, you pay lip-service to the notion that

French skiing is where it's at and that there'll never be anyone else on *planches* quite like Killy, they can be reasonably pleasant to you.

A general point about the Latin group is that, on the whole, they are much better ego-boosters. At the end of your week, for instance, they will dole out all manner of ribbons and trinkets and certificates to make you feel good.

The Mittel-Europeans

The Mittel-European group reject the lighter Latin approach. Their view is that you're not there to enjoy yourself, you're there to ski; and skiing is something to be taken seriously – it is, after all, their livelihood. Skiing is good for you, but like many things that are supposed to be good for you, it is not necessarily enjoyable. It will be made clear from the start that the Austrians and the Swiss are the real skiing nations, and that you should forget any of the half-baked notions and sloppy ideas you may have picked up on the southern side of the Alps. There is only one way to ski – the proper way, the *Skitechnik* way, the way painstakingly evolved in the German-speaking Alps and codified in one of the definitive texts like the official Austrian manual for *staatlich geprüfte Skilehrer*.

The British, in general, seem to prefer this second approach to skiing. This may seem like sheer masochism but there are certain advantages to it. The instructors' long-winded lectures and technical explanations take up most of the time which means you can get by with less actual skiing. And their taste for bizarre exercises, often without sticks, also means you have to perform less. This is because each exercise takes time to explain and they are usually performed by the group one by one. Above all, Mittel-Europeans are sensible – no adventures – so your chances of ending the day in reasonable physical shape are fair. They also take a little more interest in the class and less in their own performance.

But one or two distinctions should be made between the different types of Mittel-European.

THE GERMANS

The Germans are very much the junior partners and don't really lay claim to their own national style. They will usually defer to the others as keepers of the skiing covenant. Their main distinguishing feature is an insistence on over-vigorous warm-up callisthenics, though this is compensated for by plenty of time-wasting concentration on safety drill and correct preparation and adjustment of equipment.

THE AUSTRIANS

The Austrians, like the French, need constant reassurance that they are the Tops when it comes to skiing. Their instructors are less intellectual but equally boring, as they repeat their litanies from the *Ski Instructors' Manual*. Sometimes the class is obliged to chant these litanies in unison – possibly while performing a manoeuvre. But if you are good at remembering what you are told, even if not necessarily doing what you are told, you can usually get off lightly.

THE SWISS

The Swiss have less of a complex about the whole thing – they know they are the Number One skiing nation. They, too, want it all to be done according to the

book but they probably don't take it out on you so much. Not on your body anyway; they do, however, hit you where it hurts most — in the wallet.

There are also, of course, the Scandinavians (principally the Norwegians) and the Americans — both of whom adopt a lower key, friendlier approach; 'skiing with a human face' as it's been called. The Scandinavians go on about it a lot less than the other nations, possibly because they don't take downhill skiing quite so seriously. For them *langlauf* is the real thing. American instructors, however, can get rather carried away. They are often excessively technical, can be almost as incomprehensible as the Continentals, are obsessed with new equipment and have a tendency to go on about the Ultimate Experiences they have had or hope to have. But for all that they do try to treat you as a human being and don't push you around too much (except when the instructor is playing Coach and telling you to 'Go For It').

It will be clear from this that ski-slopes are very fertile ground for national chauvinism. Every nation, for instance, lays claim to having invented the sport. The British know it was Henry Lunn who really started the Alpine thing off by organising that first package tour to a religious conference (convened by him) at Grindelwald in 1892; and anyway miners in the Cumberland fells were already using a form of ski back in the nineteenth century. The Austrians will tell you that their peasants were skiing in the province of Krain as early as the seventeenth century. The Swiss know that they are regarded by the world at large as the skiing nation *par excellence*. The Scandinavians point out that before anything got going in the Alps it was all happening in their neck of the woods and that they've got the cave paintings and the 2500 BC Hoting ski to prove it; even the 'modern' era was kicked off by Sondre Norheim at Christiania in 1866. The Italians and the French knock all these claims down by referring to ancient Chinese and tundra skiers and then go on about defunct sects of mediaeval skiing monks in the Jura or the Dolomites. The Americans will point out that it was Snow-shoe Thompson who, in the 1850's, was the first to find a practical application for skis.

As to which is the main skiing nation, the Italians will invite you to look at the map and see which country contains the biggest slice of the Alps. The French, instead, will invite you to study the modern ski era and look at which nation has been responsible for most of the research, innovations and major developments over the past 30 years.

The British do not rise above these controversies. They feel their role is to evaluate the competing claims and to arbitrate on some of the great doctrinal schisms such as 'open pole plant' versus 'closed pole plant'. They don't hesitate to put the other nations right on particular issues.

The British have also started to clean up some of the confusing foreign vocabulary. Tidied-up stem christies, for instance, have now become basic swing. This is rather a pity, in fact, because much of the magic comes from the foreign terminology. It all sounds so much better when you don't understand what it means. We all know that there are basically just two kinds of turn – one to the left and one to the right – but it makes you feel so much better if you can talk about *'ski aval'*, *'ski amont'* and *'projection circulaire'*.

For those who just don't like foreign words, it should be pointed out that the worst fate of all for a ski-class is to have an instructor of the same nationality. There is then no excuse for incomprehension and the class has no opportunity to indulge in the collective xenophobia towards the instructor which is part of the fun.

What usually happens in single nationality groups is that the instructor spends much of his time leading the class in making catty remarks about the skiing prowess of some of the other nationalities represented *en piste*. There's an awful smugness about English, Dutch, Danish, German or American groups who take their own man along – a growing trend among these nationalities. Their line tends to be that other countries may ski better, but they can teach better. As a result you are subjected to the most boring monologues of the lot – and there's not even any escape in the evening as the chap will be in the same hotel as you.

12. Skiing Types

**'It is in the ability to deceive oneself that the greatest
talent is shown'**

Anatole France

In addition to being aware of the different national approaches to skiing, the well-prepared Survival Skier should also be able to identify the more common individual types on the slopes — most of which cut across national lines. The following are sketches of some who stand out. (Even though, for convenience, only the masculine pronoun is used, it should not be imagined that they are confined to one sex.)

THE MEASURER

Obsessed with ski lengths and talks of little else. Usually strikes in queues where skis are being carried. He stands his skis alongside yours and asks: 'What are they — 180s?' He then proceeds to tell you how he was on 175s, is now on 185s but is thinking of eventually settling on 190s.

THE SURGEON

Spends most of his time waxing and sharpening and adjusting bindings. When on the slopes can't wait for someone's skis to break down so he can show off his collection of screwdrivers. Always on the lookout for snow conditions that severely damage skis so as to make his evening surgery sessions more interesting and challenging.

THE SUN-WORSHIPPER

Usually to be found sitting, standing or lying down — almost never skiing. Face is always turned to the sun, eyes closed. Only interrupts this to apply new layer of sun cream.

THE NON-IMPROVER

Can't work out why he is in a lower class this year than he was last year and why he's now being forced by the instructor to learn things he had taped years ago. He's constantly referring back to some mythical time when his skiing was sheer poetry and the instructor thought he had real potential.

THE ADVISER

Can't ski but makes up for it by omniscience. Usually lets the instructor say his bit, then comes in with the definitive interpretation of why you cocked it up. The most amusing thing is watching him try 'o demonstrate: 'Well, it's not quite like that, but you know what I mean.'

THE T-BAR ADVISER

A very close relative who's no more competent on the T-bar than the other is at skiing. Normally seeks out novices to go up with. If you do have the misfortune to join him, he'll spend all his time explaining about T-bar technique and what you're doing wrong. 'Relax,' he'll say, convinced that the fact that you're both about to fall off is your fault rather than his.

THE PANTHEIST

Often German or Scandinavian. In love with nature, always gazing at the mountains, taking deep breaths or smiling into the sun. When people pass he beams and sighs 'Herrlich' or 'Spitze, nicht?'

THE SNOW BUFF

Usually found cupping snowflakes in hand and explaining to anyone who's prepared to listen that there are literally thousands of different types of them, and that the Eskimos have a word for just about every one. Carries small books in his bum-bag to help him identify different formations of snow crystal.

THE METEOROLOGIST

Much akin to the snow buff but more doom-laden and less entranced by the magic of the mountains. Usually occupied scanning the horizon and predicting changing weather conditions. Also has plenty to say about snow surfaces, potential avalanches and hidden crevasses.

THE SAFETY NUT

Spends most of his money on the latest bindings and spends most of his time adjusting them. Knows the drill for all emergency situations and usually sports a number of first-aid badges. His bum-bag, of course, is well stocked with medical, and even surgical, bits and pieces. Off the slopes he's usually busy attending a ski injury seminar or going to the map-reading class.

THE HAPPY WANDERER

Sets off in the morning armed with *Alpenstock* or *piolet* and returns in the evening laden with mountain flowers. Rightly contemptuous of your activities.

THE TALL STORY-TELLER

Always on about the mogul that got away and the time he came down the Devil's Elbow on only one ski or how he'd done five runs by the time you arrived on the slopes at nine o'clock.

THE MACHINERY MARVELLER

Often accompanied by children on whom he inflicts his worship of snowcats, ski-lifts, cable cars and all the other mechanical contrivances on the slopes. Never tires in his wonder and faith in these machines. Two words that would never occur to him are 'metal fatigue'.

THE HUMAN AVALANCHE

Fancies himself as a bit of a 'bomber'. Specialises in skiing beyond the limit of his generally modest talents. Perpetually covered in snow, he wastes little time picking himself up from his crashes and hurtles straight on to the next disaster.

THE CLASS FOULER-UPPER

A cousin of the human avalanche. Can always be counted on to see that no group effort goes off as it should. If, for instance, the line is peeling off from top to bottom, he'll break ranks to make sure that the order is not followed. When skiing down to the class he will invariably try to join at the top, or, if he misses his last turn, somewhere in the middle, usually managing to knock everybody down.

THE JOKER

Another relative. Enjoys standing on the back of your skis, flicking snow at you with his ski-sticks, throwing snowballs and similar activities. Also has a limited range of 'silly positions' which he keeps inviting you to watch him perform.

THE *SKI ÉVOLUTIF* FANATIC

Usually has children. Had the whole family on *ski évolutif* in France once and has never got over the discovery. Spends a lot of time in obscure resorts in places like Bulgaria, demanding to know why they don't offer *ski évolutif* or why they've never even heard of it.

THE PHOTOGRAPHER

Identifiable by his huge black bag which he will sometimes manage to get the instructor to carry for him. Amiable enough, but keeps the class hanging around a lot while he sets up the equipment – especially if it's cine. Most irritating trick is to make the class walk uphill in deep powder snow so he's got the right background for his picture.

THE LINGUIST

Has a smattering of the instructor's tongue and so volunteers to translate for the rest of the class. In fact he misses most of what's said, but as he usually feels he knows a bit about skiing himself, he'll prattle on, inflicting his own half-baked theories on the rest of the class.

THE POWDER FREAK

Is always going on about *la poudreuse* or *neve fresca* or *Pulverschnee*. He knows the name for it in most languages. Spends a lot of *en piste* time sitting back, with sticks out, imitating the motions for powder skiing. Is usually a lot less successful when he actually gets into the stuff but is always whining at the instructor anyway to take the class off *piste*.

THE IMBIBER/NIBBLER

Keeps the day well punctuated with refreshment stops at friendly hostelries, fortifying drams on the slopes or smoke breaks. Always has a flask of alcohol about his person and probably some *saucisson*, nuts and chocolate, too. Worth keeping in with.

THE EARLY BIRD

Has faded gear and old fashioned equipment and always arrives back in the ski-room just as you are setting out of a morning. Makes a point of telling everyone very heartily how there's nothing like 'first run'. This person may just be a skilful Survival Skier, but it's probably not worth getting up early to find out.

THE ACCUSER

Always has someone or something to blame for his difficulties. Either you were skiing on his tail or he couldn't follow the funny line you took. The snow always seems to organise itself just to thwart his efforts.

THE *PISTENJAEGER*

The smoothie who knows how to ski. Is actually rather bored with skiing but enjoys being admired, envied, hated, and so keeps at it. Usually performs on difficult bits that are in full view of lots of people (e.g. on 'Watch Me' mogulfields). Very helpful to attractive beginners of the opposite sex. The more flamboyant types have taken to wearing a silk handkerchief knotted around the thigh.

THE VETERAN

Has been returning to the same hotel in the same resort for the past few decades and always occupies his particular corner of the hotel bar or nearby *Stübli* where he has his own personal beer *Stein*. Spends his time there mumbling to the barman about the snows of yesteryear and the *Thé Dansants* of yore and the good old days when people went ski-touring, dressed for dinner and had intelligent discourse on the respective merits of using one, two or no sticks.

THE SKI NEUROTIC

Increasingly common. Constantly worrying about whether he's on the right type of skis, or whether he hasn't perhaps got worse since last year. Always goes to the instructor after class to ask if he might be better off having private lessons geared to his particular needs. More and more shrinks are going into full-time ski psychiatry to cater for this new breed of patient, and many instructors are on commission for referring patients to them. (Slogan in the consulting room of one Californian nut doctor: 'First get your head together, then get your feet together'.)

THE ZEN SKIER

A close cousin of the ski neurotic. Invariably American. He's usually wearing a headband, carrying a copy of *Inner Skiing* and chanting a mantra. In action, adopts funny positions to 'listen to the sound of his skis' or to concentrate on some other specific part of his anatomy. When not on the slopes he can be found doing yoga somewhere in the hotel.

THE 'ULTIMATE' FREAK

Another relative. Also usually American. He's on an unending search for the 'ultimate' ski experience; or failing that, anything he can say 'Wow', 'Holy Shit' or 'Hit me' about while he's waiting. If there's no helicopter skiing, he'll be off *piste* somewhere in unskied powder. Usually manages to find new and highly dangerous routes down, preferably involving a bit of jumping, during which he will yip at the top of his voice. He's also embarrassingly enthusiastic about equipment. All his gear is either handcrafted or the 'ultimate' product of the latest space age technology. He is, of course, already planning to trade it in as new stuff is about to appear on the market that is even more 'ultimate'. He will also be the proud possessor of a mono-ski so if you want to shake him off the simplest thing is just to go up the Poma-lift — unless, of course, he happens to be bow-legged.

THE CHALET DWELLERS

Several varieties of these. Often British. One lot are very hearty with piercing South Ken voices. They spend a lot of time swapping names of people they have in common, eating fondues and forgetting to do the washing-up. A second lot are a bit more down-market and keep talking about how they enjoy 'mucking in together'. They are always arguing about whose turn it is to do the washing-up or use the bathroom first and live on instant soup and baked beans from the local supermarket. Both groups easily drown out a third lot — the guitar-players and songsters. These people don't wash much (the others don't give them much chance) and don't wash up because they live on bread, cheese and wine.

THE PROUD PARENTS

Do their skiing through their children. First enrolled Jason with DHO when he was three and he's now in the West Norfolk under-fives slalom team. They're thinking of coming to live permanently in Switzerland. Meanwhile they travel out to the Alps every other month in a battered mini-bus plastered with ski stickers. They often team up with similar families for these trips so that the fathers can play at being team managers. The big advantage for the parents is that they feel involved in the Big Time but don't actually have to do much skiing. Their biggest gripe is that no firm has yet been prepared to sponsor their offspring: 'No wonder we can't keep up with the East Germans'.

THE SHOPPER

Spends most of his time going round the shops, trying things on and even studying items already bought on previous days. Is never sure whether things are cheaper at home or on the mountain. He only goes out on the slopes to test or show off his latest acquisition. This will always be pointed out to you for admiration, envy or approval; if it wasn't pointed out you'd never know it was new as he doesn't have a single item of gear that's old.

THE RESORT COLLECTOR

Doesn't do much skiing but claims to have skied an awful lot. You name it, he's been there — done all the right things. If it's St Moritz then his hangouts will have been the Palace Bar, the Corviglia Club and Hanselmanns. He must either spend half his life travelling or an awful lot of time studying brochures.

THE PRIVATE LESSON TAKERS

Usually a couple. They can't take the abuse in bigger classes and feel that they have latent skiing talent (usually very latent indeed) that could be brought out by a more personal form of tuition. Their instructor knows what he's being paid for and does his bit at making them feel a lot better than they are. They spend the evenings telling each other and everyone else how the lessons are worth every penny and what tremendous progress they are making.

THE REPORTER

Occupies himself by feeding you snippets of information about what's going on in the outside world, never imagining for a moment that the reason you're on the mountain is to sever all connection with the outside world. He's usually armed with a pocket transistor radio capable of picking up the moon and he gets his written information by hanging around at the newsagent's scanning the front page headlines with the aid of a selection of pocket dictionaries.

13. Après-Ski

'Rise up lads, the evening is coming . . .'

Catullus

Strictly speaking, *après-ski* refers to those other winter sports, like ice-skating, curling, or sleigh-riding, that you go in for when you come off the slopes. Everyone knows, though, that what it really means is putting on a chunky sweater and lounging around on a bearskin rug in front of a blazing log fire with one arm round a jug of *Glühwein* and the other round an attractive companion.

The trouble is that this cosy picture of skiers who came in from the cold (which may have lured us into the mountains in the first place) is not really true either. In fact, *après-ski* is more like a nightly social assault course which can take more out of you than your on-slope activities. Don't be misled into thinking *après-ski* is the easy part. If anything, it's the skiing that's got easier over the years (yes really), while the *après-ski* has got tougher.

The real problem is that *après-ski* and skiing don't go together. Skiing doesn't leave you in much shape for *après-ski* and vice versa. Night-time knees-ups and daytime knees-bends are not all that compatible. But you paid for both. You *will* enjoy both.

The good thing about *après-ski* is that you are not at the same disadvantage vis-a-vis the pros as you are on the slopes. We all have plenty of opportunity during the rest of the year to practise getting drunk, sing-songing, disco-dancing or whatever form of carousing happens to be our forte. Indeed, there are plenty of rotten skiers who are in the front rank of *après-skiers*, and it's probably true to say that among the all-time great *après-skiers* very few have been any good on the ski-slopes.

Many of the big names on the ski-circuit avoid *après-ski* altogether. But don't let any of the ski-nuts on your holiday do the same. If a keen *après-skier* like you does his bit on the slopes, there's no reason why the skiers should cop out of the bar sessions. If you are prepared to be shown up during the day, they should be prepared to be shown up at night. *Après-skiers* therefore make it their business to see that skiers don't sneak off to bed early and skimp on the *après-ski*.

If some people do insist on jacking out of the *Gemütlichkeit* (couples are the worst offenders) it's unlikely to do them much good. *Après-skiers* can usually make enough noise in every corner of a resort to ensure that nobody gets to sleep before they do.

The fact that skiing and *après-skiing* don't always marry up too well doesn't mean that skiing techniques don't come into *après-ski*. As on the slopes, a lot of time is spent posing and there's probably more ski-talking *après-ski* than during ski.

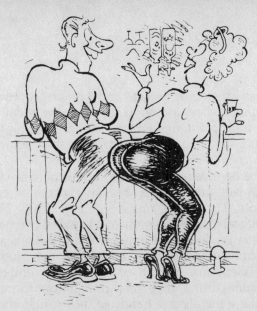

Stand back some time and watch a group of skiers standing at a bar. They'll all be bending right or left in banana position, weight on the lower foot, pushing their knees forward as they make a point and leaning into the bar as if it was the Fall Line. Similar postures can be seen at the disco. Everyone will be weighting and unweighting as they roll their knees and bump bottoms (a favourite with skiers who tend to have quite large ones).

Although this is all quite unconscious, there is also a good deal of deliberate demonstrating. Many people find it easier to execute certain manoeuvres at the bar than on the slopes, and even quite undistinguished skiers seem to feel they can pull off some of the more exotic turns very successfully when legless. But do resist any temptation to rush down to get your skis and show people how to do it on the stairs. It's more difficult than it is on snow and the landlord won't like it.

The *après-ski* begins as soon as you arrive back in the ski-room where you show off your best bruises and have a preliminary undress rehearsal for your stories of the day's escapades. The exercise continues over some form of hot grog at your *Stammtisch* in the local *Weinstube*, enabling you to further restore your circulation and your ego. This usually ends in a bit of a scramble as people make a dash for their rooms to try to get to the hot water while there's still some left.

These days it's more the thing, particularly if you're a top-floor dweller who didn't make it in time, to do your bathing in public — at the swimming pool and sauna. Exposure to heat can seem like quite a good idea after a day of exposure to cold. Those who've had enough exposure for one day stay at the poolside draped in their towelling robes and continue drinking. There's usually a bar attached or one within staggering distance. Some people even swim. For a change of scene you can always go and play with the apparatus in the gymnasium or solarium.

But the real *après-skiers* take a sauna and a massage, proclaiming heartily that dehydration and pummelling are good for you after a day on the slopes. The sauna can be fun. Most of them are mixed now and the regulars can have hours of harmless pleasure steaming it up or turning up the thermostat to drive out the novices.

You need not be deprived of the comfort of alcohol as you sweat it out. The sauna hour can, in fact, turn into a very heavy session – especially if there are Scandinavians about. They usually insist on bringing large quantities of beer and aquavit inside for instant replacement of lost liquid. If you get round to chucking beer instead of water on the stones it makes for an even headier atmosphere.

Some people can get quite carried away in the sauna – again, usually Scandinavians or Germans. Instead of lying there semi-conscious reading a newspaper and getting drunk, they keep dashing out to roll in the snow, jump into an ice-cold lake if there's one handy or, failing that, the plunge pool. They also beat each other with rolled up newspapers or flick each other with towels, presumably as a substitute for birch twigs. If the going gets too rough, retire to the solarium to work on your suntan.

After all, the bathing hour is supposed to be for the less sporty individuals. The real athletes will be outside again for another bout of hard physical exercise – ice-skating, bowling, or sometimes jogging despite the obvious difficulties in a ski resort. Some even head back out to the *pistes* – a lot of places now have floodlit lower slopes. But a word of warning to Survival Skiers: these slopes are always prominently situated to provide entertainment for more sensible people sitting and drinking inside.

The next item in the *après-skiing* programme is usually shopping. This is perhaps the most relaxing pre-dinner activity, most skiers have a strong urge to spend money which will have been largely frustrated on the slopes during the day. It's also a good morale-booster as shopping is something most people know how to do.

The shopping stroll is often combined with a stoking-up-before-dinner session, which means dropping into one of the many pastry and ice-shops and exercising your jaws and your waistband on some *Strudel, gâteau* or *cassata*. Another alternative in the old days used to be the *Thé Dansant*, which seems to have been phased out at even the poshest resorts, though there are attempts in some hotels to replace it with an American-style Happy Hour.

After this people are usually ready for dinner, which takes place early in ski resorts. Skiers, even Survival Skiers, are always hungry and eat a lot.

People no longer dress for dinner – except in their *après-ski* suits – and no longer seem to feel it's not the done thing to be among the first into the dining room. In fact, people tend to gather at the bar and charge in as soon as the dining

room doors open. It does, of course, pay to start early if you're somewhere like Switzerland and may be put to work on the slow business of cooking your own in a fondue pot.

Make the most of dinner. Linger over your myrtle tart or your *crêpe*. As soon as it's over there'll be little chance to escape from the action.

Some of the ski-freaks, of course, now go back to those floodlit slopes yet again. But most people will choose to do their sliding to and from the *Weinstube*, night-club or disco.

It is on these little expeditions to and from your local hotspot – usually from –

that most skiing accidents occur. Clearly you've quite a good chance of breaking your leg on some slippery path wearing your non-grip *après-ski* boots, slightly the worse for alcohol poisoning, being pelted with snowballs and writhing about when someone puts snow down your back.

It is after dinner that you sort out the real *après-skiers*. Those who can't handle it will opt for some tame diversion like sitting around playing cards or draughts or watching films with titles like 'White Dreams' of people hot-dogging or floating in slow motion through the powder. Ski-tourers will sit studying their maps and would-be racers will go and sharpen and wax their boards.

The true *après-skiers* will be down at the *Weinstube*, beer-on-draught 'English pub' or *Bierkeller* already linking arms and getting stuck in to their *Schunkellieder*. These usually turn into national team affairs – the Germans with their oompah songs, the Italians hitting the higher notes and trying something a bit more melodic like *O Sole Mio* and the British confusing the opposition with *On Ilkley Moor Bah't 'at*.

You may well be joined at the *Weinstube* by your ski instructor. Try not to let him upset your drinking as much as he does your skiing. He'll probably encourage you to try the local firewater, but there's no point in letting him choose the weapons all the time. He was probably weaned on this stuff.

Be equally cautious about getting involved in other local customs like *Schuhplatter* dancing, balancing on beer *Steins*, yodelling, alpenhorn-blowing or skiing down flights of stairs. However much the instructor or dirndl-clad maid may enjoin you to *'sei nicht so feig'*, these are offers you definitely can refuse. Stick with things you know how to do – like limbo-dancing or swinging from the chandeliers. But don't imagine you'll be on home ground if you move over to the dart board – if it's been there at least six months the chances are the locals will be more accurate with the arrows than you are.

If you do decide to perform any of your favourite party tricks, it's as well to remember that it can be more difficult after eight hours on the snow and one in the sweat-box. Your body may feel you've asked enough of it for one day.

You may be better off linking arms with your neighbour (one advantage of *après-skiing* over skiing is that you can use other people to hold yourself up) swaying to the music and watching some foolhardy innocent take on the alpenhorn.

Before you are too far gone you'll have to make a move and stagger on to the last stage of the evening's *après-ski*. This could be the casino or a bout of serious drinking in some murky cellar or, more probably, hopping about in *Pferdestall*, night-club or disco. The first two are likely to be the hardest – one on your pocket and one on your liver. The night spots are the most popular choice, provided you think you've still got the legs for it. It's also an opportunity to come alongside

---

Skiing Statistics

Most people ski between 40– 70 per cent better in their mind's eye than they do on the slopes.

The stranger you gave advice to in the bar will turn out the next day to be twice as good as you are.

You are three times more likely to break your leg going down the path to the disco or going downstairs in the restaurant in your ski-boots than you are while skiing.

Your lift pass will cost at least 150 per cent more than you thought it would.

At 2,000 metres a three and a half minute egg needs to be boiled for six minutes.

Your teeth are four times more likely to ache at altitude.

---

whoever it is you've been lusting after on the slopes — if you can recognise him or her out of their ski-gear, that is.

If you don't go with a partner, it's certainly a good idea to lose no time in seeking one out. It's vital to have someone to lean on on the dance floor and to help you keep your head above table level.

The more experienced *après-skiers* should also try to keep their eyes open for any of the weaker bretheren who try to slip off to bed, perhaps claiming that they've got to adjust their bindings for the morrow. One way of stopping this is to pool all the room keys. People don't normally like to be the first to draw a strange bed and an unfamiliar bedfellow unless it's a proper key-swapping party night.

One of the main things to remember on this last stage — particularly on the journey back — is to keep the noise level up. No-one in the resort should be allowed to get to sleep before you do. Just to make sure, one of your number is usually detailed to go and knock on all the other bedroom doors before going to bed. Strictly speaking this shouldn't happen much before 3 am, otherwise those already in bed will conclude that you haven't really enjoyed yourself.

If you are sharing an apartment or a room with someone who has already got their head down, make sure you turn on all the lights, make a fair old racket and ask them (several times, if necessary) if they are asleep. They also often appreciate it if you open the window wide for a refreshing blast of cold air. Remember, he who goes to bed last sleeps best.

You will sometimes come across people who don't take this in the proper spirit and, rather childishly, try to take revenge by tipping you out of bed in the early morning. This need not worry you too much since, if they don't tip you out, the chalet or hotel maid certainly will. These good people (who have the sense not to sleep on the premises) are totally unfamiliar with the concept of the lie-in and are under orders to see that all visitors are dispatched to the ski-slopes during the day.

This is one reason why it's best not to pass too often that point in the small hours when *après-skiing* more or less turns into *avant-skiing* and it no longer seems worth the effort of taking your boots off.

Nevertheless the real stayers will often remain active a while longer groping under the sheets – doing their best to keep those promises made on the disco floor. Some hold that an early morning grope is a good way of loosening up for the day ahead. Ski instructors say it can give you the idea of the sort of rhythm you should be looking for in your parallels. But it seems fair to say you may not notice much immediate improvement on the slopes the next day.

14. The Natives

'Those rascals of the mountains who practise every kind of cruelty imaginable on travellers'

Michel De Montaigne

If you ever get lost or stuck somewhere in the mountains, whether it's a precipitous by-road or a darkening ski-slope, the odds are that sooner or later you will find yourself face to face with some canny old Mountain Man who knows you are his victim. This is the native in his purest form. His forefathers made a killing whenever Hannibal and Napoleon came the way of the Alps. And now you are going to help him to get through the winter by letting him help you — at a price, of course — to find food, shelter, petrol, a mechanic, the way down or whatever else it is you need.

This man is a member of the same clan — albeit one of the wilder cousins — as those who staff the ski resort of your choice and fleece you in today's more organised and sophisticated way. They no longer have to lie in wait for travellers. They've spun a web of *pistes* and ski-lifts over the mountain and baited it with goodies to lure you up to 1500 metres for your two week spending spree.

It's important not to delude yourself about this. For, as a keen skier who has spent the rest of the year yearning for the clean air and the open sky of the high ground, you may feel yourself to be something of an Honorary Mountain Man or Woman yourself. That may be the way you feel. But to the real mountain folk the word skier means only one thing — tourist.

The appearance of the first ski-runners raring to get at the snow must have seemed like an answer to one of the eternal mysteries. For thousands of years mountain folk must have asked themselves what the point was of the snows that came every year to drive them with their livestock into winter hibernation. They've since found out. Now they know that the snow is their most precious resource, and renewable annually to boot. Their only regret is that they didn't start showing the lowlanders how to strap barrel staves to their feet earlier.

Just how slow they were on the uptake can be gauged from the fact that, as late as the end of the last century, a family in the ice-cream business in Granada in Southern Spain had no difficulty in acquiring rights to the exclusive use of all the snow on the Sierra Nevada for their trade. These rights, incidentally, have been handed down through the family until today, but they've been decent enough to let people ski on the snow and so enable the local ski industry to flourish. They put the title up for sale every now and then; so if anyone's looking for an exotic present for the girl who has everything . . .

It probably won't be long, in fact, before the whole business of snowing — that quirk of nature on which Mountain Man has come to depend — will be taken out of the hands of the Gods. Snow-making machines can only go on getting better and we will soon have the technology for inducing the right temperatures over the tops of mountains to precipitate the stuff.

Certainly Mountain Man has not been slow to take advantage of and adapt to whatever mechanical paraphenalia lowland man can dream up. It's hard to believe sometimes, looking at the complex complex of a modern ski resort, that what is being offered are still the basics of food, shelter and mountain know-how.

It must be especially hard to believe for the locals, who probably spend a lot of time pinching themselves and wondering for how much longer the goose is going to lay his golden eggs. Is it possible that these lowland masochists are still going to want to come all that way to be abused by the locals on the slopes? Can there be enough money left down there for people to continue to be able to hand over such huge sums for the privilege of going up and down on sundry mechanical contrivances in conditions that no self-respecting brass monkey would be out in? Will young lowland men with PhDs continue to want to throw it all up to become ski bums?

The locals themselves are not sure exactly what the magic formula is that keeps these people coming to spend their money in remote and inhospitable places. But they do by now have a fairly good idea of some of the basic ingredients they have to provide.

One of the most important of these is the setting. Ideally there should be an important mountain in the area to serve as a backdrop and, of course, to feature on most of the local picture postcards. Other outstanding climatic or geographical features – like a glacier or a special type of wind (*Foehn*, for instance) – also help.

When it comes to the slopes, it is usual to have a *piste* or a piece of *piste* apparatus that can claim to be the 'mostest'. Thus you might have the longest *piste*, or the widest, or the one with the biggest camber, or with the most moguls, or with the biggest vertical drop. The lift could be the longest T-bar, the T-bar with the most bends or the fastest running T-bar. Competition between resorts being what it is, many villages are obliged to qualify these claims, so you often get something like 'the longest Poma-lift on an east-facing slope in the Romansch-speaking Alps'.

Each village has a statistician who collects all this data and collates it with the latest statistics from other resorts, so as to lend a specious authority to the claims that are made.

Most resorts also have a fellow whose job it is to think up names for newly-opened slopes, *pistes*, lifts and mountain restaurants. The Americans have a particular talent for this, inventing names like 'Don't look now', 'My God', 'Watch me' and 'Never again'.

These two individuals work very closely with another important character – the local Pathological Liar. He's the one who rings up the national newspapers with the snow reports and who persuades the National Ski Club representatives that it really is possible, or very shortly will be, to ski on the Neverneve.

This last job is often held in rotation by different people in the village, since the incumbent fairly rapidly becomes discredited. Most of the locals can do the job as nearly all Mountain Men think of themselves as amateur meteorologists. It's a role that is certainly expected of them by their guests. In answer to a question about what the weather is likely to do, they can all be counted upon to turn out a first-rate performance. They'll narrow the eyes, look up, scan the horizon, sniff the air, taste it, put a finger up for the wind, scoop up a little snow, eat it and then come up with something suitably Delphic that you can interpret as you wish. Sometimes they'll offer up a more specific piece of local weather lore like 'When the wind is in the East it's neither fit for man nor beast' or 'It always snows on the fifteenth night of the year when the moon is new and the birds are flying west in threes'.

At best this will be enacted by a wizened, red-nosed, wind-tanned, bow-legged old Mountain Man, complete with pipe and stick. These old fellows used to provide some of the best examples of local colour. Unfortunately, because of the softer life in the mountains in recent years, there are fewer authentic specimens around these days. As a result an Alpine version of Central Casting has been set up and is doing excellent business providing suitably gnarled freelancers who do the rounds of the villages and pose for photographers.

Rather more likely to feature on your picture postcards are local girls and boys in folksy costume, perhaps *Dirndln* and *Lederhosen*, dancing some traditional mountain jig. These same people also perform at evening *Schuhplatter* sessions or whatever the local equivalent is.

All this, of course, belongs more to what we like to think of as a typical Alpine village – cuckoo clock houses nestling in a secluded valley surrounded by pine trees and usually requiring a major expedition to get to the slopes.

The ski-from-the-doorstep purpose-built space age resort does not go in much for this sort of thing. The nearest they get to it on their picture postcards is photos of the local marmots or reprints of the old mountain hut that used to be there before the bulldozers moved in.

Instead of having wizened old men on their postcards, these newer villages are more likely to feature personality pictures of the resort's rather famous 'Director'. Most of them have one – usually a ski teacher or architect who has lent his name to the project. You will usually have a chance of shaking hands with the *maestro*, if not actually being told to bend your knees by him, in the course of a week's stay.

Many resorts also have a local skiing hero who was born or lives nearby,

encouraging us to hope that some of his magic may rub off on us. He probably grew up in a remote mountain cabin and so had to learn to ski to get down to the village school or set the bear-traps up on the mountain.

The rest of the folk who staff the resort can be divided, for the sake of convenience, into two basic groups — those who are there to look after you and those who are there to push you around. It's a sort of Alpine adaptation of the nice/nasty principle used in interrogations.

The hard men are those out on the slopes, most notably the instructors, who order you about and put you through it even in appalling weather conditions. Even more objectionable are the people who run the ski-lifts — a universally surly breed — who always demand to see your lift pass at the most inconvenient moments, like when you're just about to grab hold of the T-bar. Their colleagues manning the cable cars where they pack people in like commuters on the Tokyo underground are equally unpleasant. Nor should one forget the ratrac drivers. You may never see their faces but they make no secret that their aim is to run you down at every available opportunity. The alternative name for their vehicle — *piste* bully — just about sums them up.

It's worth noting that gratuitous unpleasantness on the slopes is now more of a European speciality. The Americans have broken with this tradition and even have pleasant lift men who say 'Have a nice day' as you climb aboard. There are even 'ski hostesses' in some resorts to try to make you feel at home.

In the village, behaviour, in general, will be much more civilised. This is, after all, where they take your money and they have every reason to smile while doing it. The only likely exception is the ski hire shop. Here they seem to work on the theory that any trace of humanity on their part might encourage you to question whether the boots they are pushing are actually right for your feet; or whether it is normal to have poles coming up to your shoulders; or rust-caked bindings; or skis with big chunks carved out of the sole. But perhaps it's understandable. It's tough work forcing feet into boots that don't fit and overtightening bindings to ensure that people don't come back for readjustments (people don't normally bother to complain from the hospital). It must also be quite a strain calculating the enormous profits: a pair of skis hired out four times have already paid for themselves and then, as most of us know, they remain in service for ever. If it should occur to you to ask just how old your hire skis are, you will, of course, be told they were brand new at the start of the season.

The other emporiums will be rather more gracious to you. They appreciate the importance of the daily shopping ritual and try to make it as pleasant as possible. You could, after all, choose to spend the time between skiing and supper asleep in your hotel. And even if people do seem to spend an awful lot of time just looking, the shopkeepers know that before the week is out these browsers will have bought something from someone and that it may well be them. Unlike the hire business, they seem to have a certain sympathy for their victims. For there is no doubt that is what you are; if you need something on the mountain there's nowhere else you can go to get it. One word of warning, though; they can sometimes be a little mischievous with their advice, like persuading you that you really can't do without a bright yellow baseball cap or a fur-lined balaclava.

In the hotels and bars, too, people are capable of being quite pleasant – whether they make your *Lumumbas* and *Glühwein* or shake out your duvet of a morning. The most *gastfreundlich* are invariably the *patrons* of the individual establishments. Many of them are local characters and often have distinguishing features like bushy side whiskers. They enjoy their role as mine host and don't seem to mind if you have a good time.

15. Competition

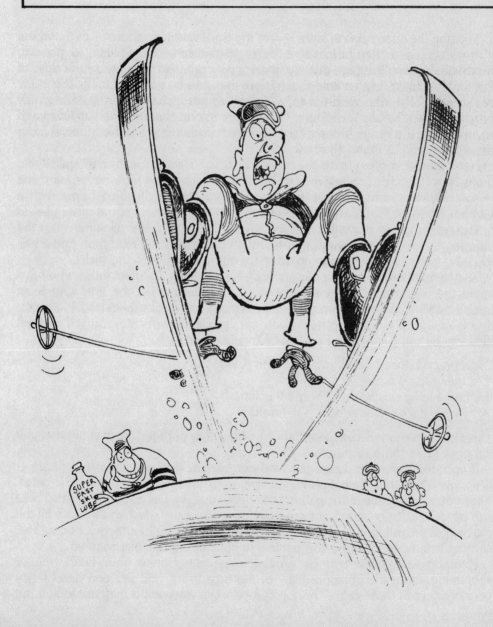

'Who's going to come second?'

Harry Jerome, to the other sprinters on the starting line

One of the big attractions of skiing – for the Survival Skier at least – is that there is no score, and therefore no necessity to subject your abilities to possibly humiliating quantification. Anyway, there's no easy way to measure the skills of the Survival Skier. His art is so much more than can be summed up by the crude calibrations of a stop-watch over a slalom course. Championship skiing may produce a neat results table but it fails to take into account all the subtleties and complexities, the range of technique and resourcefulness that the Survival Skier must command to make his mark.

Nevertheless, it often takes the novice Survival Skier some time to realise that there is not much in racing for him; and there are some who never learn the lesson. When it comes to the Big Day the temptation of going home with a Golden Arrow or Platinum Chamois pinned to his anorak or some other useless ornament weighing down his suitcase proves too much. We all suffer from the delusion that we ski (or could ski) that much faster than the next man and it's all too easy to find ourselves signing up to try our luck between the sticks.

This temptation, or indeed compulsion, is most likely to affect those who have spent the week enrolled in ski-school. The class race on the final day is an established fixture and instructors usually insist that everyone takes part. However, if you really do want to opt out you can probably extricate yourself without difficulty by using standard Survival Skiing lines like:

'Never raced since I broke my leg in the Kandahar.'
'I'm trying to ski better, not faster.'
'Left my racing skis/boots at home this time.'
'My racing days are over now, I'm afraid.'

This type of remark is best pronounced with a sigh of regret, conveying that you did once have some racing days.

If you don't want to desert the field completely, you can offer to officiate – acting as a marshal, helping with the timing or just manning one of the gates. Thus you avoid active participation but remain involved as a sort of expert. There can be quite a lot of scope in this role. You wear your faded anorak with all the old badges on and, playing the veteran who knows all the heartaches, encourage, congratulate or console the competitors in your best avuncular manner.

Pleading safety first can be another way out. Shake your head, mutter something about the irresponsibility of the organisers, and say you don't fancy your chances in those ruts – not on compact skis anyway. It may not look it but that sort of snow can be absolutely fatal. You will always be vindicated as a number of people are bound to fall and some will hurt themselves. If you like, you can always wait for the first person to fall before pulling out.

There is, by the way, some truth in all of this. Statistics show that most skiing accidents take place on the penultimate day of a week's holiday – the day of the ski-school race.

Another perfectly sound tactic is simply not to be there when your name is called. There's always so much hanging about and delay anyway that it's not unusual for people to take off in frustration and mistime their return.

Alternatively, if you want to make a bit of a show, and pre-empt any accusations that you are chickening out, just ski the first three gates. By limiting yourself to just three gates it is usually possible to perform rather above yourself – skiing faster and more stylishly than you could ever hope to over the whole course. After three gates you then miss your turn and come out at the fourth, cursing angrily to yourself.

Many Survival Skiers, however, just will not take advantage of these sensible ways out. It's quite remarkable how many normally mild-mannered and well-balanced people become transformed into kamikaze competitors as soon as they tie a race number on. Something comes over them. The adrenalin starts to flow and they're set to do or die in an attempt to settle the arguments once and for all with their arch-rivals in the ski-class.

These confrontations, incidentally, never do settle the arguments. The results are never conclusive as at least one of the two is almost bound to make a mistake and fall or miss a gate. If they do both finish, the loser will argue that he was distracted by something, or lost his way, or that the course was harder (more rutted, icy, slushy) when he went down it.

So, for those who are determined to go through with it and who refuse to see reason on Race Day, here's some advice. If you want to win, make no attempt to ski properly. Any concession to style – attempting proper slalom turns, dipping the inside shoulder to shave the sticks – will be counter-productive. The only thing that counts is the time and the only way to get a fast one is to charge down. Forget about your sticks and carving your turns. Just concentrate on staying on your skis.

Some Survival Skiers have even developed a system which effectively amounts to *schussing* down. It depends, however, on the course not being terribly well set, which is often the case with a ski-school version of a giant slalom. The important thing is not to have to change direction too much. You have to be able to plot a more or less straight *schuss* line through several gates at a time. When you absolutely have to change direction you stop in a controlled crash. This is the hard part – you can't afford to waste too much time picking yourself up. Then you *schuss* off in the new line. Generally speaking, if more than two crashes are necessary, it's not worth your while.

Another alternative which requires the same sort of 'must win' desperation, or what the Americans would call PMA (Positive Mental Attitude), is the rollercoaster. It is important here to make sure you perform last. If you get called earlier you have to pretend to be adjusting your binding or something. Then just step into the deepest ruts made by the other skiers and let yourself go. You may break a leg; on the other hand if you stay on track you may win.

The other advantage of going last is that you may not even have to do the rollercoaster. It may well be that most of the others don't finish the course, particularly on an icy day, leaving you to ski sedately down to victory in a controlled and stately snow-plough.

One reason why so many people come to grief in the races is excessive preparation of their equipment the night before. They spend hours waxing and filing their skis and the next day they find them so unfamiliar that they have no control at all, particularly as they are trying to go super-fast. Some people are even silly enough to abandon their compacts for longer racing skis – a sure way of putting paid to their chances.

There's no reason, of course, why you shouldn't make your contribution to this de-stabilising process. While not normally recommending dirty tricks like sneaking into the ski-room at night and putting the wrong wax on your main rival's skis, there's no harm in being plenty generous with the old hip flask on the morning of the race. It's amazing how effective alcohol can be to *couper les jambes*. Ideally you should carry two or three hip flasks with different types of hard stuff in each, alternating the flasks at each tippling session.

Another way to bring disaster on your rivals is to tell them during practice runs – when they are probably skiing very close to their limits anyway – that they look as if they can go a lot faster still. They are then almost sure to go over the top in the race, spurred on, if necessary, by you shouting 'Go for it' and 'Hop, hop' at them. One of the surest ways of making someone fall is to go 'Hop, hop' at him.

There's always plenty of time to lubricate the joints and massage the ego of your opponents in this way as the race never starts on time. You are bound to spend at least two hours hanging around while the course is prepared, names are checked, numbers given out and the walkie-talkies set up properly. It's also more than likely that the other classes will have their races before yours.

On the whole, apart from softening up your opponents, it's best to have as little to do with this preparatory stage as possible. Otherwise the instructors will have you wasting an awful lot of energy fetching sticks, planting them and then snow-ploughing down the course to smooth it out.

Even when they start trying to group the classes together, calling everyone to

check in at the start, you can easily afford to stay clear a while longer. You can safely ski on down and catch the lift back up at least two or three more times before you're needed.

When it comes to the race itself, just do your thing and hope for the best. You can be sure the winning tactic will be either 'Who Dares Wins' or 'Slowly But Surely'. The problem is that you never know beforehand which it will be.

At the end of the day it never seems to matter all that much who won. At the presentation ceremony that evening everyone will get an impressive medal and certificate, at the very least, to take home. From some countries – Italy in particular – whether you finished the course or not you'll go back laden with magnificent medallions, elaborately inscribed scrolls and sporting statuettes that would make you the envy of many an Olympic champion.

For many people, though, the most prized memento will be the action photo taken as they nudged past the third gate, race number flapping in their slipstream, looking for all the world like an advertisement for racing skis. This is the reason why many competitors reject the 'do or die' approach – they want to make sure they are looking their best for the picture that will sit on the mantlepiece for some time, impressing the neighbours. So they take it very easily at the start, waiting to get into the camera sights at the third gate before going into their best racing crouch and composing the face into a look of rugged concentration.

The photographer, incidentally, will always be at the third gate; he can't afford to go too far down as a lot of competitors won't reach him. So even when you are using the early withdrawal ploy, it's always worthwhile waiting until the third gate before you pull out – if you want to be immortalised, that is.

After all, just because you didn't win there's no reason why you shouldn't look and feel as if you did.

That, anyway, is the principle that is likely to guide you and your fellow losers as you drown your sorrows. Afterwards it's usually not too hard to console yourself. And in the best Survival Skiing tradition, you can expect plenty of ego-restoring support from your comrades – provided you reciprocate. You should have no difficulty in agreeing, for instance, that hand-held timing, particularly with walkie-talkie communication, is no accurate way to determine the outcome of a big race any more.

Final Rules of Skiing

All skiers end the day with a tale to tell, if not several.

If you don't catch a cold on your holiday you will catch one immediately you return home.

It will all seem to have been much more fun when it's over.

The way you say it was is never quite the way it really was.

You will come again next year.

BACK on the PISTE

Contents

Introduction

'There are three ski resorts in Lebanon. One is
occupied by the Syrians, another by the Israelis, and
in the last one you are advised not to ski off piste
because you might stray into a minefield.'

*Martin Chilver-Stainer, head of international sales at
Salomon, quoted in the* Sunday Times, *20 February 1983*

There is, apparently, still no end in sight. Neither recession, nor even, it seems, civil war, can keep us from our annual winter fix in the mountains. We'll all be in the Alps again this year clad in our gaudy romper suits, along with the rest of the madding crowd who are 'getting away from it all' on the slopes. And there, just like the rest of them, we'll allow ourselves to be herded into cable cars like so many Japanese commuters, bound for the top of yet another inhospitable Alp, where, once again, we'll brave death from hypothermia or from terminal ecstasy as we (involuntarily) seek to crash through the Mach Two barrier on our way down.

Some of us had hoped that skiing was just a passing phase that sooner or later would go the way of the trim-wheel and the hula-hoop. It was in this belief that, a few years ago, that classic handbook *Piste Again* was written, introducing the reluctant piste-basher to a few wheezes (known as the techniques of Survival Skiing) to help him cope with the whole ghastly business until the next craze came along. Unfortunately, if skiing is a phase, it is turning out to be a particularly long one — hence the need for this companion volume to *Piste Again* to bring Survival Skiers up to date with the latest developments on the slopes.

In fact, if anything, interest in skiing appears to be *increasing* rather than diminishing. It could even be said to have become an established part of the British Way of Life. These days those padded boilersuits can all be bought at C & A and Marks and Spencer. Moonboots are what children want for Christmas. And, judging by the number of school parties on the slopes, it would seem that skiing has earned a permanent place on the educational curriculum. It's even on television — so it must have arrived. Every day, on all channels, usually in the morning, wonderwomen in leotards, with names like the Green Goddess, take us through

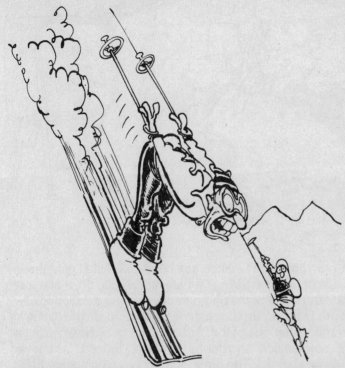

our pre-ski exercises. Then, every Sunday, there's World Cup skiing. And this despite the fact that there's never any 'British interest' in these races, since the only two British performers anyone has ever heard of (Davina Galica and Konrad Bartelski – there's two very English-sounding names for you) seem (wisely?) to have packed it in. Isn't it extraordinary that a once proud and patriotic nation should sit glued to the box every Sunday to find out that at Garmisch-Partenkirchen Hansi Skilikhjellegen has edged out Hieronymous Slalomski by 0.005 of a second to take the lead in the World Cup standings?

It may be, of course, that we simply derive some sadistic pleasure from the agonies undergone by David Vine, often dangerously out of control at the microphone, as he tries to wrap his tongue round some of the most unpronounceable names on the airwaves. (Is it true that the BBC fly out the whole of the Pronounciation Unit for coverage of the Ski Circus?) But no, let's be honest. David Vine is not really why we watch. Nor do we tune in just to get a whiff of mountain air off the tube and a glimpse of blue sky and sparkling snow as those svelte Swiss and crazy Canucks swoop down the slopes. The real reason we watch is because out there, in that red suit, just like ours, that's us scything between the sticks, just like we did last year when we were King of the Moguls. That's the way it was when we finally settled scores with our arch-rival in the ski-class. (Well, he got a medal too, but never mind). And lest anyone in the family should forget, there's that photo of us,

race-number flapping in our slipstream – taken just before we fell at gate three. (Remember that golden rule of Survival Skiing? Whatever else you do, make sure you're looking good at gate three where the photographer is always stationed).

But to come down to earth (with our usual sickening thud, sticks and skis flying in all directions), it will be recalled that one of the cardinal rules of Survival Skiing is that, wherever possible, competition should be avoided. Indeed, whenever possible, skiing itself should be avoided. The Survival Skier has other means at his disposal for competing successfully on the slopes and for getting through his day with an enhanced reputation and considerably less danger to life and limb. These standard Survival Skiing techniques are as valid as they ever were. But since publication of *Piste Again,* Survival Skiing, like Real Skiing, has continued to evolve – particularly the 'off piste' techniques. Thus, whereas *Piste Again* concentrated very much *on* the slopes, the focus of this book will be survival *off* the slopes – i.e. one of the more advanced techniques known as Armchair Skiing. To return again to the rather gruesome example of the Lebanon: according to *Euro Ski Guide* 'approximately 90 per cent of visitors to Lebanon's ski resorts *never actually ski'.*

But if this makes Armchair Skiing sound like a bit of a doddle, don't be deceived. If competition is tough on the slopes, you can be sure that it's every bit as fierce back at the lodge. Your tongue and elbows will need to be just as sharp at the bar as ever they were in the lift queue. Nonetheless, if you apply the lessons of this book properly they should help you to get through your triple brandy with as much credit as someone more athletically inclined might get for a Triple Daffy. It won't always be easy, but persevere with your Survival and Armchair Skiing techniques and in the end it will be worthwhile – particularly if you're the kind of skier who is at his best when ploughing through mountains of whipped cream and most at his ease on the slope of a reclining chair.

1.The Survival Style

'This it is also which leads some men to climb mountains, but not me, for I am afraid of slipping down.'

Hilaire Belloc, The Path to Rome

Although most readers will have been through a good many pairs of boots and skis since *Piste Again,* they will be reassured to know that the basic survival style remains unchanged. The quintessential Survival Skier is still someone who 'deep down, or perhaps not so deep down, is not that young any more, doesn't like heights or snow, would be upset if he broke a leg and just wants to get through the day with a flush on his cheeks, a few tales to tell, and his skiing ego intact'. This definition, of course, could be said to apply to just about everybody on the slopes – except for the occasional *piste artiste* or budding Bartelski. How then do we distinguish the Survival Skier from the Real Skier – particularly since most Survival Skiers have got so good at passing themselves off as Real Skiers?

Well, it isn't easy. But to the trained observer there are usually a few tell-tale signs which reveal whether a skister has learnt his skills in the Survival School. And since it takes one to know one, and since it is often helpful to be able to identify one's comrades in adversity, and since it is assumed that most readers of this book are aspiring Survival Skiers, here's a guide to some of those characteristics which set the Survival Skier apart from the Real Skier. (Needless to say, they apply to both sexes – indeed there are at least as many mistresses as there are masters of the arts of Survival Skiing.)

THE REAL SKIER

Heads straight for the slopes as soon as he arrives at the resort.

Stays in a hotel as close as possible to the lifts.

Goes skiing in mid-January or February (because the slopes are less crowded and the lift queues are shorter).

Makes sure, when he goes on a 'one week' ski holiday, that he gets seven full days of skiing.

THE SURVIVAL SKIER

Spends the first day or so getting himself organised.

Stays in a hotel as far away as possible from the lifts.

Goes skiing in mid-January or February (because there are fewer people about and therefore less chance of being spotted).

Tries to get on one of those 'seven nights' holidays which mean, in effect, only five days' skiing.

Makes sure all his gear is properly adjusted before he arrives at the resort.

Spends a lot of time fiddling with his equipment when he gets out on the slopes.

Is dressed rather too flamboyantly and is a bit of an exhibitionist.

Dresses as unobtrusively as possible and keeps a low profile.

Wears the sort of boots which lean you forward whether you like it or not.

Wears the sort of boots that don't try to tell you what to do.

Does not wear knee pads.

Takes all the protection he can get.

Has the latest hi-tech 'state of the art' equipment.

Has the sort of well-weathered gear that makes him *look* as if he knows his way around.

Is built for speed.

Is built for comfort.

Is looking for the action.

Prefers inaction.

Takes his skiing a bit too seriously.

Doesn't take his skiing anywhere near as seriously as he pretends to.

Skis to be seen.

Avoids resorts where there is no choice but to ski in full public view.

Is at his best performing in front of the sun-terrace.

Is at his best performing *on* the sun-terrace.

Gets panda eyes from skiing all day with glasses or goggles.

Has a nice even tan as he usually takes off his glasses on the sun-terrace.

Keeps a high profile on the slopes.

Keeps a high profile at the bar.

Is usually having a great time.

Tries to *look* as if he's having a great time.

Never has a moment of self-doubt.

Frequently wonders if he's going to make it through the day.

Has Positive Mental Attitude (PMA).

Detests American psycho-jargon, but *pretends* to have PMA (enthusiasm).

Knows a Telemark when he sees one.

Believes the Telemark is some sort of Central European currency.

Can identify all the surrounding peaks and lifts by name.	Thinks that one mountain looks much like another.
Has skied, within two days of arrival, every run on the resort piste-map.	Has tried to memorise the names of at least some of the runs and can talk about them *as if* he had skied them.
Knows all the best super-blacks.	Knows all the best escape routes, and back ways down.
Goes for the Big Skiing on the wide open spaces of the high peaks.	Tries where possible to ski below the tree line (where the cover is better).
Is always looking for a dreamland of crisp white powder.	Prefers to *dream* about it, rather than ski in it.
Likes skiing under clear blue skies.	Performs best when there's a bit of mist to disappear into.
Likes going off piste.	Will go off piste if it's the only way of getting to some cosy little hideaway *Hütte*.
Believes there's always room for improvement.	Knows that no improvement is possible, except in his Survival Skiing technique.
Tries to get in as much instruction as he can.	Takes the Ski-Pack with the *minimum* of hours of ski-school.
Has *every* confidence in his instructor.	Wouldn't trust his instructor with his loofah, let alone his life.
Is respectful to the instructor.	Treats his instructor with the contempt he feels he deserves.
Believes that *this time*, if he *really* concentrates in ski-class, he can make a *major* breakthrough with his skiing.	Knows that no amount of instruction is ever going to make any difference to his skiing.
Is always eager to hear about the latest techniques.	Only really takes an interest in the latest Survival Skiing techniques.
Is always looking for some useful tips.	Tends to give, rather than take, advice.

Is first out in the morning, last back at night, and careless of danger.

Is last out, and first back, and only too aware of the possibility of getting hurt.

Frequently finds himself brushing snow off the seat as he gets on the chairlift of a morning.

Has never got up early enough to experience the potential discomfort of a wet bottom on the chairlift.

Despite getting up at the crack of dawn, still finds himself queuing in the morning rush-hour.

Gets up a little later, to avoid the morning rush-hour, but still finds himself taking quite a while to get on to the slopes (usually making it just in time for lunch).

Always stays up on the slopes all day.

Frequently goes back to the village for lunch.

Makes a short stop for lunch.

Lunches long.

Doesn't mind missing lunch on occasion.

Would never, on any account, miss lunch.

Doesn't believe alcohol does much for your skiing.

Doesn't think he could get through the day without it.

Would rely on the local St Bernards if ever he were in desperate need of brandy.

Always has *at least* one hip flask about his person.

Doesn't like wasting time at the bottom of lifts.

Picks the slowest lifts and the longest queues.

Makes sure no one sneaks past him in the queue.

Denounces Queue Sneaks, but lets them through.

Would never go down in the cable car if he could ski down.

Frequently rides the car down (provided he can do so unobserved).

Is annoyed if the tow breaks down frequently.

Is philosophical about these things (and is secretly very pleased).

Always has a weather eye open for a short queue so that he can get back up top smartish.

Goes to the longest queue he can find or to the lift which has the best record for breaking down.

Gives every slope all he's got.	Saves his energy for where it's most needed (i.e. the bar).
Goes up and down like a yo-yo.	Prefers to admire the scenery.
Takes the shortest way up and the shortest way down.	Takes the longest way up and the longest way down.
Can't wait to charge back down as soon as he reaches the top.	Takes a long time to put on his skis, or adjust his bindings, at the top of the slope, and then spends a while taking in the view.
Steams off straight down the middle of the run.	Sticks to the edge of the piste where he can sideslip, and often takes the back way down.
Doesn't like being held up by anyone.	Enjoys a bit of a natter (especially with beginners, or anyone to whom he can offer help or advice).
Doesn't have much time for the locals.	Spends a good deal of time chatting to the *pisteurs*.
Is always on the look-out for super-blacks.	Tends to prefer green runs where he can survey the scene and not suffer from a sense of inferiority.
Looks for slopes that will provide a challenge.	Looks for slopes that will provide a boost to his ego.
Can never find a challenging enough run.	Finds most runs all too challenging.
Picks the steepest part of the slope to get some momentum into his *wedels*.	Does most of his *wedel* practice on the flat, in a stationary position.
Skis into the fall-line.	Skis *away* from the fall-line and spends most of his time traversing.
Holds his knees and hips into the slope, and shoulders into the valley.	Keeps as much of his body as possible between his centre of gravity and the slope behind him.

Rarely falls, but skis in such a way that he deserves to.

Has to be a bit careful because of various injuries collected earlier in his career.

Spends most of his time working on his parallels.

Spends most of his time working on his zig-zag technique (traversing from point to point).

Is a good all-rounder.

Can only do one or two things really well (which he performs once or twice a day at carefully chosen moments in full public view).

Takes the lead, using the *suivez-moi* technique.

Leads from behind, using the *après vous* technique.

Takes calculated risks.

Has a high self-preservation quotient.

Is always ready for a head-to-head race.

Prefers to compete over a good head of beer.

Is a competitor in any race he can enter.

Offers his services as an official, track marshall, or course setter.

Looks forward all week to the ski-school race.

Spends all week thinking up a good excuse for *not* participating in the ski-school race.

Always goes out skiing in the last few hours before departure home.

Has had more than enough by this time.

Rules of Skiing

FALLING

Falling is hard, but getting up is harder.

It's easier to get up after a fall if your skis are pointing across, rather than down, the fall-line.

Everyone *did* see when you fell under the chairlift.

If you have a great run, with only one fall, that fall will take place as you're skiing under the chairlift or in front of the sun-terrace.

A sure way of falling is to try to ski in time to the music.

It's when you're skiing most sublimely that you're most likely to come a cropper.

While not exhaustive, this list should give you the general idea. Of course, not all Survival Skiers have identical techniques, any more than Real Skiers do. Some Survival Skiers are pretty mobile, ducking and darting around the slopes. Others prefer to stand their ground, and to go through most of their routines in a stationary position. Some will perform best on the pistes. Others will want to go off piste – usually in search of some mountain *Hütte* where they can while away the afternoon. But though styles vary, the basics remain the same and, for the most part, they are sheer common sense – for instance, spending most of your time going *up*hill rather than *down*hill, keeping out of sight, riding the cable car *down* as well as *up*.

Naturally once you've grasped these essentials, you will probably want to improvise and develop a style of your own. And your style, of course, will depend very much on your own personal temperament. But, in general, it seems fair to describe the average Survival Skier as a companionable sort – ready enough to pass the hip flask around; perhaps a bit of a philosopher; usually willing to offer a word of advice (to anyone who will take it); and ever prepared to comfort another skier in distress. The Survival Skier is also a gentleman ('You go ahead. I'll catch up. Don't worry about me.'). But like all gentlemen, he is not always *totally* honest (for instance, he will complain loudly about the length of the lift queues, though this is precisely the reason why he has selected that particular resort). The Survival Skier will often appear to be in some pain, but will gallantly make light of it – except when a gasp escapes his lips through his gritted teeth as he binds up a limb in the locker-room. The Survival Skier is confident in his own abilities and doesn't let the Real Skiers get him down. He's been around a bit, and is wise in the ways of snow (and, if you give him half a chance, he'll tell you all about it). He's also a patient man and, if necessary, he can outwait anyone on the mountain, and even appear to be busy at the same time. (Usually, this won't be necessary as he will have teamed up with other Survival Skiers, who will tactfully look the other way at critical moments, or who will intuitively move off down the slope simultaneously, so that nobody gets embarrassed.)

But these are all basically *on*-slope techniques. And while they must be mastered, it must not be forgotten that the main characteristic common to all Survival Skiers is that *they spend a minimum amount of time actually skiing.* Thus, from here on this volume will concentrate on *off*-slope techniques, since it has become increasingly apparent that, as far as the Survival Skier is concerned, that's where the action, or rather the inaction, is.

2. Where To Go

'**Tucked away in the Engadine Valley, shut in by snow-capped mountains and unspoiled by civilisation is a small town called St Moritz. Here for 100 years the nomadic tribes of Europe have come for the winter to find grazing lands for their herds of Rolls-Royces, Cadillacs and Mercedes-Benzes.**'

Art Buchwald, More Caviar

As we've seen, the Survival Skier is not the sort of fellow who just needs a bed for the night and whose every waking hour is spent out on the slopes. In fact, as much of his time as possible will be spent away from the pistes. So he needs to look for the kind of village that lends itself to his particular skiing style. Finding it won't be easy. Despite all the claims made in the ski brochures, there is no ideal resort. All have their advantages and disadvantages. And really it's only by trial and error that the Survival Skier will eventually discover the sort of place that suits him best. As a rough guide, however, here are a few pointers about the more common types of ski-stations.

Cosmopolitan Chic

Famous for its high prices as well as its high pistes. Plenty of poodles and Porches on parade. But if he can afford it this sort of place is not a bad bet for the Survival Skier. Many of these resorts have been around since the Belle Epoque so there are plenty of the traditional activities like tea-dancing, tobogganing, sleigh-riding, curling, bobsleighing and skating to provide a legitimate alternative to skiing. Also, of course, there's the advantage of being in the company of a lot of other Survival Skiers: most of the *habitués* don't come to ski but to be seen, preferring to gamble in the casino rather than gamble with their lives on the slopes. The 'idle' rich were not idly named. To be fair, however, they do work quite hard at their *après-ski*, dancing the night away chic-to-chic in their mink ski-pants. And these resorts need not be as expensive for the Survival Skier as they might appear. You don't actually have to *stay* at the Grand Hotel (the sort of place where you leave your moonboots outside your bedroom door for polishing). The Grand Hotel is just where you do your drinking and your people-watching (spotting the Gaga Khans of this world is a favourite pastime). Afterwards you'll retire to one of the little *pensions* that can usually be found in the vicinity. And if anyone at the Grand Hotel does start to get nosy about your credentials, you can usually send them packing by just pulling down your ermine-trimmed sunglasses and putting on your best 'I want to be alone' expression. It invariably works.

Traditional Tyrol

This is what everyone likes to think of as a ski resort: a cosy village set in a Sound of Music valley; half-timbered *Gasthäuser* with carved balconies and colourful shutters; Tyrolean schmaltz in all its picture-postcard glory. Some Real Skiers, however, are beginning to desert these old-fashioned resorts for stations higher up the mountain that are closer to the snow and perhaps purpose-built. Not so the Survival Skier. The morning bottleneck at the two or three main lifts, which take you to the next lot of lifts, which take you to the next lot of lifts, which take you to the skiing, very much suits his style. And if the village is big enough and straggly enough, there'll be the added advantage of a long hike to get to the bottom station (with plenty of *Stubes* to duck into en route), or possibly even a journey by bus (which, of course, can be all too easily missed). Another advantage is that you can

never be sure, down in the village, what the weather is like up on the mountain, thus providing another good reason to play it safe sometimes and spend the day bending your elbow rather than bending your knees. A disadvantage of this type of resort, however, is that the *après-ski* can be rather hard going – *Schuhplattler* and Hokey-Kokey, and arm-wrestling with peasants in *Lederhosen*, to the oompah of a brass band that shakes the house down every night. (Beware of the hunting relics on the walls – those ancient skis and stag heads tend to come tumbling down on top of you.)

Traditional Swiss

Also folksy – with an 'i' at the end of everything, as in *Stübli, Rösti, Grüezi*. The Swiss also know how to perform in order to entertain their guests – yodelling, flag-swinging or blowing Alpenhorns. But it's all a bit less jolly somehow (Heidi country as opposed to Hi-de-Hi country). Many Survival Skiers will find this a positive advantage. But there are two drawbacks to traditional Swiss resorts: they are expensive and they are efficient. The ratracs will be out at five in the morning trying to win the award for the village with the best-kept pistes. And you'll find that the post-bus, the cable cars and the ancient cogwheel railways and the multifarious modern lifts *all* work and will get you up to the slopes in no time. In many resorts you can't even use that traditional Survival Skiing ploy of getting stuck in a traffic jam on the way to the bottom station – they've banned cars and have little electric snowmobiles to whisk you around. Another problem is that being that much higher, these resorts are closer to the slopes, which are often Big, well above the tree-line and often on the side of some famous mountain like the Eiger or the Matterhorn. This can provide a rather grim reminder to the more sensitive Survival Skier of all those mountain-mad Brits from earlier times who lie buried at the bottom. Still, if you do make it back down, there's a good chance of hot water in the hotel. (In Swiss hotels things actually work.) And even the more modest establishments usually have plenty of dining-rooms and wood-panelled *Stüblis* and other cosy corners that give the Survival Skier the scope he needs to manoeuvre.

Purpose-Built

Usually French. An ugly conglomerate of multi-tiered concrete blocks, which has won prizes for its 'architecture', and is designed primarily for self-caterers who want to have their *pieds dans la neige*. This is why many Real Skiers rather like them. Not so, of course, the Survival Skier. Skiing straight to, or from, his front door is the last thing he wants, since it practically eliminates any opportunity for time-wasting *en route*. Fortunately, however, despite all the hi-tech and Space Age planning, nothing in these places ever actually functions. The conveyor belts and electric trolleys are usually out of order, the elevators (vital to get from level to level), are always stuck and you spend a great deal of your time stumbling down flights of uncleared steps (without, however, any friendly *Stüblis* to duck into en route). One advantage is that the *domaine skiable* is usually rather large, often linked up with another *station integrée* down the road. This provides plenty of scope for getting around, so you can keep well out of the way of the people to whom you spend your evenings giving advice in the Rose and Crown. (All of these places have an 'English pub'.)

But somehow, these *station villages* are all a bit soulless, though some of them do employ 'hostesses' and '*animateurs*' to try to liven things up. Unfortunately they tend to do this mainly in French – like the resort radio station, which will be about all you'll be able to tune into on the radio in your room. If you're unlucky, however, there may just be one five-minute spot in English in the mornings telling you that, despite the weather, the pistes are all in operation (thus depriving you of one of the better Survival Skiing excuses for staying in bed).

Chalet Resort

These are becoming very popular, especially with Brits who like to ski in groups. They also tend to be popular with goodish skiers, which is, of course, a disadvantage for the Survival Skier. Nevertheless these villages, which are usually well spread out and offer a large and varied skiing area, would appear to be well suited to Survival Skiing. The problem is that life revolves almost entirely around your chalet, and it's almost impossible to escape your chalet-mates. If you do manage to give them the slip on the slopes, you can be sure the chalet-maid (most of whom ski rather better than they can cook) will spot you. Thus if you spend the evening describing pedal-jump turns, you may be called upon to demonstrate one the next day. And there's not much chance of escaping in the evening down to the village. The 'Downtown' area, such as it is, will tend to be modernish, with few hotels, and better equipped with supermarkets than *Stüblis*. Thus you tend to go there only in daylight to stock up, rather than at night to stoke up (which would entail the risk of *not* finding your way back up the long, icy path to the chalet). The *après-ski* and the entertainment therefore tend to take place back at the chalet (of which more in Chapter Five).

Cross Country

At first glance, these resorts would seem to be a good bet for the Survival Skier since they are invariably low-lying with plenty of vales and trees to get lost in. The

---

Rules of Skiing

BOOKING UP

The week you want to ski will always be just inside the high season, rather than just inside the low season (and priced accordingly).

The fact that there was a heavy snowfall in November doesn't mean there will be any snow left when you go in December.

The resort you are going to visit won't figure in any of the snow reports in the newspapers.

If you ski early or late, and there turns out to be no snow, you will be assured that this has never happened before at this time of year.

If it costs extra (like bacon and eggs for breakfast) it won't say so in the brochure.

You will pay more for your holiday than you can afford.

---

problem (or the advantage) is that there probably won't be much in the way of downhill slopes. Of course, there'll be one or two ski-lifts (so that the resort can claim to offer both Nordic and Alpine). But even the most gifted Survival Skier may have difficulty explaining to the *Langlaufers* what he's doing fooling around in the foothills when he should be powering down the peaks. And if you do duck into the woods you're liable to find they're crawling with people on skinny skis who'll have nothing but contempt for the massive boards on *your* feet. Things may not be so bad if there are other downhill skiers around (particularly the Survival sort). But if you find yourself mainly in the company of *Langlaufers,* you may be in for a tough time. They don't think too highly of piste-bashers and are almost certain to get you to try on a pair of their skinny skis and to lure you out on a loipe (which is guaranteed to shatter both you and your image).

The Resort 'Of The Future'

A building site. All mounds of red earth and concrete slabs. An embryonic purpose-built resort and a classic example of mountain blight. Not very suitable for the Survival Skier – or any other skier, for that matter. Usually situated somewhere magnificently remote, where the real estate speculators somehow managed to get 'planning' permission to 'develop' the area. Unfortunately, they can only do this when enough people have been persuaded to invest in their own 'dream' condominium or timeshare. Thus, for now, there are only a couple of baby lifts working and a few hideous apartment blocks, inhabited by people who were persuaded they could get rich quick if they got in 'on the ground floor' (they're still building the upper floors). Most of one's time is therefore spent listening to the ear-splitting racket of bulldozers and power drills, waiting for the sewerage to be put in, and asking the developers when exactly they intend, as promised, to 'open up' the mountain. Strictly self-catering – everyone goes back to their studios for lunch. About the only entertainment is the local laundromat.

Novices Only

A large low-lying village with easy wide open well-groomed slopes. This will not, however, prevent everyone on those slopes from colliding with one another all the time. Most of them will be there because the brochure said it was a good resort for beginners. It will also be cheaper. And if you're lucky there may even be no snow. Not a bad choice, therefore, for Survival Skiers who specialise in advising the innocent. Not, however, a name to conjure with and not one which will impress your more knowledgeable friends when you get home.

Locals Only

A small village, consisting mainly of chalets, with just one or two small hotels, where the locals still spend most of their time looking after the cows rather than catering to piste cowboys. The only visitors will be people from other parts of the Alps who like the place because there's some good skiing not too far away and because it has not yet been 'discovered' by people like you. Unfortunately for the Survival Skier who does stumble across it, these people also know a bit about skiing and will tend to make disparaging remarks about his antics in Schwyzerdütsch or some other incomprehensible Alpine patois. However, although he may not actually feel very much at home here, the Survival Skier will describe this sort of place as his 'ideal' resort, a place which only he knows about and which he intends to keep very, very secret.

Over The Top

A resort on or near a mountain pass – to be avoided at all costs (which are likely to be very, very high) unless you just motor straight through. The locals have been fleecing anyone coming their way for centuries. They have not lost their touch, and they are more than a match for even the most clued-up Survival Skier. Their victims used to be the Grand Tourists who got carried over the col in sedan chairs. Now they prey on the somewhat less grand, like you, who get carried away on skis.

Satellite

A very small village which trades off the name of a much bigger resort not far away. The brochures will describe it as 'just up the road from', failing to mention that the road between the two is usually impassable and that there's no regular transport, though there will be one lift to link you to the other resort's skiing area. Nevertheless, these villages do offer certain advantages to the Survival Skier. They're cheaper — you'll be staying in a no-star *pension* rather than a five-star palace. And the locals will be glad to have you, listening eagerly to your Survival Skiing accounts of daily derring-do. Nor will you be kept awake by the night-life (there isn't any), though there are those creaky stairs and the noisy plumbing. By day, of course, the Survival Skier can escape into the big ski area of the neighbouring resort.

Rules of Skiing

PLUMBING

The number of loos on the mountain is in inverse proportion to the number of people on the slopes.

The higher you go, the fewer the loos and the worse the plumbing.

Never eat yellow snow.

Mountain loos don't flush.

The chalet bathroom is always occupied.

Even if you sneak back during the day when everyone is supposed to be out skiing, the bathroom will still be occupied.

When you do get in, there'll be no hot water.

The rate of consumption of toilet paper is faster in a chalet than in any other form of accommodation.

Eastern Europe

Either old established resorts with antiquated lifts that keep breaking down, or fledgling resorts with brand new equipment which also keeps breaking down. Neither of these factors, of course, will deter the Survival Skier. The central heating can also be temperamental, so the locals tend to rely on more traditional methods of keeping warm – the Yugoslavs and Poles start the day with slivovic and vodka, while the Czechs like beer for their breakfast. This also may be no deterrent to the dedicated Survival Skier. And if he isn't up to dancing the *Kolo* or the *Czarda* in the evenings, he can always spend his time reminiscing about How It Was with local skiers, many of whom will still sport leather boots and cable bindings. Take your blue jeans along – not to wear *après-ski*, but to pay for your *après-ski*.

Cheap And Cheerful

Usually a low-lying farming village – perhaps somewhere like the Vosges or the Black Forest – where they're trying to trade in their tractors for Ratracs. They've seen resorts higher up in the mountains get rich, so they want to cash in too – even though they're a bit short of snow sometimes. Unfortunately they're also a bit short of lifts, which only operate when there are enough skiers about. And there will only be the one lift-man, who always takes a three-hour lunch break. To make up for these shortcomings the locals just keep on smiling, plying you with cheap booze and telling you what a bargain you're getting. One disadvantage for the Survival Skier is that he will probably keep running into *Langlaufers*; nor is this the sort of resort which is likely to add to his reputation when he gets home.

Just Outside Town

A popular resort, not far from a large town or city. Facilities are normally good and the place is usually large enough for the Survival Skier to get lost in – both on and off the slopes. One feature will be a gigantic car-park to cater for the inhabitants of the nearby city who drive up and take over the resort completely at weekends. This, of course, provides the Survival Skier with an excellent excuse for staying off the overcrowded pistes at these times. It's therefore ideal for the Survival Skier who's on a ten-day holiday which includes two weekends, and thus leaves him with only five 'actual' skiing days to worry about.

Mountaineering

Often more of a town than a ski resort, used as a base by walkers, climbers, mountaineers, ski-tourers, and also by skinny skiers. So it'll be full of shops selling hiking boots, skins, guns, ice-axes, ropes, crampons, back-packs and other bivouacking tackle. This may rather cramp the style of the sort of Survival Skier who excuses his ineptitude on the pistes by saying that ski-mountaineering is really his thing. If he spends his time at the bar holding forth on *La Haute Route,* he may just find there's someone within earshot who's done it – all too often. (And don't imagine that climbers can't ski – some can, only too well.) Caution is therefore recommended, even on the prepared pistes which can be pretty fierce. In short, not a resort for the faint-hearted, but big and varied enough to provide plenty of scope for the adventurous Survival Skier.

Mostest

Not so much a resort as a *zone*, a *domaine*, a *centre* – except that there is no centre. It's more a group of small stations and villages which, on their own, have nothing special to recommend them. So they've decided to join forces, to pool their limited assets and have hired a promoter to publicise the area as having 'the most beds' and 'the most hotels' and 'the most lifts' and 'the most runs' and 'more variety' of just about everything than anywhere else of comparable size – whatever that may mean. Not a bad bet, though, for the Survival Skier who likes to get around, provided the villages and the runs are all genuinely 'inter-linked', as claimed in the brochure.

3. Selecting Your Stube

**'Promote merriment, singing, fiddling and so forth
with all your power.'**

Francis Galton, The Art of Travel

Just as the Survival Skier aims to find a suitable resort and then sticks to it, so it is with the equally important matter of selecting a *Stube*. As we've already said, more reputations have been made or broken at the bar than on the slopes. Thus it's an enormous help for a Survival Skier to have a regular *Stammlokal* where the locals can be counted on to give maximum support to his stratagems. This is not something that can be achieved overnight. Mountain folk are more cautious than most, and it'll take a while and a good few rounds of grog and *grappa* to win their confidence and secure their co-operation as a supporting cast.

There are really no rules about where you are most likely to find your sort of *Stube*. It could be a snug in your *Gasthaus,* or a back room in another hotel or hostelry. And it could be situated almost anywhere in the village, even out by the slopes. But it does need to be the sort of place the Survival Skier can use right through the day – somewhere to have his morning nip and a natter about the weather; where he can get a goulash soup or a *Bratwurst* for his lunch, and perhaps another nip or two to fortify his spirits; where he can spin his yarns in the all-important *Klatsch* hour after coming off the slopes in the afternoon; and, of course, where he can find solace after dinner, and into the wee small hours, if he needs it (as he often does).

The atmosphere in your *Stube* will probably be hugger-mugger rather than chintzy and it certainly won't have some frivolous name like 'The Purple Pussycat' or 'Hawaii Five-O'. If there is 'entertainment', it'll be provided by a wooden skittle alley, bar billiards or darts – certainly not go-go dancing, video or 'space invader' machines. The liquids served will probably include the sort of brews that reach those parts that other liquids do not reach – perhaps some locally made moonshine or good mountain *Schnapps* made from the very best mash of skins, pips, stalks and all. They certainly won't serve those rotgut technicolour cocktails with a parasol floating on top that hustling Hansi palms off on the smart set at inflated prices up at the Palace Bar. Above all, your *Stube* should be very much a *locale* for the locals, as well as being a place in which the Survival Skier can socialise with and impress his fellow piste-bashers. The locals in question should be mainly members of the skiing fraternity – instructors, *pisteurs* or Ratrac drivers and the like, rather than discotheque or boutique owners. Ideally, they will include, on occasion, people like the *Chef de Piste,* the Resort Director or the Local Skiing Hero. Just five minutes spent with the ex-champ at the bar, slapping him on the back and demonstrating to him your own particular knee-rolling technique, can do wonders for your reputation – provided your fellow piste-bashers are looking on.

You'll be astonished at how much you can do to improve your skiing in just one session at the *Stube*. Sometimes you need only ply your instructor with a few drams, and the next morning it won't be 'Bend your knees, British' but *'Bravo, le Britannique'*. A few drams for the T-bar attendant and the next morning you too will be a member of that privileged clique that can stand and chat to him, leaning on the fence that nobody else is allowed to lean on, wasting plenty of good skiing time and watching the rest of them shuffling along in the queue and getting sent on up the tow. And when you do eventually decide to go up yourself, the *pisteur* won't expect you to share your meathook with anybody else. You'll go up alone – and he'll specially position the bar on your bottom for you. For a few more drams, he may even stage a little scene for you, failing to help some obviously incompetent novice to get *his* bottom on the bar properly, allowing him to crash ignominiously and then switching off the tow, causing the rest of the queue to groan loudly, and at the same time giving you his best 'Don't some mothers have 'em' expression. And if you become *really* good friends (and this can involve a very great many drams), he may even let you keep your skis in his little hut, so you don't have to trudge up and down to the slopes with them every day. In short, most *pisteurs* can soon spot an accomplished Survival Skier when they see one and will be prepared to see him right, provided he does the same for them. And with any luck, if you've chosen the right *Stube*, the rounds will be at 'local' prices rather than 'resort' prices.

But these relationships won't evolve from one day to the next. They can sometimes take years to develop. Mountain folk, especially if they work outdoors, are traditionally taciturn, whether their job is herding cows or herding skiers. The Survival Skier with savvy will therefore make himself known gradually. Bounce into a *Stube* for the first time and introduce yourself with a chirpy *'Grüezi mitenand'* ('Evenin' one 'n all') and there'll probably be two minutes of deathly silence. Even the old boys round the corner table will stop sucking noisily on their pipes and will look up from their games of cards and dominoes. And you won't particularly endear yourself to the locals by having too good a command of their own idiom, even if all this really amounts to is bunging an 'i' on the end of the few German words you know and assuming you're talking Swiss. Mountain Men distrust glibness. Thus, any address should be as monosyllabic as possible: *'Servus'*, *'Grüezi'*, 'Hot', 'Cold', 'Snow?' 'Cigarette?' or *'Frei?'*, you say, as you collapse into the nearest chair. The locals themselves also tend to talk in monosyllables – if that. Frequently a nod, a grunt or a shake of the head, accompanied by long pauses, says it all. The Mountain Man does not waste his words. Nor should the Survival Skier. So when asked a question like 'Vat do you sink, Meester Smeeth?', the most suitable response is to just grunt and snort and be generally non-committal. This will be taken as evidence of great wisdom. And be particularly careful with any questions concerning intercommunal rivalries (of which there are many in any Pistendorf). Since everyone in the village is related, you are bound to offend someone within earshot if you venture any sort of opinion.

But though the Mountain Man does not open up quickly to strangers (not surprising of a people who were used to being imprisoned by snow for six months of the year), the Survival Skier who perseveres should gradually manage to become accepted. And it needn't take too long before he finds himself wistfully reminiscing with one of the Good Old Boys (or bores) about how it was when visitors used to come up to the village by mule train. (A word of warning here, however: the Old Boys will frequently be *very* old, and *very* boring, since Mountain Men live a *very* long time and have *very* long memories).

In conversations where the Survival Skier is required to play a more active role, it is also important to avoid making any remark which smacks of frivolity. The *Stube* is a place for serious discourse, not for pastry-shop prattling. It is where the village sages discuss important matters like the price of potatoes and whether Herr X should be allowed to build an extension to his *pension*. Generally the sentiments expressed will be negative. Mountain Men are conservative and distrust change, (which, they have found, is usually for the worse), including the arrival of all these golden hordes, calling themselves skiers, who spend their time sliding – very sloppily – all over their mountain. This, of course, is also the Survival Skier's view (he doesn't include himself, naturally). For if the locals are conservative, the Survival Skier is a conservationist and doesn't like what's happening in the mountains at all, any more than they do.

This general pessimism and a mysterious mountain moodiness which seems to keep coming over the locals is often put down to the weather. In the mountains the weather, too, is a serious matter and it is almost always ominous – even on one of those sparkling Alpine days which can make even skiing seem worthwhile. (Readers familiar with *Piste Again* will remember the first rule of mountain weather: 'The weather always gets worse'). This moodiness is most often put down to the dreaded *Föhn,* when the warm wind blows down the mountain and upsets everybody. The correct Survival Skiing response, of course, is to sympathise, not to tell everyone to 'snap out of it'. The only consolation is that there's consolation to be found in the safety and warmth of the *Stube.* There will usually be a sufficient supply of liquor to last the winter, as one laments one's lot, drowning one's sorrows, one ear cocked for the rumble of a constant avalanche, and occasionally toasting The Local Hero if he happens to move up a place in the World Cup standings.

The key figure in the *Stube,* of course, and the one with whom it is essential to strike up a good Survival relationship is *le patron.* The ideal *Wirt* will spot you across his smoke-filled *Kneipe* the moment you step inside the door, reaching immediately for your own personal drinking *Stein* to fill it up with your 'usual'. And when you suddenly put in an appearance after a year's absence from the slopes, he'll make sure you get a real welcome in the hillside with hugs and handshakes all round, as he announces to the assembled company, as if you were back from the grave: 'Look who's here. It's Meester Smeeth'. (This is unfortunately an occasion when a number of rather large rounds will have to be bought by the returning Survival Skier. Still, it'll be worth it.)

The well-drilled *Wirt* will always know how to respond to the Survival Skier's cue. If you tramp in clasping a detailed ordnance survey map, he'll be only too ready to help you spread it out on the bar and to go into a huddle with you as you discuss some of the more remote trails. If you come in with your ice-axe and compass, he'll be the first to ask you out loud if it really is wise to try the Spitzenspitze at this time of year, when the weather can be so treacherous, especially on the North Face, and particularly with that pin in your knee: 'Eet steel geev much pain, Meester Smeeth?'. But he knows, despite his forebodings, that Meester Smeeth, Survival Skier Extraordinary, is not so easily daunted, and what's more, he'll make sure everyone else knows too: 'I theenk you ski down ze Beeg one again, Meester Smeeth. I know you. Every year you must come down 'er, even eef you 'ave to jump Ze Great Crevasse'.

Still, if the Survival Skier will persist in continuing to risk life and limb, there's nothing more to be said. Except, of course, to ask him 'how it was'. This the *Wirt* will take every opportunity to do (provided the Survival Skier keeps buying his rounds). Thus the *patron* will frequently have occasion to put technical questions to the Survival Skier – about the state of the snow up top, or about the advisability of triggering an avalanche on the south col of the *Spitzenspitze*, and about whether they should use mortars, hand-grenades or rockets. And, of course, if there's a big race coming up at the weekend, the Survival Skier is one of the first the *Wirt* will turn to for advice about how to set the course, perhaps even suggesting he might like to act as *Vorlaüfer*. Needless to say, the wise Survival Skier will always be ready to offer his advice on setting the course but will regretfully have to decline to be *Vorlaüfer* ('that damned pin, you know'). If he's done his work well, and paid his dues, the locals will grunt sympathetically and understand – only too well.

4. The Importance of Being British

' "Pardi!" said my host, "ces Messieurs Anglais sont
des gens très extraordinaires" — and having said it and
sworn it, he went out.'

Laurence Sterne, A Sentimental Journey

When it comes to getting the right sort of treatment, the Survival Skier should never underestimate the Importance of Being British — really British, that is — like those Victorian 'skisters' pictured in the fading deguerrotypes on so many *Stube* walls, steering themselves straight-backed down the slopes, using their single pole like punters on the Cam. Most Mountain Men still have an image of the British as this sort of type — a nation of Whympers and Mallorys, dashing from peak to peak, planting Union Jacks, or bombing head-first down the Cresta on their bob-sleds before breakfast (presumably with no certainty that they would ever live to eat it). Just as most of today's ski-freaks and 'hot-doggers' seem to come from America, so, in imperial days, the ski-nuts were mostly mad-dog Englishmen. It was these Lords of the Alps — and of just about everywhere else — who introduced the Swiss to mountaineering, and then (to the Survival Skier's eternal regret) to skiing. Not that those English antics, crashing down the slopes on their hickory boards while everyone else was demurely ice-skating, were always the subject of awe and admiration. (There were places where the locals would pelt them with stones, forcing them to confine their skiing to moonlit nights.)

Nevertheless, by and large, the British have long enjoyed a certain pre-eminence on the High Ground (or so they like to think). It seems absolutely right and natural, for instance, that the British should have been the first to scale Everest (and, indeed, that in the years between the wars, that particular mountain was, quite rightly, 'off limits' to any other nation). The French made it to the top for the first time only in 1978, though, in fairness, they did *ski* back down. Thus it doesn't seem quite right, somehow, that the man who now holds the record for skiing from the highest height should be a certain Mr Yuichiro Miura from Japan, whose *Schuss* down Everest in 1970 (with the aid of a parachute) broke the record set by one R.L. Holdsworth who skied down Kamet in 1931. Mind you, even in the imperial heyday, there was the odd nation which made the mistake of trying to tweak the British Lion's tail — like Norway's Amundsen getting to the South Pole (on skis, of course) before Scott in 1911.

If it suits his style, therefore, it's often best for the Survival Skier to come over as much this sort of chap — a bit 'off-the-wall', slightly insane, but charmingly so, and probably with a few broken bones in his body. But without overdoing it, of course, not like Austria's Mathias Zdarsky, inventor of the 'Zdarsky Swing', with his 70 fractures and dislocations suffered in an avalanche. And, as we've seen, the well-trained *Wirt* can generally be counted on to foster this image. Thus when the Survival Skier walks out of the *Stube* with his ice-axe and rope, remarking like Scott's Captain Oates 'I am just going outside, and may be gone some time', the locals will all know just how to respond. More often than not, of course, with the Survival Skier, it will be the other way round and the locals' response will have to be geared to his *appearing* at the *Stube* door with ice axe and rope, indicating that he's coming *inside* and may be *in* the *Stube* for some time.

Nevertheless, we must recognise that this traditional image is one which it is getting harder and harder for the Survival Skier to sustain. Even in the mountains, where news travels slowly, people are beginning to twig that today's Skiing Brit is not quite what he was. They're beginning to realise that the days are gone when no Englishman was a gentleman until he'd spent a winter in the Alps and that today even the most moneyed hearties in 'Val' can only afford to stay for three weeks. And as they glance through their hotel registers, the locals can't help but notice that most of the names are no longer double-barrelled, like they used to be. And out on the slopes, of course, it's all too obvious that these days most British *piste artistes* are no longer kitted out in Burberry gabardine, but tend rather to be clad in C & A's finest. The Mountain Man can therefore be forgiven for wondering if today's Brits are still made of the same stuff as those intrepid Victorians pictured on the *Stube* walls.

Well, of course, it's up to the Survival Skier to show that they are – or, at least, that *he* is – and that even in the era of the massed ranks of the British 'costa' skier,

---

Rules of Skiing

GEAR

The problem is you, not your equipment.

No skier believes this.

The newer your skis, the more ragged rocks there will be to run them over.

Every skier will be wearing about two metres worth of zips, of which 50 centimetres will be out of operation at any one time.

The more you wipe your goggles, the more they will mist up.

There will be one clip on your boots that you never manage to undo.

There will be one clip on your boots that will constantly be coming undone of its own accord.

The most comfortable *après-ski* boots are socks.

the tradition of the supreme British individualist lives on. And, let it be said, although the new breed of British piste-basher may *look* a bit different from his forefathers, he still has a lot in common with them. Like his forebears the new Brit still arrives, like the True Brit of old, very fully equipped, except that now, instead of ropes and climbing irons, he is more likely to be weighed down with jumbo tins of baked beans and jars of instant soup. And beneath that Union Jack hat you can still see at work the same inventive technical mind that devised the revolutionary Kandahar binding, with stirrup toe and steel spring, except that today his genius is more likely to be applied to finding new ways of sabotaging the hotel vending machine. It's true that we may not figure too often any more in the World Cup standings, but Britain continues to play an important role in the development of skiing technique. There is, for instance the all-purpose 'Fudge' turn, developed mainly by the British, which could be said to stand in direct succession to the telemark, the stem christie and the parallel, and which has transformed the sport for thousands of holiday piste-bashers. It is a turn which can be seen as a uniquely British compromise – neither traverse, nor snow-plough, nor stem – but rather a unique blend of all three, designed specially to help the average piste-basher to get down a slope and round the odd corner, and calculated to reduce any orthodox ski instructor to tears.

The British skiing style still retains many of its original characteristics. Like the old-time ski-runners, today's Brit also uses his sticks to reduce speed. And the typically British 'head-first stop' is, of course, very much inherited from the 'dash and crash' school of the early days. The British piste-basher is as intrepid as he ever was, climbing up the slopes in the lunch-hour when the lifts aren't working, munching the provisions he smuggled away in his cagoule at breakfast, while the Continentals laze around in deck-chairs and lunch for three hours. The British piste-basher is as contemptuous as ever of sun-tanning Alpine weather. He prefers the messy stuff we have back at home and thus often finds himself trudging out alone when the going gets rough. (As with the midday sun, it's only mad dogs and Englishmen who go out in blizzards.) And unlike the Continentals, most British piste-bashers don't take the third day off to rest – though this is actually a rather useful habit that many a Survival Skier would do well to pick up. There are also, of course, certain British traditions which the rest of the ski world have inherited, like queueing, for instance, which must surely have been introduced by the British when the ski-lift was invented.

It's true that British ski gear is now more likely to have been bought from a chain store than from an outfitter in Piccadilly. But the British still favour that characteristic 'bulky' look as opposed to the 'sleek' look of the Continentals. They still prefer to wear their well-padded salopettes and anoraks one size too big, and tote around the largest and best-stocked bumbags and packs on the slopes. The British skier

may no longer stand out — as he used to — due to the sheer drabness and unsuitability of his clobber (jeans, sweatshirt and hand-knitted woolly cap). But most British skiers still look 'interesting', though some *are* getting hard to distinguish from foreigners. And you do, of course, still see plenty of Brits wearing that traditional speciality: the socks rolled down outside the boot, thus absorbing the snow and so, by capillary action, keeping the feet pleasantly moist.

So, although many Continentals do seem to be forming the view that the Brits are not quite what they were, the locals still look on with wonder — but less at their antics than out of curiosity as to whether they can afford to pay the bill. Of course, those milords of yesteryear couldn't pay the bill either, but then they probably didn't cause quite so much damage. (Is it true that Brits get asked to pay a higher inventory deposit than other nationalities?) For, like their predecessors, British skiers are still a hearty lot, as good as ever at raising the roof and taking over a *Stube* when they're in a 'won't go home till morning' mood. Most *Wirts* are usually happy to go along with this — *provided* they can pay the bill for smashing the furniture, chucking their friends through windows, spraying one another with cans of lager, and generally having a good time. The problem is they often can't.

This is one of the reasons for the popularity with both Brits and locals of the British-owned 'club' or 'chalet-hotel', where the guests will be encouraged to remain, (preferably locked inside), during *après-ski* hours. This will not, of course, prevent them from sallying forth on occasion, perhaps in their vomit-streaked bus, armed with their aerosol cans. These adventures do, it is true, often turn into a high-spirited wrecking spree: the group may spice up the evening by looting shops and supermarkets, burning down chalets and hotels, and generally painting the town red as they sing 'Una Paloma Blanca' or 'Viva España'. By day, you'll often see those same high spirits enlivening the slopes, playfully nicking, or 'readjusting' direction signs, riding up on the outside of the cable car, and littering the mountain with colourful coke tins and orange peel. All this, of course, is a *shade* more rowdy than the conga-dancing or snowball-chucking that went on in the old days. And it is true that today's piste-basher often has a bit of a rough-diamond edge. But true Brits have always wanted to make their mark. And if we no longer have the James 'Jimmy' Palmer-Tomkinsons to outski the opposition, it's only natural that we should seek other forms of self-expression. It's also natural that now that the French, Germans and others have become much more numerous on the slopes, the British, too, should have sought safety in numbers, travelling out in hordes, staying in the same chalets and hotels and banding together on the slopes.

Rules of Skiing

WEATHER

The weather never changes for the better.

Whenever it rains in the village, someone will say it's probably snowing up on the mountain.

If, after four days of bitterly cold blizzards, you buy yourself a balaclava, it will suddenly turn mild and sunny.

The best way to warm up your feet is to put on a hat.

The sun always takes too long to come up from behind the mountain in the morning.

The weather will be at its coldest when you're stuck on the chairlift.

It is usually possible to ski all the way back down to the hotel – except for the week when you're staying there.

This phenomenon – skiing together in 'Brits only' groups – has been one of the major developments of recent years, with Brits bringing out their own instructors and organising their own ski-schools and races. After all, if you can't beat the opposition, why play with them? So British groups set up their own flags and finish gates and have their own *Führers,* equipped with armbands and megaphones, to move any foreigners out of the way. ('Will you *please* clear the piste. This is the Croydon Clappers Ski Championship.') Then they all line the side to cheer each other on, calling out to sluggish Susan: 'Come on, Sue, you can do it', while the rest of the world looks on, bemused. But when you think back, is this all that different from the Kandahar Club at Mürren taking on the Downhill Only club at Wengen, while the rest of the world looked on? The only difference perhaps is that in the intervening years the rest of the world have learned to ski and seem to have got decidedly richer.

At all events, it's in the Survival Skier's interests to persuade the locals that, *au fond,* nothing much has changed and that, even if his countrymen seem at times to get a little out of hand, at least *he* is living proof that the tradition of great British eccentrics lives on. This reputation for eccentricity must, at all costs, be maintained by the Survival Skier – not just in the national interest, but in his own. Thus when the Survival Skier finds himself behaving and dressing a bit strangely, the locals will just shrug their shoulders and say *'Oui, mais c'est un Anglais',* as if this explained everything. So stick to the resorts *we* founded, where *our* pictures are still on the *Stube* walls, and where the locals still remember us as we were in our prime. They may have concluded, reluctantly, that the British are not quite what they used to be, but they'll welcome any opportunity to be proved wrong, and that includes pandering to the Survival Skier. They don't want to see the Bulldog Breed die out entirely, and if the Survival Skier is all that remains of him then he'll be encouraged, or at least tolerated. After all, if it wasn't for those pioneering Brits, the locals wouldn't be soaking the rich like they do today. And although today's British Survival Skier is likely to be somewhat poorer than his instructor or hotelier, most Mountain Men do have the decency not to rub it in – not too hard, anyway.

5.The Chalet

'And is there honey still for tea?'

Rupert Brooke, Grantchester

Straitened economic circumstances, of course, are among the main reason why Brits have gone in for group holidays and self-catering in such a big way. Of the various options available, perhaps the most popular, and certainly the most British, is 'the chalet party'. The idea of sharing your own little home in the snow with loved ones and a few close friends is without doubt an appealing one, though the reality is more likely to be endless squabbles with a group of strangers all trying to get into the bathroom to wash their smalls at the same time. As pointed out earlier, chalet resorts are far from ideal for the Survival Skier. Unfortunately, however, the Survival Skier is likely to be as strapped for cash as the rest of his countrymen. Thus it may be that, in a choice between a shoebox apartment and a chalet package, he'll find himself opting for the chalet. In the event that such a fate should befall you, this chapter attempts to set out some of the pitfalls and to offer some advance warning about chalet-going, which despite its inexplicable social cachet, rarely fails to live down to expectations.

One of the main reasons why the myth of the chalet has arisen is because the word itself has such a nice ring to it, conjuring up chocolate-box visions of a pretty wooden villa set in the snow, amongst the pines, with a log fire burning in the grate. There are *chalets Suisses* all over the world, all of which sound absolutely enchanting, as indeed does London's own Swiss Cottage – unless you happen to be familiar with the realities of the Finchley Road. Unlike London's Swiss Cottage, however, (which has rather good bus and tube connections), your little chalet in the Alps will invariably turn out to be virtually inaccessible, from either the village or the slopes. Every time you venture down the long, icy path which will be your only link with the outside world you'll take your life in your hands, since the chap who's paid to grit the path and clear the snow never does. As a result, apart from the daily expedition to the slopes, chalet life tends to revolve very much around the chalet. This, of course, cramps the style of the Survival Skier enormously, but it does not seem to have dimmed British enthusiasm for 'the chalet party'.

Yet here, too, the idea is very much at variance with the reality. The brochures will all describe it as 'one long house party', evoking visions of a leisurely country house weekend. In practice, though, conditions will be rather basic: the food will rarely live up to your chalet-maid's 'Cordon Bleu' reputation, and the level of overcrowding will be much like that in a Third World shanty town (hardly conducive to that chalet romance that many expect to find). The extraordinary thing is that people who would look down their noses at the Club Med – such as well-heeled Sloanes who could afford to stay elsewhere – will plunge with enthusiasm into the general mucking-in routine of these mini-Butlins in the mountains. In fact they are not always quite so mini: many of the chalet operators, as we have seen, are now taking over *pensions* and hotels which they turn into 'chalet-hotels' or 'super-chalets' – actually not all that super, but a lot cheaper to run than a proper hotel – and once again it's that magic word 'chalet' that enables them to get away with it. The attraction of the chalet-hotel is that it's guaranteed to be an all-British affair, and thus fits in with the general trend towards tribalism that's become apparent in most ski resorts. This is one way of ensuring that pride in your performance either on or off the slopes won't be undermined by any of those awful foreigners, though they will provide you with something to talk about: constant astonishment will be expressed in the chalet at how numerous other nationalities are – the so-called 'F-Factor' (Frogs) and 'K-Factor' (Krauts).

Unfortunately all this deprives the Survival Skier of the possibility of playing one nationality off against another, and of making the best possible use of the locals. But he usually won't have much choice but to go along with the general xenophobia, which is usually running high – even before departure from Gatwick. This is the main chalet airport, particularly for flights to Geneva, where the aim is to get well plastered on the duty-free, to identify potential chalet-mates, and to loudly hail anybody you vaguely recognise – particularly if you have that sort of Sloaney voice which *carries.* There'll also be a certain amount of one-upmanship about which chalet operator you're with (ideally, of course, none – you're staying in a *friend's* chalet). The order of the Top Ten companies is constantly changing (depending on which has the most attractive chalet-maids this year and whether they can also cook). Frequently companies will drop out of the ratings altogether since many are only one-man-and-a-maid outfits and go bust after a season or two. If you're very lucky your company may go bust just before you're due to leave, thus providing you with an ideal Survival Skiing excuse for not skiing this year. Ideally this will happen towards the end of the season – perhaps Easter, the peak chalet-going period – by which time it'll be too late to book in anywhere else.

The Survival Skier is advised to keep a low profile during the journey out. He only really needs to swing into operation when the coach or mini-bus rolls up at the bottom of the path to the chalet. This will, as we've said, be some considerable distance from the chalet itself – the bus never parks outside the front door. The Survival Skier will be at an advantage here if he has succeeded in remaining a bit less plastered than the rest of the crew. Then he can scramble up the slope to the chalet ahead of the opposition and be the first to make contact with the rep. or chalet-maid who will appear at the door in her company-issue Puffa jacket or her butcher-stripe pinny (in an effort to persuade you, even at this early stage, that she *can* cook, and is not the type who just issues survival rations). Being ahead of the field is important, since some chalets operate on a 'first-come-first-served' basis. So

it pays to get in quick. If you've brought your own chalet-mate with you, just bag the best double room nearest the bathroom and furthest from the fun-and-games room, after checking first that it's not a double that can be turned into a triple or a quadruple. If you're on your own, go for a single. But if you find you do have to double or triple up (usually the case), try to share with people who may go along with your style of Survival Skiing. For more on potential chalet partners, see chapter six.

Even if you don't have your own chalet-mate, it may be as well to try to stay in a chalet which contains mainly established couples (or even families), since they will be more likely to leave the Survival Skier to his own devices. Obviously, this sort of preference needs to be signalled in advance and some companies invite you to do so. In practice, though, this is unlikely to do you much good. Even if preferences have been relayed beforehand and the chalet-girl has made up a list of who's to share with whom, this will be completely at variance with what people actually want when they arrive. For the chalet-girl's list will never take account of the fact that since it was made up, A will have fallen out with B, or got picked up by C, or made friends with D. And since chalet-goers are often mate-hunting singles, this makes for a great many possible permutations.

It is not always easy to find out in advance whether you'll be sharing your chalet with a bunch of Sloanes, or a bunch of hooligans (the two are not mutually exclusive), or even a bunch of skiers (there are actually people who come for the skiing). There is, however, a tendency for certain chalets to always be occupied by the same types of people. You'll soon find out which type as you study the decor, read the rude comments and messages on the chalet notice board, see what sort of literature and dead plonk bottles are left lying around, and generally discover whether the place is reasonably habitable, or is the sort of joint that gets smashed up every week. You'll also be able, as you all stand around drinking your free introductory *Glühwein,* to size up your chalet-mates, and the chalet-maid (or maids), or even the chalet-man. The latter is a rather new phenomenon, often pre-varsity, filling in his gap year. He should not be confused with the Strongman or Snowman, who makes the daily deliveries, brings in the logs, drives the chalet car, and is *supposed* to clear the path and unblock the sink and do a great many other things which it's useless to mention since they won't usually be done.

In general, the larger the chalet, the more things won't work. Thus the 'chalet-hotel' is often in pretty poor shape. This is partly because of the battering it gets

---

Rules of Skiing

CHALETS

There won't be enough coat-hangers.

This does not matter since skiers prefer to drape their gear on radiators, chairs, bedposts etc.

They do this as a way of demarcating their territory.

Getting into, or out of, bed will invariably involve clambering over someone else.

Someone's feet will smell.

There's always something in the chalet that doesn't work.

It will be a different something every day.

The chalet car and the chalet mono-ski will always be booked on the day you want to use them.

Breakfast never takes place on time.

from its guests (during those heavy *après-ski* sessions) and partly because the management have deliberately seen to it that certain things do not work. The lifts, for instance, will have been shut down, as will the pool and anything else that needs maintenance and supervision. The locals still aren't sure what to make of these places. It's certainly enabled them to sell off a lot of ropey old hotels and *pensions,* and it is a good way of confining British furniture-wrecking habits to British-owned establishments. On the other hand, it does mean less custom in town (the guests never stray far from the chalet 'duty-free' bar) and it does mean fewer jobs for the locals. This is because the 'chalet-clubs' are all operated by underpaid British chalet-maids, with perhaps a chalet-manager in charge – usually a bored or redundant businessman who liked the idea of spending a winter in the Alps (he doesn't usually come back for a second). One thing you can be sure of is that the locals will admire the British business savvy behind these operations. Who else could take the crummiest hotels, reduce the facilities, run them with a few underpaid, untrained staff, and manage to pack in twice as many guests as ever before – and all on the strength of a cleverly-worded brochure, written in 'nudge-nudge' language, assuring punters that the 'intimate' British chalet-hotel is *the* place to stay and the envy of the rest of the village.

The chalet-hotel is therefore best avoided by even the most hardened Survival Skier. The *après-ski* can be very tough going – plenty of throwing up and swinging on chandeliers. And the entertainment and Alpine ambiance will consist mainly of video games and knobbly-knee contests. Another problem is that though chalet-maids often cook passably well for ten, they are rarely trained to cope with 70.

But whatever sort of chalet you stay in, the chalet skiing day normally follows a pretty standard pattern. It begins with breakfast, where the central issue is invariably the porridge. For some obscure reason, British chalet operators tend to make this a key feature in their brochures ('a good bowl of hot Scottish porridge to start your day'). The problem is that this British speciality as served in the Alps usually bears more resemblance to a mogul slope (the porridge is a favourite subject for chalet-party witticisms), and more important, *it's never ready on time.* This is because porridge is one thing that your chalet-maid will not have been taught to cook on her Cordon Bleu course. She will thus be blissfully unaware that cooking porridge requires her to get up *early.* The fact that she doesn't get up early may just be her way of trying to get people to settle for various other kinds of soggies or muesli. But this never succeeds – British chalet skiers have been *promised* porridge and they will insist on *getting* their porridge. They also tend to insist on quite a lot of other things not calculated to endear them to their chalet-maid: they will want a second boiled egg, and a lot more rolls; and *brioches,* and *pains au chocolat,* to take out with them for refuelling during pit-stops on the slopes. They also tend to top up their hip-flasks from the bar when she's not looking. All this provides additional

aggravation for the chalet-maid who will be as keen as her charges, if not more so, to get out on the slopes and spend the rest of the day skiing. She must therefore use breakfast time to do all her other chores, like bed-making, baking the tea-time cake, doing the washing-up from the previous night's blast (or clearing away the debris), and persuading the unidentified body on the sofa to go back to his own chalet for breakfast.

Actually, the general confusion at breakfast-time can serve the Survival Skier well. Since breakfasting and departure from the chalet is usually a staggered affair (depending on such factors as whether you bother to wash, and how insistent you are about getting your porridge or your second egg), the Survival Skier can usually slip off on his own. If he does find himself caught up in the last-minute mustn't-be-late-for-ski-school crowd, he can always pretend he's forgotten his lift-pass and go back, promising vaguely to meet up with his chums later on the slopes. Once on the slopes, the chalet-skier can apply standard Survival Skiing techniques, skiing solo or *en groupe*. If, however, he decides to ski *en groupe,* he must do his utmost to ensure that the group, if at all possible, does not contain people from his own chalet. He can thus avoid his chalet-mates until that next major event in the chalet programme – chalet tea, often billed as the 'high spot' of the day.

Once again, the central issue for discussion and banter is likely to be the chalet-girl's cooking. For however lovingly and expertly prepared her cake, she will almost certainly not have been advised by her Cordon Bleu school that eggs take a lot longer to cook at altitude. Chalet-girl cakes therefore all tend to have a familiar, almost endearing, leaden quality. She may also have difficulties with those poverty-stricken members of her party who couldn't afford to eat on the slopes and thus tend to treat chalet tea as a late lunch, invading the kitchen to forage for bread, cheese and any plonk that's going. Tea-time, of course, is one of the times for ski-chat, consisting mostly of the usual tales about how many black runs were skied, tumbles taken and disasters encountered or narrowly missed. Most of this ski-speak will be at a fairly banal level, so the Survival Skier is once again advised to adopt standard practice and stay somewhat aloof – unless invited to comment on some highly technical matter such as torsion coefficients or the state of the powder on the *other* side of the mountain. In fact, the smart Survival Skier will be well advised to skip tea, in order to *try* to get into the bathroom. There are never enough bathrooms in any chalet. And there certainly won't be enough hot water – not at any rate for those who linger over their tea. If you don't get in there quick, you never will, since it's during that period after coming off the slopes (rather than in the morning or late at night) that most of the washing (including socks and smalls) seems to take place.

The next set-piece will be dinner, when your chalet-girl faces her sternest test of the day. If she's shrewd about it she will encourage her guests to get well sozzled beforehand (particularly if it says 'unlimited wine' in the brochure). This isn't always easy, since the vino usually tends to be well-watered rotgut, but with a little persistence she can probably get them well and truly chucking the bread about before the time comes to tuck in. They will thus be less likely to notice that the 'four-course' meal was really 'two-course'; or that they didn't really teach *co-ordinated* cooking at her Cordon Bleu school, which explains why the veg. usually arrives about 15 minutes before the main course. The cuisine is generally 'English international' – with variations. Some chalet-girls specialise in overcooked soggy (British style) food, some in raw and undercooked (*nouvelle cuisine*) dishes. Some

prefer the warm-it-up-and-serve style, straight from the supermarket. The thing you can be sure of is that the meat will usually be veal or chicken (often undistinguishable from one another); the garnish will always be chopped parsley; and, if it's pasta, it'll be lasagne. Needless to say, many chalet-girls, understandably, prefer not to eat with their guests. The chalet chatter will continue much as at tea-time, except that now people will have their stories better rehearsed. By the time they adjourn to the sitting-around area, puffing on their duty-free cigars and bringing with them any left-over vino, they will be almost word-perfect.

What happens now by way of *après*-dinner *après-ski* can vary enormously. It can be anything from a group of bored males playing Scrabble to a group of excited Sloanes playing 'Do you know?' (as in 'Do you know Henry Hooray?'). Or it might be high jinks, with people running around in their underwear, or putting on their

skis to *schuss* down the chalet roof; or lighting farts; or setting fire to other people's hair; or sending out a raiding party to ambush innocent passers-by. This goes for up-market 'I say, shall we?' chalets as well as for down-market 'wot a larf' chalets.

Of course you may just find yourself with a nice quiet group of people – it's unlikely but possible (though the only way to be sure of this is to rent your own chalet). But if you're in one of those chalets where there's a 'quiet group' and a 'not-so-quiet group', you'll invariably find that it's the rowdies who set the pace. And don't think you can opt out by crashing early. The sleeping arrangements in chalets always ensure that the livelier elements have to climb over at least two or three other bodies to get into bed, thus affording them ample opportunity to put the boot in before they themselves finally crash ('crash' being the operative word).

6. Chalet-Maids and Chalet-Mates

> **'La belle Dame sans Merci
> Hath thee in thrall!'**
>
> *John Keats,* La Belle Dame Sans Merci
>
> **'Company, villainous company, hath
> been the spoil of me.'**
>
> *William Shakespeare,* Henry IV, Part I

Although her presence may at times be fleeting, the chalet-maid is, without doubt, the key figure in the chalet for the Survival Skier. Thus he can do himself a lot of good by getting on the right side of her – offering to help with the washing-up, sneaking on people who help themselves at the bar without logging up their drinks, not complaining about the porridge, bringing in the crates of booze that the Snowman leaves outside the door, emptying the *poubelles,* not throwing up in bed etc.

If you're male, of course, she may initially be suspicious that you're yet another of those tiresome types who feel the chalet-maid is not just there to do the cooking and cleaning. Certainly, there are chalet-maids who are looking for a mate, but this usually means the sort of city slicker who could keep her in Hermès scarves for the rest of her days, rather than the average Survival Skiing male. And anyway, for the moment she's probably blissfully happy with your ski instructor or the disco-owner. But whatever rapport develops or, more probably, does *not* develop between you, most chalet-maids (like the *pisteurs*) can recognise a Survival Skier when they see one and are often prepared to play along with him. For one thing, many chalet-girls are Survival Skiers themselves. They will take great pride in giving advice to their guests about slopes and technique, but will very rarely allow themselves to be observed skiing. In fact, many chalet-girls – particularly if it's the start of the season and they've never been a chalet-girl before – can't ski any better than any other novice. Nor will they necessarily be able to ski much better at the end of the season – just as spending six months at a Swiss finishing school won't necessarily mean that they can speak French. Chalet companies, incidentally, have now all but replaced those prohibitively-priced Swiss institutions as places for the British bourgeoisie to get 'finished-off' (often literally): learning to cater for ten, speak French (well, some) and find a husband. So if you're in luck you may well find a chalet-girl whose skiing is as poor as her cooking and her French, and who will be only too delighted to sneak up to the slopes by the back lift with you. You can then both trek off piste, spend the day in a little *Hütte* (*bewirtschaftet,* of course) and then return in the evening to tell tales to the rest of the group about how marvellous it was off piste, and to ask them how they're getting on with their star turns.

On the other hand you may just be unlucky enough to run into a chalet-girl who is not there to learn French, practice cooking or find a husband. She is simply there to work on her jet turns before joining the rest of the British Olympic ski team. That is to say, she's a whizz on boards, and therefore probably will not want to spend her time sloping off with you. All need not be lost, however. You may find that although you won't want to actually *ski* together, you can *talk skiing* together (preferably back at the chalet in front of the other guests). This can often work out quite well, since, as we've seen, the Survival Skier talks a lot better than he skies. Thus you may find yourself having some fascinating technical discussions with her, with the rest of the chalet listening in admiration. And who knows, if you praise her cooking loudly enough, she may even praise your skiing. You may also find that you have not one, but two, potential accomplices. All the best chalets seem to be staffed by pairs of birds. If so, this should double your chances of finding a willing Survival Skiing partner.

There are, of course, a great many varieties of chalet-bird. Some tidy and make beds. Some don't. Some are supposed to and don't. Some sleep on the premises. Some sleep off the premises. Some sleep with the clients. Some sleep with the local *Pistenjaeger*. There'll be nothing standard about the girl inside that standard-issue Puffa jacket. Even though the advert she answered the previous June asked for 'a superb cook with a warm, intelligent, mature personality who should speak French, drive, ski and not smoke', she may be all or none of these things. She can be a teenage deb; or a hearty husband-hunting Sloane; or a stern disciplinarian who makes sure you don't bring anyone you shouldn't back to the chalet. It's even

---

Rules of Skiing

CHALET-GIRLS

She has a boyfriend.

He can ski better than you.

Chalet-girls are more obliging and less bored at the start of the season than at the end of the season.

Some chalet-girls can cook; some chalet-girls can ski; some can speak the language. Very few can do all three.

She spends more time skiing than cooking and cleaning.

She says she knows where it's all happening – but she never takes you.

When things go wrong, she usually blames the Snowman.

possible she won't be English – though that wouldn't seem quite right somehow; it's bad enough being ordered around by someone of your own nationality never mind a foreigner. There are some things, though, that chalet-girls do have in common – they've all done a Cordon Bleu cookery course (it's just a pity you have to be the guinea-pigs before they get a *real* job doing directors' lunches); they all claim to speak the local language; they're all sunburnt (by the end of the season anyway); and they all live in their ski-gear and boots (ski or moon).

And whatever type they are, you can be fairly certain they'll appreciate the Survival Skier's support when they make their excuses to ditch the assembled company. So when the others all start moaning that *tonight* was the night she promised to introduce them to the social scene in the village, you pipe up in her defence with: 'Poor girl, she must have some time to herself'. For this is something else that chalet-girls have in common with the Survival Skier – they all want to spend as little time as possible with the other people in the chalet. That isn't to say that the girls can't be sociable sometimes – if they're between *Pistenjaegers,* or if there happens to be someone in your group they find 'interesting'. Indeed if it's someone's birthday, they can usually be counted on to stay for a chorus of 'Happy Birthday to You'. And there are those famous 'chalet-girls' picnics' as Easter approaches. She may even be prepared to ski with her guests – if they're prepared to fork out a bit for her freelance instruction or pay for her services as a 'guide'. Generally, though, she will prefer to spend her spare time with a ski instructor of her own. And the longer the season drags on, the less time she is going to want to spend with her charges – to be fair, she *has* heard all those stories before, including yours.

Incidentally if she does go in for any freelance coaching it almost certainly won't endear her to the locals any more than do the activities of your resident ski bum. (He's the chap who hangs around your chalet company and offers to show you the slopes and sharpen your skis for a 'special' price – normally the same price as in the village shops, except that there they do it properly.) Some ski bums also find employment as Snowmen: driving the mini-bus, shovelling snow and doing other odd jobs. But whatever their function, ski bums and Snowmen are worth keeping in with. These chaps can usually ski a bit, normally know a Survival Skier when they see one, are invariably short of cash and are far from being incorruptible. In the normal way of things you wouldn't see much of these fellows, except in passing. But, as we know, there's always something wrong in the chalet – fuses blown, boiler on the blink, fridge breaking down, sink blocked etc. So, if the Survival Skier makes it worth his while, the ski bum can usually be persuaded to spend most of his time in the chalet 'fixing things' and at the same time having erudite conversations with the Survival Skier, expressing admiration for his deep powder technique: 'Don't tell me. You must have learnt that in the Rockies'.

But however successful a relationship he strikes up with his chalet-girl or

Snowman, the Survival Skier is also going to have to learn to live with his chalet-mates. Some, clearly, will be more livable-with than others. So here's a guide to some of the more recognisable types (who, despite the use of the masculine pronoun, can, of course, be of either sex):

THE LIFE AND SOUL

The chalet's self-appointed *animateur* and a permanent source of irritation. Feels that the party needs a 'life and soul' and that he's the man for the job. Is therefore constantly chattering away, repeating the same old jokes, organising games of charades and telling you to 'Smile – it may never happen'.

THE BATHER

Often female. Gets into the bathroom at six a.m. and emerges about ten minutes before the ski-lifts are due to open. It's the same after skiing. She's always in there first, clutching her collection of lotions and bath essences, and reappears later (much later) to ask innocently of the queue outside: 'Oh, have you been waiting long?'. (Her chalet-mates meanwhile have been getting steadily sloshed, and so they may by now be as unaware of the passage of time as she is.) A male version of this type is the photo-nut, who takes over the bathroom to use it as a darkroom.

THE PISTE SNOB

No shortage of these in any chalet. Starts off at tea-time by asking you where you went, then spends the rest of the evening telling you where *he* went – a lot further, of course, *much* faster, and down *much* blacker pistes. If perchance you find you've both skied the same piste, he, needless to say, will have come down the *more difficult* way.

THE DEEP BREATHER

It's well known that the British like draughts. But the fresh-air freak carries it a bit too far. He'll be constantly flinging open windows and doors so that he can take in great gulps of Alpine air and generally ventilate the premises. One problem is that he also has a habit of doing it at night – at two a.m., for instance (so he can look at the stars), or at six a.m. (so he can watch the dawn come up).

THE ORGANISER

The one who got the chalet-party together, thus getting himself out to Pistendorf for free or at half-price. He's also got himself a nervous breakdown in the process, having spent the last six months worried sick that the whole thing would fall through, since no one would commit themselves until the last minute and those who did kept dropping out.

THE WHEELER-DEALER

A cousin. But this one doesn't suffer from nervous collapse as soon as he gets his group out to the resort. Instead he spends the whole time buzzing around with his notebook, already trying to sign people up for next year, or for his summer skiing group, at 'special rates'. Also sells insurance on the side, gets a cut on the lift-passes and a commission for wheeling you all off to the disco. More of a tour-guide than a chalet-mate.

THE DOSSER

Prepared to sling his hammock anywhere – and usually has to. He frequently arrives at the chalet at the last minute, unexpectedly, after being told by the tour

operator that he can stay if he doesn't mind 'making do'. He doesn't. He'll kip anywhere. So it's his body you stumble over when you go to the loo at night, or his bedsocks that give breakfast that 'special' flavour (he often sleeps under the table).

THE ROYAL

Should really be staying at the Palace in St Moritz, but is trying a chalet this time 'just for fun'. Unfortunately he expects much the same sort of service from the chalet-maid as he'd get from the Badrutts' staff. Finds it hard, therefore, to understand the 'maid's' refusal to bring him tea in bed in the morning, or to run errands for him, or to clear up after him, or to lay out his monogrammed pyjamas.

THE GANNET

Wolfs about half of the cake at tea-time, getting his choppers into the last piece before anyone has a chance to respond to his: 'Well, if no one wants that last little bit . . .'. If you're in the kitchen preparing yourself some tea and toast, beware. Before you know it, he'll have marmalade on that toast and be washing it down with the quickbrew, leaving you with nothing but an empty pot and some washing-up to do.

THE HOARDER

A cousin – except that this one brings in his own supplies. He treks down to the supermarket and back every afternoon, and returns loaded with parcels of goodies to gobble. The fridge and cupboards in the kitchen will be chock full of his store of provisions : tins of baked beans, spaghetti bolognese, etc.

THE WALKMAN

Has discovered the ideal way of avoiding any contact with his chalet-mates. Either on slope or off, and even in bed, he'll have that damned headset over his ears, interrupting his listening only to change tapes. If you say something to him, he just smiles back and carries on clicking his fingers.

THE MOTORIST

Whereas the rest of you flew to Pistendorf, he drove. Will therefore spend most of every day describing his journey out, much as other people spend their time describing their adventures on the slopes – dices with death, precipices avoided etc. The rest of the time he spends worrying about the journey back, studying his map, checking which passes are open, fiddling with his snow-chains, and wondering whether he shouldn't buy a set of those studded tyres.

THE BARMAN

Fancies himself with a cocktail shaker and duly appoints himself chief barman, dutifully logging up everyone else's drinks for them – though frequently forgetting to note down his own. Or perhaps he just feels you'd like him to 'have one himself' in return for his advice on how to really make a lumumba, Jägertee or chisky.

THE PRANKSTER

The one who nicks the road signs, causing the rest of the chalet to live in permanent fear that the police will burst in at any minute, or that a horde of angry Germans will charge in to take their revenge for the time when he locked them in the sauna. On party nights, of course, there'll be no holding him back as he follows each merry jape with an even merrier jape. Try to stay out of his way.

THE WHOOPER

Specialises in whooping or yippeeing at the top of his voice during moments of great elation or on party nights. This acts as a signal to other chalets and hotels in the neighbourhood that your chalet is not to be tangled with, and may be about to go on the rampage. Can often yodel a bit too. Often Scottish, and if so will certainly have brought his kilt with him.

THE WAXER

Spends all his spare time in the ski-room waxing his skis and filing his edges and will even do yours for you if you slip him a few francs. This may simply be his system for keeping as far away from the rest of the chalet party as possible. On the other hand, he may just conceivably be another Survival Skier.

THE MECHANIC

A close cousin. Also possibly a Survival Skier. On the slopes, he's always crouching over his skis with screwdriver in hand, and most of his *après-ski* time will be spent fiddling with his bindings in the ski-room. He's the sort of chap the Survival Skier can sometimes team up with, though he does have some irritating habits like pointing out that your carefully adjusted bindings should really be one centimetre further forward.

THE DRESSER-UP

Would have been happier in an earlier skiing era, before jeans and moonboots became *de rigueur après-ski* wear, and when people actually dressed for dinner. He's brought along several pairs of shiny disco trousers, so he's always anxious to go out on the town. If the others can't be persuaded to leave the chalet, he'll try to organise a fancy dress party instead – even though everyone's had quite enough of wearing fancy dress all day out on the slopes.

THE UNDRESSER

Lets it all hang out. Frequently parades in underwear and will often appear for tea or dinner in nightie or pyjamas. If anyone's required to drop their trousers to raise a laugh, he will be the first to volunteer.

THE ADOPTER

The one who takes seriously that line in the brochure which says: 'And tea-time is when you invite friends around to the chalet to swap tales of the day's adventures on the slopes . . .'. This won't make him very popular, since there's never enough cake to go round anyway. His guests often turn out to be *pisteurs* (perhaps he's a Survival Skier) who have gargantuan appetites and like to move straight on from tea to aperitifs – much to the annoyance of the chalet-girl, who's usually seen this particular *pisteur* all too often; every week he finds one of these adopters to latch on to.

THE SINGER

Chalet groups tend to pride themselves on being able to 'make their own entertainment'. So when the chalet-girl asks if anyone can play the guitar or piano, he pipes up: 'No, but I can sing'. This often turns out to be a slight exaggeration. But thereafter he'll be unstoppable, leading any small-hour carousing with his piercing warble while you lie in bed tossing and turning and wrapping your pillow even more tightly round your head.

THE FOOD FADDIST

Harmless enough, but can take up a lot of time and space in the kitchen at breakfast preparing his special concoction of muesli, blackstrap molasses, yoghourt and stewed fruit. Make sure the chalet-girl doesn't let him interfere with dinner or you may find he'll persuade her to do the cooking with snow-water, or do something equally ghastly.

THE EXERCISER

As if strenuous activity on the slopes was not enough, he'll also spend all his *après-ski* time and his *avant-ski* time exercising and performing his aerobic routines or his yoga. Again, harmless enough unless he invites *you to* join him in these pursuits – jogging on ice can be dangerous and rubbing snow in your face just isn't as much fun as he cracks it up to be.

THE SAUNA-NUT

A close cousin. This one believes that the secret of life is the sauna bath. So even if your chalet doesn't have one (or, more likely, if it's broken down or has been shut off) he'll simply trek into the village with all his towels as soon as he comes off the slopes. He'll be back for supper, rubbing ice in his face and then proceeding to tell everyone, once again, how much better he feels for his sauna and how he's installed one at home.

THE WRECKER

Accident prone. If you hear a crash in the middle of the night, it'll be him dropping a milk bottle as he takes it out of the fridge. If the lights go out, it'll probably be her fusing them with her hair-dryer. None of this is intentional. But it does mean that the Snowman who helps out at your chalet will be in almost permanent residence to repair the damage.

7. Skispeak

'Be careful to mix some truth with your lies.'

Etienne Rey, Eloge du Mensonge

Readers familiar with *Piste Again* will be aware of the tremendous importance of mastering the art of 'ski-speak'. A strong line in chat is probably the Survival Skier's single greatest asset. Generally speaking, of course, this skill will be of most use during *après-ski* hours, particularly at the bar. And it is here that we will usually find the Survival Skier in his best form. But ski-speak can also be a big help in getting around successfully *on* the slopes. So even though on-slope survival techniques are a bit outside the scope of this volume, here are a few hints about talking your way around the pistes.

The Survival Skier will most often find himself using his ski-speak on slope to extract himself from a tricky situation, such as when his chalet-mates suddenly round a corner and find him in a state of collapse and disarray in the middle of the piste. In this sort of situation, it's absolutely vital for the Survival Skier to react quickly, perhaps announcing breezily: 'Those damned pedal-jump turns – I'll get the hang of them one day' or 'That's what comes of trying to do a Legspin Helicopter without a proper jumping platform'. With any luck, it'll be the other way round and you'll be the one to round the corner to find your chalet-mates all lined up being put through their paces by the instructor, or perhaps sprawled out with their noses in the snow. In this instance, you needn't say anything. You can simply skid to a stop, with as much control as you can muster, preferably positioning yourself above them so you can look down on them condescendingly for a while, as if to say: 'That was me, once – a long, long time ago'. Then after a few minutes you can begin to look bored, and turn your attention to something else, perhaps scanning the horizon or inspecting the snow before traversing off. (Survival Skiers spend a lot of time scanning the horizon or inspecting the snow.) If queried about this, the Survival Skier can casually mention that the *Chef de Piste* has asked him to keep an eye out for potential avalanches. This will then provide him with a cue to launch into a brief discourse on different types of snow texture.

If you happen upon your friends while they are not in the presence of their ski instructor, then, of course, a bit of a chat will be required. The basic rule is that any remarks addressed to one's friends on slope should be enthusiastic and hearty. However foul the weather, however many times he's crashed, however sheer the slopes, the Survival Skier will never let on that he's spent the day wishing he was somewhere else. 'Enjoying yourself?' he will say, patronisingly, trying to convey that he at least has been having a whale of a time. Once again, when coming alongside anyone to stop for a chat, try to park yourself *above* them – ideally on a rather steep part of the slope (you don't of course actually have to ski down from

---

Rules of Skiing

CLASSES

Ski-school never starts at ten a.m.

Any similarity between the way the class skis and the way the instructor skis is purely accidental.

No one will be sure where or when the class agreed to meet again after lunch.

There will always be at least one ski-class assembling just as you come off the lift, blocking your path and everyone else's.

The day your class goes off piste in deep powder is the day you choose to wear your jeans and a sweater.

On race day, your class will go last.

---

this point). This not only gives the Survival Skier a sense of superiority; it also makes your friends feel obliged to ski off first – the old *après-vous* technique. In fact, if they're not very experienced, they will probably even want to go off first, just to show you what they can do. Then, when they've executed a marvellous turn, of which they are obviously, and quite rightly, very proud, call down to them: 'Ye-es. That wasn't *too* bad. But try pushing round more with your knees. *Kniespieltechnik* is *so* important'. And, remember, at all times, talk about *their* skiing rather than yours. (This will usually be no problem as *their* skiing is what they're most interested in.) And never let them feel at ease. The Survival Skier should apply the same technique used by ski instructors: first destroy their self-confidence; then offer them a few hints, which will, of course, lead to a 'big improvement'; and, finally, shower them with enthusiastic praise ('I knew you could do it'), which, at the same time, is a way of complimenting yourself on your own instruction.

Another good rule for the Survival Skier is try to ensure that he's only seen on the higher slopes – say between 2,000 and 3,000 metres. Thus a standard opener when you pull up beside someone for a chat is: 'What are the lower slopes like?' thereby implying that most of your time is spent either up to your neck in off piste snow or with your nose in the clouds near the top of the *Spitzenspitze*. Not that you will wax enthusiastic about the upper reaches of the *Spitzenspitze* – in fact it's becoming a bit of a bore and a bit overcrowded: 'Isn't it about time they opened up the *Oberspitzenspitze?* Then we could get some real skiing in'.

As well as the question of status, there are certain real practical advantages to skiing from the highest possible point (even if it does take you most of the day to get down). First of all, the top station will nearly always be reached by cable car, which means no messing around on uncomfortable tows or freezing to death in chairlifts (though it can also be a bit nippy at the top of the *Spitzenspitze*). Another advantage is that there will always be a lot of people who want to go to the top, so that getting up there will be a long, slow haul, thus wasting a lot of good skiing time. This is something the Survival Skier will, of course, complain about vigorously if he comes across anyone he knows in the cable car: 'You know, what with all this hanging around, it'll take about three-quarters of an hour to get to the top of the *Grand Diable*. Then you're down at the bottom again in two and a half minutes to start the whole business all over again'. The Survival Skier will not, of course, venture to actually demonstrate how he gets to the bottom in two and a half minutes. So he may have to find a system for slipping away from the friend he's met in the cable car. One effective method is to exchange a few more words with your friend when you get out of the station and put on your skis. Then, still grumbling about all the hanging around, you suddenly shoot off in a dramatic *Schuss* down the *back* side of the mountain, calling out: 'I've had enough of this. I'm going to find myself a more interesting way down'. You then duck out of sight behind the nearest large rock, and take stock of your surroundings. You usually have a choice of either heading for the nearest *Hütte* or, alternatively, clambering back up to the cable station (once everybody's gone and the coast is clear). You can then take the cable car down (keeping your head low) and wait for your friends at the bottom, asking them nonchalantly when they arrive 'What kept you?'. When the Survival Skier does cut loose from the company like this at the top of a station, the break should be short and sharp; otherwise your friends may be encouraged to follow you. It's the same when ditching someone on the T-bar by jumping off before you get to the top. Call out: 'I'm going to find another way down. See you at the restaurant', (i.e. 'You go your way and I'll go mine').

But the Survival Skier won't always be trying to give his friends the slip and, often enough, he will be prepared to give his friends the time of day – particularly when they are comparative novices and look as if they might appreciate a few tips. A good rule when offering advice is to try to use as many technical words (preferably foreign) as possible. This will make your protégés feel that what they're doing is that much more impressive. The same applies to your own ski manoeuvres – if you're caught in the act of trying to execute something fairly ordinary and fail dismally, give it a fancy foreign name, and you may just get away with it: even though what you were doing may have looked like a rather sloppy stem christie, you were really trying to set yourself up for a Moebius flip; or you made the mistake of trying to change a compression turn (*Kompressionsschwung*) into a flying weight transfer turn (*Fliegendes Umsteigen*) once you were past the point of no return (*Keinruck-kehrspunkt*).

This sort of talk also makes it abundantly clear to the novice why it is that *you're* not skiing in a class. Clearly they don't really have instruction for the sort of things that you are trying to perfect. At times you have to be a bit more explicit: you let slip, for instance, that you came to the resort on hearing that they had a *'couloir* course' which specialised in crevasse techniques. This, unfortunately, turned out not to be true, so you then decided to do a little ski-jumping ('well ski-flying really') to work on your 'hang', but found, to your surprise, that they didn't have a proper jumping hill either. Thus it is that you can be found on the piste like everyone else, reduced to practising your *Gelände*-jumping. That's why, though he may be putting his usual brave face on things, our Survival Skier will often be a shade downcast. It wouldn't have been so bad if he could have done a little ski-kiting, but unfortunately weather conditions wouldn't permit that either. And standing on the piste watching the antics of lesser mortals in their compact skis has not exactly improved his spirits. Indeed, watching the piste-bashing masses at play has made him feel that perhaps the noble art of ski-running is not quite what it was in his day. Still, it's nice to see people enjoying themselves. He must confess, though, that he's not at all sure he likes what's been happening in the Alps – one more reason, he may conclude, why he's going to stick more and more in future to ski-touring and ski-mountaineering. Unfortunately even on the very high ground things are no longer as tranquil as they once were; and, if things go the way they have gone in the *Vallée Blanche,* then even the more remote high mountain routes won't be safe for very much longer.

With any luck (and a little practice) you may even be able to make all this sound sufficiently convincing to explain why, when your friends came round the corner, they found you collapsed in a heap with your sticks between your legs: the reason was very simple – you had merely been practising riding your sticks broomstick-style, like the old one-stick ski-tourers of yesteryear.

8. Apres-Ski-Speak

'But he'll remember with advantages
What feats he did that day'

William Shakespeare, Henry V

Although a strong line in chat is a big help while actually skiing, it is during *après-ski* time that ski-speak really comes into its own. For, once off the slopes, ski-talk becomes without question the main activity – and not just for Survival Skiers but for *all* skiers (most of whose accounts of their on-slope doings will be as much at variance with reality as the stories told by Survival Skiers). As a result, the competition at the bar these days can be very tough indeed. Don't, incidentally, be misled by all those other activities apparently going on during *après-ski* time (everything from aerobics to flower-arranging): whatever else people may appear to be doing, what they are really doing is chatting about their skiing.

One problem with ski-speak is that there never comes a time when you can say you've got it mastered. Whereas with most Survival Skiing techniques a good grasp of the basics will last you a skiing lifetime, this is not the case with ski-speak. Chatting techniques do keep on evolving. New terms and new gambits are constantly being developed. And the range of subjects the Survival Skier must be able to turn his tongue to gets ever wider – covering everything these days from wind-speed coefficients to mountain mushrooms. Nonetheless, at the risk of rendering this book rather rapidly out-of-date, here are a few tips about the current state of the art of ski-speak.

Perhaps the most significant development in recent years has been the use of medical terminology. Survival Skiers have not been slow to catch on to this and many have now made medical chat as important a part of their repertoire as technical chat about the mechanics of skiing. In fact, the two areas are quite closely related, and medical know-how can be used very effectively to counter technical know-how. As you might expect, the Americans, who have long been deft users of medical terminology (having 'tonsilectomies' rather than having their tonsils out), are very much the leaders in this field at the moment. A big advantage of being a medical specialist is that it's a very good way of endearing yourself to your fellow skiers. Everybody has things wrong with them and will enjoy talking to you about their ailments, particularly if you can add some tone to the conversation with obscure and impressive medical terms. The key areas are the back and the knees since this is where most people have their twinges. And skiing, of course, does tend to bring these twinges on. Even perfectly healthy individuals are going to collect plenty of aches and pains in the course of a day on the slopes and will therefore appreciate a 'consultation' with the Survival Skiing medic.

It's helpful, of course, if the Survival Skier can establish some credentials in this field – ideally something like the old-pin-in-the-knee – which, although it's something he doesn't like to talk about, he will occasionally curse about under his breath (particularly when it prevents him taking chances in skiing down a rather steep slope). Thus his words will carry some weight when he recommends his 'patient' to try a 'knee-brace' or an 'anti-rotation brace' to stabilise the quadriceps. His words will carry even more weight if he can arrange to be seen chatting during the day to the man who tows the blood-wagon, examining with him his selection of metal clamps and frames with which he fixes people up if they have an accident on the slopes. The important thing is to always relate your 'diagnosis' to actions performed during the course of skiing. This is what will make your diagnosis carry more weight than anything that a local GP could come up with. A GP, for instance, can hardly be expected to know much about the relationship between the head of the tibia and the bone fracture forces generated by the torsion coefficient of badly adjusted ski-bindings. By the way, always try to get bindings into the conversation early on since most people worry about them a great deal, and suspect that though they may be called 'safety' bindings they're actually rather unsafe.

The Survival Skier will, of course, try to put things over as *simply* as possible, explaining to his patient that in his particular style of wide-stance skiing it's the *extensor* muscles, like the *gluteas maximus,* which are in a state of maximum contraction, while, somewhat surprisingly, the *rotators,* especially the *middle gluteal,* are partially relaxed. If, perchance, your patient should appear to be in any way mystified by this, you can sketch out a diagram ('a bit simplified') with plenty of intersecting arrows and curved lines showing exactly how the servo forces involved in weight-transfer are affected by torsional stress, depending on the position of your centre of gravity at any given moment and of course taking into account their direct relationship to the weight distribution of your body mass, in so far as this is actually applied through the spinal column to change direction in a friction turn.

It may be that even such a straightforward exposition of biomechanics as this will still leave your patient somewhat mystified. And he may even be a little ashamed that he is not able to provide you with even such elementary information as his bone density coefficient, ('Worth checking out, old boy'). But not to worry, the Survival Skier won't lose patience and will boil it all down to essentials: 'Basically, your type of stem turn is exerting pressure on the lower patella. So your best course would be to try to counter-rotate more. If you don't, then the lower third of your tibia will be very vulnerable to a spiral break, particularly with those high boots of yours. I've seen it so many times'. Above all, be reassuring. It may never happen, you tell your patient. And now that he understands exactly what the problem is, he should be perfectly safe – particularly if you've got him so worried that he decides to give up skiing entirely. In some cases people may be slightly ashamed of what they've got wrong with them – perhaps something like fallen arches. But once you've got it out of them and dressed up their rather banal complaint with a lot of fancy jargon about pronation and canting, recommending to them that they try wedges under the boot, they'll soon begin to feel better.

Occasionally you will find people who, like the Survival Skier, tend to keep a stiff upper lip and are reluctant to discuss their ailments. But persevere, and you will find that they too (like the Survival Skier, grunting with pain through his gritted teeth because of that 'damned' pin in his knee) will admit that all is not well. The plain fact of the matter is that no lowlander feels well at 2,000 or 3,000 metres. It's just not natural to be at that height, without our usual supply of pollution-rich oxygen. So if your friends can't sleep, or their hands are trembling, or they feel faint, don't tell them they've just been over-eating and drinking too much. Tell them it's a mild case of altitude sickness and explain to them a little bit about hypoxia and hyperventilation. They will appreciate this much more than being told to lay off the booze.

In addition to mastering new fields like the application of medical terminology to skiing, it's always a good idea for the Survival Skier to have expert knowledge of a particularly rarefied form of skiing. This might be ski-orienteering, or dog-sledging across glaciers, or barrel-jumping (in your youth of course), or *ski-jöring* (skiing behind a galloping horse – except when you did it just after the war which meant being towed along by US Army Jeeps). The Survival Skier should, of course, always have enough detail at his command to follow through any of these conversations if pressed. Thus, if the conversation has switched to remote ski areas ('Such a pity about the war in Afghanistan – there used to be such good skiing in

---

Rules of Skiing

PROGRESS

All progress is either theoretical or illusory.

You ski worse on the second day than on the first.

When you feel you're skiing a lot better, no one else will notice any improvement.

It's when you're skiing your best that things are most likely to go wrong.

Most skiers believe that there's a knack which, once grasped, will make it all come right.

No one *ever* finds it.

If you start getting it right, things will immediately start to go wrong.

the Hindu Kush'), and the Survival Skier gets asked 'Ever ski in Chile, down Roca Jack?', he can sink back in his chair and ask rhetorically: 'Have I skied down Roca Jack? Have I skied down Roca Jack? My goodness me, I was skiing down Roca Jack long before these *kilometro lanciato* boys had ever heard of Portillo. Used to ski down Roca Jack with Old Jack himself. And it was a damned sight steeper in those days – not the mere 45 degrees it is today. It took more than a couple of pisco sours to get up enough courage to point your skis in the right direction. And a pisco sour at that height really *did* go to your head!'.

Yes, the Survival Skier will usually have been around, and will be as ready to wax lyrical about the lightness of texture of West Coast powder as about the heavy stuff in the Himalayas ('some great skiing once you get above 6,000 metres, but unfortunately the *après-ski's* not up to much, nor the food – mainly dried bear biltong and yak's milk'); or perhaps to reminisce about ski-touring in the High Atlas ('wonderful landscape but *après-ski* a bit limited – mainly squatting around a pot of couscous swapping sheeps' eyes with the locals').

The Survival Skier also, of course, gets around in more familiar ski areas a little closer to home. He tries, for instance, to drop in at the Palace in St Moritz at least once a year. However, if asked to pick a favourite resort, he will invariably come up with some totally obscure Alpine station that no one else in the assembled company will ever have heard of. Thus, the message to all aspiring Survival Skiers is that if you're going to make your ski-speak work for you, you've got to do your homework beforehand, and develop a wide-ranging repertoire.

You must also try to inflict your ski-speak on as broad a range of people as possible. It's no good just sitting in a corner of the bar all night talking to a bunch of high-technology buffs about minimising drag coefficients or a reversed somersault turn. The Survival Skier does not limit himself to one particular group. He's a good mixer. He moves around – amongst the pros, amongst the novices, amongst the Brits, amongst the foreigners and, of course, amongst the locals. As we've already said, you'll do more for your reputation by knocking back the firewater with the old-timers down at the *Stube* than you will by spending your time eating puff-pastry with your chalet-mates.

Another reason why the Survival Skier won't want to spend too much time with any particular group is that he doesn't want to get a reputation as a Ski Bore. And anyway, he is, after all, the strong silent type – isn't he?

9. The Locals

**'Some centuries since, when a stranger strayed into
one of their valleys, their simple forefathers would
kill him and share out the little money he might have
about him. Now they know better. They keep him
alive and writing cheques.'**

C. E. Montague, The Right Place

If a Survival Skier is to succeed in putting himself over as the sort of chap who knows his way around the world's high spots, it's rather important that he should also be seen to know his way around Pistendorf. A reputation for being able to converse in fluent Bhote with your Sherpa guides in the Himalayas can rapidly become somewhat tarnished if you can't so much as exchange a *'Grüezi'* with the locals in the Alps. It's not too much good being able to tell your fellow piste-bashers where they serve the best pisco sour in Portillo if you can't give them the low-down on where it all happens in Pistendorf. This should not, in fact, present too much of a problem. As we have seen, our Survival Skier will be spending a good deal of his time in one of Pistendorf's steamiest *Stubes,* so he should be better clued up than most on what's what and where's where.

What your fellow piste-bashers will be particularly keen to know, however, is *who's who* in Pistendorf. Most piste-bashers like to feel they're in with the locals – though the locals aren't always that easy to get in with. As a result, most piste-bashers tend to end up getting to know each other rather better than they do their hosts. So a Survival Skier who can offer a little inside gen on who's who can do a good deal for his reputation. Unfortunately, mountain folk, with their traditional taciturnity and suspicion of strangers, don't easily give that much away about themselves. But this need not cause you too much difficulty. The fact is that most mountain men are much like most other mountain men. The people in Pistendorf won't differ very much from the people in Oberpistendorf or Unterpistendorf, or indeed from the people in almost any other Pistendorf you may care to mention. So for those Survival Skiers who may not have had the opportunity to undertake all the necessary research into the genus *homo montaniensis,* here's a potted guide to some of the stock characters you can be almost certain to find in almost any mountain village:

THE VILLAGE ELDER

One of a group of (usually bearded) sages who constitute the village Politburo. No major development will be undertaken, no new ski-lift opened, no hotel extension built, until this caucus of mountain wisdom has deliberated upon the matter and pronounced. A *Stammtisch* will be reserved for them at one of the local hostelries and it's here, elbows wearing ever deeper grooves into the table-top, that all the big decisions will be pondered over and taken. Even when there aren't any decisions to be made, those elbows will stay firmly implanted as the elders continue to ponder over a game of dominoes or shuffleboard. On Sundays you'll find them all done up in their best brass-buttoned jackets with the green velvet trim and matching knickerbockers. This is mainly for the benefit of the village priest who's invariably a village elder himself.

THE PATRIARCH

A leading member of one of the half-dozen families who actually run and own most of the village. Everyone in Pistendorf is either related to, or employed by, one of these families. The patriarch is not however usually one of the village elders – his many vested interests disqualify him from membership of this supreme council of the wise and the good. And even though the patriarch may be the owner of Mount Pistendorf itself he won't dare put another lift on those slopes without the elders' approval. Not that he won't get it – he does, after all, also own the very hostelry where the elders gather to ponder. The fact is that he's usually a bit too busy supervising his various business operations, each of which will be run by one of his scions or other members of his extended family. There may also be the odd feud with another of Pistendorf's leading clans to keep him occupied. These days, however, the local clans more often find themselves closing ranks to keep out the big money outsiders who are trying to buy their way into the village.

THE SAGE

Often a retired village elder – and therefore very, very ancient. He'll have a long memory, an even longer white beard and will usually be found sitting on a bench sucking on a long-stemmed curly pipe. His main function is to provide visitors with local colour, and to dispense mountain lore and wisdom. So he does his best to dress the part, perhaps sporting a bright red embroidered waistcoat which will come out well on your colour snaps. Visitors are usually less happy with his soothsaying, which tends to be somewhat doomladen – if he can be persuaded to pronounce intelligibly. More often than not questions will be met with a long pause as he sucks on his pipe, whistles through his one remaining hollow tooth, and eventually answers with some non-committal monosyllable.

THE FARMER

A rare find in the mountains these days, since most of them have discovered it's much more profitable to milk the tourists than to milk the cows. Sondre Nørheim, that Norwegian grand-daddy of all downhillers, showed them the way back in the 1860s: apparently too lazy to make a living as a tenant farmer, he proceeded to think up the telemark and the parallel 'christiania' instead, as well as inventing the sort of skis that have been causing the rest of us problems ever since. But though you won't find too many real farmers in Pistendorf any more, there will be some who do a pretty good imitation. Pistendorfers know that their visitors appreciate a touch of rurality. So a few of the locals will go in for what's called 'agro-tourism', which basically means keeping the logs neatly piled up in their weathered wooden barn and sending the occasional cow out to graze under the pylons, clanking its cowbell noisily to put the visitors in rustic mood.

THE RESORT DIRECTOR

Usually an ex-champ recruited by one of the newer purpose-built resorts, which needs his name and reputation to give the village a bit more *cachet*. In theory, he's the resort administrator. But in practice he's more of a PR man, usually surrounded by a bevy of attractive 'hostesses'. He spends most of his time skiing around asking everybody if they're happy, and if they're making progress with the new miracle system of coaching he's devised specially for the village. Even if you're not making progress, you'll be so intimidated by the great man's reputation, and so overjoyed at having the chance to shake him by the hand, that you'll probably omit to tell him his system doesn't work.

THE MAN FROM THE MINISTRY

This fellow is also an outsider. But unlike the ex-champ, he's a real administrator appointed by central government to oversee the tourist trade. He thus spends most of his time on the blower to 'The Ministry'. Not unnaturally the locals tend to view this *apparatchik* with some suspicion — particularly in view of the rumours circulating

---

Rules of Skiing

LIFTS

A lift that breaks down will keep breaking down.

The lift always stops when you are going up the coldest and most exposed stretch.

By the time you get to the bottom you'll have forgotten how cold it was going up. So you'll go up again and find out.

The lift you thought linked up with another one doesn't.

The greatest insult is to decline to go up on the T-bar with someone.

If you spend much time and effort to reach a remote lift, it will stop working or turn out to be owned by another lift company.

Your lift-pass will not be valid for your last morning before departure.

about his salary and his rather grand title of 'Tourist Director'. They rather suspect that he's just there to keep an eye on them and that they'd be just as successful at keeping their pistes profitably congested without his 'direction' and 'co-ordination'. And whereas the locals do have a sneaking regard for someone who can ski a bit, like the ex-champ, it's hard to feel the same way about someone whose mission in life is to compile statistics.

THE *PISTEUR*

Perhaps the ultimate Mountain Man. Impervious to the elements, and built to last, his solid frame and wind-burned face can withstand the fiercest of blizzards and sub-zero temperatures. His forbears used to make a living carrying milords in sedan chairs over Mont Cenis and the other Alpine passes. But since the lowlanders have discovered it's more fun to tumble up and down the mountains by themselves, he's found easier ways of making a living. This basically consists of keeping the pistes tidy: shovelling snow, operating lifts, driving sno-cats, collecting dead bodies, and generally watching other people suffer and make fools of themselves. But though his robust constitution is his main asset, he does have a few professional secrets to help him avoid death from exposure: those little wooden huts dotted around the mountain, for instance, are usually well-stocked with firewater and other traditional means of warming up the system.

SKI-LIFT ATTENDANT

One of the most common types of *pisteur*, renowned for their surly taciturnity, although they will sometimes chat to one of the pros or respond to some palm-greasing by a Survival Skier. Their speciality is making life for the average piste-basher just that little bit more difficult than it need be by asking to see your lift pass when he's already seen you go up and down 20 times; or when you've just zipped it away; or when you're just about to climb on to the tow. Other favourite irritants include shovelling great mounds of snow into your path as you go up the tow (in theory to fill in the dips); closing the lift down five minutes early after you've just broken every other bone in your body scrambling down the hill in order to fit in one last run; always making a point of being in his little hut, *and staying there for a good ten minutes,* whenever the lift breaks down. You and your fellow piste-bashers will of course retaliate by continually smashing down the little fence that he keeps on re-erecting to indicate where you're supposed to queue. Still the ski-lift attendant is one of the traditional characters on the slopes, and it's a pity to see that some resorts are phasing them out and replacing them with turnstiles and little plastic cards.

THE PISTE-BULLY

A more dangerous type of *pisteur* altogether. Armed with sno-cats or ratracs, these bulldozing bullies spend their time roaming the slopes chasing down innocent

piste-bashers. In theory they're supposed to be 'grooming' the piste and flattening out the moguls. But don't you believe it – *they're after you.* One of the most common ways of coming a cropper is when you're skiing sublimely down a superb stretch of piste and then suddenly hit a patch that's just been ploughed up by the ratrac, which sends you sprawling. Their favourite technique for mowing down a victim is the sudden change of direction, catching the hapless piste-basher unawares. But ratracs are at their most deadly when hunting in pairs, chasing down and cornering their prey by expertly co-ordinated criss-crossing pincer movements.

THE *CHEF DE PISTE*

This man is the *padrino* of *pisteurs*, the Godfather of slopemen. He's the one who decides which *pisteur* gets a cushy number on the bubble lifts and which *pisteur* gets the North Face drag-lift which keeps on breaking down and where the temperature never rises above minus five. He also determines your skiing day. It's his inspection which decides which pistes can be opened, whether it's too windy for the cable car and which crevasses should be roped off. He is not, however, infallible. As we all know, even the least adventurous piste-bashers do sometimes get gobbled up by avalanches or disappear down crevasses. The problem is that his directions never seem to get transferred accurately to the piste-board down in the hotel or village; all the runs declared to be open will in fact turn out to be closed and vice versa.

THE VET

Mountain vets tend to have two roles – not just animal doctor, but animal trainer as well. In fact, as there aren't that many animals at altitude, his veterinary duties don't consist of much more than attending to the occasional pregnant cow. It's animal-*training* that takes up most of his time. First, there are all those St Bernard dogs who have to be trained to deliver barrels of brandy to stranded skiers. Second, and rather more difficult, is getting the marmots to take up their positions all over the mountain, particularly in the spring. Each marmot has to be carefully stationed so that they can *just* be spotted – *but not too easily* – to provide amusement for eagle-eyed skiers going up in lifts and cable cars. He also has to train them to give that characteristic high-pitched whistle to draw attention to themselves, before they duck quickly out of sight to tease the marmot-spotting skiers.

THE LANDLORD

All the best *Wirts* or *patrons* do their best to look the part – white whiskers, ruddy cheeks, ample girth, waistcoats – and are generally known by their Christian names (usually something like Rudi or Hansi). They will liberally dispense bonhomie as they preside over their hostelry, and they will indeed have reason enough to be jolly. Piste-bashers have been conditioned to expect ski holidays to be expensive, so they're happy enough to pay his high altitude prices – even for that almost pure spirit made from crushed pine needles that he buys for next to nothing from the clandestine still up the mountain. And there'll be none of those notices saying 'Please don't ask for credit as refusal often offends'. Instead he'll merrily encourage you to run up those bills, cheerfully offering to 'chalk it up'. You thus spend more than you intended, and also give him a chance to add on a bit more when he presents you with *die Rechnung* at the end of the evening or at the end of the week.

LE PATRON CHAMPION

This is an ex-champ who's hung up his skis and now earns a living as a bar or hotel owner. All his trophies will be on display behind the bar or in one of the public rooms, including a battered pair of boards that got him his gold medals in the Kamikaze Kilometre and the Suicide Slalom back in whenever it was. This is not because he's any less modest about his skiing prowess than any other Mountain Man. It's simply that his establishment is not exactly the best-run bar or hotel in town, and the main reason piste-bashers go there is because of his legendary reputation, perhaps in the hope that some of his twinkle-toe technique may rub off on them. In the event, they never get much out of him since he's more the strong, silent type than a silver-tongued smoothie. In fact, in the end, its usually the piste-bashers who find themselves giving *him* a few tips.

THE EXPAT *PATRON*

There will usually be at least one Brit or American who's set himself up in Pistendorf as a publican or bar-keeper. His establishment won't, however, be one of Pistendorf's several imitation English pubs, all of which will be run by the locals. Instead 'Bill's Boozer' will usually be a rather dimly-lit dive, decorated with yellowing prints and curling posters, a place for serious drinking rather than mountain merrymaking. Bill himself will tend to be a sort of Alpine Hemingway *manqué*. His clients will be single males in melancholy mood leaning forward on their bar-stools and moaning to Bill about how life isn't what it was or should be. The main attraction is being able to moan to Bill in one's own mother tongue. And to make his guests feel even more at home, and to give them something else to talk about, Bill will have Pistendorf's best and indeed *only* selection of obscure British beers or virtually unknown American bourbons. Younger versions of Bill sometimes arrive and decide that what's missing in Pistendorf is a bar where you can hear hard rock or progressive punk. But they never seem to last long. People in ski resorts seem to prefer the old *Schuhplattler* and *Schunkellieder*.

THE PERFORMER

These people provide Pistendorf's more traditional forms of entertainment as spoon-players, *Schuhplattler* dancers, arm-wrestlers or Alpenhorn-blowers. In fact you'd probably find that in their homes these people prefer listening to jazz records or progressive pop. But since their piste-bashing visitors seem to have a preference for waltzes played by brass bandsmen all kitted out in *Lederhosen*, they do their best to oblige. In fact these performers are often part-timers. During the day they may well be your chambermaid or your bus-driver. It's only in the evening that she plaits her hair like Heidi's and Hansi dons his knickerbockers and braces. They then roll along to the local hop to perform their Alpine Reel and provide the 'local colour' their visitors seem to expect by way of amusement.

THE SKI-BUM

Often an Australian or American. Is nuts about skiing and could give any of the local hotshots a run for their money. Unfortunately he doesn't have a certificate to prove it, or a work permit. So the locals refuse to give him a job as a ski instructor. He thus leads a somewhat marginal existence, living in his dormobile, doing odd jobs and getting off with the chalet-maids – much to the resentment of the locals. In fact, it's the chalet-maids who often keep him in business, introducing him to their guests as an 'alternative' instructor, who's a lot cheaper than one of the local instructors and actually speaks English. The problem is that since his activities are not strictly legal he has to keep well out of sight of the ski-school, so you end up spending the afternoon way off piste, and getting somewhat pissed off in the process.

THE NOMENCLATOR

His job is to think up and allocate names for all the resort's hotels, pistes, discotheques etc. This is actually not too arduous a task since ski-resorts like to stick to a limited selection of names that have stood the test of time (no exotic formulations like 'The Dog and Parrot'). Hotels, for instance, are always the Edelweiss, Alpenrose, Sporthotel, Alpenblick or Schwarzer Adler. Discotheques will be 'The Stork Club', 'The Purple Pussycat', 'The Pink Panther', 'Number One' or the ever-popular 'King's Club'. Pastry lounges will be 'The Shangri-la', 'Tiffany's' or 'Tea for Two'. But where he can exercise a bit of artistic licence and use his imagination is when it comes to naming the pistes. The main object here is to make them sound that much more hair-raising than they actually are, for example The White Devil, Dead Man's Gulch, Hell's Highway, Never Again, Do or Die, Rather Not, You First, I'm Going Back, and Say Your Prayers.

THE PHOTOGRAPHER

This man's livelihood depends on the simple statistic that one in two people who arrive at a ski resort forget to bring a photo for their lift-pass with them. The automatic coin-operated photo-booth will, of course, always be out of order – the photographer sees to that. Thus he manages between 7 and 8.30 every morning to make more than enough to live on, taking exorbitantly-priced mug-shots of piste-bashers desperate to get out onto the slopes. Later there'll be the obligatory ski-class photo which we always seem to take back home with us. Not exactly the most creative camerawork, perhaps. But he will get his chance to show his mettle as a lensman on Race Day. There he'll be, stationed at gate three, just before you crash out of the course, doing his best to snap you in a pose that will make your friends at home believe you actually know how to ski. He can also be a bit of a papparazzo at times, snapping you at the night-club when you're having a grope with someone you shouldn't; or lurking outside as you tumble arse over elbow when your unsteady legs go their separate ways on the icy path. (The negatives of these better forgotten moments never come cheap.)

THE SKI-HIRER

This man works on the assumption that if you need to rent skis and boots from him you probably can't ski anyway, so he needn't waste too much time fitting you up. He'll look you over, have a guess at your foot-size, pain threshold and level of incompetence, and then hand you a pair of boots and boards, giving you the sort of look that defies you to bring them back. All dialogue will be discouraged and questions about the age of the equipment on offer will most certainly not be appreciated. In fact you can count yourself lucky if you're allowed to try them on in the shop. When you rent skis you take what you're given – usually a pair of battered boards with a very blunt set of edges. (They don't like to file them too much because this wears them down.) The rust-caked bindings will, of course, be over-tightened so that you don't keep on coming back to have them readjusted – you just break your leg instead. This system ensures that the hire shop turns around most of their clientele during the morning and evening rush hour. They are then left in peace for the rest of the day, except for the occasional dissatisfied customer who has the nerve to come back at lunch-time to complain.

THE SKI-REPAIRER

Often part of the same outfit as the ski-hire shop. His 'surgery' is usually round at the back or down in the basement. A hard man to fool. He's not likely to be taken in when you explain that the battered little compacts that you'd like him to fix up for you are 'just an old pair' you use for crevasse work; or that really they belong to your sister or to your wife. This man need only glance at a pair of boards to know exactly how well or how badly you perform on them. You'll do yourself no good by pretending that all those gouges in the bottom came from leaping over rocks or careering down off-piste precipices. He *knows* you just scraped them on the gravel outside the hotel because you were too lazy to take them off and carry them those last few yards. And anyway the mere fact that you've come to see him is significant – and enough to earn his contempt. Real skiers file their own edges and wax their own skis.

THE *GARAGISTE*

The *garagiste* is still usually more Mountain Man than mechanic. He just happened to have a piece of land near the main road and was the first villager to twig that the automobiles bringing the skiers up the mountain needed to be filled up periodically with black liquid. So he invested in a solitary petrol pump and now enjoys a total monopoly as the only dispenser of auto-fuel in Pistendorf. There'll be almost an air of conspiracy as he slowly pumps this vital resource into your tank. He likes you to feel grateful for this service because he's not exactly the most popular man in the village. By no means all the locals are convinced that there's any real need for a garage. After all, skis and sleighs have always been a perfectly effective means of transport in years gone by. And the internal combustion engine does tend to make such a mess of the snow. Some villages, as we know, ban cars altogether. In fact the *garagiste* doesn't make his money so much from providing petrol as from fitting snow-chains for people who can't do it themselves, or from digging out cars that get buried in snow drifts. But if you ever happen to need a spare part, he'll be no different from any other garageman: it'll cost you.

THE TAXI-DRIVER

Like the *garagiste,* the taxi-driver also usually enjoys a monopoly in the village. Thus, unlike lowland taxi-drivers, he doesn't spend his time cruising around looking for a fare. You find a taxi in a ski resort by looking up 'Taxi' in the phone book, and by ringing him up, and negotiating a rate for the job. Only then will he get his precious vehicle out of his garage and come and fetch you and take you wherever it is you want to go. This service never comes cheap, since he knows that no one in a ski resort will ever ring for a taxi unless they're absolutely desperate, and the last post-bus has gone, and they've been unable to cadge a lift any other way. The other difference between mountain taxi-drivers and normal taxi-drivers is that they see their job as simply driving the taxi, rather than driving and talking you to your destination. For this, at least, much thanks.

THE SLEIGH-DRIVER

This chap doesn't come any cheaper than the taxi-driver. But at least he drives the sort of vehicle you feel you ought to be driven around in when you go to a ski resort. He's also more of an entertainer than the taxi-driver. He may look like some senile dwarf, but you'll find he doesn't need any help as he loads your bags on to his sleigh when you arrive at the railway station. And before long that white-bearded chin of his will be wagging away and he'll be telling you about how it was in the old days, before they built the cog railway, when people used to come by mule train, and when skiing folk did things in style. You'll even feel slightly ashamed, as you unload, that all your luggage is made of nylon and plastic, not canvas and leather, *comme il faut.*

THE ANNEXER

Pistendorf is full of little chaps with big ideas, and the annexer is perhaps the most typical. He was once the owner of a charming little *Gasthaus,* with shutters and windowboxes – the sort of place that made Pistendorf Pistendorf. But he's

gradually bought up the bits of land on either side of it, and now every year he tacks on a new addition – annexes, swimming-pool, sun-terrace, boutique, *Stübli* etc. As a result his once quaint, but now unrecognisable, little *Gasthaus* has more mod cons and facilities than most luxury hotels. All this tends to give the local elders a good deal to scratch their beards about. There they are trying to ensure that Pistendorf retains its essential character, and along he comes with yet another planning application – this time asking if he can tack on a ten-pin bowling alley. His is not an ideal place to stay since the builders are in almost permanent residence.

THE SKI-SHOP OWNER

This chap's operation, too, has expanded a good deal over the years. As the manufacturers have kept on inventing new items of gear – things we don't really need, but have to have – so his shop has taken up more and more space to stock them all. The equipment he sells is actually much more expensive than it would be in your end-of-season ski sale back at home. But piste-bashers tend to assume that because they're in a ski-resort, the ski-gear there *must* be cheaper. The ski-shop owner also knows that it's when you're in Pistendorf that you're at your most vulnerable. Everybody will buy some new item of gear in the course of a week – even if it's just a new bobble-hat. And it's after an awful day's skiing on your battered old skis (the ones you bought last year) that you're most likely to be tempted by visions of transforming your skiing by acquiring some of that gleaming new high-technology he has on display.

THE DISTILLER

Every bar in Pistendorf, as in all ski resorts, will have a good selection of evil-smelling mountain *grappas* made from all manner of crushed stalks, pips and berries. But like every other ski-resort, Pistendorf will also have its own special local brand of ferocious firewater which the barman will keep locked away under the counter and which will only be produced when the door is bolted and the drinking starts to get really serious. Pocheen has nothing on this infernal beverage, about 2,000% proof, and distilled (if that's the word) clandestinely up on the mountain in an innocent looking *Hütte* by a family of moonshiners who have been handing down their dastardly recipe from generation to generation for centuries. No one quite knows what they put in it, and not everyone is sure that it's safe for human consumption. But when the tax inspector comes up the mountain, no one ever gives the moonshiners away. Pistendorf would not be Pistendorf without this potion. And anyway it's such fun serving a snifter (one is always enough) to innocent piste-bashers and then watching them go into convulsions as the beastly brew percolates to those parts that no other brew has ever been known to even approach.

THE *CONTRABANDISTE*

Most Pistendorfers number more than a few brigands amongst their forefathers. And, as we know, tradition dies hard in the mountains. This is one of the reasons why Pistendorfers have adapted so well to today's more sophisticated methods of perpetrating daylight robbery on innocent piste-bashers. Very much a part of this tradition is the local *contrabandiste*. Pistendorfers, who never got much help from the ruling bureaucrats down in the valley, and who used to be cut off for nine months of the year anyway, have never quite understood why they were supposed to pay those 'big city' taxes. So in the old days local smugglers used to keep a steady supply of tax- and duty-free goods circulating around the mountain tops. And there will certainly be at least one operator who continues to offer this valuable service in Pistendorf today. Even visiting piste-bashers have been known to snap up one of his bottles of duty-free or one of his digital quartz pedometers which fell off the back of a sleigh. (If you're looking for him he's usually the man in the corner of the bar wearing the bulging overcoat and a pair of running shoes, with his *eye* constantly on the front door. He tends to use the back exit himself.)

THE LAW

This is the fellow that the *contrabandiste* is watching the door for as he lurks in his corner of the bar. But Pistendorf's equivalent of Mr Plod usually knows better than to barge in when delicate negotiations are taking place or when the *patron* sets out the snifters for a serious session on the local moonshine. Mr Plod would never have got his job if he didn't know the importance of discretion. Anyway he's usually much too busy keeping an eye on the tourists (they're the ones who tend to really get out of hand). So much so that there are times when he finds it very hard to sympathise when the piste-bashers come to him (as they do every day) with sob-stories about how their precious skis and ski-boots 'disappeared' when they forgot to lock them away overnight.

THE DOCTOR

That classic skiing salutation *'Hals und Beinbruch'* more or less sums up what life's all about for the local quack. The surprising thing is that after all the practice he's had with broken tibias and clavicles he can't do a better job at repairing them. Have you ever heard of anyone who broke a leg or a collar-bone skiing which was not incorrectly treated and did not have to be completely reset when the victim got home? Perhaps that's why the locals steer clear of their quack. Unlike many rural folk who credit medics with magical powers and think that medics know the answer to everything, Mountain Men remain unconvinced that the quack knows the answer to anything. They know that the local herbal tea is the only internal medicine that works; and that nothing beats the local moonshine for dabbing on cuts, grazes and bruises. They also have great faith in prudence – making sure that *Hals und Beinbruch* is something that only happens to tourists.

THE MUSHROOM MAN

If anyone in the village is credited with magical powers it's the local fungologist. Mountain Men revere the mushroom and when autumn comes and the air is moist and the fungi start popping up under the trees, they head for the woods to search for their supper. Thus there's a lot of respect for the mushroom man – usually an ancient sage with a trufflehound nose and an encyclopaedic knowledge of every conceivable variety of agaricus, whether bisporus, campestris, arvensis or downright deadly poisonous. He often teams up with the local chemist or homeopath; and together they run a consultancy for people who are uncertain whether their ceps, morels and girolles are the real thing and won't give you something rather worse than indigestion when you fry them up on toast. The mushroom man also sells jars of dried mushrooms which he seems to be able to find throughout the year. He must go out at night because no one has ever managed to follow him to his secret mushroom-growing places. (The village cynics say he just keeps a bed of well watered horsedung in his backyard.)

THE SKI-MANUFACTURER

No one outside Pistendorf has ever heard of the locally-made skis. But after a week in Pistendorf you could be forgiven for thinking they're world-famous. They're advertised on every other billboard in the village and the local manufacturer is, of course, in with all the local ski-shop owners who are amply rewarded for pushing home-produced Pistendorf *planches*. There'll be many a visiting piste-basher who'll decide he can't pass up the opportunity to pick up a pair of handcrafted Pistendorf wonderboards at factory prices. It's a good job that most people buy them at the end of their holiday and not when they arrive.

THE LAUNDRYMAN

Being rather traditional places, most ski resorts have resisted pressure to open up a laundromat — that even goes for the new self-catering villages. This is extremely fortunate for the local *blanchisseur* who specialises in being both expensive and slow. But like a number of other tradesmen in Pistendorf he does have a monopoly. Thus he can continue losing and savaging any clothing submitted to him by innocent piste-bashers with little fear of losing his livelihood. He also does rather well out of all the items that aren't ready when the piste-bashers depart and which they therefore have to write off and leave behind.

THE CAKEMAKER

He supplies the local cafes and confiseries with all those *Himbeertortes* and cream-topped triple-deckers which lie in wait for the unwary piste-basher when he goes out on his pre-prandial stroll. The cakemaker gets away with it a) because people get very hungry when they come off the slopes and it seems a long time till dinner and b) because people tend to feel they've suffered so much on the slopes that they deserve a bit of a treat. So much for the F-Plan. Yet believe it or not, all those piste-bashers, in their heart of hearts, *do* know better, even as they succumb to their second *Strudel*. They've all read all the right books about calories and cholesterol and they all know just how long it's going to take their system to break down all that whipped cream (if it ever manages to). It's a good thing the cakemaker doesn't know what a menace he is to society – he'd find it very hard to live with himself.

THE DISCO-OWNER

This chap has discovered that you can take an old barn or disused cellar and put up a sign outside saying 'Nite-club' or 'Disco' and charge people twice as much for drinks as the other bars in town. Many Pistendorfers have their doubts about these sorts of places. But they're what the piste-bashers seem to want, and no Pistendorfer ever tried to stop another Pistendorfer who was on to a good wheeze. They also provide employment – as 'disc-jockeys' – for younger Pistendorfers who don't make the grade as ski instructors. Rather a new profession in Pistendorf, this, but one that's catching on, and which does seem to have certain advantages. It's rather extraordinary really that these failed ski instructors should be making it rather more successfully with the visiting piste-basheuses than even the most dashing of Pistendorf's *moniteurs*.

THE GUZZLER

Every resort has one. He's usually a *pisteur,* perhaps a lift-man, built like a barrel, as hard as a rock, with insides to match. It's his capacity to down anything, including the local moonshine, in quantity, for hours on end, and still walk out of the bar in a straight line that has earned him his awesome reputation. This talent also provides him with a valuable source of extra income as there are always some hard-drinking piste-bashers ready to challenge him at downing a yard of *vino* in one. He can normally see off three or four opponents a night. And as he steps out in the cold night air at two in the morning you half expect him to be found the next day, a stiffened corpse, still standing but frozen in mid-stride. Instead he'll be manning his lift as usual, making a nuisance of himself, with no sign whatsoever of any ill-effects from the night before. (Actually, it's training that's his secret. If you watch carefully you'll see him empty at least three hip flasks in the course of the day, just to get himself in trim for the evening to come.)

10. Apres-Apres-Ski

'Maybe the biggest problem in life is how to spend it.'

Burt Blechman, Maybe

In the beginning there was ski, then came *après-ski*, and now, for better or worse, we have *après-après-ski*. That is to say, piste-artistry is now an activity that goes on all the time right through the year. Gone are the days when people started talking about it just before Christmas, put in their obligatory two weeks on the slopes soon afterwards and then chucked their skis into a corner of the garage and forgot about it all till the next season. But year-round skiing need not be to the disadvantage of the Survival Skier. As we have seen, the further he is from the slopes, the better the Survival Skier tends to perform. So if he's twice as good at the bar as he is on the piste, he ought to be about 20 times as good when he's performing on his own home ground. In fact, the Survival Skier's reputation back at home is much more likely to be determined by his performance in the local pub than by his performance in Pistendorf – particularly if he's been wise enough to go skiing in a resort where none of his friends go.

But be warned. *Après-après-ski* competition in your own High Street can be pretty hard graft, and the 'out of season' ski programme can be very loaded. It's no longer just a case of putting a little dubbin on your boots, 'easing the springs' on your bindings, and occasionally spinning the odd skiing yarn down at the local pub. Off-season Survival Skiing is now a full-time activity and the only thing for the committed Survival Skier to do is to get stuck into it. If you do take this sort of positive attitude, you should find that the results will be very effective. In fact, if you do your stuff well enough in the off-season, you may find you can actually get out of going skiing altogether and sneak off to the Caribbean instead.

As with skiing and *après-skiing*, perhaps one of the most important things about *après-après-skiing* is to have all the right gear. This does not mean just having the usual 'state of the art' skis and boots that you cart off with you to Pistendorf. It means nothing less than equipping your whole house in such a way that it would be an attractive proposition for Franz Klammer if he ever decided he needed a *pied-à-terre* in your neck of the woods. This means that as soon as anyone steps inside your front door they will know they're in a Survival Skiing home. The coat rack will be slung over with assorted anoraks and ski-hats; there'll be the odd ski-pole in the umbrella stand; and lined up in the hall will be not the row of traditional British wellies, but the family's collection of moonboots. As you enter the living-room these initial Survival Skiing impressions will be more than confirmed. The focus of attention is likely to be the large open fireplace with perhaps an Alpenhorn or one of those ancient museum-piece skis suspended over the mantelpiece, much as an oarsman mounts his oar on the wall after the Boat Race. You

may also have a special shelf for all your trophies – you will certainly have
accumulated enough in your ski-school races over the years. Skiing books will
abound on your bookshelves – a number of them, ideally, in foreign languages.
And there'll be plenty of other items of ski-decor: the 'personally autographed'
photo of Jean-Claude Killy, the blown-up photo of you and your family snapped at
their finest moments in their 'gate three' positions, and the odd poster or two –
perhaps that classic two-metre wide panorama of the mountain tops of the Alps.

But the centre of *après-après-skiing* activity will be elsewhere in the house.
Somewhere there'll be a room, perhaps the attic or a box-room, but more likely the
conservatory or the garage, *which is completely given over to skiing*. Some
Survival Skiers even build a special extension or their own little skiing *Hütte* at the
bottom of the garden. The garden *Hütte* is, of course, the best option since it will be
the most conspicuous to passers-by. It should be made of pinewood (perhaps
using some of the planks left over from when you had your sauna installed); and
you can put Tyrolean shutters on the windows, just to ensure that your *Hütte* is not
mistaken for the standard British woodshed or potting shed. Some Survival Skiers
like to do the same thing with their house, putting up shutters and window-boxes of
geraniums and perhaps renaming their abode 'Ski Heil' or 'Alpenblick' (even if it
does overlook the gasworks). If you can afford it, and if you're a true Survival Skier
you can't afford *not* to afford it, you should also get a big wooden balcony tacked
on to the front of the house. Here you can emerge on a frosty Saturday morning in
your ski-pants and moonboots and wearing your 'Off Piste Skiers Do It Deeper'
T-shirt to perform your knee bends, consult the giant thermometer on the wall,
scan the horizon, and, if conditions look right, head off up the road on your roller
skis to do the shopping. If there's the merest sprinkling of snow, of course, you'll be
out on your cross-country skis.

The centre of activity, however, will be the ski-room or *Hütte*. This year's skis and poles will all be neatly lined up in the storage rack. But in another corner of the room you can be sure to find a thicket of discarded skis and poles, of varying lengths, testifying to the progress you and your family have made (or haven't made) over the years. In yet another corner you'll probably find a jumble of rusting old cable bindings and sealskins, now somewhat moth-eaten despite your periodic sprinklings with Para-di-chloro-benzene. On the walls there will, of course, be the usual posters, maps, ski-ads, team photos, stolen piste-signs and stickers like 'Do it in the snow', '. . . and on the seventh day, God went skiing', or 'Skiers are piste artists'. The focus of the room, though, will be the workbench (unless you can afford your own wind-tunnel). Here on the bench you'll find all the paraphernalia that you'd find in any decent ski-workshop in the Alps – clamps, blow torch, bunsen burner, various tools, files and scrapers, plus sandpaper, steel wool, linseed oil, turpentine, P-tex, assorted waxes and waxing corks.

Now, all this may seem like a rather high price to pay just to avoid actually having to go skiing. But many Survival Skiers, in that great British tradition of pottering about and doing-it-yourself, do rather enjoy fiddling around with all this gadgetry: stripping and reassembling their bindings, getting at them with the white spirit and pipecleaners, waxing and scraping, and rewaxing, and paraffin waxing, and then starting all over again. And, of course you never run out of skis to work on. There are not just yours to do. There are the rest of the family's as well. And every member of any self-respecting Survival Skiing family will have at least two pairs of skis. Then there'll be the novelty skis, like the Scorpians and the mono-skis, to tinker with. Some Survival Skiers have found that it pays to extend this service. Rather like a local MP, they set up a sort of 'surgery', inviting their friends to bring along their battered boards for expert care and attention. This has the advantage of luring them into your lair so you can impress them with all your technology and know-how, and also enables you to earn a few bob on the side.

As well as getting his house properly fitted up, the Survival Skier must also make the most of his car. This will, of course, be four-wheel drive, have a ski-rack on the roof, and perhaps be decorated with 'Go Faster' stripes to match his ski-pants and the odd 'I ♥ SKI' decal. The Survival Skier puts on snow tyres every winter, despite the fact that he always goes to work by train and that if there's any snow it's almost impossible to open the garage doors. He'll also have a set of studded tyres in the garage, along with a large selection of snow-chains. The reason for this great pile of ironmongery is that, like all Survival Skiers, he is engaged in an eternal quest for the perfect (or at least, adequate) set of snow-chains, i.e. a set that are reasonably easy to affix and detach. Unfortunately, as we all know, despite the claims of every snow-chain manufacturer that his chains are the simplest in the world to operate, it just ain't so. (And anyway, the instructions are usually in

German.) Nevertheless, our Survival Skier can be counted on to persevere, continually experimenting with different types — ladder, zig-zag, or cross-tracked — reserving the utmost contempt for anyone who resorts to using those easy-to-clip-on tyre-grips. This means, of course, that our Survival Skier will have to spend a good deal of his time practising putting on different types of snow-chain against the stopwatch. Ideally, he likes a bit of a blizzard to do this, so he can train under 'real' conditions. In the event, of course, that he ever did find himself really stuck in the middle of the Alps, he would, like everybody else, drive back to the nearest garage and ask them to fit the chains, or at worst, cheat by jacking up the car (instead of trying to fit them by driving endlessly backwards and forwards over them).

With all this paraphernalia the Survival Skier will need a largish vehicle, perhaps a station-wagon, or at least a hatchback with a sizeable boot. There needs to be room for his portable ski-lift complete with motor and nutcracker wire, as well as the shovel, a couple of sandbags, and of course, those damned chains. And he always keeps his cross-country skis on board just in case, while out for a spin, he should chance to pass a skiable patch of snow. The back end of the car also needs to be big enough to accommodate the family St Bernard.

Now all this can make après-après-ski sound a bit like hard work. And, it must be admitted, not every Survival Skier is happy spending his evenings P-texing away amid the comforting scent of waxes, removing brakes and bindings, ironing his skis, and then having to repeat the whole process because he's got the new base higher than the edge. It's not everyone's idea of fun to spend his weekends replacing lost screws, filing edges, sandpapering tips and tails and reconditioning snow-chains. Many Survival Skiers, as we have seen, tend to be more the outgoing type. Clearly they need to be able to perform these chores, so that they can show off when there's an audience around. But they won't want to spend *all* their spare time polishing their moonboots and reproofing the family's ski-clothes.

Fortunately, the ability to fine-tune a pair of skis is not the only way of making one's mark on the *après-après-ski* scene. The successful Survival Skier will also be an active member of his local skiing community. He'll probably hold office as an official of his local ski-club; perhaps as Secretary or Treasurer, besides belonging to half-a-dozen other national and international ski associations, as well as being a founder member of the local yodelling society. He'll be a leading light in all the local campaigns to put your neck of the woods on the skiing map – such as the campaign to get your bailiwick twinned with Pistendorf; or the campaign to get the local council to put up an artificial ski-slope. If the council just won't see reason over this, then the Survival Skier will be a prime mover in trying to get together a co-operative or syndicate to build its own slope. Nothing, of course, ever comes of these schemes, which is fortunate since the Survival Skier is no better a performer on the Dendix than he is on snow. If, in fact, there already is a local dry ski-slope, the Survival Skier will tend to remain somewhat aloof, and stay away from it on the grounds that the plastic can spoil you for real snow and that he doesn't want to scratch all his hi-tech gear to bits. He can also claim that a couple of spills on the

---

Rules of Skiing

LOSSES

Someone will lose something going up the ski-lift.

It may well be you.

The things you will lose most frequently are your balance and your self-confidence and your way.

The other item most frequently lost will be your rubber ski-clips.

When a ski is lost in deep powder snow, it will be found in the last place anyone digs – if it is found at all.

If you lose a contact lens in the snow, it's not worth looking for it.

Better to have skied and lost, than never to have skied at all.

Dendix have left him almost permanently crocked up, which is why he's now campaigning to set up a mud-skiing group instead (it's softer when you fall).

The Survival Skier will, above all, try to be the link between your club and the wider world of skiing. Thus he's always the one to organise the annual outing to the ski show. This is the high point of his skiing year, marred only by the fact that the ski show signals the start of the ski season proper and thus the imminent prospect of finding himself out on the slopes again. As soon as he gets his troop to Earl's Court he invariably makes straight for the Skiholics Anonymous stand, hailing everyone in sight by their first names to show his club-mates that he really is somebody in the skiing fraternity. Then while his charges wander round collecting brochures or watching the go-go skiers on the artificial slope, he'll get to work negotiating special rates for his club with various chalet companies (and freebies for himself), as well as making contacts with some of the Big Names to persuade them to come down to the club to give a talk. If nothing else, he will at least get his address book filled up with the names and phone numbers of assorted ski-bums and chalet-girls. And he will probably come away with a few new ideas, so that when he gets back home he can get busy organising *Schwyzerdütsch* classes or setting up a ski-video swapping service.

A good deal of this sort of activity may well take place in his own home which will be all rigged up to show those Dick Barrymore movies and other slightly obscene-sounding productions like *Deep Snow* or *White Dreams*. During these screenings he will, of course, take the opportunity to make a few technical comments, rather than just gasping with awe like his club-mates, as Wayne Wong and the other powderhounds bounce through the bumps. Sometimes there's rather more scope for expert commentary if you show one of the golden oldies like Arnold Fank's *Der Wunder des Schneeschuhs* (1920) or simply invite friends around to watch *Ski Sunday* (and to listen to your critical remarks about the technique and style of those World Cup hopefuls).

But *après-après-ski* shouldn't all be taken too seriously. After all, skiing is a sociable activity and the Survival Skier is a sociable fellow. So friends will frequently be invited round for fondue or raclette evenings or for one of his mid-summer *Glühwein* parties (which invariably take place on a blazing hot day so that you have to go out on the lawn, rather than snuggle together in the *Hütte*). And the talk won't just be about skiing. As with any other British social occasion, the conversation will range from the weather to what they stock or don't stock at the local supermarket (which unfortunately does a very poor line in mueslis, is always out of blueberry soup and doesn't seem to have even heard of *Schinkensemmels*). Inevitably, though, there will be a tendency for the conversation to turn from ski-food to skiing.

This is perhaps only to be expected in a country which has more ski-experts per head of population than anywhere else in Europe. The evening will usually end with a session on the *Schnapps,* of which our Survival Skier will have a good selection, ensuring that everyone goes home yodelling, or trying to. Thus these evenings are invariably more successful than those occasions when you all trudge down to the local pub in your moonboots to be told by the landlord, once again, that he's never stocked *grappa* and has no intention of starting now.

Survival Skiers therefore do best to confine their activities to their own haunts in the company of other Survival Skiers. One regular venue is the local ski-shop, where our Survival Skier will be found every Saturday morning, offering advice, checking on the new gear, and peering down the grooves of skis for those who don't know a straight line when they see one. The ski-shop owner will usually be happy enough to have the Survival Skier around to lend a hand. If the Survival Skier knows his stuff, he can be good for business, so much so that the owner will turn a blind eye if the Survival Skier operates a sort of exchange and mart on the side – swapping children's clothes, ski mags and videos and taking orders for ski calendars and Christmas cards.

Of course, it helps a great deal if the Survival Skier's family are willing participants in all these activities. It's not much fun bouncing up and down on your own on your trampoline at home. In fact, the Survival Skier would much prefer to see his children doing the bouncing and practising their aerials. It was really for them that he built that polystyrene pit in the back yard so they could work on their starting technique. It was for them that he installed the conveyor belt in the spare bedroom so they could spend more time rolling their knees. This permits the Survival Skier to take on the role of coach, making his critical remarks as his children practise their triple somersaults. In fact, the Survival Skier's own best attempt at an aerial is likely to have been one of his more spectacular falls in Pistendorf. (If, perchance, someone happened to snap him as he was involuntarily upended in mid-air, it's not a bad idea to get the picture blown up – this can then be shown to one's children as a good example of how to perform a Wongbanger, *with Spread.*)

Many families are quite happy to go along with all this. Children don't seem to mind having their names put down for DHO at birth, or being seen as future Olympic stars, or being sent off to skiing camps, while the *paterfamilias* keeps a detailed written and photographic diary of their progress. The one drawback is the drain this can prove on the family finances. All those Alpine expeditions and yodelling classes don't come cheap – not to mention the equipment, especially the machinery the Survival Skier needs to install in the *Hütte* to develop his prototype 'ultimate' ski. One might even draw a parallel here with the fabled Søndre

ADAM ZAPPELL
YODELLING
CLASSES

Norheim, also basically a lazy man, who spent all his time working on his ski designs and is said to have reduced his family to such poverty that his wife was seen surreptitiously begging for food in the village.

In short, *après-après-ski* life is not just one long chalet party. There's work to be done and workouts to be suffered. There will be many long nights planning routes over Alpine passes, or hunched over your P-tex candle dripping polyethylene into your ski soles. There will also be the occasional weekend of unparalleled misery up at Aviemore. Few *après-après-skiers* manage to escape this.

But, in the end, it will be worth it. True worship of Vil (the Icelanders' appropriately named God of Winter) will eventually be rewarded. And, as we said at the outset, if you do your work well enough, you may find you don't have to go skiing at all. You can just send your children off to represent the family on the slopes and to collect the medals. This enables you to sneak off on a well-deserved holiday in the Caribbean, where you can lie under the coconut palms dreaming sweet dreams of snow crunching under ski-boots (other people's, fortunately).

Totally Piste

CONTENTS

For Christina

INTRODUCTION

**'Here we are again,
with both feet planted firmly in the air'**

Trade Union leader, Hugh Scanlon

Hugh Scanlon was actually talking about the Common Market. But his remarks could equally well have applied to skiing, which is something else that Brits seem to have got roped into against their better judgement. And, as with the EEC, there is no immediate sign of our opting out.

Every year, more and more of us are to be found freezing our assets on the high ground, crossing skis with bad-tempered foreigners in the lift queue in a vain effort to prove to ourselves that there is life after birth. Instead of staying sensibly at home and catching a cold, we head for another extreme experience at Ice Station Zebra and catch pneumonia. Clad in our brightly coloured romper suits, feet jammed into those steel traps, we set off down assorted heart-stopping precipices like misguided missiles on what may well prove to be a one-way ticket to (ski)Boot Hill. Even if we did manage to get out a cry of 'Help', our words would probably freeze in the air.

What is it about The Big Chill, Monster Mountains and the possibility of sudden death that turn us on? Surely people have realised by now that Life at the Top means no more than High Anxiety. Or even worse: it's not just bone-*chilling* up there, it also can be bone-*breaking*.

Far from leaving your troubles behind, they are only just beginning. Even the law says that skiing is a 'dangerous sport'. And there's no question that it ought to be issued with a government health warning – not so much because it's dangerous though, but because it's *addictive*. Nevertheless, even if we are plonkers on planks rather than poetry in motion, and the highest we really want to go is the third floor of Lillywhites (to buy all that snazzy gear) we are still getting hooked in ever-increasing numbers. There are even weekends when Ski Sunday gets a bigger audience than Match of the Day.

Deep down inside, of course, we all know that if God had wanted us to ski he would have given us long feet; that man is a warm-blooded animal; that just because people were sliding around on boards 2,000 years ago doesn't mean it's natural; that skiing is the ultimate trivial pursuit and one sure way of saying goodbye very quickly to all the money stuffed into our zip-fastened trouser pockets.

Nonetheless, this hasn't stopped vast numbers of Brits from getting twitchy knees at the onset of winter; starting to walk up stairs instead of taking the lift; muttering to themselves skiing prayers like 'Blessed are the piste-makers' and 'Snow Snow, Quick, Quick Snow'; and wondering whether to invest in a four-wheel drive.

Perhaps it's just the snob appeal of it all. There is no question that skiing is a very snowcial sport and that snowbberry abounds on the slopes. So spending some time being downwardly mobile seems to have become a *sine qua non* for the 'upwardly mobile' or for those with aspirations to High Snowciety. Even the Pope skis, not to mention the Royals.

Whatever the reason, there would appear to be no stopping it. There is snow hiding place. So for the moment we are going to have to learn to live with it and make the best of things. It was with this objective that almost a decade ago this author wrote that classic handbook for hesitant skiers, *Piste Again*, in the belief that 'most skiers are not that young any more, don't like heights or snow, would be upset if they broke a leg, and just want to get through the day with a flush on their cheeks, a few tales to tell and their skiing ego intact'. It suggested a few ways and wiles (otherwise known as the techniques of 'Survival Skiing' or 'piste de résistance') to help reluctant piste bashers to survive, and occasionally even to *succeed* on the slopes – showing them how to cope with 'the high life' until the ski boom died away. 'Eddie The Eagle' has, of course, since shown the world that lack of ability need be no barrier to success on the slopes.

The fact is, however, (even though *Piste Again* is the name of one of the newest discotheques in Gstaad and is still being sported on t-shirts) that *Piste Again*, and its companion volume *Back on the Piste*, have not kept pace with events. Far from fading away, skiing has kept on developing: new instruction techniques; a revolution in gear; more advanced forms of hooliganism in the snow wars between different nationalities on the slopes; the boom in summer skiing and in cross-country skiing; and much else besides.

Hence the need for yet another volume in the *Piste* series to bring Survival Skiers right up to date with all the latest wheezes for getting by on the slopes, and giving them some advance warning of what they may be letting themselves in for this season. So if you're in any doubt whether fluffy earmuffs are in or out; if you aren't sure that 'ski sauvage' is quite your style; if powder for you is the 'Johnson's Baby' variety; if your skis don't exactly 'kiss' the snow; if you prefer to ski with the handbrake on; if you'd rather contribute to the black economy than the white economy; if you only sidestep up the slope when there's a worthwhile objective (like a café), this book may be for you. Plank-hopping is never going to be completely painless, but with the help of *Totally Piste*, you should have the 'snow how' to ensure that your skiing is pretty much all downhill, and that, at least, you return with your limbs all present and correct.

○ RESORTS

The snow reports in the newspapers will bear no relation to the conditions when you arrive

If they say it's *possible* to ski back to the hotel, that doesn't mean it's possible *for you*

Ten minutes walk from the lifts does not mean ten minutes in your ski boots

If the bus is free it won't be frequent

The year the weather is really bitter is the year you will have chosen a high resort with North-facing slopes

The 'basic holiday price' is approximately one third of what it will actually cost

The duvet is never long enough

1 THE SNOW SHOW

'The idea is to look like a cross between subway graffiti and Papua New Guinea. The skier, even at a dead stop, will snap, sizzle and smoke.'

Martie Sterling, American writer
on 1987/88 winter fashions

Times change. It's not actually so long ago that almost the only colour worn on the slopes was regulation navy blue – though you did see the occasional flash Harry in black with a white sweater. In *Piste Again*, of course, we did recommend the 'old-timer' look – getting yourself up like the old hand who knows his way around. These days, however, designer-dressing is the norm – even for budget-buying Brits; and rambling on nostalgically about leather boots and cable bindings can make even the Survival Skier seem a bit too long in the tooth. You can all too easily find yourself boring the salopettes off your younger skiing companions. Thus an increasing number of Survival Skiers have decided to update their act and invest in the sort of rig which now passes for style on the slopes.

This need not be, it should be noted, what the ski fashion pundits have decided is this year's 'in' look or this month's 'ultimate' Space Age material. The fact is that everyone has so many ski outfits these days that no one on the slopes has any idea what is *this* year's look, what is *last* year's and what is *next* year's.

So the Survival Skier can safely ignore 'the new look' being pushed by yet another ex-skiing champ who is now wowing them with his zany line in gear rather than his line down the slopes. These garments, needless to say, will all be made of a new fifth generation silicone wonderfibre that is thirty per cent warmer, diamond-tough, accelerates faster and insulates as it breathes. (This actually means that the manufacturers have found yet another way of making nylon or polyester and a new type of synthetic filling to do what goose or duck down used to do. But by making it sound revolutionary enough, they can charge more for something that's cheaper to make.)

This new material will inevitably be run up by the ex-champ's little Japanese designer in Paris who this season will perhaps have decided that we should all be in sherbert and cerise billowy one-piece wraparounds – with magenta and fuchsia tail-drapes to show off our slipstreams. That's for the chaps, of course. For the girls he's come up with a little prison grey number cut like a pair of battle fatigues and decorated with alphabet soup and quadratic equations.

Survival Skiers, however, would do better to dress dangerously in styles of *their own* choosing. Ideally your outfit should look as if you put it together yourself and should always include various bits and pieces that apparently have a special significance for you (like that blood-stained bandanna you were left clutching when your friend slipped down a crevasse). You might also wear an item or two that are somewhat impractical (e.g. fur gloves, leather trousers) since this does rather tend to proclaim that you ski well enough to get away with it (i.e. you don't fall).

This sort of approach should make at least as much of an impression as the latest designer one-piece with all the accessories coordinated. But, do bear in mind, that, like the ex-champ's, your gear also should 'go for it' – if only to distract attention from your rather less than intrepid skiing. Remember – snow business is show business. Skiing is a high visibility sport (occasional blizzards and whiteouts notwithstanding). Not for nothing are those bindings called 'Look'.

Dressing up is also part of the fun – even though it can take you all morning to peel on one of those 'second-skin' fluorescent Lycra racing suits. (Not a bad bet, actually, for the Survival Skier who likes to take his time before appearing on the slopes.) And the gear does give you a sense of security – we feel protected somehow in those seven-league boots and padded clothes.

In order to make an impact (apart from when you collide with other skiers) the Survival Skier should bear very much in mind *where* he'll be skiing. Thus, for example, at a serious Swiss resort, the Survival Skier will probably be dressed rather frivolously à la française, clowning around in laid-back gear, clutching a mono ski or one of this year's new ski 'toys' under his or her arm. (Survival Skiers, of course, can be of either sex – though for convenience we'll tend to use the masculine pronoun in this book.) At a French *station, par contre*, or amongst the Martini set, our Survival Skier will be kitted out with all the latest 'down to business' hi-tech gear worn by last season's racers. (Never mind if the equipment exceeds your skiing abilities – that's all part of the game.)

Most frequently, though, the Survival Skier's aim will be to look as if he doesn't take his skiing too seriously (which *might* explain some of his deficiencies in technique). So feel free to wear the sort of outfit that would look more at home in the disco, or perhaps something more sober, say a tweed coat. But even if you are going for the laid-back or uncoordinated look, do make sure you get all the details right.

Nothing the Survival Skier wears should be unplanned. Not that anyone – let alone a Survival Skier – will own up to all the time and effort they have put into their appearance, working on their chic technique rather than their ski technique. All the *talk*, both during ski and après, will be about skiing. You never *mention* the clothes. This is true even of the increasing number of resorts which have all but stopped any serious skiing and are now almost completely given over to posing and people-watching. (This is a phenomenon that had to come –

the fact is that there is not really enough time for both skiing and posing. You either dress to ski or ski to dress.)

It does help, though, if the Survival Skier knows how to make his way around the slopes, looking, for all the world, like a *real* skier. (Readers familiar with *Piste Again* will know the drill.) If ever you're curious, by the way, about how much skiing someone actually does, you can usually tell by just looking at their hands: the hands of the poseurs will be as tanned as their faces from all those hours spent lounging on the sundeck; the skiers' hands will be white since they've been wearing gloves most of the time. 'Banana' boots are another giveaway – showing you've spent more time walking around in your ski-boots than skiing in them.

You even keep your gloves on, of course, in spring or summer when skiing in swimwear – or even in the altogether (though this can be a bit expensive on the sun cream). Remember – these days – 'anything goes'. It's hard to imagine how much fuss Suzy Chafee caused all those years ago when she was photographed nude on skis for *The Sunday Times*. Today we've got to the point where, for

those who really want to maximise their all-over tan, a French designer has come up with a transparent ski suit made of a material which just lets through those tanning UV rays.

But although now anything goes, there's still a good deal of 'U' and 'non-U' attached to ski-clobber. And this can inhibit the Survival Skier who wants to cut a dash. What, for instance, will those little bobbly head antennae do for your image? Would you make a better impression with the latest double-glazed goggles, or with those wraparound tinfoil 'glasses' that seem to be all the rage? Should your gaiters be attached or detachable? And what kind of headband — wide or narrow, plaited or tubular, with eye-piece incorporated or not? And are those beer-can holders on the tips of your skis the way to win friends and influence people (or to get them under the influence)?

So, to give you an idea of what's 'in' and what's 'out' *at the moment*, here are a few pointers. But do bear in mind that things won't stay that way for long.

○ HEADGEAR ○

Most kinds of hat, including the red, white and blue so patriotically sported in the past by Prince Charles and others, are very *old hat*. If you are determined to wear something on your head, though, you might get away with a fur pillbox, quilted caps in prints and florals, or perhaps a tweed cap or Basque beret. And if you want to be dramatic, cowls or snoods are also absolutely OK.

What has come in to replace the hat is the headband in its many variations — wide, narrow, smooth, 'Fergie' furry, interknotted or flat, natural or synthetic, even in some cases, incorporating a peak. Some of the more exotic woollen ones are in fact not that far short of a hat. But they do still conform to the essential requirements of a headband: they stop your glasses from falling off, keep your ears from getting cold or getting sunburn, and — most important of all — *they don't ruin your hairstyle.* (Needless to say, they should not itch.)

Those fluffy earmuffs are not the thing at all anymore — though earmuffs combined with headband or incorporated with a Walkman earpiece or built on to your sunglasses are acceptable (and very useful if you want to avoid listening to other people's advice in the lift-queue).

○ SHADES ○

It's now glasses rather than goggles, worn on a leash or a multi-coloured coil cord around the neck. (Only Sloanes are still wearing them on the head.) Established brands are best — Ray Ban, Yves St Laurent, Bollé, Wayfarer. The classic 'catseye' Vuarnets tend to make you look a bit American — but they're OK *if white.* Mirrored lenses are giving way to tinted; and the shade of the lens is probably now more important than the colour of the frame – and should be 'interesting'. (Try 'shooting' green or bronze.) Wraparounds and Porsche-style designs tend to look as if you are trying a bit too hard, as do visors on your sunglasses, high-altitude nose protectors and leather side shields. But, a pair of those American cult Oakleys with all their interchangeable bits and bobs is acceptable, as are those teeny 'sunbed' eye-pieces.

The Survival Skier, however, should try to make do *without* glasses – the macho 'crows-feet' look is rather in, and does avoid the 'panda' effect. But if you do stick to your shades, don't forget the demister. (This is perfect for the Survival Skier who needs to waste time – smearing it over his glasses, and then smearing it off again because he can't see through them.)

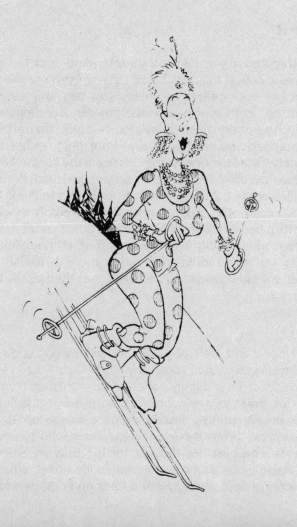

○ FACE ○

Women are now in full make-up and jewellery on the slopes (as indeed are some of the men). This, of course, means pearls for not a few Sloanes; lip-salve dangling on a neck cord for others. Avoid, however, those earrings and pendants with ski motifs, or shaped like ski sticks or whatever. Out, too, is the Black and White Minstrel look, with whitened lips and the splash of zinc on the nose (or piece of baco-foil). Instead, you should be using a neutral absorbent, high factor cream – it doesn't do to have a red or shiny nose. Lip gloss is very OK, though, as is technicolour 'war-paint'. If the weather turns nasty, a face-covering Balaclava is acceptable – but should be made of silk, cotton or very fine wool rather than the classic knit variety.

○ NECKWEAR ○

Try to go bare-throated if you can – thus extending your tan down as far as possible. The classic cotton roll-neck is still OK – *if worn unrolled*. But not those 'tubi-grip' affairs or 'neck-gaiters' – unless you can suggest that you often enough find yourself up to your ears in the powder. Bandannas or chequered Arafat-style Kaffiyehs are very much today's look – especially the big ones you can wrap around your neck several times and knot tight, rather than the loose front-knotted variety. Avoid the ones in the colours of the various Swiss cantons.

Scarves are also fine, provided they are *not* worn so much around the neck as just generally trailed about the body. The only exception to this is the little red (or sometimes yellow) scarf, with or without tassles, preferably made of cashmere. This should be worn tied at the front and tucked down your bib so as to be just visible at the throat when skiing. When you strip off at the restaurant, however, the Survival Skier can and *should* show rather more of it. (NB. The two ends should *not*, under any circumstances, descend lower than *nipple* height.)

○ TOPS ○

These should be loose, and preferably light and billowy so there's plenty of room for lots of other layers below. Just about anything will do – from a flak jacket to a balloon-silk windshirt; from a duffely poncho to a nightshirt; from a puffy jacket (or a real Puffa for Brits) to a windbreaker; from a flying jacket to a ski-shirt (preferably in a crinkly printed fabric); from a sweat-top to one of those fashionable ski-smocks (even though the top does tend to keep rubbing up against your nose). The best bet, though, for the Survival Skier, is to choose something that doesn't look as if it was designed for skiing. Whatever you wear, it should have plenty of flaps and tucks and folds and drapes and pleats, as well as a sprinkling of rivets and press studs for good measure, and as many complicated pockets and zips (the longer the better) as possible – for all your little accessories.

Underneath you should have a fair old combination – sweatshirt, t-shirt, granpappy Yukon vest, lumberjack check flannel shirt, woollen waistcoat, or whatever. Just about anything will do, in fact, except a sweater (the ones in the traditional striped or Nordic design are a real no-no). Everything should be kept in place by your braces – very 'in' now and found in a variety of styles.

Unfortunately, it will not be possible to buy many of these garments without a logo or motif. But this should be as discreet as possible – perhaps a little egg (denoting your membership of one of the speed-skiing clubs – *or so you will say*). Avoid anything with a t-shirt slogan like: 'Skiers do it in the snow'; 'Piste Again'; 'Just because I sleep with you tonight doesn't mean I'll ski with you tomorrow'; 'I love Switzerland'; 'No problem'; 'Summer stinks – Think Snow'; 'Eat my powder, suckers'. Worst of all is probably the name, or even logo, of your chalet company. You might, however, get away with something like 'Vasaloppet 1982'. Anoraks autographed by assorted championship skiers are also very much out.

Remember, too, that everything on your jacket should be detachable and discardable – sleeves, cuffs, pockets – so that it can speedily be converted into a natty little gilet. (When you do cast off your sleeves, though, don't forget to hang on to the goggle-strap watch on your upper arm – very 'in' these days.)

Be very careful, incidentally, about plumping for unknown Italian or American makes of anorak. Italians tend to have short bodies and Americans long arms. And neither the 'bum-freezer' look, nor the 'gorilla' look is very 'in' right now.

○ BOTTOMS ○

Stay well clear of salopettes – they're just too sensible. But you could try the sort of loose-fitting overalls that you might have borrowed from your local painter and decorator. If anything, though, there does seem to be a trend back to the traditional Keilhosen or stretch pants – with stirrups (for all those powder hounds). Few other garments since have shown off the line of the underbody quite so well. If, however, underbodies are not quite your line, why not try a pair of parachute pants or baggy trousers in natural materials, which make it look as if you've just walked in off the High Street. (This is totally impractical, of course, and so gives just the right effect.)

If you're in any doubt, though, you should be safe with Killy-cut trousers. Alternatively, try a bulky combination of over-trousers, trousers, and under-trousers, topped by multicoloured triple-decker gaiters. Another colour detail you might like to incorporate is the technicolour crotch, (reinforced if you ride a lot of Pomas) and contrasting with the rest of your outfit, that you can really show off when you take a tumble. (Not very often, of course, in *your* case.)

When the weather is warmer, you might try a pair of Bermudas or striped boxer-shorts – partly bare legs and arms (sleeves pushed up to your elbow) are very 'in'. (This is probably a development of the traditional type of ski wear where there was always a space at the top of your boots, and between your gloves and your sleeve, for the snow to accumulate.)

You should avoid blue jeans – unless you're a ski bum or a chalet girl, or can afford to wear them with a fur top. The fur, of course, should be *real*. There's more and more of it about on the slopes – mink head-bands, full length fur coats, even. So it's quite OK to work a bit of mink or reindeer trim onto your outfit.

The traditional one-piece jumpsuits and catsuits are still very much around – despite the difficulties of getting the top off for lunch and the bottom off *after* lunch. But they do tend to look a bit too designerish and tidy for the Survival Skier, whose aim is to look like his own designer.

One last touch that you might consider wearing down below is the knee brace. These are now being made in some rather snazzy colours and do make it look as if the Survival Skier has *earned* the right to take it a bit easier on the slopes these days.

○ GLOVES ○

These, of course, should be leather *not* vinyl, though some of the new hi-tech synthetics – in printed fabrics even – are OK. Wrists should be longish, perhaps gaiter-style (but not the half-sleeve glove, or detachable sleeve glove). If you really want to cut a dash – and are not too worried about frostbite – you could try a pair of those aerodynamic surgical gloves that the KL boys wear.

Avoid those sheepskin-lined gloves – they're a bit too pansified – though silk warmers underneath are OK. The Survival Skier should use electrically-heated gloves or 'warmpacks' *only if he must* – but do make sure no-one sees them. (This also goes for any other 'heated' ski garments.) Those blow tubes sticking out of your gloves, for instance, are an immediate giveaway.

On no account should you wear mittens – despite the advice given in so many British instruction manuals. (Try getting your lift pass out of your pocket with them.)

○ MATERIALS ○

Most of your clobber will probably be made of synthetic 'high performance' fabrics – *perhaps* treated so that you don't slide for half a kilometre when you fall. (The high gloss shiny look is back unfortunately.) But try to work as many natural materials as possible into your outfit – cotton, leather, wool, silk. The latter is very much in – especially worn next to the skin – and is very easy to handwash overnight. (NB It's no longer done to wear the same underwear for a week's skiing – even if it is made of Chinese Imperial silk.) You might also try silk longjohns or those all-in-one 'scarlet teddies'. After all, the Survival Skier needs all the thermal insulation he can get.

The new man-made materials – Goretex, Thinsulate etc. – also do a pretty good job. But Survival Skiers concerned about their creature comforts should make sure that everything they wear has been tested in polar or Himalayan conditions. It goes without saying that this is unlikely to be the case with a good many of the more exotic 'in' designs – i.e. your pearlised zebra one-piece with leopard-skin trim, or your quilted satin blouson, or your Batik print shirt with appliqué finish.

○ COLOURS ○

Generally speaking, wear as many colours as possible – preferably clashing – unless you are going for the military drab effect. And try to make them as *interesting* as possible. The manufacturers do their best to help here by the names they give them – yellow becomes yolk or saffron; pink or cherry red is cerise, or even *orchard* cerise; orange becomes sunset; red becomes raspberry. Either that or there'll be an appropriate qualification – *peacock* blue, or *glacier* blue, or *ice* blue, or *pacific* blue.

○ LABELS ○

Preferably none. But since nothing can be bought without a manufacturer's logo, or a designer label these days, you'll probably have little choice. (Isn't it about time they started paying us to wear their brand names?)

The established brands like Ellesse, Killy, Belfe are still very much around. But you may score more points by supporting the challenge of one of the newer designers – Grosjean, Luhta, Schoeffel, Descente, Dubin, Mäser, Bognor (the man who came up with the first mink ski gilet). In this case, though, do be consistent – your sun-cream too should be Vichy rather than Boots.

○ HOLDALLS ○

The biggest change in recent years has been the demise of the bum-bag – with only the occasional Brit resisting the trend. Some people try to soldier on wearing their bum-bag *under* their jacket – for the 'Duck's Arse' effect. But this is not recommended.

Instead of the bum-bag, we have ski wear that consists of little else but pockets and miles of zips (preferably with plaket closure in front, or wind protector behind – unless you *like* air vents). As we've said, the Survival Skier can't be too careful.

Bags as such are not entirely out, however. Jazzy handbags, usually slung from the shoulder, made of fabric that matches your suit are making inroads, as is the belt pack (a sort of bum-bag in disguise), or the hat doubling as a bum-bag, or the bum-bag that's built into your clothes. Avoid, however, those kangaroo 'hidey' pouches or backpacks in the shape of Pandas or Koalas. If necessary, one of the standard types of rucksack is acceptable, or preferably, your own custom-made ski bag.

This should give you the general idea. But, of course, it's how you put it all together that counts. (See next chapter.) As we've seen, the key thing for the Survival Skier to remember is to *personalise* his or her outfit. There's no reason, however, why you shouldn't be practical about it. What about a panic button, for instance; or a snorkel (for powder skiing); or an oxygen mask (which you used for high skiing in the Himalayas); or a racing number tie-on (kept as a souvenir)? Other useful items are a snow-proof wallet (the Survival Skier often needs to dish out the odd backhander and to refuel on the mountain); a thermometer built into your anorak to keep tabs on the air temperature and wind chill factor (Survival Skiers can't be too careful – people have been known to die from hypothermia); an altimeter; and a well-padded behind for shock absorption or for 'sitting it out' till the weather improves. A pair of rubber knees can also come in handy.

○ MOUNTAINS

The mountain looks closer than it is

The mountain gets steeper as you get closer

It always looks steeper from the top than from the bottom

Skiing ability declines in inverse ratio to the proximity of the mountain

Whenever you stand and stare you can always see two people trekking uphill on a distant mountain-side

The day you set out to do the Vallée Blanche is the day you forget to bring your passport

At least once on every ski holiday you will think you are going to die alone on a deserted mountain-top and be brought down in a body-bag

2 PUTTING IT TOGETHER

'Later the Princess [Diana] spent the afternoon trying to ski incognito.
She wore goggles, pulled her hat well down and turned up the collar of
her fashionable ski suit in an attempt to hide her face. But then she
fell full-length.'

Daily Telegraph report of the Prince and Princess of Wales'
ski holiday in Liechtenstein

Now it is just possible that the previous chapter may have left you somewhat
confused. But that, unfortunately, is the way the ski scene is tending to look at
the moment. There are a tremendous number of different 'looks' around. To
give you an idea of the range, here are some sketches of types you may well see
around the slopes.

○ MICHELIN MAN (OR WOMAN) ○

One of the classics — the mobile duvet look once much favoured by British
skiers who believed in lots of clothing worn under puffy ski suits bought a couple
of sizes too big. (For a budget version, try stitching together some lagging from
an old immersion heater.) A little bit impractical and dated, but perhaps an idea
for the Survival Skier who prefers to sit it out at the *top* of the mountain. If you are
prepared to go to the trouble of acquiring a genuine ex-NASA spacesuit
complete with bubble helmet, you *may* make quite an impression.

○ SNOW WHITE ○

White belted body-hugging one-piece suit, preferably made by Event or some
such, for the real snowbird. Usually a splash of colour somewhere though
(probably red or yellow) just to make sure you don't miss her. In fact, she's
probably about as pure as the driven slush — but you'd never guess it from the
outfit.

○ RAMBO ○

The ultimate 'macho' look — for men *and* women. Not over-expensive either.
You can find everything you need in your local army surplus store. Try parachute

pants and battle fatigues in camouflague colours, with khaki socks worn *outside* your boots. Head should be swathed in a bandanna, knotted behind, and trailing, which can also be used as a tourniquet or for binding up wounds.

◯ SHEIK OF ARABY ◯

Two versions of this. The upmarket djellabah-style top in cashmere or angora draped around you from the head down in folds – sort of 'Salome of Saas Fe'. Or, for the peasants, the Arafat-style dishcloth held in place by a headband – sort of Lawrence of Avoriaz. For a touch of the 'Mujehaddins', try the Vallencant look – flowing chiffon bandanna knotted at the back of the head and trailing.

◯ SAILOR ◯

Yellow wellies, puffa or anorak with drawstring hood, blue sailing style trousers, but perhaps padded for extra warmth. Not the most practical ensemble – but might just be one way of explaining why your skiing is not all that it might be – you're too busy on the boat for most of the year.

◯ DRAPER ◯

The key garment here is the long anorak-cum-coat. Can either be teddyboy three-quarter length or full length. Started off a few years ago with those long quilted jackets worn very loose by the younger set. Now comes in a variety of materials – denim, gaberdine or whatever. Avoid, however, those fluorescent raincoats that are now making an appearance. For the right effect, this look should remind you of those longish coats they took to wearing in Sergio Leone spaghetti westerns. Should be worn with the right air of decadence.

○ ROCK STAR ○

Anything slinky, sexy, heavily crinkled in the right places (perhaps by your waist-nipping gold lamé belt), and generally totally inappropriate for the slopes. A Paisley shirt would do at a pinch, or perhaps a similar printed or star-spangled top in psychedelic colours. A suitable outfit perhaps for the Survival Skier who likes to ski by floodlight and then hop straight into the discotheque. Don't forget the bloodshot eyes to complete this look.

○ CROCODILE DUNDEE ○

Stetson, lumberjack shirt over polo neck – the traditional 'down-home' look favoured by American skiers. Or, for that extra something, leather fringed ski suit, or perhaps a reindeer-fur jacket or reindeer-skin legwarmers, and a husky in tow. Not really the thing in the Alps – unless you want to show you've been spending some time recently in that over-the-head Rocky Mountain powder.

○ MATA HARI ○

More one for the girls – but not exclusively so. Give yourself that air of mystery in sombre colours with a cowl over the head attached to a loose-fitting cloak-effect garment – all Dolmen drop-sleeves for that 'batwing' look, and plenty of material so that you can either drape it or wrap it around you.

○ APRÈS SKI ○

Any sort of après-piste outfit, but worn *on* the slopes – or on the sundeck. For the skier who makes no bones about his or her priorities. Big fur coats are one option – at the risk, for men, of being confused with Liberace, Nureyev or a male model. Expect to see a lot of developments in this look over the next few years as après-ski gets closer and closer to ski. You can even find après-ski boots that slot into special bindings – but these can come a bit expensive.

○ COURT JESTER ○

Any sort of clowning-around harlequin outfit will do – perhaps a candy-striped or pirate-striped pair of baggy pants that bounce up and down on elasticated braces. At the other extreme, what about a sort of dinner jacket ensemble, with black bow tie worn on a bare neck?

○ HEAVENLY TWINS ○

Matching his and hers outfits, or even hers and hers, or even his and his – usually 'created' by one of the new designers. All a bit too twee – unless you can pair-ski as a coordinated duo, sort of Torvill and Dean on skis, in which case you *might* get away with it.

○ COMMANCHE ○

The Indian brave look – face streaked with primary-coloured splashes of zinc oxide face paint, usually on cheekbones and nose. (This comes off best if you're very brown. Spend some time under the sunlamp before coming out.)

○ TRAILER ○

Very 'in' this one. A look that has gradually evolved over the years. Used to be just the 'kerchief knotted around the thigh (most commonly red polka dot against a pair of faded blue jeans). Nowadays, though, you can let it all hang out. As much as possible should be worn undone and flapping. And there should be plenty of drawstrings, powder cords, leashes, bandannas, straps and rip cords 'trailing' in your slipstream. It does help if you can ski a bit so that you actually *have* a slipstream.

○ LIFTS

The one chair which is wet and which the attendant fails to brush the snow off will be yours

When you drop a stick or a glove from the chair-lift, it will always be while crossing the most inaccessible piece of terrain

The fact that a lift starts moving is no indication that anyone will be allowed to go up on it

This will not prevent a large queue from forming

The longer the queue the less likely the lift is to open

The jerk on a Poma only comes after you've stopped expecting it

The more unsteady the skier the more likely the lift attendant is to shovel snow onto the track ahead of him

If, according to your calculations, you are skiing at a speed that will enable you to cross just in front of or just behind someone going up a drag-lift, you have miscalculated

If you make a dash for the only lift that's still running, it will be closed the moment you get there

---

3 SLOPEMANSHIP

'Top Three? I think I'll finish in the top one.'

Olympic downhill gold-medallist, Bill 'Bigmouth' Johnson

Along with his outfit, the Survival Skier would do well to equip himself with some of the various types of 'toys', like sno-boards and so on, now to be found on the slopes in increasing numbers. These novelties have actually added a new dimension to the basic techniques of slopemanship which were outlined in *Piste Again*.

The Survival Skier should take advantage of the nervousness that most people feel about this gimmicky gear, and make them very much a part of his own repertoire. Less so, perhaps, in the up-to-the-minute French-style resorts, where you do find a number of people who actually know something about these things, but most emphatically when you find yourself in one of the traditional resorts.

The thing is that most skiers won't yet have tried them. (Memories of learning how to stagger about on standard equipment are probably still too painful in most cases.) This means the Survival Skier should be able to start 'one up'. He can probably even afford to roll up at the restaurant and park his monoski, or his funboard, or his wings, or his voile, or his parapente and confidently but casually invite his ski-chums to 'have a go': 'Go on. It's damned simple really' (though he might add warningly *once you get the hang of it*). If the Survival Skier has picked his crowd right, he almost certainly won't find any volunteers.

Problems may arise, of course, when the Survival Skier himself actually has to perform. Fortunately, both monos and ski-surfers are basically designed for the powder. So the Survival Skier can just confidently disappear off-piste well out of sight. After having spent an hour or so in some cosy little Hütte (preferably bewirtschaftet) he can then reappear on the piste. To allay any suspicions that people may have about what you've actually been doing, a little Father-Christmas cottonwool sprinkled liberally about your hair and body can make just the right impression from a distance. This will have 'melted' away, of course, by the time anyone gets to inspect you more closely. A bit of 'frosting' on the goggles is also a nice touch — try the sort of sugar and alcohol mix that you use for your pink gin.

The 'voile' and 'bird-sail' wings may pose more of a problem. But you can always busy yourself preparing the wings, fitting them to your poles, and folding and unfolding your voile, intermittently eyeing the mountaintops for a suitable peak to sail off. Even better would be a proper army parachute if you can get hold of one – you can spend all day sorting it out. Easiest of all, though, are those mini-chutes you strap to your back and inflate by pulling a ripcord if you feel you are going to go under in an avalanche. They look rather forbidding, but provided you can get a bit of speed up, you can inflate at will and nothing too serious should happen.

With a bit of careful preparation, the skilled Survival Skier might even be able to persuade his admirers to look on him as a sort of latter-day Roger Moore in *For Your Eyes Only*, expecting at any moment that you will rocket off as you suddenly pop another toy. And, on the subject of rockets, how about getting hold of a pair of those turbo-powered skis the French are now working on for the 'Kilomètre Pulsé'. In your fluorescent skin-tight suit and gigantic aerodynamic helmet you should make quite an impression with these. Hardly your fault that conditions are never right to 'run' them or that it might be a bit dangerous for others on such a crowded piste. You can always rev them up a couple of times to show onlookers what you mean.

One novelty to beware of perhaps are those plastic H-shaped plates that you fit to your ordinary skis to transform them into a monoski. It can be difficult to explain why you can't use these *on the piste*. This contraption, however, might prove interesting to the Survival Skier who would like to experience *for once* – if only momentarily – the joys of actually skiing parallel.

Where you can really give yourself away with these things, as with monoskis, is trying to go up in a lift. Making your way through the queue will be quite a slog – whether you keep both boots in your bindings, or take one foot out to 'scooter' along. Once you're on the chair that 'strait-jacket' feeling from having your knees locked together as you go up can be very unsettling. And just try going up a drag lift on a mono or snurfboard with the button or T-bar jammed in your crotch – and threatening not to unjam if you fall off.

Something else you can give a miss are Scorpians (almost forgotten now) – although those half-metre long 'baby' skis are OK. (Why not just tuck a pair into your rucksack along with your biathlon rifle?) What can really cause a bit of a frisson at the restaurant is turning up in a bobsleigh (or, if you can't afford one, an old converted motor-cycle sidecar). Try and get up a bit of momentum for 20 metres or so as you approach the café (making sure there's a convenient *uphill* slope to run out on), and then climb out in your best devil-may-care manner, tether it like a horse to the sundeck railings and leap neatly on to the terrace, stripping off your helmet, and your elbow and kneepads. You can then proceed to regale the assembled company with tales of some of your more hair-raising experiences, and explain why you prefer bobsleighing to tobogganing down the Cresta: 'You need to be pie-eyed to toboggan well. I like to keep my wits about me.'

It's on such occasions that you can really install yourself at the restaurant, stripping off your Ski Patrol jacket so that people can admire your 'Dangerous Sports Club' t-shirt. No harm either in taking your boots and socks off in order to get really settled in. (But make sure your feet are well sprayed – you don't want to deter your audience.)

At other times, too, of course, Survival Skiers should make themselves comfortable at the restaurant, draping themselves and their gear around their deckchair. Then, by the time they've managed to get themselves together again, they'll be able to exclaim: 'Is that really the time – and I've got a squash court booked at 3.30' – thus absolving themselves of having to hit the slopes again.

It often pays to go to some length to establish the right sort of daredevil aura. You might, for instance, allow yourself to be seen one day hanging outwards by your knees from the hotel balcony (making sure, of course, that you have a couple of concealed and trustworthy collaborators holding onto your feet, which – to be on the safe side – should also be attached with climbing ropes).

You won't, incidentally, cut quite this sort of figure circling around the café in a snowmobile, or one of those mountain bikes with big knobbly tyres, or an electric buggy, or ski-bob, or even cruising around in your 4-wheel drive Audi Quattro, or Toyota Landcruiser. When it comes to these sort of vehicles, the Survival Skier will earn more admirers by leading the campaign for SSSH (Society for Silent Snowmobiles Here).

Far better to use your imagination and roll up on a piano, or a milkcrate, or a tin tray, or a bin-liner, or any number of other silly objects. In fact, this perhaps conveys best the sort of attitude the Survival Skier should have to the whole range of 'toys' currently on the market: 'alright for the kids', and 'for a bit of fun' — but not to be taken too seriously.

Many Survival Skiers might rather stay well away from such gimmickry altogether, preferring to rely on the time-honoured methods outlined in *Piste Again* for establishing their reputation around the slopes. Even these techniques, however, are being constantly refined by Survival Skiers just to keep ahead of the game. And although they may choose not to make use of the new 'toys', there are other props which they might well take advantage of.

If, for instance, your traverse is not as strong as it might be, one way of distracting attention from this deficiency is to glide around with a stopwatch in your hand and walkie-talkie nestling in your blouson (but clearly visible — aerial sticking up).

If even your traverse is pretty shaky and the snow plough is your limit, then perhaps the answer might be to display yourself ploughing down the slope carrying an enormous collection of ski gear and clobber explaining that 'your friends have changed into their mountaineering gear' — but climbing is 'not your thing' any more since you took that tumble last year on the north face of the Eiger ('Good thing those sniffer dogs found me'); so you've volunteered to be a sort of Sherpa Tensing and take their ski gear back to the hotel (good fellow that you are). This ploy, of course, does require some investment in additional skis and clothes – though you might be able to just use an assortment of items from your own extensive wardrobe.

Another useful prop is one of those huge tripod-mounted stop-clocks that stand beside the starting gate at top races. Why not set one of these up on the piste, and then spend some time crouched low on the slope below 'tracing a race line' with your hands. A nice additional touch is to wrap up part of the clock box with one of 'your' old race tie-ons (marked, say, 'World Cup, Kitzbühel': 'So glad they gave me the old number 7 for the Streif last year – my lucky number').

Even with the 'just off piste' technique, you can make very good use of whatever props you have available. It's easy enough to rig up a kind of bivouac beside the piste, using your skis, poles, anorak, backpack – against which you can then lounge, soaking up the sun, like someone who has just been hard at it for three or four hours and needs a bit of a rest. If this is your speciality, it's worth getting hold of the sort of skis which provide the best support for lounging – nice and broad, comfortable binding for the small of the back, padded toe-piece to rest your head against.

As pointed out in *Piste Again*, when simply standing by the piste, it's important always to have something to keep you busy – which these days might be fiddling with your boot controls, waxes, or whatever – until there's a suitable moment to move off (i.e. when no-one is looking).

But you can also rely on stance alone – and the Survival Skier should spend some time working on this, and keeping up with all the new 'looking on' postures – a number of which depend on making good use of your *poles*. (Fortunately, they seem to be making them stouter these days and they are less likely to bend if they have to take your whole weight.)

For the more advanced Survival Skier, there's the one where you hoist yourself into a sitting position on your poles, supporting your legs by planting your skis vertically in the snow. You won't be able to hold this for too long, and it does need a bit of practice. But if you can sit there relaxed and beaming for a minute or so while your friends come whizzing and crashing past down the piste, you should be able to suggest a sort of effortless superiority.

For the Survival Skier who prefers something a little simpler, there's always the classic 'stand easy' position, one leg bent and forward of the other as you support yourself on your poles at around chest level. This works best if you look slightly pooped, as if just taking a breather before dashing on down. A variant of this is the more crouched position, sliding backwards and forwards on your skis and pushing on your poles as if getting ready to jump-start, and doing your best to look like the kind of skier who thinks nothing of skiing down the roofs of off-piste huts and cottages. You might also try doing a few press ups on your ski poles from time to time; or jumping yourself around 180° on your poles (not as hard as it looks).

When it comes to actually moving off down the piste, the Survival Skier will usually traverse in a kind of easy zig-zag (see *Piste Again*). But here too your poles can come in very handy. One way of disguising the fact that the traverse is actually your standard method of skiing down is to aim on each traverse for some collapsed novice, and then offer your pole to help him or her up. Be careful though that they don't drag you down with them. It's always worth being solicitous to novices, by the way, thus adding to your coterie of admirers. When you see them later in the village, always stop to enquire: 'Did you manage to get down OK?' (Omit to mention that you *rode* down in the cable car.)

You can also make good use of lifts *going up*. (The Survival Skier, of course, will always pick the ones with the longest queues and spend a good deal of time at the bottom, *just to one side of the queue*, casually leaning on his sticks and chatting up the lift-man. It's a pity so many resorts are now introducing those little plastic cards.) When you do eventually go up in the chair, why not try sitting side saddle, or tangling your skis up in the bars. Done with the right sort of aplomb this can earn you more admiring glances than the piste-artists below you slaloming down between the pylons. If it's a double chair, of course, these sort of antics may not altogether be appreciated by your companion.

On a t-bar or poma, you can also jiggle about (this is even being encouraged in some French resorts – 'to get the feel of your skis'); and it's often a good wheeze to come off half-way, ducking off piste into some nearby forest. Pick your spot carefully though. You don't want to have to plough through too much wilderness to find yourself a congenial refuge – with the risk of ending up with more snow up your nose than there is on the piste. (If you are ever spotted buried in a drift, it's probably best to pretend that you were practising 'digging yourself a snowhole'.)

One problem though is that it's getting harder and harder to escape into some cosy mountain Hütte as more and more skiers are going off piste. It might, therefore, be worth pushing on off piste to the next village, finding a nice hotel with indoor pool and sunlounge to work on your tan, and then reappearing in your own resort at the end of the day to announce: 'Found this marvellous suntrap up in the wild on the other side of the mountain'. Lest any of your friends ask you to take them there, it may be worth adding 'Nearly got a nasty touch of frostbite on the way back though. Rubbed myself with snow. But could hardly get rid of it. Thought at one point the skin was frozen solid and I'd have to chip out some flesh. Lucky I had my ice-axe with me.' (One tip: get the taxi-driver who brings you up from the other village to drop you a hundred metres or so short of your resort, leaving you to shuffle in on your skis. Otherwise people might have a few doubts about your story.)

4 INSTRUCTION

'And everybody's going 'Shoosh, shoosh, shoosh. I feel the
snow. I feel the cold. I feel the air.' . . . They all felt something.
But I felt nothing – except the feeling that this bullshit was
absurd.'

From the song 'Nothing', A Chorus Line

Even though increasingly skiers seem to be looking to state-of-the-art equipment to help them to achieve The Big Breakthrough, there are many who still
think that ski-school can do something for them. Somehow, somewhere, many
of us believe, there must be a Skilehrer, moniteur or maestro who will be able to
bring forth all our latent skiing ability.

This belief has been fostered by the proliferation in recent years of new
'methods' of tuition – although there still don't seem to be many schools which
teach the really useful skills; like how to keep your balance in the cafeteria in wet
ski boots while carrying your lunchtray to your table; how to say 'help' while
travelling downhill at 45 mph; or how to make a successful excursion to the loo
while wearing salopettes or a one-piece.

These days, it's no longer just a toss-up between the classic Austrian, French,
Italian and Swiss methods. In more and more resorts, you'll find competing ski
schools – offering everything from the traditional methods to 'inner' or 'guru'
skiing, not to mention mono lessons, powder classes, mogul clinics, racing
schools, hot-dogging practice, ski voile and so on.

This was perhaps to be expected. The traditional 'bend ze knees' and 'one two
three – after me' methods haven't really achieved dramatic results. (If people ski
better now, it's probably not so much because of the tuition as of the technology
and because skiers are now spending that much more time on the snow.)

This is hardly surprising really. No one who learned to ski as soon as he could
walk (i.e. most instructors) actually *knows* how he does it. He just does it. And the
reason he can do it is because he's been skiing since he could walk. And this
experience of a lifetime on planks is not something you can very easily transmit
in a week of ski-school. How can someone whose skis defy gravity understand
the problems of people who can't even point their skis downhill? How can
people who have one left foot and one right foot put themselves in the position
of punters like us who as often as not take to the slopes with two left feet – and
clay ones at that?

Nevertheless, the 'new' ski-schools *claim* to be able to do just this. And even

some Survival Skiers are being seduced by their ideas – despite the fact that deep down they know that all classes mean drill of one sort or another, and that good instruction is not really compatible with the Survival Skier's more individualistic approach.

But like other skiers they too continue to nurture the hope that the locals can pass on some of their knee-flashing magic – despite the fact that the skiers we most admire on the piste are often precisely the ones that our instructor will proceed to tell us are doing it all wrong. Instead of showing us how to emulate those elegant upright skiers who swoop serenely down the piste, they remain committed to putting us through the old thigh-squeezing squats as if they were training us up to be Cossacks.

It is, in fact, a favourite technique of instructors to pour scorn on the local hot-shots who dazzle us with their windshield wiper turns under the lifts:

> 'That boy should learn to *ski* before attempting that sort of thing'
> 'Now, if he'd just practice that without sticks (like you've been doing), he'd get the whole thing a lot cleaner'

At least, the instructor will tell his (somewhat sceptical) class, they can be content that they are doing it the *proper* way.

But what is the *proper* way? One year they're telling us to ski feet together — and next year it's feet apart. Remember the way they used to tell you to keep *all* your weight on your downhill ski? And what about that 'unweighting' that used to be all the rage, and all those hours we spent trying to work out the difference between 'upward' unweighting and 'downward' unweighting, religiously following our instructors' advice to practice every night on the bathroom scales.

Survival Skiers would be well advised not to get involved in these doctrinal controversies. Far better to let the 'experts' fight it out among themselves about what we *ought* to be doing and concentrate instead on trying to do what you do a bit better than you did. The fact is that you can be pretty sure that this year's orthodoxy will be next year's heterodoxy.

Nevertheless, many a Survival Skier will probably want to see what some of the new 'schools' and 'methods' have to offer. (There may — unlikely but possible — just be one that will work for you.) Here then is a guide to some of the options.

○ **PSYCHOLOSKI** ○

These are the new methods, like 'inner skiing', which seem to have most caught the imagination — tempting skiers with the notion that here maybe, just maybe, is a system that can unlock all that inner potential that we all feel we possess. They also appeal because they're said to be 'non-striving' learning theories — i.e. gain without pain. Just a question of listening to your own 'inner voice', 'letting the force be with you', and helping Self I to make contact with Self II.

In practice, though, as anyone who has ever watched an inner skiing class, let alone taken part in one, will know, it's actually jolly hard work: skiing without your sticks; skiing on one leg; 'skating' on the flat; pretending you're a gorilla on skis; trying to ski 'like the worst novice you ever saw'; skiing blindfold or with your eyes shut; playing egg and spoon races; passing balloons between your legs; imagining you're sitting on the lavatory (you will probably wish you were — skiing does tend to make you constipated, either as a result of nervous retention or by freezing up you inner tubes).

Whether all or any of this helps you to ski any better than good old 'bend ze knees' is arguable. And anyone reared on the old methods may find it very hard to 'trust your body' (after all it's let you down often enough in the past). And is it all any more enjoyable – despite the fact that inner skiers are all encouraged to go around chanting: 'Smile – you are having fun'?

The problem for many Survival Skiers tends to be that if you haven't been sufficiently brainwashed by the silly exercises, your inner voice does tend to keep saying to you 'Now why on earth am I standing here behaving like such a bloody idiot?' Can they really be serious? I mean: 'stabbing at circles of snow to get rid of your troubles'; or 'saying thank you to moguls'; or 'talking to trees'. I ask you.

One might even ask if these methods are really all that new. After all, skiing Sloanes have for years at the shout of 'Dead Ant' been flopping onto their backs on the snow, wiggling their legs and arms in the air. And much good has it done *them*.

Still, some of the theoretical discussions can be quite interesting ('Does the snow know whether it's cold or not?'; or 'At what point does one turn finish and the next one begin?') And there are ways for the savvy Survival Skier to make it easier on himself: You can always spend a fair amount of time staring silently into space, and if quizzed, say simply 'I was meditating', or I was 'trying to feel At One with the mountain' (both of which responses will probably take you straight to the top of the class). Another nice thing is that you can always pull out for a couple of days saying: 'I think I should stay away a bit until my mental attitude is right.' There are some things to be said for a ski-school which specialises in 'understanding'.

○ 'MAESTRO' METHODS ○

This is not all that far removed from traditional methods of teaching. But there will be one new 'slant' – perhaps 'fluency' or 'flow', 'rhythm' or 'dynamic balance' or 'the pre-turn turn'. These 'systems' are usually promoted by a recently retired 'ski champion', who will claim that these were the secrets which took him to the top and which will revolutionise your skiing. Don't you believe it. In fact these methods would under normal circumstances not be taken much notice of – were it not for the reputation of the retired champion, desperately trying to cash in on his name before he is entirely forgotten. The 'maestro' will have got together a 'school' of disciples to promulgate the method which you may even find does help you to ski a bit better. The only problem is that when you go back to conventional ski-school, they'll tell you you're doing it all wrong.

○ SKI 'CLINICS' ○

These cater very much to drop-outs from other ski-schools and are often set up by a 'maestro' without the champion's reputation from one of the non-skiing nations, like Britain. His line, therefore, tends to be: 'I may not be one of the greatest skiers of all time – but I am a great ski *teacher* and I understand the problems of people not born on the Alps.'

Like the 'maestro', he too will have his own variant on traditional methods which you will subsequently have to unlearn when you go back to conventional ski-school. You may also be confused by his insistence on not using the Standard Alpine terminology. Thus stem christie becomes 'plough swing', parallels become 'basic swing' and 'wedel' becomes 'short radius turns'. He will also have a lot of new terms of his own – like 'relaxed mode', 'stretched mode' etc.

What may appeal, though, is the opportunity that will be given to you to pour forth your tales of how you've been mistreated and abused by every other skiing instructor you've ever come across (and who hasn't?) His methods should, therefore, suit the more chauvinistic Survival Skier who enjoys being with an instructor who spends much of his time explaining how all the other nationalities on the slopes are doing it all wrong.

The problem is that your guru will require you to display total faith in his theories, as he expounds his original ideas and his conviction of the need to improve teaching skills *in the Alpine nations*. And if you show the slightest doubt, he can get rather tough on you, putting you through endless silly exercises and making you keep confessing to the rest of the class ('Now what were you doing wrong this time, Peter?') This, incidentally, he will probably call 'talking it through'.

○ SHORTCUT ○

Another new method where the gimmick is that it misses out a stage i.e. you go straight from snow-plough to parallel. But what, the Survival Skier might ask, do you fall back on? Some of us prefer a good old stem turn to using our bottoms.

○ MONO-SKIING ○

For anyone who already skis on two planks as if they were one, mono-skis shouldn't prove too much of a problem. It might even be easier – after all you've only got *one* board to worry about instead of two and, as the mono skischools will tell you: 'All you need is a basic sense of balance'.

Unfortunately, of course, this is precisely what most Survival Skiers lack, and when you fall off a mono – as you are going to do a lot at the start – climbing back on board ain't that easy. Even standing around (that Survival Skiing speciality) isn't that easy: any attempt to take a breather on a mono – on the piste anyway – is agony on the ankles (whether you're on the type where the heels are locked together, or where they're slightly apart). You also tend to oversteer and find yourself paddling madly with your ski sticks to point yourself back down. And those sharp turns, flinging your whole body around, are not recommended if you suffer from a slipped disc. If you do catch an edge, of course, you're going to provide much more spectacular entertainment for onlookers than you would falling on two skis. You may just get your own back though – since, despite the restraining straps, runaway monos are not uncommon.

Monos, however, might have some appeal to the Survival Skier who has never absorbed anything about skiing on two planks – and so won't have to *un*learn anything. At least there aren't any tips to cross. And as we said earlier, you can make quite an impression – provided you can just about master the art of traversing and then disappear off-piste.

○ SNURFING ○

Once again, the propaganda is seductive – no hard boots (you can even wear your docksides), no poles to get in the way, no long skis to get crossed, and they're a lot quicker. (This last might perhaps not be quite such an appealing feature to the Survival Skier.)

Its promoters also claim that it's easier than skiing or mono-skiing. ('Just face sideways. You can pick up the basics in a couple of hours'), and that here, at last, is a type of skiing where 'anything goes'. (You, perhaps? Or some other part of your anatomy?) They do assure you, however, that it's impossible to break a leg snow-surfing – even though the bindings do *not* release. If you do take a tumble, by the way, do try to see that you end up facing up the slope in a kneeling position, not flopping *down* the slope on your bottom.

One advantage for the Survival Skier is that you can use *all* of the mountain (like monos, surfers are at their best *off*-piste) – so there is some scope for doing your thing out of sight i.e. chatting up the barmaid in some cosy mountain refuge.

Another advantage with both snurfers and monos is that liftmen often refuse to let you go up – thus providing the Survival Skier with another excuse for *not* performing. (You'll have to pretend, of course, that you've never heard of those short surfboards which clip onto your skis.)

○ SKI EVOLUTIF ○

No longer all that new and a teaching method that hasn't spread much beyond France. A sort of variant on the oldfashioned system when you *started out* on very long skis and then changed to shorter ones when you couldn't get the hang of it.

The problem is that once you've got the hang of a comfortable length of mini-ski, you've then got to change to another. It can also come a bit expensive. (There are some who claim it was probably invented by a Frenchman who manufactured baby skis only to find that business was dropping since two year olds these days seem to move straight on to two metre planks.)

Not really a thing for the Survival Skier since the idea is supposed to be to teach you how to ski from scratch – and the Survival Skier should be a bit above this.

○ HANG-GLIDING ○

Hang-gliding on skis, usually with an instructor. (You don't *have* to have someone with you, but the Survival Skier may prefer to.) Actually not as hard as it looks. You only need to be able to ski well enough to take off and land (preferably upright).

Not a bad bet for the reputation-building Survival Skier – if he can afford the cost. (If you do go up, it's worth trying to ensure that you can only be seen by your skiing chums from quite a distance. That way they might not notice the instructor up there with you, whose presence would, of course, detract a bit from your image as 'Icarus on skis'.)

Other variants are delta-skiing and paragliding. But the Survival Skier should be careful here – the idea is to perform *without* an instructor.

○ SKI SAILING ○

As with snurfing, could be one for the Survival Skier who knows how to windsurf. The way these boards are sailed is not dissimilar; and you can 'carve', jump, slalom (uphill too) or even 'tack' and 'jibe' up the piste – standing side-on in your après-ski boots. If you'd rather stick with your usual skis, you can also get a sailboard rig mounted onto a crossbar attached to your skis.

As with monos and other 'new way' inventions, there is the big advantage for the Survival Skier that lift operators don't like them – even when you go up on another pair of mini-skis carrying your rig. You won't be very popular either with other people in the queue – though if you swing your sail crossways it can be a good way of preventing queue jumpers.

Of course, you can try getting uphill with one of those ski-parachutes, using the wind to blow you up. This can make quite an impressive sight – until the wind drops and you collapse downhill with all your kit and caboodle (also quite an impressive sight but one that will do rather less for the Survival Skier's reputation).

For the less ambitious Survival Skier, who is more attached to the rig than to the experience of sailing it, there is one very handy cop-out. The fact is you really need a clear piste for this sort of thing (and where do you find a clear piste these days?) So you can just hang around at the bottom, looking mournful and amusing yourself with a bit of sail-tweaking.

○ THE UNDERGROUND SCHOOL ○

One way to minimise your 'tuition' costs. These are schools run by various types of ski bum (often Australian or American) who get their clients by undercutting the recognised schools. Since, however they are not strictly 'legit', the class will tend to have to assemble behind some chalet at the edge of the village (probably where your instructor's chalet bird/girlfriend works) and then head straight into the powder. The problem is that these boys often don't seem to have heard of the 'fear factor'. They just love to ski and that's what you may find yourself doing a bit too much of the time. Any dashes across the piste will probably be over some little frequented stretch of concrete washboard so that you're not spotted by the official skischool. So do make sure you have no loose fillings in your teeth. However, if a Survival Skier can survive a spine-crunching afternoon with him, it would at least mean you could probably ski anything.

○ SPEED SKIING ○

This used to be restricted to the 'Kilometro Lanciato' boys. But it's now being offered (though not quite a kilometre's worth) at some of the modern French resorts. Not all that hard actually – if you've got the nerve. Just point your skis downhill and go. With any luck a fall will slow you down sooner rather than later. If later, then you may just turn out to be one of the few Survival Skiers that didn't survive. Still, no guts, no glory.

○ SLALOM ○

There are schools for this too these days. Fortunately the new World Cup rules *seem* to indicate that the aim is to knock down all the spring-loaded poles with your shoulders as you go down. Might just, therefore, suit the Survival Skier who had been doing it this way – admittedly with the *whole* of his body – long before they ever changed the rules.

○ OFF-PISTE SKIING/POWDER ○

Has become popular with skiers who feel they are a bit above conventional instruction and that 'real men' no longer ski on the piste. Also a lot of people don't want to be taught anymore and are looking for more of an 'off-piste guide'. 'Powder has come to the people.'

Quite why it has become so popular is hard to say since skiing through powder usually feels more like skiing through polyfilla. It may just be all those glorious looking pictures of people (who know how to do it) skiing through the Bugaboos. But at least it will cure you of the habit of looking at your skis since you won't be able to see them.

In fact a good deal of time will be spent reassembling yourself after 'headplants', wiping the snow out of your goggles and trying to get your skis back on with ice-cold fingers after extracting them from under a tree root or a wire fence. There will also be a lot of searching for lost equipment in the snow — and so need not be too bad for the Survival Skier who enjoys a breather (provided he doesn't volunteer to help with the digging).

As mentioned earlier though, the Survival Skier might do just as well for himself by standing at the edge of the piste making a display of poking at the powder to check for consistency; and then positioning himself at the bottom of a beautiful set of snaking powder tracks, and looking back up at them as if they were his own handiwork (or rather footwork). 'Bit of a climb to get up there', he could say to anyone chancing to pass, 'but worth every minute for that run down'.

○ HELI-SKIING ○

If you are going to go into the powder, why not go the whole hog. Actually there are quite a number of reasons why not – avalanches, whiteouts, and the prospect of being buried in the powder for ever if you end up in one of those 3-metre tree holes.

If, however, you survive, it does mean you'll probably never have to ski off-piste again. 'Once you've heli-skied, nothing else could ever do', you can tell them, and then proceed to reminisce about the day you skied 40,000 vertical feet before lunch.

Some Survival Skiers, however, have been known to have second thoughts when they actually get up there. If this turns out to be your case, your best bet might perhaps be to set off an avalanche when no-one is looking, or to take your high altitude radio with you and claim you've just heard about a storm blowing up. This might just persuade the rest to take the next helicopter back down – that way it wouldn't look as if you were the *only* one chickening out.

○ POWDER

The day you decide to go off-piste is the day everyone decides to go off-piste

Going off-piste is usually more for the instructor's sake than yours

Whatever you are doing wrong, the instructor will tell you to lean forward more or to sit back more

If you carry your skis 'properly' over your shoulder when you approach the helicopter, the main rotor may see to it that you return home with a very short pair of skis

The ski that gets lost in the powder will be found further away than anyone thought – if it is found at all

The deeper the powder, the more likely you are to have forgotten to zip up one or more of your pockets

The line you took through the trees is never the line you intended to take through the trees

If you head for a slope of virgin powder in order to make the first wiggle in the snow, someone will get there before you

○ COULOIR SKIING – SKI EXTREME – SKI ESPACE – APOCALYPSE SKIING – SKI SAUVAGE ○

A nice simple sort of skiing – there are basically just two options: you will either live to tell the tale, or you will die. Perhaps worth considering for the Survival Skier with big *cojones* who enjoys a game of Russian roulette with his Glühwein.

The advantage is that if you do come through – and someone gets a picture of you on your way down (make sure he shoots it at about 1/2000th of a second at least) – you may never have to ski again. (You may, of course, never be *able* to.) You will be able to rest on your laurels forever after – occasionally rolling up at the restaurant with your pair of special couloir skis that Sylvan Saudan helped you to design.

It might be easier though to get your photographer friend to photograph you on these skis standing on a jagged, but level, piece of terrain, with a look of terror on your face, doing your own version of Saudan's 'hop turn'. You then get the picture mounted *sideways*, so that it looks as if you're hurtling *down* a couloir. If any other skiers ask you why you're not seen on the slopes too much these days, all you need to do is take the picture out of your wallet, say that's really the only kind of skiing for you but that you've rather lost your nerve since you took that tumble last year. They should understand.

○ MOGUL SKIING ○

An excursion to Bump City to do battle with the Munch Monsters which probably won't appeal to most Survival Skiers. In any event, surely the technology should soon be getting to a point where they'll be able to eliminate bumps altogether. So there doesn't seem to be much point in learning how to ski them. Anyway, confusion still seems to rage about whether to ski *through* the bumps, *over* the bumps or *around* the bumps.

○ SKI VOILE ○

This is skiing with round glass-fibre wings attached to your arms or to your poles to help you 'fly through the air'. Despite assurances about 'high speed stability' and 'air-flap' braking, many Survival Skiers may find they are happy enough with the more modest flights they take on the piste when they come over an unexpected bump.

○ SKI ARTISTIQUE ○

Ballet, moguls, aerials. A great many of these flips, are not unlike the positions many Survival Skiers will have found themselves in at one time or another – whether it be a Spreadeagle, or Royal Christie or belly flop (you are often expected to practise in a wet-suit in a swimming pool).

No reason, though, why the Survival Skier shouldn't pretend to be a bit of an Evel Knievel on skis — adding, however, that he prefers to do his own thing: 'I just don't like the way hot-dogging has become codified these days. These people are acrobats, not skiers, and ought to be kept inside a circus'.

○ **VIDEO** ○

Used by all sorts of classes these days. The only advantage is that you will spend a lot of time sitting around — preferably inside — 'talking about it'. Picking out the faults that everybody else is making is actually quite fun. But when it gets to your own, it can be a bit of a blow to your skiing ego. (To quote *'Piste Again'*: 'No-one skis like he thinks he skis'.)

○ SCHOOL

It is easier to imitate bad skiers than good skiers

No-one who can really ski well — like the local hot-shots — ever learned in ski school

The more people in the class, the less time you will spend skiing, and the less attention will be paid to the instructor

There are always more people in the class than you were led to expect

In any ski class between one third and one half of the pupils will assume that they are the best in the class

At some point in the week at least one skier in the class will be advised by the instructor to undo the top clip of his boots

The part of your body you actually lean into the turn is not the part of your body you thought you were leaning into the turn

5 SELECTING YOUR INSTRUCTOR

'Do you want us to fall over?'

Prince Charles

As you may have gathered from the previous chapter, many of the new methods may just promise a bit more than they actually deliver. And some Survival Skiers have come to the conclusion that they are no worse off sticking to the traditional methods.

Here, too, though, there have been some useful recent developments. There is, for instance, a trend now for ski schools to display on their notice boards photographs of all their instructors, with a brief indication of their specialities. Thus you do have more of an opportunity to select your instructor and to pick someone who suits your particular style.

Not that you will necessarily learn a lot from the picture. The older instructors often provide photos of themselves taken a couple of decades previously. And whatever the photo may look like, the chances are that in the flesh your instructor will tend to be the archetypal unshaven garlic-scented bandy-legged weatherbeaten hunchback with a cigarette dangling out of the corner of his mouth; or, it it's a woman, a sort of Alpine Amazon. So much for the bronzed Killy lookalikes of legend. This can actually make it all the more frustrating: if this bow-legged simian can do it, surely a beautiful talented person like you should be able to make a better fist of it.

In fact the descriptions under the photos often can be of more help if you can interpret them properly. 'Has taught at resorts all over the Alps' probably means he hasn't been able to hold down a job in any of them. 'Can instruct in English' as likely as not means he doesn't speak English. Whatever his or her recommendations, however, it's probably better not to expect too much of your instructor. After all, any job where you're unemployed half of the year, paid a minimum wage, and work in freezing conditions is going to produce some fairly frustrated individuals – particularly towards the end of the season.

True, he or she may just *love* skiing – but skiing with a bunch of clowns like you? (There's *not* a lot of competition among ski instructors to take the least competent classes.) Perhaps the most candid appraisal you will get from your ski instructor is that look when he first claps eyes on his new class, and which often amounts to: 'Here we go again. Another prize set of duffers. Don't I get 'em.' They do say an instructor can tell how someone skis just by watching them ride up the t-bar.

But even though they are probably better at assessing you, than you are at assessing them, it pays for the Survival Skier also to be able to suss out his potential mentors at an early stage. The following profiles may help to give you a clearer idea of what to look for.

◯ **THE DRILL SERGEANT** ◯

Believes in teaching skiing by numbers, putting you through endless agonising knee-jerk exercises, playing silly games (like jumbling up everybody's skis in a pile and getting you to fetch them), and generally getting you to do things that are even more difficult than skiing. 'Now I want you to jump from big toe to big toe holding your sticks in the air.' This will provide some light relief for other classes who will enjoy watching him put you through your paces. They'll always know where to find you – your instructor's 'fog horn' voice can be heard all over the mountain.

○ THE CONFUSER ○

Specialises in telling you too much, all at once: 'Get your weight forward – now *use* your pole – and *watch* where you're going – don't forget to look for your *hands*.' In the unlikely event that you do manage to do all these things, he still won't be satisfied: 'And which way were you supposed to be facing – do I have to spell everything out?'

○ THE FLATTERER ○

Knows that the ego of the recreational skier is a fragile thing and that you'll think the more of his instruction if he can persuade you that you are better than you really are: 'You certainly wear your skis well'. This is not an altogether misguided theory since in skiing, confidence is all. Might, therefore, suit the Survival Skier who wants reassurance that he can do no wrong. Even when you just manage to stay upright after a nasty bump, arms akimbo and one leg in the air, he'll offer something like: 'Nice piece of recovery skiing that.'

○ THE TRICKSTER ○

The sort who makes sure he stays one up on his class by never letting the class settle down to *their* pace. There will be some nice easy skiing; then without a word of warning he'll be getting you all to do little jumps or leading you straight into a field of moguls the size of haystacks, or down The Big One. He also always seems to be skiing that *bit* too fast, or more likely that *bit* too slowly for a particular piece of piste. In this case the Survival Skier might be better advised to just do his own thing and ski on past him. ('See you at the bottom, boss.')

○ THE GLOATER ○

Has discovered that the best way to boost his class's ego (and the class's faith in *his* teaching ability) is to spend a good deal of time gloating at even worse classes – or perhaps better classes just as they are in the process of attempting some 'Ski That?' precipice. Your class can then stand there and watch them all fall down, and then ski off down an easier route, noses in the air, with your morale much boosted. A type of instructor who might well suit the Survival Skier.

○ THE OBSCURE ○

Not a bad choice for the Survival Skier as you can always pretend (with some justification) that you don't understand what he says: 'So *that's* what you wanted me to do'. Not that he will give up easily. And he can get quite menacing if you keep on failing to get his drift: 'You no understand English?' Make sure you don't let him get away with this and reply clearly: 'No, *you* don't understand English'. Unintelligibility is actually quite a common failing among ski instructors. Try learning in Scotland, for instance; or with one of those Brits who has read all those ski manuals and jabbers away at you all the time in arcane Skinglish.

○ THE SALESMAN ○

Has a little thing going with his cousin who owns a ski shop. Will, therefore, spend most of his time trying to persuade each member of the class (and they very often don't need much persuading) that they would ski much better if they were on a different type of skis. Fortunately, *he* knows somewhere where you can get a good discount, and he will be only too happy to help you to select a new pair one evening.

○ THE REALIST ○

Makes no attempt to conceal his belief (probably well-founded) that most of you in his class are probably never going to make it: 'You *may* get the hang of it – in about ten years time.' (Ha! Ha!) Better this, though, than the type who believes it's possible for even *you* to learn to ski, and keeps on promising an imminent breakthrough. (You are bound to disappoint him – and yourself.)

○ THE RE-EDUCATOR ○

Spends most of his time explaining to you that everything you've learnt everywhere else is wrong. So now it's his sorry lot to try to correct all those sloppy habits you've picked up in Italy or Andorra or somewhere. (For an Austrian or a Swiss this can explain everything – even *your* performance on planks.) The problem is that he usually insists on going right back to basics: 'Now we must learn again the first lesson – falling down. Tomorrow we learn the second lesson – getting up.' Not the sort of instructor the Survival Skier would be looking for.

○ THE ROMEO ○

May not exactly be the hyper-smooth demi-god that ski instructors are popularly imagined to be. But that won't stop him trying. He'll take every opportunity to massage the thighs of his female charges as if they were downhill racers being

prepared for the 'off'. With these protégés he will tend not so much to demonstrate positions as to physically 'arrange' their bodies into the right stance. The advantage is that he'll probably leave the rest of you pretty much alone. If he does start pushing you around, though, it may not be a bad idea to 'plant' one of the little goers in your class on him — so that the next day she can criticise *his* performance (under the duvet).

○ THE FAVOURITISER ○

Similar type. Picks out one or two favourites in the class on the first day — often including the most attractive female — and devotes all his attention to them. They are the ones who get to ski behind him all the time, go up on the lift with him, and receive the benefit of most of his advice. May suit the Survival Skier who prefers to be left to his own devices by the instructor.

○ THE THEORETICIAN ○

Believes theory is as important as practice, and will spend more time talking than skiing. Not a bad bet, therefore, for the Survival Skiier who enjoys talking technicalities, and brushing up his ski-speak. The problem is that all these explanations about what makes a ski turn (interesting though they may be) won't necessarily make *you* any better at turning on skis. And you'll also find, when you do perform, that all those complicated instructions he calls out to you bear very little relation (unfortunately) to what you're actually doing, i.e. just trying to stay upright on your skis as you bounce through a mogul field.

○ THE BOOZER ○

Often an oldtimer with a paunch and a red nose, who believes it's important to 'bend ze elbow' as much as to 'bend ze knees'. Much of your time, therefore, will be spent adjourning to hostelries near the slopes and sitting around to 'discuss your problems'. On the slope too, he'll probably be able to supply the class with some fortifying firewater and other goodies from his backpack – just to help you 'relax'. For obvious reasons, not a bad bet for the Survival Skier. And if you ensure that you too always have a couple of hip-flasks to pass around, you'll probably find yourself top of his class.

○ THE SPEED-MERCHANT ○

The one with the extra-long 'demo' skis. Often an ex-downhiller who never made it into the big league. He will just keep disappearing off the end of the world, and expect the class to follow. No sooner will they catch up with him, skis flapping in their faces, teeth chattering in time to their skis, than he'll be off again: 'Last one down buys the drinks.' An afternoon with him can thus come a bit expensive for the Survival Skier who likes to hang back a bit.

○ THE TOUGHIE ○

The instructor who is always detailed to take the class where they've put all the 'Type-T' personalities – the daredevils, doers and delinquents. His first priority, therefore, will be to clip their wings a bit – leading them up and down the Abbatoir Piste at double time and off the sort of precipices where your suntan immediately fades when you get to the edge. Probably, therefore, not one for the Survival Skier – though there is a certain aura attached to being a member of the 'Suicide Squad'.

○ **THE SONGBIRD** ○

Has a bit of a voice, or can yodel, and enjoys displaying these gifts as he leads his troupe down the piste. All very jolly. The trouble is that this will just draw attention to your class; and that's the last thing the Survival Skier wants. Even worse are the ones who see their class as a potential chorus: learning to ski is hard enough – without having to learn the words of 'La Montanara' at the same time.

○ THE REGRADER ○

The instructor who is never content to stick with the class-members he has been allotted, and is, therefore, constantly looking to promote some and to demote others. ('OK. If you too stupid, down to next class.') In fact, this may just be a subtle way of encouraging the weaker brethren to shape up: just imagine! The shame, the ignominy of having to join the class that you've been spending your time looking down your nose at – and most of whom you will now probably discover are better than you are.

○ THE ENGINEER ○

More of a do-it-yourself-man than a skier. Gets much more pleasure from adjusting all your equipment than he does from teaching you how to ski, and will have a rucksack full of tools to tune up your bindings and your skis. Not that this will make any more difference to your skiing than instruction would. A good choice, perhaps, for the Survival Skier who is not looking to put in too much mileage. If necessary, you can always get him to stop to 'check the adjustment' of one of your spoilers, or fiddle around with some other part of your equipment.

○ RUNS

One man's schuss is another man's precipice

If you have one good run, don't expect to have a second

You will have more bad runs than good ones

You are more likely to fall if you look up at the chair-lift

Only the perfect skier never looks up at the chair-lift

The colour of a run is never the way you would rate it

A black run in Italy is not the same as a black run in France or a black run in Austria

It's easier to get onto a black run than off one

6 TRAINING YOUR TUTOR

**'That's enough for today.
Let's all go back to the restaurant.'**

John Lennon, after his first ten minutes skiing in St. Moritz.

Now, some of these types we've mentioned may seem a bit fearsome — but perhaps not as much as they once would have done. For another positive recent development is that instruction is increasingly being seen as a *two-way process*, and not simply as a case of 'Achtung, bereit, los' or 'follow-my-leader'.

This means that the skilled Survival Skier should be able to see to it – and earn the respect and gratitude of his classmates into the bargain – that your instructor also comes in for a bit of training. No harm at all in making him go through his routines a few times, then shaking your head and getting him to try them again. You could also try placing someone directly behind him to ski on his heels, and so bring him crashing down — which won't be the best thing for his image — though it wasn't exactly his fault.

With this sort of approach you should be able to get your instructor *in tune with you* by the end of the week, if not before: stopping when *you* want to; doing the exercises *you* prefer; sticking to the pistes that *you* choose (declining his suggestions that you go off piste); lunching late or early as *you* decide (and make sure *he* is back on time — *you* can be late, but *he* can't). Make it clear from the start that he is your hired hand and that he'd better be civil or you will just have to find someone else.

Perhaps the most effective training technique to employ is the one which many instructors themselves have been using for years on their pupils — first destroying the class's confidence, and then spending a week rebuilding it. It can be easier to turn the tables on your instructor than you may think. Some of these types — even though they may look indestructible — have surprisingly fragile egos. And their confidence can often be as easily shattered as yours. A few well-chosen remarks on that first morning may be all that you need:

> 'How long have you been teaching exactly?' (Perhaps to a younger instructor.)
> 'So that's how they're teaching Christie's now, is it?'
> 'Have you ever taught *English* people before?'
> 'How dare you address my friend like that — it looked like a perfectly good turn to me.'

'How do you expect us to do it, if you can't do it right?'
'Try again old son. Walk up here and see if you can get it right this time.'
'Would you mind demonstrating that again?'
'Get your hands off me' (if he tries to rearrange your limbs into the correct position).

You could also try forgetting his name from time to time: 'Now look here. What's your name again? . . .'

And don't neglect the effect of the odd remark made to your classmates, which he will also be able to overhear: 'The only reason he does those turns better than us you know, is those special skis of his.' (If he offers to swap, it may be wiser to decline the offer. This might prove a bit embarrassing for you.) Or perhaps: 'We learnt more in three hours in Pistendorf last year than we have in the last three days with this chap.'

Another good idea is to mug up a bit of ski jargon and to ask him questions he can't answer. It pays to be knowledgeable about instruction – especially with the younger type of instructor. Make it very clear that you've had more instructors than he has had classes. Then, when he elaborately demonstrates a turn, whisper loudly to your classmates behind your hands: 'You know I really do think he's the best skier in the class' or 'Well that's certainly not what the last instructor told us.' Take every opportunity to enter into a discussion, contradicting him and arguing. If nothing else, this will at least give the class a chance to take a bit of a breather – which may be much needed if he's the type that sees to it that your class always has priority on ski lifts.

Another way to slow down the pace if your instructor's English isn't too hot is to get the class to keep scratching their heads and look puzzled and then try to interpret what he has said for one another's benefit. This, of course, can be great fun for the 'interpreters' who can then become surrogate instructors with the chance to try out some of their own theories. Skiing, of course, does tend to bring out the instructor in all of us.

Or, if your tutor has a habit of launching into particularly boring monologues, just clamp on your Walkman and look bored. If he takes exception to this, say: 'I was just listening to an instructional tape – to try to pick up a few useful tips.' You might also threaten to change class. Many instructors are quite sensitive on this score. They don't mind demoting people, but don't like their pupils to demote themselves, in case it reflects badly on them.

Now all this may sound a bit cruel. And, as we've said, instructors can be delicate souls – quite sensitive to how much their group likes them. (Nor do they want word to get back to the other instructors that they are unpopular, or that they can't speak English as they claimed when they got the job.) Many instructors also do want to be obliging, and, if encouraged, will be happy to keep

trotting out the ski stories at the café so that you don't have to go back to the slopes too soon. Nor are many of them too bothered if your skiing is not up to much. Some don't even like you to make too much progress. After all, they do like to feel needed.

In fact the best way to boost both your ego and his is to start the week pretending to be a prize duffer – or rather more of a prize duffer than you usually are. You can then proceed to make a dramatic improvement during the course of the week, earning yourself constant praise and also making him feel good about his instructional skills.

The truth is that a lot of instructors need reassurance every bit as much as their pupils – not, however, that they can *ski*, but that they can *instruct*. So once you've got him well-drilled, no reason not to start saying a few nice things about his instruction. He, in turn, may start saying nice things about your skiing. All in all, just the sort of 'two-way process' that modern instruction is supposed to be about.

7 GEAR

**'The first person to arrive in Mürren (in the twenties)
with a zip on his jacket was a fascinating sensation;
he got so fed up with people pulling the zip up and down
that in the end he fitted a padlock to its top.'**

Peter Lunn

When it comes to hardware, the rule is much the same as for softwear – the Survival Skier should have *as much of it as possible*. Some of it may even help. *Piste Again*, of course, did recommend sticking to tried and tested equipment – say hickory skis and bamboo poles – and maintaining a healthy scepticism about some of the more new-fangled inventions. But the fact is that people do now ski much better than they used to (a bit too well in fact for the Survival Skier who doesn't like to be shown up) and this just may have something to do with modern technology and wonder-materials like Kevlar and carbon fibre.

Also, as we've said, most of the chat around the slopes will be about skiing and equipment, even amongst the piste poseurs – so you can feel a bit left out if you're not bang up to date. So do be knowledgeable about the latest techniques and equipment – particularly the bits and pieces which *you* have acquired.

Don't worry about getting out of your depth. The Survival Skier, like everyone else, should go for the state-of-the-art stuff. Don't worry that it may be too good for you. No ski gear was ever designed for the mediocre skier. He or she does not exist. So, as with clothing, the Survival Skier should 'go for it' – provided he can afford the sort of equipment that ought really to be kept in a bank vault.

Top of the range gear may even add a little something to your performance. With any luck, in fact, it shouldn't be too long before the manufacturers really start living up to their claims, and the skiing itself is actually done for you. Computers at the foot of the slope and in your boots will process all the data about snow-coefficients, windspeed and so on, to help you to decide which ski to wear; and once you're skiing they will 'read' the snow for you, transmitting all the right messages to your laser-guided skis, and to your poles and to your body, which will be cocooned in a totally integrated solar-energised air-flow system.

Unfortunately, however, we're not quite there yet. The Survival Skier still has to do quite a lot for himself – though you'd never realise it from flipping through some of the brochures and ski mags. They all make it sound as if the equipment already needs a minimum of assistance from you. But many of their claims and counterclaims are actually quite confusing. To help you get all of this into perspective, therefore, let's have a closer look at what's currently available.

○ **BOOTS** ○

In the last few years boots seem to have superseded skis as *the* focus of interest. And in most lift queues, you'll find that far less time is spent looking at each other's clothes and skis than in examining the controls on one another's shin-bangers. (One recently introduced model in fact has no less than *nine* fit and performance controls – a sort of plastic box decorated with knobs, dials, ratchets and levers.)

Not that this means that beginners are any the less likely to put their boots on the wrong way round. Nor that your ankles and shins will get off any more lightly than they used to. You stand as good a chance as ever of getting an attack of 'the boots' – your feet imprisoned in those great triangular blocks, calves bent forward at an unnatural angle, and being rubbed up the wrong way in at least three separate places.

Now, that isn't the theory, mind. The idea of all these controls, with everything adjustable, is that you get a *perfect* fit, geared exactly to *your* type of skiing. The

fact is, though, that there are so many fine-tuning possibilities that you'll *never* get your boots set up-right – despite the 600-page instruction manual and the half-day course they gave you in the shop about how to 'drive' the boot and how to set it up to compensate for your hammer toes, fallen arches and knock-knees (all based on a diagnostic computer read-out of your 'pressure emphasis' and other personal characteristics).

One advantage of this for the Survival Skier is that you can spend a great deal of time on the slope fiddling with the controls on your boots, as you adjust for cant, flex and forward-lean. All quite an advance on just playing with your clips. The pity is that you still have to *bend down* to do it. How long are we going to have to wait for the manufacturers to come up with a remote-control box conveniently built into your anorak?

Needless to say, this sort of activity can also take up a fair amount of your *après*-ski time – recharging the boots, adjusting the central heating system, and checking that the avalanche locaters are working OK, or the piste-reading sensors on the toe-piece, or those reflectors at the back for night-time skiing. Still, this is one way of keeping away from the disco action – though it won't necessarily be much more peaceful, with all those flashing lights on your boots and on your 'boot charging unit'.

One last tip. Difficult as it may be to walk back to the chalet in your boots, on no account should you use those 'boot walkers' that clamp on to the bottom. This will mean that your lack of 'bootmanship' will be revealed to all who will see that you can't even set the flex adjuster to 'walk' position so that they move easily in the forward plane.

○ SKIS ○

The paradox about skis is that we all now buy our own on the basis that this will work out cheaper than renting over a period of three or four years, and we then proceed to invest in a new pair each season. The Survival Skier shouldn't worry about this too much, however, since, as we've seen, he or she needs as many pairs of skis as he can afford – piste skis, off-piste skis, hard skis, soft skis, slalom skis, downhill skis, as well as various types of novelty ski – so that he can spend a good deal of time chopping and changing to suit the conditions. To paraphrase the Duchess of Windsor: 'No woman can ever be too rich, too thin or have too many pairs of skis'.

As a general rule, the Survival Skier should be seen with the *longest possible* skis. And this indeed is the trend. Compacts have been succeeded by mids, and then by 'clipped' full length. (So much, incidentally, for the theory we were all led to believe, that it was compact skis which caused moguls: compact skis are long gone, but there is still no shortage of bumps on the piste.) Avoid those 'boutique' skis, by the way. They may have a certain 'limited edition' snob appeal and be easier to ski on, but they'll do a good deal less for your reputation than your detuned racers.

Even if you aren't very tall, there's no reason (except possibly lack of skiing ability) that you shouldn't have long skis. How else are you going to be able to hold your head up as you wait for the cable car? So make sure everyone else in the queue is looking *up* at your ski tips. No matter that your instructor will be entirely contemptuous when he sees this. After all, it's not him you're trying to impress. One answer to this problem might just be those adjustable-length skis. (It might be worth noting that Lego have now started making ski equipment!)

The other important thing is to 'know your skis'. You've got to be as ready as anyone to hold forth on the merits of laminated carbon-fibre or assymetrical edges or vibration-dampening modules or whatever. This should pose no real problems – just read carefully the manufacturers' blind-them-with-rubbish puffs. (Have you ever come across a ski without a 'unique construction'?)

But do try not to fall too much in love with your skis. There are people who would happily take their skis to bed with them – and may even do so. (There are always people sneaking down to the ski-room at night and then back up the stairs.) Thus it can be a bit disheartening when your pride and joys are irreverently bunged into the back of the bus or the train with all the others. The Survival Skier, however, should *not* be the type who puts transparent film on his skis to stop his customised graphics from getting scratched; or has his name studded in diamonds on his custom-made sliders, or his own silk-screen design printed on. He knows that disposability is the name of the game. So don't bother with one of those burglar-alarm attachments.

Even though the Survival Skier should be well versed in the manufacturer's claims, he should also display a certain scepticism: he's not blind to the tendency of Kevlar to 'delaminate sideways'; or to how the effects of torque and sidecut often can cancel each other out. Not that this will prevent him from ensuring that he has all the new rubber attachments on his ski tips, the latest design in spoilers and air flow systems, and assorted knobs and counterweights to dampen those spine-crunching vibrations. He knows, though, that sooner rather than later the hole in the tip will have become as redundant as the parablack. (Whatever happened to those things, by the way? Why don't we need them anymore? People don't seem to be crossing their ski tips any less than they used to. Perhaps there just wasn't any room for both them and the mileage-gauge we'll all soon have on the front.)

The Survival Skier, however, shouldn't just leave it to the manufacturers to make all the improvements. He should be seen constantly peering down the barrels and 'air channels' of his skis, tuning up his edges, dulling the ski tips, rounding off or sharpening up the tails (split or otherwise), adjusting the length of his powder retaining straps, drilling holes in his boards and moving the bindings backwards and forwards, and painting yet another substance onto his black graphite bases.

Waxing, of course, is back in fashion now. So much for those 'thermal' skis. The Survival Skier thus has yet another good way of keeping himself busy beside the piste. It's worth bearing in mind that you can also wax *to travel more slowly*. It's just a pity that sprays have rather put an end to the ritual of brewing up your wax. (Some resorts even have piste-side drive-in 'waxoramas'.) There seem to be sprays for everything now – your skis, your boots, your bindings, your clothing, as well as for assorted parts of your body.

One type of 'innovation' that the Survival Skier would, however, do better to ignore are all those gadgets for carting your skis around – those shoulder straps, clips or 'ski-totes', or those little wheels for pushing your skis around on. Any skier worth his salt has a little groove in his shoulder for lodging his skis (or, in the case of the Survival Skier, perhaps a little foam pad inside his anorak instead). One thing you might find useful though is the ski-box or roof-boot for the top of the car. This can be rather handy for keeping all your equipment in. (You may need two or three.) And, at a pinch, they would do as a coffin if the unexpected happens and you end up going home as 'brown bread'.

◯ **BINDINGS** ◯

The fact that you are that much less likely to end up as 'brown bread' these days is in no small measure a consequence of binding technology having got so good (as well, of course, as developments in the techniques of Survival Skiing). Never mind that they are now starting to make them out of plastic and rubber – they do still seem to do the job.

So it always seems a bit thankless that we should just chuck our bindings away and replace them whenever we get a new pair of skis (conveniently forgetting when we order our new skis to allow for new bindings in the final cost). But clearly, there's no reason why bindings should be an exception to the law of disposability which applies to all ski gear. And lest you should contemplate transferring your old bindings to your new skis, there are always some new refinements which would make this seem unwise. The binding-makers also seem to like to persuade us to keep on swapping brands, as they all take it in turns to lead the field – from Marker to Look to Salomon and back again to Look and Marker. The question is, with the introduction of micro-chip electronic bindings, will the Japanese also be willing to continue to alternate in this gentlemanly fashion?

This might perhaps be a subject for speculation for the Survival Skier, who should be as adept at talking about bindings as about anything else, holding forth on technicalities like 'equaliser' features and Twincam toes and the prospects of the plate-binding staging a comeback.

○ **POLES** ○

Sticks are also something that tend to be bought very much as an afterthought. Once you've got the skis, after months of agonising about the pros and cons of different types of plank, you are more than likely to settle for the first pair of poles the salesman hands you. (HIM: 'Here, try these for size.' YOU: 'They seem about right. I'll take them.')

But since some skiers weren't actually bothering to change their poles, the stickmakers have also been making annual alterations to ensure that we have to keep up to date. So we've gone from straps to sword-grips and back to straps. And every year there's a smaller basket on the end of your poles – whether they're the latest telescopic type, or elliptical ones, or wiggly 'corrective' angle poles, or designer 'wrist-assist' sticks in flashy colours with see-through handles.

One word of warning to the Survival Skier. You'd do better not to let yourself be tempted away from your Scott's by those poles that unfurl to make a sort of deckchair when clipped across your upended skis. This really does make you look like too much of an armchair skier. If you do want to lounge about on the piste like this (and no reason why you shouldn't), better stick to the 'old way' – propping yourself up against your skis, or perhaps using your bandanna or your poles to improvise a backrest between your skis.

○ GEAR

On any skiing holiday, you will spend as much time zipping up your clothes as zipping down the slopes

The more comfortable your boots while skiing, the less comfortable while walking

The likelihood of your boots hurting is substantially increased if that was the last pair in your size in the hire-shop, or if you rented them at home before coming out

No ski glove has yet been designed which keeps the tips of your fingers warm

At least one of your ski poles is always bent – either accidentally by you, or on purpose by the manufacturer

The fact that the binding released correctly when the assistant yanked it in the shop is no guarantee that it will release properly on snow

Just when you think you are going to get through the week with your new ski bases unscathed, you'll hit the rocks

○ **SOUND** ○

After 'Bend ze knees', probably the most common cry on the slopes these days is: 'Damn – my Walkman's bust again'. More and more skiers are now wired for sound; and for the Survival Skier this does have certain advantages. It means, for instance, that you can't actually *hear* when people are laughing at you. Nor will you have to listen to the crack when you snap a tendon or fracture a limb.

It also means that *you're* the one who gets to choose what you're listening to – not the chap who operates the loudspeakers on the pylons; or the person with the Walkman next to you in the queue. (The problem of 'sound overspill' is probably going to get worse rather than better with the introduction of 'sound jackets' – anoraks with inbuilt speakers and power boosters.)

There is one drawback though. As we know, the Survival Skier is someone who does enjoy giving others the benefit of his advice – it seems a pity that there are going to be fewer and fewer people around who are in a position to listen to him.

8 ON THE LEVEL

'Wait till I count my fingers. I may have lost one.'

'Scotty', in *The Thing from Another World*

Many an innocent Survival Skier has had the 'bright idea' of taking to cross-country for a couple of days as an easy and acceptable way of avoiding the agonies of Alpine skiing and the sheer cost of downhill high tech. It usually doesn't take long, however, for them to radically revise their opinions: shuffling along on skinny skis is not quite the doddle it looks.

Certainly, when you start out, it can seem like a distinct improvement on downhill. You can take your time and linger over breakfast – none of that early morning rush for the lift. You can then spend a while quietly in the 'salle de fartage' (the waxing room, incidentally, not the 'farting room' – though it is often characterised by its distinctive smell).

It's when you actually set out though and start moving that your ideas may begin to change a bit. The fact is that *you* are the one who has to move the skis – unlike downhillers, langlaufers don't rely on gravity. And after you've shuffled along a bit, it may suddenly begin to dawn exactly why those oldsters were taking their time at breakfast, and tucking supplies of food into their backpacks: the truth is that few activities on the planet burn up more calories per hour than this 'soft sport for oldies'.

It's then that you begin to see in a somewhat different light those genteel geriatrics shuffling along in kneesocks and knickerbockers. For one thing, a good many of them aren't quite that geriatric: they can't be – not at the speed they shuffle past you (who will more likely be going slowly nowhere while expending a great deal of energy). Nor, on careful examination, is a lot of the gear quite so old-fashioned. A fair number of skinny skiers will be clad in aerodynamic skintight fluorescent suits (though they often still stick to the long hat with the bobble). In many ways, in fact, loipegear is sexier than downhill gear – though you couldn't say the same about their tomato red faces once langlaufers get into their stride.

But whatever the pros and cons, there's no question that the popularity of cross-country has been growing dramatically – even among Brits. And the compleat Survival Skier, therefore, should also be able to hold his own in the ruts. Gone are the days when the Survival Skier could afford to look down on skinny skiers (jeering at them 'Telemark please' whenever he caught sight of one).

Fortunately, there are one or two techniques that can make things easier for the Survival Skier. As with 'avoidance skiing' on piste, for instance, there is always the option of ducking off the beaten-track and spending your time getting well-oiled in some little mountain hostelry. After all, traditionally, cross-country is supposed to be a sport for loners and nature lovers who enjoy getting out into the countryside, listening to the silence in the fir-glades, interrupted only by the birdsong, the babbling of brooks under the ice, browsing deer or the occasional nibbling winter hare. That's all part of the 'kick' of cross-country skiing.

If, instead, you stick to the loipes (which are fast becoming as crowded as the pistes) you'll find there isn't much scope for creative lingering. Practitioners tend to just charge along the marked rails, head down, in their tramlines to the next signpost. (If downhillers are said to go up and down like yo-yos, langlaufers could be said to go round and round in circles – and extremely *large* circles at that.) Après-loipe tales told at the end of the day tend to concentrate overwhelmingly on how many kilometres you covered and how long it all took you.

So lying low in the woods in a sheltered spot is not such a bad idea. Then when the Survival Skier feels like a bit of company and wants to establish his presence, he can re-emerge from between the trees, duly fortified by the solid and liquid provisions in his knapsack, and park himself at one of those junctions where three or four loipes cross. There are often a fair number of people standing around at these places since it is never clear which arm of the sign is pointed in which direction, and any map will not agree with the signpost.

In fact, all loipe groups include a map-reader who will insist that though the sign may *look* clear, according to his map, there is a *better* way. (This is rarely the case – though I suppose it depends what you mean by better.)

Ideally, the Survival Skier should take up his position at the loipe junction at one of those moments when the coast is clear and there is no one else around. Then when people do appear, he can stand there looking puffed, loaded down by his well-stuffed pack (as if he's been on the trail for days) or perhaps towing a sled and offering, on the basis of *his* experience, advice on the best route to take.

Another ploy is to set out from your base on a lollipop-shaped loipe. You should be able to make it up the stick of the lollipop and a bit beyond – onto the start of the circuit. You can then turn around to head back (slowly), pretending to anyone you meet that you've actually been *right round* the circuit in the other direction.

On no account, however, should you actually try to complete the course. All loipes are actually longer than the direction indicators show and it will always be a good deal further than it looks on the map. Another rule to remember is that it's always shorter on the way out than it is on the way back – so beware of straying out too far. There's also no point in trying to select your route so that you have the wind with you in at least one direction. You can be absolutely sure that if the wind is against you on the way out, it also will be against you on the way back.

For the Survival Skier who really wants to cop out though, and enhance his reputation into the bargain, there's probably nothing to beat the 'early bird' routine. This involves arriving a bit late for breakfast, in a damp pair of kneesocks, with a bit of frosting in your hair, looking a bit pooped and sweaty. (A few physical jerks outside in the snow beforehand should see to this.) You then breeze in, looking flushed and pleased with yourself at having 'got in your twenty kilometres' before breakfast, and being generally hearty to all and sundry: 'Nothing like getting out there just when the birds are waking up'. That, of course, will be the last anyone sees of you on the loipes that day.

In fact, heartiness is one of the most important skills a langlaufer has to master. Cross-country skiers are for ever pronouncing 'Herrlich, nicht?' and wishing one another 'Viel Spass'. Such greetings are very much the thing when you meet other langlaufers en route. However puffed they are, they'll offer at least a 'Guten Tag', to which (if they've got in first) you should reply: '*Schönen* Guten Tag' or '*Wunderschönen* Guten Tag'. It's all part of the cross-country philosophy that 'Langlaufers laugh longer' – as well as 'love longer' and 'live longer' (or so they say). The Survival Skier may well have his doubts about this latter claim. No statistics have yet been produced of how many cases of cardiac arrest occur on loipes each year. But all those little shrines dotted around the mountains would seem to indicate that it's a fair old number.

When the Survival Skier is out on a loipe and not skulking in the woods, he'll generally do best to stick to the well-trodden trails. But do stay well away from those smaller circular nursery-type loipes where everyone can watch everyone else going round. It can be a bit embarrassing to keep on being lapped by people who are either half or twice your age.

Out on a proper trail, it should be easier to cut a better figure. But do be careful not to give yourself away. You can show yourself up very easily by the way you handle yourself on the track. The pros, for instance, swop ruts without thinking twice about it; the amateurs tend to hang onto their ruts no matter what. In some respects, though, it does pay to be the weaker skier. This should mean you are left to plod along in the well-trodden tramlines, leaving it to the stronger skier to ski wide – perhaps even having to make some new tracks.

At times, of course, there will be some joker coming straight at you in *the opposite direction* in your right-hand track (probably another downhiller, 'giving it a go'), and turning the whole thing into a game of 'chicken'. This is when you should loudly voice your contempt for the sort of people they are now letting onto the loipes and offer a few lessons in the highway code – making the point clear with the tip of your pole if necessary

Another type to beware of are the overtakers. These are often German and tend to use the same technique as they do on the Autobahn, haring down in the outside lane flashing their lights at anyone in their way. On the loipe the lights and horn will be replaced by an 'Achtung' – though some have taken to blowing a little whistle as they charge past, weight thrust forward, and head down. Once again, though, stand your ground – make sure that if anyone is going to come a cropper, it won't be you (And don't neglect the possibility of letting a ski stick *accidentally* drift between the overtaker's legs.) It's this sort of encounter which provides yet another reason to choose to go round the loipe in the *opposite* direction to the one being taken by most people.

Incidentally, try to avoid overtaking yourself – although it is one of the rules of cross-country that no one else's speed ever coincides with yours. For if you do forge ahead of someone, it's a pretty safe bet that before long you will be overtaken by the person you passed – the old 'tortoise and the hare' syndrome.

The downhiller should find that there are certain advantages to having learnt his skiing skills on the piste. Langlaufers, for instance, tend not to be much good at going downhill. Even something like the snow plough (elementary to most downhillers) can represent the height of technique to the langlaufer. In fact, you often see langlaufers using the lifts on the piste these days trying to get their skinny skis more used to downhill.

One of the nice things about cross-country, though, is that people tend not to be so critical of your technique, or to spend too much time developing their own. It is burning up those calories that concern them most. Of course, a few of them are starting to get the hang of the 'new' skating step – though there is a good deal of resistance to this from the traditionalists as it destroys the tracks. Thus, most continue to be content with the old kick-glide-kick diagonal stride.

So it's worth the Survival Skier trying to get a few of the more advanced techniques off-pat i.e. the skating step, fancy sidesteps from rut to rut, and, above all, that racing flick (lifting up the heel of the rear ski – even if the longest you can keep this up for is about forty metres). With any luck you should have reached the trees by then, muttering loudly to yourself as you disappear: 'Und jetzt, mit *tempo*'.

Where the downhiller can also come into his own is après-ski, or rather après-loipe. The sad fact, though, is that you may well find yourself on your own – though there's more après-loipe these days than there used to be. However, langlaufers tend to be the 'early-to-bed' type, who look down on downhillers and their after-hours cavortings as rather decadent.

○ CROSS-COUNTRY

You never get enough glide for your kick

Your degree of contempt for cross-country depends on whether you've ever done it or not

All XC trails have more uphill sections than they have level or downhill sections

Multiple trail junctions are always situated so that maximum number of langlaufers reach them at the same time

All XC clobber is either too hot while you're moving or too cold when you stop

Never believe a returning langlaufer who says the route is pretty level, or that 'You can easily do it by nightfall'

Whenever you're convinced this must be the very last bend, there'll be one more to go – at least

The fact is too, of course, that langlauf doesn't leave you in much shape to shake a leg of an evening. Most langlaufers tend to go either tomato red or deathly pale after their day's efforts. And it's not just your legs that go. Your stomach muscles, your torso (and also for some obscure reason your big toe) also tend to be very much the worse for wear.

So, even though 'ski de fond' may be good for you it is not exactly 'ski de fun' (which may be no bad thing for a jaded Survival Skier). It can be nice, for a change, to go to a resort that goes to bed at night.

9 SUMMER SKIING

'What do you do in the summer time?'
'I wait for the winter.'

Tycoon Roland Young to ski-instructor
Greta Garbo in *Two-faced Woman*

The one thing that could be said about skiing was that, at least, come Easter or so, it was all over for another year. You could just hang up your boots and try to forget about it. In the last few years, though, the more reluctant piste-bashers have come to the rather unsettling realisation that it is possible to ski 365 days a year – and not just on the Dendix. Even in the Alps, however, you do tend to get some funny looks from customs-officers when you roll up at the airport in August with your ski gear.

More and more glaciers are being 'rigged up' for summer skiing, and since, even in winter, summer skiing tends to be a standard conversation piece, it is something Survival Skiers should know something about. In fact, not a few Survival Skiers have actually been induced to try it out – tempted by the notion that it might be more *pleasant* to ski in your swimsuit on a warm summer's day. (And that it might provide a good excuse for opting out during the Winter.)

Certainly, there are some advantages for the Survival Skier. First, the only hotel near the glacier will be booked out and over-priced. This means you'll have to stay way down the valley in the company of a few pensioners on walking tours in a sort of Alpine ghost-town, and will thus be able to spend some hours every morning getting up to the skiing. It can actually be quite fun travelling up a series of cable cars, watching out for the marmots, spotting wild flowers and glimpsing cascading waterfalls. Fortunately, the gigantic mounds of mashed potato that form in the soft snow (to call them 'moguls' would be a euphemism) will make it impossible to ski in the afternoon – *thus limiting your skiing to half a day only.*

On the debit side, though, it does mean that you're going to have to get up at the crack of dawn – if not before – if anyone is to believe you have any serious intention of skiing. (The lifts are often open at 7 a.m.) The aim is to hit the slopes, skis chattering, while the snow is still icy hardpack, and getting in your skiing before you develop creeping paralysis of the knees, and start revealing all the deficiencies in your technique. (Unlike in the powder, in this sort of porridge you just get *stuck*.) By the way, try not to be put off by the ominous creaks and groans that you will hear from time to time as the ice shifts under the pistes. However it is not wise to venture too far off-piste in the summer – crevasses have been known to swallow ratracs, to say nothing of off-piste bashers.

Needless to say, these are not the sort of conditions in which the Survival Skier will usually perform at his best – either on the piste or at the restaurant. (There often won't be that much open in the way of poseur piazzas up on the mountain in mid-summer.) The advantage, though, is that there will be very few people around to actually take any notice of the Survival Skier's piste performance, and that glacier slopes are almost by definition open and gentle. Most of the people you find up there are die-hard ski-nuts at 'race camps' or 'ski clinics', or the members of national ski teams keeping themselves sharp and clocking one another with a stopwatch. The Survival Skier can thus spend his time admiring the view – though ski areas above the tree-line in summer do tend to look rather forlorn without their blanket of snow.

Unfortunately, there very often will not be anyone companionable to admire these views with. So much for all those ads of bikini-clad lovelies propped up on their skis, soaking up the sun. Actually these bikini pictures are all taken in the spring. (Incidentally, if you do ski in your swimsuit make sure you don't fall – snow crystals can very easily scrape off a couple of layers of tan.)

You may well find, therefore, that summer on the high peaks is simply very

often not what it is cracked up to be. For though in the winter the mountains do seem to drum up consistently clear weather, surprisingly they often fail to do so in the summer. You find it's fine and sunny down in the valley – but mist, blizzards or clouds up on the glacier (which, as we've said, can provide the Survival Skier with a reason for not going up). If you do go up in the mist, though, it does mean no one is going to be able to cast a critical eye on your performance.

Queues too tend to be in rather short supply in the summer – also somewhat unfortunate for the Survival Skier. The 'race camps' and 'clinics' seem to spend most of their time lined up on the piste discussing the technicalities of technique, fiddling with their electronic timing devices, and leaving you to go up and down the few lifts that will be working.

One tip: stay well clear of these people in the afternoons. The 'racing camp brigade' may well invite you to join them at their lectures, or video watching, or ski tuning sessions; and the individual ski nuts will want to do nothing but talk skiing, and High Factor suncreams. The latter tends to be *the* big topic of après-summer ski conversation. For though it can be icy cold in the morning, when it does heat up later the sun can easily burn a couple of layers of skin off you. Don't incidentally, miss out any bits when you apply the cream – like the tips of your ears. (They even say you should alter the position of the parting of your hair every day to ensure you don't get a line branded into your scalp.)

Summer skiing may thus have some points to commend it for the Survival Skier who wants to work on his face tan and pick wild flowers in the afternoons. He may, however, miss the camaraderie of the more jolly recreational skiers you find in the winter, and to whom most Survival Skiers' act is more specifically geared. The fact is there often isn't really anyone much up there in the summer to pose for or to perform your tricks.

○ MISHAPS

The surest way of making your tips cross is to look at them

Whenever a novice falls on a track it will be where the track is narrowest, and where it will cause the maximum inconvenience to oncoming skiers

If you schuss down into a dip, however fast you go your momentum will never be sufficient to get you up the other side without poling

The nicer a mogul looks, the more likely it is to have ice on the other side

The pocket you keep your money in is the one you always forget to zip up

If a plastic bag is blowing across an empty ski slope below you, it always moves at such a speed that at some point it will wrap itself around the tips of your skis

Just as you think no one's going to come round that corner, someone will

The part of the mogul you intended to turn on is never the bit you do turn on

10 SNOW WARS

'Seven times fall. Eight times get up.'

Japanese proverb

No, there's certainly no stopping them. Those Japanese have kept right on coming – in bigger and bigger numbers. And if the land of the rising yen keeps on living up to its economic reputation, it surely won't be that long before a good deal of the Alps are *owned* by Mitsubishi or some other Nipponese conglomerate.

The Japanese, of course, are not the only ones. About sixty nations now claim to be 'skiing countries'. Unfortunately though, a lot of them don't stick to sliding around at home but have taken to invading the Alps and Europe's other ski regions. All a far cry from the early decades of the century when the Brits had the slopes all to themselves – though it is true that in the very early days there were some places in the Alps where the natives would pelt the Brits engaged in their aberrant activity with stones, forcing them to confine their 'skiing-running' to moonlit nights.

The regrettable thing is that the 'stone-throwing' syndrome does seem to be coming back. And as more and more skiers crowd onto the pistes, friction between national groups has become all too common – though some of this is no more than healthy competition. Who can wear the snazziest gear? Who can turn the town upside down most effectively at night?

But all too frequently the competition is a good deal fiercer. One sign of the times, perhaps, is that last year the authorities in Zermatt introduced Switzerland's first 'Ski Police' force. Fist fights and shoving and arguing in lift-lines were apparently just some of the problems. 'They throw off their gloves and fight,' according to a senior officer. 'The Americans and English are best – they seem to know how to stand in line. But the others – Swiss, Italians, Germans, French – are not and we had problems.' Other resorts, too, are said to be trying to ban 'Pistenrowdys' from the slopes.

It's nice to see though – at least according to the Zermatt Ski Police – that the Brits are not apparently living up to their 'football hooligan' reputations. It should be pointed out though that a number of bar-owners don't seem to agree. There are some which will not admit Brits or Swedes. In fact it's those 'Big crazy Swedes' who seem to be *persona non grata* more than anyone else. They may be few in number but they certainly have made their mark off the slopes.

Perhaps this is because Brits have still not felt the need to make full use of all

those techniques honed at Highbury and Anfield. The day may come though when we will just have to display our skills with the old aerosol; or at spraying the opposition with cans of fizzed-up lager; or showing that we're a match for everyone at sliding poubelle-liners into the tips of oncoming skiers; or tripping up into a heap a group of 'enemy' skiers as they come up behind you on the lift; or dropping a well-aimed ski pole from the chairlift at some Continental Pistenjaeger flashing down between the pylons below you; or mowing down 'hostile classes' as you career into them on a kamikaze schuss; or surreptitiously 'pulling the plug' on the Walkman of the person in front of you in the queue; or jumbling up the skis of a hostile class while they're inside the restaurant at lunch (perhaps – if you have time – coating their boards with 'go slower' wax); or even – though this does seem a bit dastardly – offering your worst enemy a swig of firewater *spiked with pure alcohol* from your *other* hipflask before challenging him to a race.

The fact is, though, that xenophobia is often regarded as all part of the fun on the slopes; and any British Survival Skier worth his salt should know how to defend his national colours if need be, keeping a stiff upper lip (and weight planted *firmly* on the *lower* ski) when some foreigner comes haring down at you shouting 'Piste!', 'Achtung!', or whatever, and making sure you get your knee in his groin *first* when the inevitable collision results.

All this is undoubtedly one of the reasons why piste-bashers tend to ski more and more in their national groups. It's a form of self-protection (safety in numbers). It also perhaps explains the British preference for staying together in chalets. And on slope you can enjoy yourselves making catty remarks about the way other nations ski. However well any other national group *appears* to ski, the golden rule is to be contemptuous of their efforts. Here you will probably be aided and abetted by your instructor. (It's a growing trend to take along an instructor of your own nationality.)

Although you can happily take to task all or any of the other sixty nations sliding around on the slopes, do not, however, let anyone get away with rubbishing British skiing. Admittedly, amongst themselves, for instance, Brits may run down Cairngorm. But interrogated by any other nation you should make it clear that Cairngorm is 'fantastic'. (You can forget to mention the huge queues, lack of loos, absence of civilised cafés, uncivil service, and high prices.) No, you can tell them, Scotland is paradise compared with some of these Alpine resorts – makes you wonder why you come. And don't feel inhibited about making your views plain about some of the other skiing nations – especially when you're not directly addressing a representative of the country in question. For instance:

○ SWISS ○

A nation of goatherds and hoteliers, trying to preserve the illusion that they make money out of banking and cuckoo clocks, when really they are earning a living by overcharging you for the use of their snow.

○ AUSTRIANS ○

Pretty much the same – except that put them in a ski instructor's uniform and it's as if they were wearing jackboots.

○ ITALIANS ○

Their biggest contribution to skiing has been the pasta and pizza joints now found all over the Alps. Not to be taken seriously on the slopes though – flashy fair-weather skiers, who spend more time chatting than skiing. (Perhaps wisely as most of their ski lifts are reputed to have been obtained fifth-hand.)

○ FRENCH ○

The people we all love to hate – particularly as they now tend to be where it's at in skiing in both fashion and technology (even though they seem to spend most of their time on slope lunching). For the masochistic Brit, though, France is *the* place. If you like to have a go at the Frogs, pick somwhere like Courchevel where the locals will all look down at you. If you really want to rile them, just lay claim to 'our' boy Jean-Claude Killy, telling them that his name is really 'Kelly'. (His forebears were actually Irish Celts – not *quite* British, but near enough.)

○ GERMANS ○

A bunch of langlaufers rather than skiers. 'Schwobs' as the Swiss would say abusively or 'Piefkes' as the Austrians call them. And you surely can't call the Zugspitze and its surroundings a skiing area. Anyway it all seems to have been leased out to the US army.

Another point to bear in mind is that even in resorts where the Brits are a majority, always pretend that you are being over-run – the K-factor (Krauts), the F-factor (Frogs), not to mention the S-factor (Sloanes). A good line to take is that Pistendorf was so much nicer before that other lot arrived. Nor should you make any attempt to pronounce the local names correctly – thus Saulze D'Oulx becomes Sowsy (or 'Saucy screw' as some would have it), Meribel becomes Maybel, and St. Moritz becomes Morrers.

Of course, we all have our own national characteristics and that is what makes the ski scene interesting. Brits, for instance, have this habit of wearing their swimsuits in the sauna, but are the first to strip off on the slopes. To non-Europeans, of course, all this may seem a bit daunting. They may not realise that inter-European aggro is all part of the fun, and has been for centuries, and that we actually *enjoy* this sort of thing. So how are those other nations who are now beginning to appear amongst us in ever greater numbers going to fit in – notably the Japanese and the Americans?

○ JAPANESE ○

In a way it's a pity the Japanese have had to come to terms with this unruly scene. The ones we have seen so far have seemed to be a disciplined gentle bunch – though we shouldn't forget they too have their crazy side: the term 'Kamikaze skier' wasn't coined for nothing; and it was of course Yuichiro Miura (now director of Sapporo Ski School) who schussed down Everest (with the aid of a parachute) in 1970.

Make no mistake though, they are making inroads – especially where gear and clobber is concerned (and that, as we've seen, is really what it's all about). Even French moniteurs have now been equipped with Descente suits. And YKK, of course, is the biggest manufacturer of zips in the world. Their gear, though, does tend to be pretty flash – even changing colour according to the temperature. And when it comes to really 'flash trash', they must surely be way ahead with their new 'disposable' cameras. Fortunately, they haven't yet got the hang of making good skis – though they have put up the trade barriers to prevent European and American imports.

Once on the planks, as you might expect, they don't give up easily, and they

tend to keep bashing away from dawn to dusk. One problem is that you very often don't see them coming – not last year anyway when they had a penchant for white ski suits. And since they do tend to be rather small, you could have a whole class of them through your legs before you knew what hit (or hopefully) missed you.

An indication of the extent of their obsession with skiing is the 'urban slalom' building being put up in Tokyo – a six-storey refrigerated building in the city complete with spiral slopes, three lifts and nine artificial snow machines.

So don't underestimate them. They are pretty well bound to get there in the end and they are prepared to take their time about it. Japan itself is reputed on weekends to have the longest ski lift queues in the world and the largest concentration of skiers (twelve million plus). (They may perhaps just be the Ultimate Survival Skiers – and we may in time be able to learn from them.)

The ones you will come across in the Alps, though, will tend to keep very much to themselves – like everyone else, skiing in national groups – and going through their exercises in rigid formation, rather like the Austrians, often all dressed the same with a big brand name on their outfits, carrying a small backpack – *and apparently eager not to cause trouble.*

Let's try to keep it that way – misunderstandings can so easily occur. When they talk about 'Yuki', for instance, they mean 'snow' – not that they think Euro-snow is yukky. There's also that mysterious 'Wa' they're always on about, which apparently translates as 'harmony'. So don't misunderstand a Nip hurtling down the mountain murmuring 'Wa' under his breath. He is not making a declaration of war and there would not normally be any need to fear imminent attack. Just say politely, 'Ah ha! wa' (though apparently it isn't done to talk about 'wa' since it then disappears). And this might upset him.

○ THE AMERICANS ○

You'd have thought the fall in the dollar would have kept their numbers down. But it doesn't seem to – any more than the falling pound has been deterring Brits from getting their annual winter fix in the Alps. And like those gentle Japanese, they must also experience a certain culture shock when they find themselves pitched into European-style 'snow wars'.

The thing is that 'stateside' skiing, whilst very 'macho', is also an altogether more friendly business – wishing one another frequently 'Have a nice day', rather than the European 'Out of my way'. Americans don't even seem to have heard of jumping the queue (or rather 'not standing in line'), or jostling on the T-bar (perhaps because they're more used to chairs). And instead of spending their time fighting for elbow room and unsettling their partner on the drag-lift, they just introduce themselves (despite the name badge on their anorak if they are part of a group), and settle down to tell you their life-story, wishing you cheerfully 'A good day's skiing' when you get to the top.

And they really seem to mean it. Americans, it seems, do come to *ski* rather than to pose (as evidenced by their gear). Like the Japanese they too seem to have come to Europe for some ultimate skiing experiences – though they are not so much looking for 'Wa' as for runs that will 'Wow' them. They do have a rather disconcerting habit of yipping at the tops of their voices whenever these 'Wow' experiences occur and they find themselves airborne coming off the top of a bump made of some of that European 'white gold'.

No less than with other nations, though, there is the problem of the language barrier. Americans are forever heading back to 'the lodge' or to the 'condo' (while we all go back to our hotels and apartments); or waiting for 'trams' (perhaps they use those over there instead of 'cable cars'); or hitting the 'trail' (as they set out to bash the 'piste'). Even their well-intentioned warnings are not much help as they call out to you 'Watch out for the tiller', just as a ratrac is about to mow you down; or calling out 'timber' or 'track' instead of 'Get out of my way. I am out of control'.

The only time they can get a bit touchy is when you start making unfavourable comparisons with US skiing. Admittedly they are over here because the Alps are a sort of snow-worshippers' Mecca. But when it comes to Vail versus Saint Moritz, or American powder versus European powder, they certainly aren't going to concede defeat. And as for that 'European ambiance', well there's more than something to be said for good old 'down home' US skiing.

Like the Japanese, they too are making inroads. Europe still seems to be ahead in equipment. But the Americans are the ones who invented modern snow – the stuff shot out of a cannon. (It's thanks to them that Europeans will probably now be able to go skiing in December again; and also the fact that there are more and more Kleenex dispensers at the bottom of the slopes at modern resorts to wipe your goggles.)

Let's just hope it doesn't go too far and we find ourselves sustaining ourselves on slope on hamburgers, beer and popcorn rather than saucisson, pâté and white wine, or that, like them, we start spending 'Happy Hour' in gigantic parking lots at the foot of the slopes with stuff from the picnic cooler, rather than in some good old European steamy Stübli.

○ ACHES AND PAINS

The chills and spills will outnumber the thrills

Falling is more fun when someone else does it

It is more painful when someone else is watching

If your leg breaks it won't be in a way they know how to fix at the resort

You won't discover this 'till you get home

Flying through the air with the greatest of ease is a lot simpler than landing

The side of your body on which you fall is always the side with the pocket in which you have both your keys and your sunglasses

It's when you're going your best that the worst will happen

If you don't get skier's thumb, you'll get skier's toe

11 APRÈS-SKI

'Keep it simple. Don't eat too much, don't drink too much, and don't smoke too much – but don't do too little of them either.'

Hermann 'Jackrabbit' Smith-Johannsen,
who skied till he was 105 and died at 111

As pointed out in *Piste Again*, on-slope activities are not exactly the most compatible with off-slope activities. And it takes a hardened Survival Skier to keep his end up at both. In recent years, if anything, things have got worse, to the extent that it's almost *impossible* to do both – unless you pick a resort with one ski lift and six discos or, alternatively, a resort which is famous for the *non*-existence of its night-life.

Sadly, though, there are fewer and fewer of these places about. At the bigger resorts there's now hardly anything that's *not* on offer après-ski. They've all got massive sports complexes with swimming pools, tennis, squash, aerobics, yoga, ice skating, shooting galleries, golf driving-ranges, courses in this, that and the other, floodlit skiing, and all manner of bars, dives and night spots for whatever your taste – Schuhplattler, knobbly knees contests, snow dances, hell-raising, wood-chopping, disco-raving, bar-hopping or just plain hard drinking. Far from being 'dolce far niente', après-ski is now very much 'dolce far *molto*'. And this is perhaps the explanation for the growth of the poseur-phenomenon we mentioned earlier. It's just about the only way of ensuring you still have the legs for what happens 'après-piste'.

One problem is that these days après-ski is getting going *far too early* – if you are going to stay the course through to the small hours that is. First, there's the now established phenomenon of the extended lunch on the slopes, after which it's considered quite normal to head straight for one of the après-piste bars at the foot of the slopes. Thus we find ourselves nipping in for 'a quick one' *as early as 4 p.m.* to rub noses, thaw out and start exchanging lies about what we did that day. (This can even be a bit too soon for the most quick-thinking Survival Skier to have got his stories sorted out.)

Inevitably, of course, the quick one usually turns into a quick one *or three*. And so, against our better judgement we head for another smoky cave for 'real drinkers'; or to a dance-bar to work off the effects by dancing in our ski boots. (God knows ski boots are hard enough to walk in – let alone dance in.) The result is that after a few more grogs at Pub 21, and Pub 37 and then Pub 45 (or was it 46?) – Alpine pubs so often seem to be numbered – you head for your chalet or hotel with your double-glazed eyes (no you didn't forget to take your goggles off), your mouth tasting like the inside of a ski instructor's glove, and your head like the inside of a telephone exchange (and no – it wasn't your Walkman that was playing up). Incidentally, the Survival Skier would be well advised to do his après-piste drinking at the *bottom* of the slopes – not at those bars halfway up the slope, where you will then have to *ski* the rest of the way down.

Now all this wouldn't be so bad if you could just go back and sleep it off in the sauna, and then clear your head with a bit of walkabout before dinner – the good old promenade through the village, visiting the ski shop and the supermarket, and doing a bit of celebrity-spotting, or sitting in a café over an ice-cream and hot chocolate. The problem is that the locals have got it into their heads that what their visitors want straight apre-piste is *even more* physical jerks – not the old Apfelstrudel and thé citron at the local Konditorei. So they've been investing like crazy in all those sports facilities we mentioned earlier – in an effort, it would seem, to finish us off for good.

The Survival Skier, unfortunately, with his reputation to think of, will not be able to opt out of this session completely. After all, his performance as a skier will often be judged by the showing he makes après-ski. So try not to clutch your aching limbs too obviously when you climb out of the jacuzzi; and don't stagger, red-faced and lank-haired out of the sauna saying 'I can't take it anymore'. Stick, however, to this sort of activity rather than to a couple of sets of squash or a quick game of ice hockey. Leave that to the ski hooligans who enjoy bashing foreigners and who have brought their hurling sticks along. Survival Skiers will probably prefer to spend this time inspecting their bruises rather than acquiring more.

As far as the rest of the evening goes, the Survival Skier should find he is rather better prepared. He should, for instance, have spent the off-season eating three to four big meals a day, and bending the old elbow at frequent intervals in order to get in shape for his holiday. (This won't however leave you looking your best for 'strip fondue' – drop a piece of meat, and drop a piece of clothing.) In fact even ordinary fondue is probably better avoided; there's always that frustration of dropping bits back in just as you get them out, and then chasing in vain the last piece of bread skidding around in the bottom of the pot.

By this stage of the evening, though, the Survival Skier should have got his stories of the day's exploits on the slopes sorted out – so that they seem almost plausible – or at least as plausible as anyone else's. Thus he should be a match for any of the black run bores over the old raclette and plonk particularly as by now he will probably be hungry enough to eat his ski socks and polish off his inner-soles for dessert. And, with any luck, you will be served up something that slides down even better.

It's after dinner though that the Survival Skier will have to show that he can really cut the mustard. The fact is that even if you are not at Saint Moritz, all skiers will be expected to put in an 'après-ski' show. And after staring death in the face all day, a lot of people like to get their own back by dressing to kill at night. So, you'll be decked out in your après-ski ensemble (smart or unsmart according to where you are) – perhaps in your crocodile skin ski pants and diamond-studded moonboots. (Fortunately moonboots, like ski boots, have now also gone hi-tech and the new type of undersole should help you to stay upright.) If you've still got the mammoth's foot type, the dress-conscious Survival Skier will, of course, have fluffed them up them with a hair-dryer. These days there are even après-ski skis – small rubber jobs. But you'd probably be safer in your moonboots or your wellies or perhaps on a pair of snow shoes instead.

The Survival Skier who will get the most out of the evening is the one who can enhance his on-slope reputation by now going in for the sort of activities that would appear to require a certain amount of skiing ability. This is your big chance to make your reputation *on* the slopes *off* the slopes (as well as providing a handy excuse for not appearing the next day – if things don't go quite as intended.)

So you might just think of volunteering for the:

– torchlight skiing party. (Despite the 'torchlight' it should be too dark to spot your skiing inadequacies.)

– the candlelight toboggan race. (Being well tanked up is the main qualification for this – so you should be OK.)

– the moonlight snow-dance. (You don't actually have to do it on skis – even those little rubber ones.)

– skiing in fancy dress by floodlight. (If you're suitably disguised i.e. totally unrecognisable, you can always pretend afterwards that *you* were the masked 'mystery' figure who skied like a dream and then disappeared.)

– bar-hopping on skis. (You can probably manage this if the bars aren't too far apart from one another – preferably adjoining.)

Don't however get too carried away in your choice of activity – jumping over barrels on ice skates, for instance, is harder than it looks.

Having now established your reputation, you can start to have some *real* fun. After all, the night is still young. Now's your chance to go to the sort of places and to do the sort of things which you would take infinite pains to avoid at home. So take your pick – head for the Pferdestall, or Bierkeller, or Club 77 or Five-to-Five Bar for whatever takes your fancy: 'Hot Legs' contests; moonbooted

---

○ NOSH

The higher you eat, the higher the price and the less haute the cuisine

The chances of you banana-skidding in your ski boots on the tiled floor of the mountain cafeteria, increases in direct proportion to the amount of food you are carrying on your tray

The number of calories consumed at the après-ski tea or booze-up will be at least double the number of calories burned up during the day's piste-bashing

Ski-slope meals are better at getting your stomach moving than your skis moving

There's always a queue for the loo

The piste map is harder to read after a good lunch

If there was some stale bread and hard cheese left in the morning, it'll be fondue that evening

congas; hokey-kokeys; passing hot potatoes around between your legs (in the nude if you're doing it properly); some *real* 'snow' – the imported variety that you sniff at chic resorts. (Anything seems to go in après-ski these days – you even find transvestite floorshows in some resorts.)

Chances are though that you'll probably find yourself doing the 'flake-out flop' to an electronic zither or 'Ländler Band', in some sweaty dive, working up a thirst for Stein after foaming Stein. Either that, or some *real* hell-raising, wearing lampshades on your head, putting fondue down other people's shirts – the sort of thing, in fact, that puts the 'Hooray' into Henry.

The locals have actually now begun to realise that there is less interest than there was in the folksy side – Schuhplattler, flag-waving, Alpenhorn-blowing, and so on – and more interest in getting a real skinful of concoctions that you wouldn't dream of pouring down your neck at home: Jägertee, chisky (cherry brandy and whisky), snakebite (a lethal brew of beer, cider and vodka drunk by the pint), spiked vin chaud (in half pint mugs), cocktails made out of whatever the barman has left over, or perhaps one of the 'Cresta' classics like Bullshot (vodka and consommé, well-chilled). In short, the kind of concoctions that gave an international notoriety a couple of years ago to that bar in Denmark where the landlord would serve up his customers with his own dastardly 'special' – at the same time getting his customer to bare his behind for a belt on the arse, (the idea being that this was a drink with a real 'sting in the tail').

This certainly seems to be the direction ski resorts are heading – ensuring you get enough lethal liquor down your throat so that you can hardly push open those heavy Alpine doors for a final bout of mayhem on the way home, crashing your electric trolley or your toboggan or your bin-liner a few times en route, whilst performing a few other gratuitous acts of violence along the way (nicking roadsigns, lighting fires etc.), and perhaps stopping off for a visit to the crêperie or for some Bratwurst and chips. (Skiers tend to be at their hungriest at 4.30 a.m. and 4.30 p.m.)

Of course, you can just stay in and play chess, go to a skiing lecture or a concert, play with the computer (some big hotels are even offering these now), attend a course in photography or Alpine flowers, or have a quiet game of scrabble. Incidentally, don't on any account take on the locals at space invaders, or 'mini-foot' (i.e. table football) – you'll come off a worse loser than you would at one of the more hairy activities we outlined.

But no Survival Skier worthy of the name should be seen to opt out like this. And, painful as it may be, après-ski does *just* beat staying in your room boozing out of a toothmug. Anyway, you've little choice. As we've said, if you can't exactly cut the mustard *on* the slopes, you've got to show you can hack it *off* the slopes. And with any luck, it won't be too long before the Japanese take over. Apparently, their idea of après-ski is a Japanese bath and a spot of shinto-worship.

○ COMPANIONS

An 'experienced' skier is someone who got to the resort one day before you did

The likelihood of someone talking about tip-rolls and gut-flips is in inverse proportion to his ability to perform them

The skier you most want to avoid is the one you are most likely to bump into – literally

The size of a chalet party bears no relation to the size of the chalet

If you meet the romance of your life on the T-bar and spend the journey up discovering how much you have in common, chances are that when you get to the top you'll find that what you don't have in common is skiing ability

The best opportunity you will ever have to inspect the nostrils of people you don't know will be in the 9.15 a.m. cable-car

The chalet girl is having a better holiday than you are

12 SUMMIT MEETINGS

**'People say it's piste-bashing by day
and duvet-bashing all night.'**

Ski-bum quoted in *New Society*

Many skiers spend a good deal of the year getting into shape – trying to get that skier's body. Once on the slopes, though, it's often more a question of how to get that *other* skier's body – and that also goes for a fair number of Survival Skiers. If you've studied the previous chapter, though, you may wonder if you'd be in any position to do anything with that other body if you did manage to get at it.

Nevertheless, skiing romances do still seem to take place and this prospect is probably still one of the main reasons for going. The very term 'ski lodge' with images of being cosily curled up in front of a log-fire for two is almost synonymous with romance (although today's multi-occupancy chalets have rather destroyed that Hollywood illusion). Also, of course, the majority of skiers are single. (Why on earth then do Americans have to have those 'singles' snow-weeks?)

Certainly, as we've seen, people do tend to shed their inhibitions while skiing – whether it's playing 'strip fondue' or getting together in mixed saunas. And although most people (well some) are looking for good clean fun on the slopes, it's often good *dirty* fun they're looking for after sunset – not just a waltz round the ice-rink and a foxtrot at the tea dance. (These, surprisingly, are coming back into style by the way – despite the absence of people under thirty who can foxtrot.) The line here for the amorously inclined Survival Skier is: 'We don't seem to be terribly good at this – perhaps we could do something else together.' Or: 'Neither skiing nor dancing is the best aerobic work-out, you know.'

After all, it does make sense. To quote a reply recently given to a British reporter who asked a girl from Alaska how she managed to cope with those harsh dark days of winter: 'I find someone nice and stay indoors.' The problem is, as always, the 'finding someone nice'; and the odds are rather against the males who tend to heavily outnumber the girls on the slopes. The Survival Skier, however, should start with certain advantages – given the dash he probably cuts on the piste. In the end, surely, all that posing practice should pay off.

The snag, though, is that it's not always easy to see what there is underneath all those layers of ski wear. Of course, personality is a lot more important than looks – but there are limits. This, incidentally, is one of the few advantages of summer skiing – on the one day the sun shines all will be revealed. And you can offer to smooth some of that factor 20 suncream all over him or her – especially in those delicate parts. Furthermore, summer skiing does leave you free in the afternoon. . . .

In winter, though, the Survival Skier's best bet is probably the swimming-pool, the sauna or the jacuzzi if you want to check out what you might be getting ('Who's got the biggest knockers/biggest dong?' is actually one of the standard après-ski games.) Fortunately, sauna hour is usually early enough in the evening so that, if necessary, you can suddenly remember that you had other plans. If all seems well, on the other hand, you can then offer to take his or her pulse, or offer a little gentle toning up on the massage table: 'The thighs do tend to get so tensed up during skiing, don't you find?'

Skiers incidentally do tend to have fairly meaty thighs – especially powderhounds, or heli-skiers, who are the real 'thigh guys'. So if you're a real Survival Skier (i.e. you hardly do it at all) it might be best to decline an offer to reciprocate. Otherwise your potential partner may begin to suss that you're not actually all that you seem. Out on the slope, though, the Survival Skier should be

able to *seem* as if he or she might be just the job to team up with for a little after-hours pole-planting.

Do make sure, though, that you set up your liaisons *on* the slopes. Expecting to meet that special someone après-ski is a non-starter. To the Survival Skiing male it may often *seem* that there are more bumps and curves parked on the barstools in the village than on the slopes – but these usually belong to chalet girls who won't be interested in *him*. And most ski resort discos are so dark and awful that there's no telling whom you may be leaving with, or of what sex (and these days you can't be too careful).

The great advantage of the slopes is that you do meet on neutral ground and there are plenty of opportunities for those 'chance' encounters – perhaps engineering discreet collisions and offering to help put his or her skis back on. (Incidentally, the Survival Skier should try to make it look like the other person's fault – he doesn't want to make himself out to be a worse skier than he is.) If you actually can ski, of course, then you can just cruise over and say: 'Do you fall down often:' or 'Isn't this the life?' If the reply is 'Not with you around', you picked the wrong victim. It's also easier on the slopes to get a conversation going – unlike at the disco you can usually hear one another.

The Survival Skier's big advantage is his sincerity. Given his general disinterest in skiing, he or she can genuinely look into his prospective partner's eyes on a mountain top as if his new friend was the most important thing in the world – on that particular mountain anyway. The Survival Skier should not forget the importance of flattery. Make sure you say that he/she is 'looking good'. They'll really appreciate it. (After all, the outfit did cost £500.)

With his skill at getting around the slopes the Survival Skier should also have a headstart. In your case, though, it will tend to be a case of appearing *alongside* at the right moments, rather than getting round yourself in full view of your partner – particularly if he or she is a better skier than you.

Not that incompatibility of skiing levels need necessarily be a major barrier to romance. In the unlikely event that you're the stronger party, this enables you to offer a little personal advice and tuition. And if you're the weaker – well, it's surprising how much other skiers can enjoy taking you under their wing. Some Survival Skiers even pretend to be even more incompetent than they really are and find that this works wonders. But this is perhaps not to be recommended if you're a male trying to seduce the local snow queen.

Far better, though, to find yourselves close to one another in the lift queue treading on one another's skis ('Do you always jump the queue?') Even better perhaps is the cable car queue, where your towering extra-long skis should make quite an impression. Should you find yourself sharing a t-bar or a gondola with him or her, there are all manner of possibilities for breaking the ice – although with today's new super-fast lifts you do get less time than you did.

You can, for instance, offer a listen on your Walkman from your spare earphone (try to remember to wipe off the earwax of the previous person you loaned it to); or share your blanket on the double chair – who knows, you may soon be picnicking together on it; or you can offer any number of the other little bits and pieces from your bum-bag – your 'hand warmer', your suntan lotion ('What a lovely colour you are – you just need a splash of this to get the shade absolutely perfect'). The fact that this person undoubtedly has a similar supply of bits and pieces about his or her person does seem to indicate that if he or she accepts, this could be the start of something.

You can then feel pretty sure that he or she won't take it amiss when you rub the snow off his or her bottom on alighting from the lift; or help him or her off the t-bar with a little shove on the behind – particularly if you have been rubbing boots together all the way up the t-bar. (One tip though for the Survival Skier – t-bars do tend to attract foot fetishists; so bear this in mind when you are scouting out the lift lines.)

But even if your relationship is at an even more advanced stage, it does pay not to get too carried away on the ski lift. An embrace on the t-bar can leave you in a nasty tangle indeed. Even the arm round the shoulders can have unforeseen consequences – unless you actually want to roll back down to the bottom of the slope intertwined. A similar fate is likely to befall you if you and your beloved rashly take out one of those mono boards for couples – at least if *one* of you is a Survival Skier.

Better to leave all that groping until you meet for lunch. Here on the terra firma of the restaurant there should be no hazards in helping one another to peel off those clothes and undo one another's boots – with probably mounting curiosity and excitement on both sides as you get closer to discovering what exactly lies beneath. Another tip here for the Survival Skier: Don't forget to wear silk next to your skin – it does feel so sexy if your friend does get his or her fingers to it.

So far we have tended to concentrate on getting the gear *off*. But that, of course, can be to diminish the role of clothing on the slopes. After all, as we said in the opening chapters, the object of ski wear and skiing is to be a sex object – never mind the burnt skin, peeling nose and chapped lips. And the clothes can be used to send all manner of sexual signals. The Survival Skier would do well to study these carefully in order not to make any nasty errors. For instance, leaving your bandanna undone tends to mean 'Come here and knot it for me'; whereas wrapped around tight and knotted behind usually means you are unavailable.

Needless to say, the Survival Skier should keep his actual performance on slope to a minimum from now on – unless he wants to undo all his good work. Skiing ability is so often equated with sexual performance. If necessary, try to ski in another group. And women should, on no account, ski in a higher class than their spouses. (The problem is that, as at dancing, women often make better skiers.)

It's when you get off the slopes that things are going to get more difficult.

What with the sardine-syndrome in much ski-lodging, hardly anyone has a room to themselves any more; and you will also probably feel obliged to put in a bit of après-ski – which, as we saw in the previous chapter, doesn't leave you in much shape for anything else. One word of advice here: stay away from the Ski Instructor's Ball – if you want to hang on to your partner.

A good Survival Skiing line in order to cut back on the après-ski, and also making you seem like a bit of an old hand at the skiing game is: 'I can remember the days when we had to make our own après-ski.' (Nudge, nudge). You could then suggest a romantic midnight toboggan ride, or a horsedrawn sleigh for two, or a stroll down a lamplit path for winter walks as you head for even more intimate togetherness.

Thereafter, things may be a little less romantic. Stepping through piles of smelly socks and puddles of vomit to your corner of the chalet, or sneaking up a creaky stairway in a mountain pension to a bed with more lumps than a mogul field is hardly an auspicious start to any après-après-ski. Your room or hers – it'll probably be just as bad.

You may, however, earn your partner's respect for being able to make love in some pretty unorthodox positions — one leg on the radiator, simultaneously wrestling with the 'thermo-bot' you brought with you in case the radiator clapped out, doing your best not to put your foot in the mouth of the person in the bed next to you (despite his snoring), and writhing around as if you're wedeling (as those bedsprings press into your spine.)

○ APRÈS-SKI

The moguls get bigger as the day goes on — and bigger still when you get to the bar

By lunch-time you will have had enough

By the end of the afternoon you will have had more than enough

At the end of the day it will hurt even where it didn't during the day

The people with the highest profile at the bar will have the lowest profile on the slopes

The après-ski action is always somewhere else

At the end of the day there is always someone who has skied further or steeper

The best après-ski activity of all is going home

13 SKIING DOUBLE

**'They have style, the best of these
high altitude drunkards.'**

Robert Schultheis, on Tibetan folk in
Mountain Gazette

Après-ski *on* the slopes has become an increasingly worrying phenomenon. Forty per cent of skiing accidents in Austria last year were attributed to drinking (so the title of this book 'Totally Piste' is not entirely inapt).

The Survival Skier, of course should always be wary of *other* skiers who get out of control because of alcohol. But he should be equally wary of the 'piste-police' trying to crack down on his own boozing. After all, the reason many of us go is to get 'more piste for our pound'. And, as we've seen, most Survival Skiers need as much Dutch courage as they can get and are not in the habit of relying on St Bernard dogs for their brandy supply. Thus, they are often not exactly innocent parties themselves in those late afternoon collisions.

The Americans, incidentally, are getting the right idea. Some resorts now have teams of 'Thirstbusters', wearing taxi-cab yellow jumpsuits, who cruise the slopes with special patented back-packs that dispense hot apple cider and cocoa for a buck a pop.

The fact is that most Survival Skiers often find themselves more in need of moral fortification on the slopes than of the sexual gratification we discussed in the last chapter. The Survival Skier may not exactly have 'bottle' but he usually has 'a bottle' (or two) — not just to refuel (you burn up a lot of calories ducking around the slopes) but to offer to all those pisteurs he needs to keep in with, ensuring they come up at appropriate moments with reputation-building remarks like: 'That must be the tenth time this morning you came down the Black Buzzard.'

It would also be a pity — not least for the Survival Skier — if the tradition of the odd wee nip as you get around the slopes were to be outlawed. It's a tradition that goes a lot further back than Survival Skiing. There's hardly a high mountain range in the world where for centuries mountain men have not been putting away some special lethal liquid down their cast-iron stomachs to keep them going — jealously guarding the secrets of their fermentation methods from the lowlanders (and the law). And the same goes for the Alps — whether it be Zwetsch, Weinbrand, Mirabelle, Pflümli, Obstler or some more deadly form of 'anti-freeze' like Neaule. And what about all those piste-side Stübli or other watering holes — do we want to put them out of business? Let's not pretend we just go there to listen to the instructor tell us what we had been doing wrong; we go for the grog, and then more grog — preferably served in half-pint mugs.

But as well as providing an often much-needed form of central heating, Survival Skiers and others do find that a little lubrication *helps* their skiing. You often tend to be at your most adventurous after a couple of Jägertees to round off your lunch. (There must be a reason why so many of those bars are called 'Whiskey-*a-go-go*'.) How often have you heard people emerge from the restaurant at 3.30 p.m. and (after spending half an hour or so trying to locate their sticks and poles) pronounce: 'I always ski so much better after a good lunch.'

After all, isn't that what the instructors have all been telling us since way back — that the secret is to ski 'relaxed'. Even cross-country instructors (altogether a more puritanical sort) are always calling out 'locker bleiben' ('Stay loose'). The fact of the matter is that if the hipflask were passed around on the slopes a bit more frequently there would be no need for all those weird ways devised by the 'inner skiing' schools to help you relax.

It's also true that in skiing, as in anything else, you have to make the most of your natural assets. And since most Survival Skiers have spent years of their lives developing hollow legs, it seems a shame not to use them. Perhaps, in time, who knows, they'll get as rubbery and flexible as those of your instructor.

Not that this is a theory to which your instructor will all that often subscribe; though like most mountain men, they are not usually averse to a bit of a nip themselves – particularly if it's the Survival Skier who is passing the hipflask around. ('After all, it's always five o'clock somewhere.') If you do this often enough, you may not become the best skier in the group, but you'll almost certainly be the most popular.

It's something of a pity then – not least for the Survival Skier – that the authorities are trying to cut down on pit-stops at piste-side hostelries or those breaks on the slopes for a little noggin. One does wonder whether they have considered the medical consequences – many a skier trapped on a mountain has just managed to avoid succumbing to hypothermia by having a hip flask handy, as well as using it as an antiseptic. Admittedly there is now a school of thought that alcohol can cause a *loss* of bodyheat and in itself induce hypothermia. But Survival Skiers (who tend to rely on their own experience) would be advised to dismiss this as just another modern theory and rely instead on their own experience and that of 'fellow' mountain men over the ages.

So it does seem rather a pity that Survival Skiers have now been reduced to buying those hollow-shafted ski-poles to surreptitiously carry their booze around in. (If you drop one of these from the ski lift, of course, then you've *really* got something to worry about.) Nor will these poles do anything for your skiing – especially for someone like the Survival Skier, whose equipment needs to be so *delicately* balanced: a litre of firewater washing around inside your sticks can destroy your rhythm entirely. (One tip worth remembering: try to empty each shaft evenly so that you stay roughly in balance.)

In some respects, though, it must be admitted that the authorities do have a point. There have been cases where people didn't just drop their stick on top of someone from the chairlift: having consumed the contents of their sticks they fell off the chairs themselves onto skiers below. That's 'vertical drop' for you.

Fortunately, however, a satisfactory solution seems to be emerging – both to the piste police and to skiers who enjoy a tincture or two in the afternoon. The key to this is the 'long lunch' which, thanks largely to the French and the Italians has now become an established phenomenon on the slopes. Understandably these lunches tend to be mainly of the liquid variety – since though food at the top of the mountain has got better, it often seems a bit 'tired', as if it had made a big effort to get up there.

Survival Skiers need only refine this brilliant concept a bit further, and it should be possible to virtually eliminate the need to do any more skiing for the rest of the day. (If queried, of course, don't blame this on your well-filled hollow legs – say instead that you're 'very sensitive' to the 'flat light' situation that seems to occur so often in the afternoon, impeding visibility and making the bumps look flat.)

Then, with your ski clips undone you can simply catch the cable car down.

Better that — and more congenial — than sitting up on the slope boozing and waiting for the piste-patrol to bring you down. With a bit of practice, the concept could perhaps be refined even further — extending your après-ski to dawn and then staying off the slopes (in the best interests of all concerned, since with a hangover your skiing is likely to be somewhat erratic at best).

And don't believe that one about a blast of cold air being the best cure for a hangover. As we've seen, medical science seems to be overturning a lot of these old theories; with any luck they'll now recommend you to stay in bed with a little warm Jägertee. Perhaps it all just goes to prove the central philosophy of the *'Piste'* series — that the best way to succeed at skiing is to do your own thing.